CRUEL SUMMER

SEASONS OF REVENGE
BOOK 2

MORGAN ELIZABETH

To everyone who has ever been called 'unlikable.'

Fuck them.
Every single one of them.

A NOTE FROM MORGAN

Dear Reader,

Thank you so much for choosing to read Cruel Summer!

From the moment I put Tis the Season for Revenge into the universe, so many of you asked for Cami's story—our bitter, vengeful queen who loves her besties most of all. (Though they might sometimes tie with her love for revenge.) Some of you were concerned you wouldn't like her, that she went too far in her quest to help Abbie get revenge on Richard. I get that, but I hope you can see how that's only a single aspect of her personality and how flawed people exist—both in books and in real life. My goal is *always* to write realistic, relatable characters that make you think or make you feel seen and I hope I did that with Cami.

I grew up watching Mean Girls and it's a comfort movie to me. When I wrote TTSFR I didn't immediately know I'd be writing a 00's rom-com inspired revenge series, but god, has it been fun!

Cruel Summer contains mentions of anxiety, bullying, alcohol, and fighting. As always, this book contains liberal use of profanity and lots of spice. Please always put yourself first when reading—it's meant to be our happy place.

I love you all with my whole being.
-Morgan Elizabeth

PLAYLIST

Cruel Summer—Ace of Base
Good Friends—Maren Morris
Colorado—Renee Rapp
The Feels—Maren Morris
The Last Great American Dynasty—Taylor Swift
Into Your Arms—The Maine
You Outta Know—Alanis Morissette
Cinema—Harry Styles
Cruel Summer—Taylor Swift
Woman—Mumford & Sons
If You Go Down I'm Going Down Too—Kelsea Ballerini
Stay-Rihanna
Act My Age—One Direction
The Archer—Taylor Swift
Coffee Shop Soundtrack—All Time Low
Lavender Haze—Taylor Swift
You—Miley Cyrus
The Only Exception—Paramore

ONE

TUESDAY, MAY 16

CAMI

This is a terrible, terrible idea.

I'm doing it anyway, but I would like the record to show taking shots with your best friends the day before you start a new job is definitely *not* a good idea.

"To Cami's new job!" Abbie shouts with a smile, her blonde hair moving and reflecting the low light of the dive bar.

"To Cami!" Kat says before all three of us down our shots, and Kat and I shove a lime into our mouths instantly. Abbie makes a face akin to someone who is moments away from heaving before chugging the sweetest juice (pineapple) she could get from the bartender.

"Dear god, that was horrific," she says, the same way she always does when she encounters hard liquor.

"Yeah, but it makes you all warm and tingly, and that's the best part," Kat says, then she gives a little shimmy attracting every eye in the bar, including the cute bartender who has been nearby since we walked in. He leans on the bar in front of us with a smile, like he finds us entertaining.

He's got a good smile. I tracked him from a mile away—his light-brown hair cut short, the muscular build and wide shoulders stretching the black staff tee shirt he wears, and most importantly, the dimples he keeps showing us with each smile.

The man has *dimples*.

"Need anything?" he asks, his smile growing, the dimples deepening.

He's definitely smiling at Kat, my gorgeous best friend with all of her curves and beautiful dark hair and perfectly tanned skin.

"French fries!" Abbie says.

"French fries, got it. What about for you?" he asks, tipping his head to me.

"What about me?"

"What can I get you?" He has nice eyes, too. Hazel with flecks of gold, laugh lines at the edges.

"Oh. Nothing, I'm good."

"Nothing? You should eat something," he says, clearly trying to up our tab for the night.

"We'll tip you well either way, I promise," I say, and his smile comes out again.

"Not worried about a tip, angel. Worried about the fact you've had three shots in thirty minutes. You need something to sop it all up."

"Angel?" I ask with a glare. A bartender assigning drunk women pet names is a *major* ick.

"Must have hurt when you fell from heaven."

My mouth drops open with shock and a healthy mix of indignation and, though I'll never admit it, admiration

"Did you really just say that?" He laughs a bit, standing straight and wiping the bartop in front of him.

"Yeah. Dad jokes and cheesy pickup lines are kind of my thing,"

"Oh my god, I think I love him," Abbie says, the cartoon-like hearts in her eyes nearly visible.

"Right?" Kat, the hopeless romantic of the group, says.

"Does that actually work?" I ask at his egregious attempt at humor.

"Honestly?" he asks, those dimples coming out again. "No, but I normally save the jokes for my daughter who always gives me a pity laugh."

My eyes move to his hands without my permission, checking for a ring that doesn't sit on his finger, and my face burns like the sun when those *fucking dimples* come out when he catches me looking.

"Oooh, a *daddy!*" Abbie says, and it's almost cute the way a flush spreads across his cheeks.

"Stop, I bet she's so cute. Look at his *eyes!*" Kat says, and I know in her mind she's crafting what his daughter looks like.

Also, possibly what their child would look like with his eyes and her tan and smile.

Kat has the most gorgeous smile on the planet.

But my mind is stuck on the word *daddy* and, again, without my permission, I start picturing what he would be like without the tee, sweaty and on top of me.

I drunkenly shake my head to dislodge *that* thought because *absolutely not*. Obviously, I very much do need something to soak up all of the liquor in my stomach because I'm losing my mind. But, I mean, if someone called him Daddy in bed, would he blush the same way he just did or would he—

"So fries and . . . ," the bartender says, and I shake my head, breaking from the inappropriate thoughts of hot men and bedroom activities I genuinely have no time for.

"Mozzarella sticks," I say, forcing my mind to focus on the task at hand. "And another shot."

The dimples come out again and a shiver runs through me.

Fuck, I'm drunk.

"I'll get you a shot after you eat, deal?"

"What the—" I start because who does he think he is, telling me how to drink and when, but my friend cuts me off before I can throw a fit.

"Deal," Kat says, turning to me and giving me wide eyes. "It's a deal."

He smiles, and then he's off to put in our order, help other customers, and, to my surprise and pleasure, to pour me another shot.

"We should head out," Abbie says two hours and too many drinks later. "You have your first day of work tomorrow."

"Ugh, don't remind me. Whose idea was this anyway?" I complain, the world spinning.

"Yours, babe. Abbie wanted to get takeout and have a pajama night in the room."

"That's because she's *boring* and has a *boyfriend*, even if he's the most perfect specimen of a man on this planet."

"He so is," Abbie agrees, and then we all move to stand.

"You girls need me to call you a cab?" the bartender asks, coming out from behind his bar as I wobble. His words startle me, and when I stumble in my too-high heels, he reaches out, grabbing my waist with both hands and leaving them there until I steady on my feet.

A thumb brushes my skin where my top doesn't quite meet my skirt and it burns in a really, really good way.

"Your hands are warm," I say.

"Are you okay?"

"That was a good opening for a dad joke, you know. You totally wasted it," I say, and I get the dimples again.

Shit.

The dimples are cute.

"Yeah, well, right now, my main focus is making sure you get where you're going in one piece. Let's call it an IOU. Come back and see me and I'll give you a good one, yeah?"

"Don't tempt me, I might be here every night," I say, the filter between my brain and my mouth absolutely drowning in tequila and bad decisions.

"Okay, let's get you home," Abbie says with wide eyes.

"We're just going across the street," Kat tells the bartender clearly, liquor never affecting her the way it does Abbie and me, the forever mom of the group by default.

It's been this way since college. We'd all go out to a bar or to some party, all drink the same amount, and at the end of the night, it was always Kat gently pushing us back to the apartment we shared or saving us from the clutches of yet another scumbag frat boy.

"The Beach Club?"

"My *boyfriend* has an apartment there," Abbie says, and the way she says it reminds me again of how freaking perfect they are for each other.

Damien Martinez was put on this Earth to take care of Abigail Keller, and you can't convince me otherwise. He's truly the best thing to ever happen to her, and the guilt from how I acted last December still weighs on me. He's also the reason I got this job at the club, planning parties for the elite of Long Beach Island all summer long.

"Ah, got it." Quickly, he looks over his shoulder where an older man is standing at the window for the kitchen and a few people still sit at the bar. "Rhonda!" A pretty middle-aged woman sporting a dark-brown bob streaked with grey looks up. "You got the bar covered for a few minutes?" She looks around before nodding. "Thanks. Gonna walk these three over to the Beach Club."

"Got it, boss," she says, then she turns to grab an empty bottle off a table before walking to a customer and speaking with them.

"That's really not necessary," Kat starts, and the indignation of someone telling her she can't handle us creeps into her eyes, as if he's accusing her of not being a good enough friend.

See?

Mom of the group.

And just like a mom, she can always handle her children best of all.

"I know that, but if I don't make sure you get over there in one piece, I'll be thinking about it all night. You don't want to do that to me, do you?" he asks with his kind smile.

It's *too* kind.

He's *absolutely* got a thing for Kat.

Which, of *course* he does—she's beautiful and gracious and approachable even when she's a drunken mess.

"I promise that's—"

I decide to throw him a bone, partly because I know Kat, and she can be utterly *blind* to a hot man flirting with her, and partly because the room has started to spin and I *really* need to lie in a bed.

"Come on, Kat. Let the hot bartender walk you across the damn street. Jesus, get a hint already," I say with an exaggerated eye roll, my words laced with exasperation I don't necessarily mean.

"Cam, I don't—"

"Come on, dimples. Walk us back to our accommodations," I say to the bartender, cutting her off, threading my arm through Abbie's, and heading for the door.

When I look over my shoulder, I don't miss Kat saying something to him with a clearly apologetic look in her eyes or the way he smiles back at her, those dimples coming out again, before moving his hand in an *after you* type of move.

And that's the last moment I remember of the night.

TWO

WEDNESDAY, MAY 17

CAMI

A groan leaves my lips as my alarm goes off, the pounding in my head reminding me, yes, taking shots last night was a terrible, no good, *very bad* idea.

It was fun, but it sure was fucking *stupid*.

"What the fuck is that?" Abbie asks, lying next to me in the giant bed of Damien's condo above the Beach Club.

"My stupid fucking alarm," I say, my eyes squinting as I try and figure out where I need to tap in order to stop the incessant blaring.

"Well, stop it." The words are moaned from the other side of Abbie, where Kat is.

"I'm trying!" I say, my finger stabbing at the screen frantically until, finally, the room is overcome with blissful silence.

Turns out, though, the headache is not from the alarm searing my not-yet-awakened brain.

It's my *hangover from hell*.

"Fuck," I groan, flopping onto the bed as I toss my phone back to the side table, where it bounces off and lands on the floor.

I don't have it in me to care.

"Yeah," Abbie agrees as I rub my hands into my face. She slaps my hands away. "Stop, don't do that. It's bad for your skin." When I pull my hands away, the base of my palm has dark mascara on it.

"So is sleeping in my makeup, but here we are."

She sits up and stares at me, glaring.

The woman is hungover, barely awake, and I know she's ready to rip me a new one about my skincare or lack thereof.

"How many times have I told you *not to sleep* in your makeup, Camile!"

"Abbie, she could barely get her ass onto an elevator last night. Do you think she was in the right mindset to *wash her makeup off*?" Kat says from her other side.

"Then she shouldn't have drunk so much."

"Wasn't it you who made the game *take a drink every time the bartender tells a dad joke*?" I ask.

"He told so many," Abbie says, flopping back onto the bed, an arm going over her face. "Who knew one person knew *so many dad jokes.*"

"He totally knew we were playing a game," Kat says, sliding out of bed and grabbing three of the water bottles we were mindful enough to buy yesterday before digging in a bag for headache medicine. She slides back under the covers with us, handing us each a bottle and doling out meds.

"Oh, totally. He kept saying them and laughing when we'd all groan and take a drink."

"Did he really?" I ask.

"Yeah. I'm fully sure he knew what we were doing."

"No way," Abbie says. "That's irresponsible for a bartender, isn't it?"

"I don't know. He also kept making us eat, so there's that."

It's probably the lone reason I'm not hovering over a toilet this morning—the incessant delivery of French fries and other bar snacks throughout the night.

"Yeah, what was up with that?" I ask after downing my entire water bottle and stretching. I don't feel great, but it seems I might have made it out with just a headache and some sluggishness.

After my assessment of my body, I realize the silence before noticing Kat and Abbie are looking at each other, half smiling, half confused. "Wait, what?"

There's another look between my friends before Abbie answers.

"Cam, he wanted you."

"He *wanted* me?" I ask with indignation, forcing my legs to move to the side of the bed and touch the ground. The carpet is plush and extravagant like much of the Beach Club, I'm finding, but I can barely focus with the way my head is still pounding.

"Well, duh. He stationed himself in front of us the whole night." I roll my eyes which proves to be a terrible idea, the throbbing ratcheting.

"The bar wasn't that big, Kat."

"And there was the way he kept watching your face every time he told a shitty joke," Abbie counters.

"Because I kept making fun of him while *you two* kept entertaining him."

"He *walked us across the street*," Kat says, like it means something monumental.

The hopeless romantic.

I'm pretty sure she could find a serial killer romantic if you gave her enough time.

"It's his job to make sure his patrons get home safely." Kat groans with my words.

"Why is she like this?" Abbie says, lying back with a huff and shaking her head.

"We all know the answer to that," Kat grumbles under her breath.

I don't have time or energy or the mental fortitude to dig into that so instead, I stand, leaving them while I use the bathroom and brush my teeth, taking in my hair and trying to decide how much work I'm going to have to put into my appearance to cover the evidence of going out last night.

It doesn't seem like the damage is *that* bad thankfully.

When I reenter the bedroom, Abbie and Kat are both sitting, seemingly more awake, and unfortunately, Kat has the *look*.

It's part mother hen, part pushy teacher who wants to see you succeed, and together, it spells out trouble.

"You need to go back over there," she says, staring at me as I dig through my overnight bag, trying to find the outfit I packed for today. My car is loaded with all of my worldly belongings Jenga-style, so I'm ready to move into my new apartment for the summer after my first meeting with the owner today.

But her words have me pausing and looking at her.

"What?"

"You need to go back to the Fishery at some point today."

I stand, slowly turning to face my best friend and crossing my arms on my chest.

"Why would I need to do that?"

Because after making a fool of myself last night, I fully *planned on never entering that place again.*

"To pay the tab."

I blink at her.

I look over at Abbie, who is conveniently looking at her phone, avoiding my eyes before I look back at Kat.

"Why didn't we pay it *last night?*"

She bites her lip, doing everything in her power to look anywhere but at me.

Kat absolutely *hates* confrontation. So much so, it actually makes her break out in full-blown hives occasionally, but she'll do it when she thinks it's important.

I don't know why her *important* needs to land on the day I'm starting a new job.

"Funny story, I left my wallet in the room yesterday," she says with a very, *very* fake laugh and a twirl of her perfect dark-brown hair.

Bullshit.

Such fucking bullshit because Kat is the one who, anytime we go *anywhere,* double- and triple-checks to make sure we have everything we need for a night out—ID, cash, cards, Band-Aids, charging packs for our phones, hand sanitizer, a granola bar in case someone gets hungry—literally everything and anything.

"I didn't," I say, staring her down. "I could have paid. I *should have* paid, but you both told me as soon as we got there it was a stupid fucking celebration for my new job and I wasn't allowed under any circumstances to pay for my own drinks."

"Yeah, but by the time I realized I didn't have my wallet, you were so gone it was just more important to get you home."

"And Abbie?" I ask, raising a brow at her. "Abbie could have paid."

"Don't drag me into this," she says.

"So you're saying there's something to be dragged into?" I raise my eyebrow as I turn in her direction, trying with my entire being to fight my instinctive defensiveness.

Abbie stands now, hands lifting in a placating manner like she's approaching a tiger who hasn't eaten in three weeks.

"Cam, you've got that face telling anyone in a ten-mile radius you're annoyed, and Kat's wringing the comforter in her hands, panicking you're going to be mad at her and second-guessing everything she's ever done in life. Yeah, there's something to be dragged into. *Obviously.*"

"You spend too much time with Damien," I say under my breath. "You're becoming too logical."

Abbie smiles with a nearly angelic look of pride.

"I know. Isn't it fun?"

I shake my head, looking at the ceiling.

"Okay, let's cut the crap. Why are you forcing me to show my face at a bar I got embarrassingly smashed at last night?"

Kat looks like she might explode for a good three second before she finally blurts out her answer. "Because he *likes* you!"

There it is.

My hopeless romantic bestie.

"Kat—"

'Wouldn't it be precious? You get your dream job and the day before you start, boom! You meet your dream man."

"Katrina—"

"Okay, dream man was a bit much—he's no Damien Martinez—but maybe a fling! Just something fun!" She shimmies her shoulders with the words.

"Kat, honey, I'm here to work. I'm here to get references and to network. I'm here to build my *own* business."

If you don't know Kat, you probably wouldn't notice, but her lips drop just a hair in disappointment. It's too small of a movement for other people to see but not too small for her best friends to notice.

"It's not my dream job, Kat," I say, my voice lower, placating.

"It could be," Abbie says, throwing in her two cents and tipping her head to the side. "It could be your dream job. Working on high profile events for five months out of the year? Shit, they're paying you enough you could live easy the rest of the year. Travel, do whatever you want. Stop being a workaholic. You could make friends here, make a life here."

I sigh. Abbie wanted to stay out of it until she didn't, and now she's throwing her hat in the ring.

Goddammit.

Two against one.

"It's not my dream job, guys. I'm here to work with rich bitches and plan a wedding and a bunch of events for the club and to *network.* And I'm definitely not here to make friends or meet some kind of . . . dream man."

"Why can't you do both?" Abbie asks, her voice going low and soft.

"Both?"

"Both. Network and make friends. Network and have a fling. Network and give a hot bartender a chance."

"I don't need friends. I have *plenty* of friends."

Both of my best friends stare at me and blink.

"Name them," Abbie says, calling my bluff.

"You two," I start, and Kat tips her head in a *go-on* motion.

My mind runs through names and . . .

Fuck.

"Leroy."

"Leroy is 75, newly retired, and is now living in the Bahamas."

"Are you being ageist, Kat?" I ask.

"He's a *million miles away from you*, Cam, the giant age gap aside."

"Are we not going to be friends when I'm living here and you're back in the city?" Abbie sighs and shakes her head.

"You're being obtuse on purpose. He was your boss for five years, Cami. Sure, you guys had lunch together daily, but . . ." Her voice trails off, driving her point.

My mind easily fills in the gaps.

But that was absolutely the extent of any friendship you're trying to imply.

I stare back at the eyes of my two best friends, feeling the all-consuming need to be right taking over.

"I have . . . I have Damien!" I say. "We're friends. He got me this job!"

Damien Martinez overheard me whining to Abbie about how my boss who ran an exclusive Sweet 16 party business in the city was retiring, leaving me without a job. He then proceeded to tell me I would be great at general event planning and should start my own company.

Unfortunately, as I told him, I would need to create a network of contacts and grow my name recognition in order to work with the kind of clientele and budgets I enjoy working with.

As it turns out, his partner at the law firm, Simon Schmidt, is old friends with Jefferson Kincaid, the owner of the Beach Club. In a few days and just one phone interview, I was gainfully employed.

"Damien is *my boyfriend.*"

"And *my* friend," I counter.

"Honey, love you, but you spent the entire month of December trying to talk me out of telling him about our revenge scheme, threatening to ruin my relationship with him before it really even started."

We haven't touched on this at all, Abbie in her blissful bubble of happiness and love, but I should have known it wouldn't last forever.

"Look, Abbie, I'm sorry. I—"

"I don't want to talk about it, Cam. I love you. I know you, I know your past, and I know your heart. It wasn't cool, but we're good. "

"Yeah, but—"

"I think you should give the summer a chance," she says, cutting me off. "We'll be even if you do."

There's no longer the hint of a hangover in either of their faces. Instead, their looks are well-meaning and full of love and . . . shit.

Concern.

There is concern in their eyes.

"What do you mean?"

"I mean, you've already written this summer—and anyone you might meet—off as nothing more than a work opportunity."

"It is—" I start, but she doesn't let me continue.

"It doesn't have to be."

"You guys," I say with a laugh I don't feel at all. Neither of them smile when I do.

"We love you, Cami."

"We want you to be happy."

"I *am* happy."

"Are you?"

"Where is this coming from?" I ask, turning fully toward them instead of continuing to look in my bag and staring.

My friends look at each other before Kat sighs.

"We've been meaning to having this conversation for a while, but it never seemed like the right time."

"A while."

"We're worried about you, Cam."

"What the fuck is this? Is this like a fucking intervention or something?" There's frustration and anger in my voice. I don't mean it to, but the panic in my chest is building and turning into defensiveness.

"It's not an intervention, Cam—" Kat starts, but Abbie cuts her off with a shake of her head.

"No, it is. It is an intervention of sorts."

"Why, because I won't give some random bartender a chance when you're trying to set me up? A bartender who was also so very into Kat, might I add." Kat sighs and Abbie rolls her eyes.

"God, you're so fucking stubborn sometimes, Cami. No, it's because lately, it's looking like there's no *universe* where you're going to give *anyone* an honest chance. You're self-sabotaging and it's not healthy," Abbie says, and with her words, all three of our heads move too, her own eyes going wide like she can't believe she said that.

To be fair, I also can't believe she said that.

Maybe being around her hot lawyer boyfriend all the time is helping her finally grow a backbone.

"I give people chances," I say, my voice dipping a bit.

It drops with a hint of shame, because I'm lying.

Abbie isn't wrong—I probably wouldn't give some random, cute bartender the time of day.

I probably won't be opening up to anyone I meet here for anything beyond a professional relationship, be it friendly or romantic. It's not personal, not really.

I just think, generally speaking, people give out chances too easily, like they're trading cards or sticks of gum or Oprah giving out cars.

You get a chance and you *get a chance and you, over there, get a second and third and fourth chance!*

But the reality is, giving everyone you meet an opportunity to prove themselves opens you to be hurt, a lesson I've learned in the past.

So instead, I make people *earn* their chances.

I give everyone I meet a series of tests to decide if they're worthy of my time and energy.

And I never give second chances.

It's my thing, really.

Abbie's thing is being pink and outlandish and making everyone stare at her, making everyone wish they could spend some more time in her stratosphere.

Kat's thing is falling in love in a millisecond and then getting bored just as quickly and moving on without a second glance.

Mine is testing people.

Unfortunately, not many people pass.

In fact, in my ten years of making sure people really, truly mean it when they say they like me (or even more unbelievably, when they say they *love* me) only two people have passed.

Abigail Keller and Katrina Flores.

My best friends in the entire universe, but also the pains in my ass right now.

You know, I should have seen this coming. To be fair, I've been waiting for the other shoe to drop for months since I crossed a line I had no place to in December.

I just didn't think it would be *today* or *here*.

"Look. We love you. We love you and it kills us to see you so unwilling to let others in. You're an amazing person, Cami. Other people deserve to get to know that side of you," Abbie says. Kat's hand moves to her mouth, and she chews at her nail nervously, knowing it's her turn to add on.

"It's not healthy, how quickly you push people away and write them off," she says finally, her words shaky like she's afraid I'll take it wrong and cut *them* off for good.

"I don't know what you're talking about," I say, voice lower as I move my hands through my overnight bag again, digging as if I need to find something in there even though my outfit is already set aside.

"Yes, you do, Cami." I keep moving my hands in my bag, keeping myself busy. "Babe, stop trying to look busy and sit with us," Abbie says, and now her voice is soft and kind like she's talking to a scared animal.

I stare at her before finally giving in, walking over, and sitting on the edge of the bed farthest from them. "This is a waste of time. We don't have long before you leave. There's seriously no need to even be having this conversation."

But even to my own ears, my voice isn't convincing at all.

And mostly, it's because *she's right.* I push everyone away if they even *seem* like they might let me down at some point.

I cut people off before they can hurt me because if I'm the one doing the cutting, it doesn't hurt as bad.

If I'm the one to become distant, I can accept that.

A defense mechanism, a therapist once told me. *You pull away before people can hurt you, but that's no way to live, Camile.*

That was my last session with her.

I never admitted it then, not even to myself, but didn't like how close to the truth she got.

"I'm just saying . . . we're worried about you." Abbie twirls a strand of blonde hair between her fingers.

"Look, just because you're happily shacked up with the hot lawyer doesn't mean all of us need or want that."

"It's not about having a man or romance, Cami," Kat says.

"You mean the woman who is always looking for Mr. Right, the woman who *always* wants to be in a relationship, is telling me, the one who hasn't been in a committed relationship *for over ten years,* that it's not about men?" I ask, a sleek, manicured eyebrow raised.

See?

A test.

Even when I know to my soul someone loves and cares about me, I just can't help it.

It's not fair to them, I know, but part of me can't believe anyone loves the truest version of me, so I show them my worst and see if they'll stay.

I watch the quip hit true, watch an almost imperceptible flinch in Kat's eye before she speaks.

"You're hurt because we're calling you out. I get it. It's valid. But it's long overdue, Cami," she says, shocking me.

"And just because you're hurt we're calling you out does *not* mean you can be ugly to us," Abbie adds, her voice firm.

"I don't know what you're talking about."

"You're starting a new job and we're all so excited for you—"

"A job I only have because Damien talked me up to the owners —" Now, it's Abbie's turn to cut me off.

"No, a job you have because he saw how fucking good you are at what you do and knew you were looking for a new opportunity," Abbie says with an eye roll.

And it's then her happy façade cracks, revealing the truth beneath it.

The frustration.

The pain.

The *worry*.

In a single movement, I understand just how deep this goes—how much it's been worrying them, how much *I've* been worrying them

"You meet people and instantly think the worst of them. You think they're going to hurt you, they're playing you, or manipulating you."

"And sometimes, they *are*," I say, tipping my chin and crossing my arms on my chest.

Abbie's face goes soft.

"And sometimes they are, Cami, but how do you expect to figure out who is and who isn't if you decide someone is going to fuck you over before you even know their name?"

"And once you know their name, you make decisions, placing them in your neat little categories," Kat adds on.

I do that.

I *totally* do that.

"Think about what would've happened if you had met us *after* Jason, Cami? Would we be friends?"

The name still tears through me, a mix of sadness and embarrassment and rage I've never taken the time to work through.

But for some reason, I do as they ask of me.

I think about their question.

Where would they be if I met them now?

Abbie would probably be placed in the *annoying girls who are way too happy all the time so I can't trust them* category.

Kat would be in *flighty people who have little to no substance behind them, so what's the point of even talking to them.*

Well, fuck.

Neither of them is that.

And when I look at it through that lens, I actually get a bit sad, thinking I wouldn't have these friendships if I was encountering them as *today's* version of Cami.

My mind goes through all of the ways my life would be different if I had met Kat and Abbie *after* Jason broke my heart.

I don't like it.

It also makes me think about all of the people I've cut off before getting to know. What amazing relationships and opportunities have I squashed without realizing it?

I sit there for long minutes, contemplating my life, and my friends sit silently with me as I process this new insight.

Finally, *finally*, I look to them and nod.

"Okay," I say. "You're right."

A mix of joy and disbelief break out on both of my friends' faces, and it's then I know I made the right choice.

"You're going to give it a try?"

"I'm . . . going to be more open. Generally. If I cut you guys off before you made it past my walls, I'd be miserable. It . . ." I stop speaking, trying to put my thoughts into words, but nothing coming to mind really fits the bill.

"Thank you. Thank you, guys," is what I settle on, but when Kat's eyes shimmer with wet and relief washes over Abbie, I know it was all I had to say. I shake my head and roll my eyes like they drive me crazy, trying to escape from this hellhole of emotions I don't want to face.

But with that, my friends move, tackling me onto the bed in one giant girl hug, laughing as they do.

It's not until they're piling into Kat's car to head back north and I have a thick layer of concealer under my eyes that Abbie pulls me into a huge hug.

"I'm proud of you and I'm here for you," she whispers low, and I try not to focus on the lump growing in my throat.

"I love you, Abs. I love you, and I'm so sorry. I'm sorry about December when—"

"I know. I know, babe. We're good. Just . . . give it a chance, yeah?" she says, and the *yeah* makes me smile, thinking of just how deep Damien Martinez has infiltrated her personality.

"Yeah, Abbie. I love you."

And then, they're off and I'm once again on my own.

And I usually like it, being alone and able to focus on *me,* but for the first time in a long time, alone feels . . . lonely.

THREE

CAMI

Once again, my nosiness has put me into a shitty situation. I should have listened to Abbie when she told me *not* to Google the family I'd be working for this summer. She said I'd get in my own head and make judgments before I even walked into my new office.

She was right, of course.

I never should have typed *Jefferson Kincaid* into the search bar as soon they left me with an hour before my meeting, and I definitely shouldn't have hit *go*.

It's not Jefferson, the owner of a multitude of high-end boutique hotels and private clubs across the country, who has the panic creeping before I enter the building.

It's Melanie Kincaid, soon-to-be Melanie St. George.

I never should have read the tabloid article that called my first client at the Beach Club a *Bridezilla of catastrophic proportions*.

Or the one reading, *Fired three wedding planners already!* The article whose headline exclaimed, *Hotel heiress to wed finance power-house in the wedding of the season* should have been a safe bet, but it dove into deep detail of how she could be heard yelling at her previous wedding planner from a block away.

But I rarely take Abbie's advice, even if I sometimes regret it.

And I really, really regret it right now as I contemplate turning around and running for my life.

Who needs consistent income and a roof over your head anyway, right?

But backing out would make *Damien* look bad, and he's too good to Abbie for me to screw him over.

When it was presented to me, the job sounded perfect—a full-time position from May to September planning the club's events, starting with a Memorial Day brunch and ending with a Labor Day wedding for his daughter. But the most exciting part of the job is, over the summer, I will not only be allowed but *encouraged* to network with the wealthy men and women who frequent the club and build a clientele to help me start my own business.

It even included *room and fucking board* at the fancy hotel.

It was too good to be true.

There has to be a catch, I told Abbie weeks ago. There had to be a reason no one else had already snatched up this job, someone more qualified or well known.

I distinctly remember saying, "Something isn't right. I should super sleuth and figure out why no one wants this job."

That was when she *told me* not to search them, made me *promise* not to.

She actually reminded me of her promise when we were in the room this morning after our heart-to-heart.

But of course, I didn't listen like a moron, instead going straight to my phone as soon as I got to my car to drive and find a coffee shop for some much-needed caffeine.

Big mistake. *Huge.*

I sigh, my head hitting the steering wheel of my car. My phone buzzes with a text.

Abbie: Good luck! Love you! Don't get in your own head.

How do my friends know I'm panicking?

Kat: And don't forget to pay the tab at the bar tonight after work! Consider it our fee for the intervention.

Me: Fuck off.

Kat: Too soon?

I ignore her, letting my silence be the answer as I turn off my car and open the door. Stepping out, I decide to leave my things in there to deal with later because my hands are shaking enough without having to handle all of my belongings as well.

According the itinerary Jeanne, assistant to Jefferson Kincaid, sent me last week, I'll be shown to my new home soon after this first meeting.

God, even his name sounds rich, like he only wears Rolex watches and imports his wine from some valley in Italy and has a driver to take him anywhere his little heart desires.

Reaching for the front door, still lost in my thoughts, I sigh as ice-cold air conditioning hits me. It's only May in New Jersey, but the early heat wave makes it very much welcome.

As I walk in, a woman stands behind the front desk with fair skin and nearly black hair pulled into a ponytail, soft curtain bangs framing her face as she smiles at me. According to my research and some insight from Damien, the Beach Club is a giant building with beach-front access, two huge pools, and other amenities on the lower level, like a spa, salon, dining area, and, apparently, multiple areas for events. Above the first level are offices, suites, and condos which can be rented for the summer. It's clear no expense was spared when designing and decorating the lobby of the club with marble everything and white, silky fabrics for the curtains—the cleaning bill *alone* must be thousands a month.

"Hi, how can I help you today?"

"My name is Camile Thompson. I have a meeting with Jefferson Kincaid today?"

"Oh, you must be the new event coordinator," she says and her face changes, the look going from welcoming to something adding fuel to the fire that is my anxiety.

A flash of *pity*.

Oh fuck.

"Yes, I am." I straighten my shoulders, unsure of what to do or say.

"We're all so very excited about Melanie's wedding." The words hold a measured amount of insincerity wrapped in artificial joy, like she's going through the motions and afraid someone will overhear her being anything but exuberant. The man next to her snorts a quiet laugh.

"Don't let them scare you off, too, okay?" he says with a tip of his head in my direction.

The nerves already brewing start to expand and grow.

I've met two people here and both are giving the vibe this is going to be an . . . experience.

"Glen, hush," she says, swatting at the man, her eyes wide and her voice quiet before she turns to me, a cordial smile plastered on her face. "Don't listen to him. He's just a grump."

"If I'm a grump than those women are the devil incarnate," he says under his breath, and the blood drains from the woman's face.

It drains from my own body as well.

I was made aware upon accepting the position the biggest event I would oversee this summer season was the wedding of Melanie Kincaid to Huxley St. George. Melanie Kincaid, according to my online sleuthing, is a woman of the *Real Housewives* variety and, allegedly, is gunning for her own spot on one of the California seasons, where Huxley St. George runs his worldwide finance company.

She's also the daughter to my new boss, the owner of the Beach Club.

When I read a Page Six feature about the socialite supposedly running off her last event planner, I convinced myself it was some kind of exaggeration or misunderstanding, something to sell magazines and garner attention.

But now, I'm wholeheartedly second-guessing that.

"Don't listen to him. He's mad because the twins turned him down."

Who the hell are the twins and why do the words seem like they're rotten?

"They didn't so much as turn me down, rather Staceigh told me there was no way I would ever be on her level in this lifetime," he says with a sour look.

Okay.

Well, that makes this a little less terrifying. Clearly, this man is just annoyed some woman didn't fall for his questionable charm and now he's making it seem like *they* are the problem.

Internally, I roll my eyes.

A bruised man's ego leading to an attempt at ruining a woman's reputation.

So *freaking* typical.

Men.

I roll my eyes at the male concierge and look to the woman who originally greeted me.

"Again, ignore him. He's bitter. I have a note here to send you up when you arrive, so take the elevator on the left to the fourth floor. Mr. Kincaid's executive assistant will be waiting for you."

"Thank you so much," I say with a nod then move toward the elevator she pointed to.

As I hit the button for the fourth floor, I force myself to take deep breaths, to remind myself even though this isn't my dream job, it's an amazing step forward in my career.

If I can make sure this summer goes off without much of a hitch, I'm golden.

Eyes on the prize, I remind myself as the doors open with a ping.

FOUR

CAMI

Jeanne walks me into Jefferson Kincaid's office and it's hard not to be impressed. That's the point with a man like this after all. He wants people to feel impressed when they walk in, to feel just a hint of panic they *aren't good enough* when looking around at the luxury.

It's all dark, rich woods and a giant bookshelf filled with documents and old editions of books I'm sure cost more than my apartment in the city did for an entire year. The giant glass windows overlook the beach, sparkling ocean lapping at the golden sand.

It's impressive.

But not impressive enough to set me off kilter.

I've been around his type for nearly my whole life, learning how to read and interpret and morph myself in the presence of old wealth in order to fit in better.

The number one lesson I learned while attending one of the most exclusive prep schools on the East Coast for high school was people who work this hard to impress others *always* have intentions. It's never accidental.

The first is they want to remind you how much money and power they have and, ideally, how much you *do not*.

Because of my ill-advised searching, I know just how much wealth and power Jefferson Kincaid has. I know the companies he has in his portfolio, know he inherited the Kincaid Group from his father, and I know the Beach Club of Long Beach Island, though it becomes his office headquarters in the summer, is mostly a pet project.

So, I don't need the reminder of his wealth and power, and it doesn't do its desired job of throwing me off.

The second reason people put so much effort into their appearance is they want to use the reminder of money and power to make you feel *nervous*. To remind you of how much lesser you are to them, how you will never *be* on their level. Because if you walk into a room trying to do business and become nervous, you're so much less likely to argue with whatever Jefferson says. That's how you remain in power.

Intimidation.

Thankfully, it doesn't make me nervous.

It makes my back straighten, my smile turn fake, my chin tip up because I'll be damned if I let some crusty old man tell me how to feel just because he has more money than God.

"Ah, Camile, so happy to see you've made it," Jefferson says, walking over to me and giving me a firm handshake before waving to an uncomfortable looking chair. "Take a seat."

I smile politely and try not to stare too long at the pretty young woman sitting in one of the other chairs across from Thomas. She's petite with light-brown hair and a perfect fake tan, her contour better than half of the best makeup influencers I've seen, her clothes expensive and on trend.

But that's not what has my interest piqued.

It's the way her hands in her lap are moving, picking at a loose thread on her skirt.

She doesn't want to be here.

Interesting.

Next to her is a perfect blonde I instantly recognize as Melanie

Kincaid, soon-to-be Melanie St. George.

The *bride* and daughter of Jefferson Kincaid.

"I'd love to introduce you to my lovely daughter Melanie," he says. She gives me a stunning, warm smile and I move to shake her hand. "Melanie is the one getting married this Labor Day weekend."

"I'm so very excited to hear all of your ideas and get your event planning started," I say with confidence I don't necessarily feel.

Does the idea of planning an extravagant wedding in two months make me want to barf a little?

Yes. Yes, absolutely it does.

Do I also know this event specifically also comes with an unlimited budget, which makes almost anything possible?

Also, yes.

And the way Melanie smiles, kind and warm and so far from what the tabloids have framed her as, eases the anxiety further.

A positive outlook, I remind myself. *I'm entering this summer with positivity.*

"This is my granddaughter Olivia," he says, hand moving to the woman in her early twenties. She gives me a smaller smile, not necessarily less warm than her mother's but less . . . open. The smile is still sweet, though, and it's endearing.

"So nice to meet you," I say, shaking her hand as well before sitting in a chair at the long table.

"We're so excited to have you here with us this summer. After this meeting, you can go down to Janice and she'll show you to your new home for the summer. If anything at all is missing, please let us know and we'll be sure to amend it."

"Thank you so much. I'm sure everything will be perfect though." Jefferson smiles and I think in that moment, I decide I might like him.

Maybe Abbie and Kat were right. Maybe it really is all about the mindset.

"Well, keep it in mind. I really wanted to set up this meeting to say hello and introduce you to the lights of my life, both of whom you'll hopefully be working closely with this summer." I smile, slightly confused as to what he means.

"My granddaughter Olivia graduated college this week and is hoping to start her own PR firm in the fall." Olivia's jaw goes tight but a small smile hits her lips, and I can't quite decode it.

"You're free to say no, but I would love to bring her on for the summer as your assistant or an intern. We have so many events going on and although we have an in-house team to handle food and setup, another hand would probably be beneficial for you."

Oh fuck.

Goddammit.

I should have known this would be too good to be true, for this opportunity to come without strings.

"Olivia's father is from LBI and she grew up here as well as spent her summers at the club. She'll be a great asset to you in gaining contacts across the island as needed as well as handling working with the different departments here at the Beach Club."

I force my jaw to loosen and for my shoulders not to creep up to my ears with anxiety.

"I think that could be very helpful. A day or so a week, maybe?"

"There's no expectation, more like an offer for you. I'd handle paying Olivia a stipend for her hours working here." *Interesting,* I think. A rich girl needing a stipend for an internship. "And, of course, she would report directly to you."

"If Olivia is interested, I'd love to have her," I halfway lie. Although I prefer to work alone, I can't deny working with someone who knows this area would be helpful.

She gives me a stiff nod, but her smile has smoothed from nervous to warm. Maybe she's just as nervous and anxious as I am.

"I'll have Jeanne send Olivia your information so she can get on your calendar and you can talk about the details. How does that sound?" he asks, and he has such an adorable grandfatherly look about him, it's hard to say no.

"That would be great," I say, smiling at him again,

"Oh yay! How exciting!" Melanie says with a clap of her hands while her daughter just smiles.

This family is . . . so very far from what I expected.

And once again, I find myself questioning if maybe Abbie and Kat were right. If I make my mind up on people long before they get the chance to show me who they are and I've been sabotaging all of my relationships for years.

"It would just be *so fun* to have my daughter help you with the planning of my wedding!" Melanie says before lifting my worst nightmare.

A five-inch-thick baby-blue binder held in her perfectly manicured hands, *Wedding Stuff* printed on the side.

The anxiety I thought had washed away starts to creep back in.

"Absolutely. Speaking of which, I have a last-minute lunch to attend this afternoon, so I was thinking the girls could meet with you and have an impromptu planning meeting, if you're okay with that?"

I am so *not* okay with that.

I am unprepared.

I haven't done more than the basic research for this event yet, and I definitely don't have my planning materials with me—my inspiration boards and notebooks and day planner and timeline.

None of it.

But this job is important, and I'll be damned if I let anything or anyone make me lose this opportunity.

I've got this.

I'm Camile fucking Thompson.

I once planned a Sweet 16 worthy of *My Super Sweet 16* in 24 hours with a feral demon child of a client *and* I convinced her favorite K-pop artist to fly to the States and perform for her.

I can plan a rich chick's third wedding, easy peasy.

"Absolutely," I say with a smile. "I'm eager to get this going. Do you have any kind of paper or pens I could use? I wasn't expecting this, but I can transfer whatever notes I take into a document tonight and we can get this ball rolling."

This is actually great, I think, putting on my *positive thinking* attitude that I borrowed from Kat. I'll get a head start and I'll show them right off the bat what a hard worker I am.

"Right here," Jeffrey says, handing over a stack of notebooks branded with the Kincaid Corporation's logo. "When you leave, make sure you have Jeanne add you to my calendar for lunch tomorrow and we can talk more about the club and your new position. Melanie and Olivia will be there, and I believe the twins will be as well, correct?"

"Yes," Olivia says, her throaty, low voice breaking through the quiet room.

"Unfortunately, I have a spa appointment all day tomorrow. That flight from California really took it out of me and I'm in dire need of a massage and a sauna."

"Of course. Well, Camile, the girls, and I will have a great meal down at the Surf, yes?" Heads nod and Jefferson stands, grabbing his suit jacket and a briefcase.

"Okay, well, I'll see you all tomorrow," he says, shaking my hand one last time and moving toward the door.

"I'll let you ladies talk about everything!"

"Bye, Daddy!" Melanie says with a big smile and a delicate wave.

I'm beginning to actually get *excited* to work on Melanie's wedding now, watching how she is so incredibly different than what those stupid tabloids made her out to be. Abbie was so right. I never should ha—

"I thought he would never leave," Melanie says as she sits once more at the table, this time in her father's seat, voice bored.

When I turn back to look at her, I'm looking at a completely different woman. The smile has melted, the softness of her face gone and replaced with harsh lines.

I don't speak, but when my eyes move to her daughter, hers are pursed in a *goddammit* kind of way.

Uh oh.

"This is everything I want," Melanie says, clicking her perfectly

French manicured nails on that Tiffany-blue binder that is now taunting me. "There's no budget and I need it all to be *perfect*. I'm marrying a *St. George* after all."

I blink.

Once, twice, three times before I realize she expects some kind of awe-filled response.

But again, I know the type, so I don't give it to her.

Instead, I put a hand out, gesturing for the binder.

"Wonderful, I can't wait to see what you've put together and how we can make this the event of the summer," I say, my voice firm and friendly but business like.

She stares at me for a what feels like centuries but isn't more than a few moments before she gives me the tiniest of approving nods and slides the giant ass binder my way.

"First few pages are everything I need you to have completed by Friday," she says, seeming to dismiss me. When I open the binder, there's a list filled with bullet points, the font as small as can be.

There must be at least seventy items on this goddamn list.

Fuck.

Fuck, fuck, fuck.

The tightness in my chest slowly rises as I gloss over the items, my eyes not even reading them through the fog of anxiety. Instead, I put one hand under the table and begin tapping my fingers to my thumb rhythmically, one at a time, focusing on the movement until I land back into the room instead of floating above it lost in panic.

"I'll begin working on this right away. This one, item fifteen?" I ask, running a nail down the list and reading one at random. I know if I leave here with zero questions, it's a sign of weakness. "When you say cream linens, are we talking warm or cool undertones?"

With my words, there is the tiniest glimmer of a change in her face.

She's not sold on me, but I've impressed her.

I've passed one of *her* tests. It's ironic, in a way.

"Cool," she says with a tip of her lips.

Most people would go for a yellow undertone, a warm color. Very rarely can you even *find* linens with a cool undertone without having them made custom.

It's then my thought is confirmed.

This *entire list* is a test.

From the note about a quartet to play her down the aisle to the very vague request of a sendoff, every item is to see if I'm worthy of planning her wedding.

The smile on her face tells me she thinks I'll fail, just like her other, what was it? Four wedding planners?

It's clear this is a game of *let's see how far we can push the help, how miserable we can make her until she snaps.*

Except, they don't know I can be just as brutal and catty. My skin is thicker than any human's should be and my mother raised me to face this kind of mean-girl treatment, dissect it, and use it as ammunition to win.

"Any other questions I have—where should I direct them?" I ask.

"Olivia. And CC my assistant Cornelia. Her email and cell number are on page three."

In that moment, I decide every aspect of the planning process will be carefully tracked in emails. Every approval, every detail available to reference later. Melanie Kincaid may be a bridezilla, but she's never tried to crush me.

"You can do this by Friday, yes?" Melanie says, an eyebrow raised. "I don't know how much you know, but my last planner just left me high and dry for no reason. So unprofessional."

Yeah, no shit, I think. *Maybe because you're a psychotic bridezilla and not in the good, fun way.*

"Mother," Olivia says, and with the word comes a flash of annoyance from Melanie.

Also interesting.

So very interesting.

"Either she can do it or not, Olivia. You should learn that now if you plan to do your little PR thing. People judge you instantly based on what you're willing to do. Your portfolio and references mean nothing if you can't accomplish tasks in a timely manner."

Olivia opens her mouth to argue and for some reason, sympathy comes over me. My mind moves to what this could be—a blossoming friendship where I take this girl under my wing and teach her what I know.

"You're so right, Melanie. I can't wait to prove myself to you. I look forward to working with you, Olivia," I say, and the look on Melanie's face tells me I survived this round.

FIVE

CAMI

I take a few more notes from Melanie before she jets off to some appointment, then I coordinate to meet with Jeanne tomorrow to be set up with my computer and keys before I finally take the stairs to the lobby.

Once again, I'm smiling at Janice, and like last time, she speaks before I do.

"How'd it go?"

"Well, I met Mr. Kincaid and his daughter and granddaughter." Her mouth purses like she wants to say something, but she doesn't. "So, Janice, right? That's your name?" I tip my head to her name tag and she rolls her eyes.

"Yes, my mother gave me the most old white lady name known to man and I'll never forgive her for it. And Cici. Please, call me Cici."

"Got it," I say with a smile. "Cami." She returns the smile with a nod before grabbing a huge key ring and stepping from behind the desk.

"Alright, Cami. Are you ready to see your new home for the summer?"

I like her. She's fun and bubbly and way too happy, like a mix of

Abbie and Kat, and something about that makes me feel slightly at ease. It's like I might have someone on my side during what I'm thinking might be some of the most chaotic months of my life.

"I'm not in a rush, if you have other—"

"Stop, I'd give anything to leave my station. Hold on, let me grab Glen. Your things are in your car?" I stare at her, unsure. "Your bags? Clothes, knickknacks . . . You did brings things, right? I was under the impression you were . . . moving in." Her head moves and she pushes some papers around. "Jeanne told me to make sure housekeeping cleared out room 29 for you, but maybe I'm mistaken—"

"Oh. Yes. I am. But I don't need anyone to help me. I can—"

"Glen can help. Trust me, it's literally his job. GLEN!" she yells, and then finally, the man from earlier comes from the back, glaring at Cici. "Get your rack, we gotta help Cami move her stuff to her new apartment." She says it like we're old friends.

"Why can't you do it?" he asks, and she rolls her eyes before sighing.

"Because I'm a woman and I have weak, delicate arms and you're a big strong man."

He rolls his eyes and she smiles sweetly.

"I promise, it's no big. I can—" I start, but this time, it's Glen who cuts me off.

"I'm just fucking with Cici. No worries, let's just make sure Carol will cover the front desk," he says before picking up the old corded phone and dialing in whom I assume is Carol.

This place is strange. So very strange.

But ten minutes later, my belongings are on the rack and the three of us are in an elevator. I now have a card to scan to get to the locked floors where my office and apartment will be, as well as a stack of information about the restaurant, coffee and juice stations, and other amenities.

"So, the meeting went well?" Cici asks in a friendly tone.

"Yes. It was . . . good. Very . . . informative." That sounds good. A very political answer.

"Was Melanie a mega bitch?" Glen asks, and Cici turns, smacking him in the stomach. "Ooof, the fuck, Janice?" She hits him again.

"That was for calling me Janice. The first one was for being a douche. Stop it. You're going to scare her off and I think I'm going to like her."

"I was just asking," he says and looks like a lost puppy in a kind of cute, kind of pathetic way.

When I look at Cici, it's clear she leans more toward the "cute" description of it as she smiles at him.

"They were fine. Melanie seems a little . . . intense."

Glen snorts before rolling his lips between his teeth and widening his eyes.

"Intense. That's . . . a good way to describe her," Cici says, then the elevator dings and she starts walking, leaving Glen and me behind. I'm not sure what to do, but when she looks over her shoulder and moves her hand in a "come on" sign, I start to follow her. "Don't worry, he's got it." I catch up with her and can barely keep her stride before she starts talking again. "Melanie has been coming here every summer for as long as I know. She fucked a local one year, got knocked up, and well, you met Olivia."

"Yes, I did. She seems . . . quiet."

There's a look in Cici's eyes telling me this is where her wealth of easily shared knowledge stops.

"She is sometimes." Her hand moves to a door with a gold 29 on it and she slides a key into the lock, turning and pushing open the door. "So, you didn't meet the twins yesterday but they're bound to show up eventually."

"Yeah, I'm supposed to meet them at lunch tomorrow. Who *are* the twins?"

"Melanie is marrying the tech tycoon Huxley St. George. He has twin daughters, Staceigh and Laceigh. Don't even ask how their names are spelled. I promise you don't want to know."

I kind of do, but I don't ask.

"They are the devil incarnate. Started coming around three summers ago when Melanie started dating their dad. They hate the Beach Club but still spend the whole summer here, bitching about how much they hate it."

We walk into my new apartment finally and the room is *so much more* than I expected. It's a lot like Damien's room but smaller, just a full-sized bed in the middle of the space with lush white bedding and a sage-green love seat in the corner. The dresser, side table, and bed frame are all dark wood to match the wood floors, but everything else is pure white. I poke my head to see a small kitchenette and a decently sized bathroom before my eyes catch the giant window beside the bed.

An ocean view.

God, this alone might make it worth the chaos of Melanie's wedding.

"The twins are . . ." Cici looks around the room, watching as Glen closes the door behind him after he tugs the luggage cart over the threshold.

"Psychotic, just like every other member of the Bitch Pack."

"The Bitch Pack?" I ask, grabbing a bag from the stack.

"The Bitch Pack is what the locals and staff call the twins and their crew of lackeys. There's a dozen of them or so, depending on how many of them are in the good graces of the twins at any given moment." Cici jumps onto the bed and bounces once as she answers.

"And they're . . . not great?" I ask, biting my lip.

Cici answers before Glen does.

"Like every group, some of them are cool, so it's not everyone who is . . . extra. This is the twins' fourth summer here and they're probably the worst of the worst. Wait." She stops speaking before looking at me, a hint of panic in her face. "This doesn't leave here, okay?" She looks at me as if she thinks I might rat her out, like she forgot we just met and isn't sure if I'm friend or foe. I smile.

"You're good. I know the type. I'd rather get the info from the staff who work with them regularly then get blindsided." Relief crosses her face.

"I like her, Cici."

"Me too," she says before explaining. "So, each year, the twins end up picking someone to absolutely terrorize." My eyes go wide. "Full-on queen-bee stuff. Talking shit, spreading rumors, tricks to make them miserable."

"Four years ago, it was Ci—" Glen starts before he stops. "Sorry." She sighs and shakes her head.

"A few years ago, I was their target. It's a long sordid story, but Olivia and I both grew up on the island and we were pretty good friends. The first summer after college, she comes back with the twins and . . . for whatever reasons, the twins decided I was target number one."

"Oh god, I'm so sorry," I say.

"It's fine. I promise. It was forever ago and they've moved on to bigger, more exciting fish. Honestly, we're all excited for this wedding because once Melanie is all wifed up, she probably won't be spending her summers at the Beach Club which means the twins probably won't be dumped here either." She unwraps the little pillow mint on the bed and shoves it in her mouth. "So, we're all really riding on this wedding going well, you know. No pressure." There's a joking smile on her face.

"Yeah, no pressure."

"Hate to break up the gossip session, but can you let me know where to put these bags? Carol cannot be trusted at the front desk for long," Glen says before we all move to get my luggage off the rack.

"Food—where's the best place to go?" I ask Cici as I walk back to the lobby with them. I need to move my car now that I have a parking

pass, and I know I should also probably some groceries for my apartment.

"There's a grocery store on the island, but it's not the best. If you want a lot of selections, you'll have to cross the bridge, but there's also a bunch of good restaurants around, plus you get a meal each day at the restaurant near pool one. There's also a little café downstairs but it's not the best." She circles a few locations on the map of the club for me.

As much as I probably should, the grocery store sounds like the worst option right now, and the café or restaurant in the building don't sound much better. I'm both too exhausted to buy and then *make* food and way too stressed out to deal with maybe running into a potential client and having to be "on."

With my meetings crossed off my mental to-do list, the drain of the surprisingly long day is starting to seep into my bones. And not just because I didn't sleep well or because I'm still a little hung over. Now that the most pressing moments of my day are done, I'm back to contemplating what Kat and Abbie told me this morning and trying to figure out how to move forward with their advice.

"Across the street is the Fishery. It's a little dive that's been around forever and has a bunch of fried food and good drinks. It's mostly locals but bennies go in the summer, too." She pauses and smiles at me like she knows what I was thinking about having to deal with clients and employers. "Don't worry, the Beach Club members rarely ever go over there."

I smile back at her.

"Thank you."

I don't tell her how I very much do *not* want to have dinner at the dive bar where I made a drunken fool of myself last night.

"Not today because I've got work and to be totally honest, you look beat." She cringes like she's nervous I'll be offended, and I laugh because it's not a lie. "But soon, we should do something." She walks over to the desk in the corner with a little branded hotel notepad on it and writes something down. "That's my number. Text me later so we have each other's numbers and hopefully we can set something up."

"Thanks. That's . . . very kind. I don't know anyone around here, so a friend would be . . . A friend would be nice," I say, and it feels both weird and very out of character for me, but maybe that's what I need while I'm here: to get out of my comfort zone and branch out.

Cici's smile is kind when she speaks again. "You know, you seem cool. I hope you can handle it, Melanie and the Bitch Pack and the club. Don't let them scare you off, okay?" she says with a kind smile.

I decide then and there that I like her.

"Oh, don't worry. I have a lot of experience with their type. They can't scare me off easy," I say with a friendly look.

"Well, I'm glad." The phone rings at the front desk and she stares at it like she wishes she could throw it against a wall. "Alright, well, I should answer that. I'll see you around, yeah?"

"Yeah," I say with a smile before walking out of the lobby and into the salty air and sunshine.

SIX

CAMI

Leaving the Beach Club feels like I'm leaving a dream world and walking into reality.

The island is interesting because before Memorial Day, it seems it's pretty empty around here, businesses preparing for the influx of visitors and the holiday but still down-to-earth, normal people working normal jobs at normal businesses.

It's a stark contrast to the luxuriant extravagance of the Beach Club.

I like it.

I like it a lot.

The Beach Club feels like a show—I've only been there for a day but it already very much feels like a place where I need to keep my mask on firmly no matter what. But as soon as I step out, I'm . . . strangely at home.

Except, as I look both ways before crossing the road over to the Fishery, I can't help but wonder if I'm making a huge fucking mistake.

I should stay in my safe bubble and definitely not walk across the street and make a fool of myself.

I should *not* show my face at this place, that's for damn sure.

I should call in and give them my credit card number and leave a giant tip and never ever ever walk through the door.

But also . . .

I'm hungry. Actually, I'm on the cusp of *hangry* and the French fries here last night were insanely good and I don't know where anything else is *and* I have to pay my tab, so here we go.

Walking in, I'm reminded why eating here is a great idea, although if the same bartender is here, I might need to get it as take-out. The bar is dark and small but clean and smells unbelievably good. The bar spans the entirety of the back with a kitchen window and a door on the right with *office* written on it positioned behind the bar and small high-top tables throughout.

I decide to get it over with, walking to back bar and sitting on a stool. Looking around, the server from last night seems to be here but not the bartender, so my anxiety dips just a hair while I wait for her to come over so I can explain. While I wait, I reach over to grab a worn paper menu, reading it over as music blares over the speakers. It's a full 180 from where I just came from—instead of formalities and tight smiles, it's deep laughs and casual clothes and the smell of fried food.

It's like I'm back in a comfort zone I didn't realize I missed.

And that's important since my best friends have so openly forced me to *leave* my comfort zone.

"Shrimp basket is my favorite," a voice says, my stomach dropping to the floor, and when my head lifts, there's a man leaning on his forearms, smiling at me.

Even without the haze of drink and best friends, it's still a *good* smile.

It's the kind of smile Kat would love, would say she can tell he makes good pancakes and gives good hugs, but Abbie would said it's the kind of smile that screams he knows what to do with his hands.

At least, the new version of Abbie—the one who is confident and gets orgasms on the regular.

"Shrimp basket?" I ask with a raised brow.

"Oh yeah. Fried shrimp, a shit ton of fries, a couple hushpup-pies." That smile widens and I remember he also has dimples.

Fucking dimples.

What higher power looked at this god of a man with his light-brown hair, not quite a buzz cut but not quite long, and his scruff and his wide, white smile and his broad fucking shoulder and said, you know what he also needs?

Dimples.

Let's give him some dimples to nail down the fact he's going to drop some damn panties in his lifetime.

"Alright. I'll go with that." He smiles like he approves and strangely, it has an effect on me.

Earning the approval of this man, for some reason, makes me warm all over.

No, no, no, Cami. You're here on a mission. Get dinner, pay your tab, go to bed.

"So, how bad were you this morning?" he asks as he taps a screen then faces me again, leaning on his forearms.

Well, fuck.

Part of me had thought he didn't recognize me.

"Not that great. Even worse when my friends told me they left without paying the tab and I would have to come in after making an ass of myself to pay it." His face goes blank for a moment before the *stupid fucking dimples come out again.*

"Yeah, well. You all were pretty messed up last night. Where are they tonight?"

"Back home. They just came to help me get down here."

"Home being . . ."

"The city. I'm here for a new job over at the Beach Club."

"Yes, I do remember you saying that." I give him a tight smile before speaking.

"So, about that tab, how should I go about paying it? Add it onto this or . . . ?"

The dimples deepen before he answers. "Let's make a deal."

"A deal?"

"You tell me what's going on in your head, and I'll forget about the tab."

"What?"

"You talk through whatever has that stressed look in your eyes and I'll cover your tab."

"I can pay it," I say, the idea of exposing even *more* of myself to this stranger absolutely a horrible one.

"I know."

"Then why do you want to cover it?"

He sighs before leaning on the bar again, locking eyes with mine. "You've got the look," he says.

"The look?"

"I've owned this bar for a while. I know the look."

"What's the look?" I ask with a small smile.

"You're contemplating something." My smile grows with his words because he's not wrong, and coming from someone who feels like she does a pretty good job at showing specific sides of myself, I think that's impressive.

"And you're pretty good at your job."

"I know," he says with a cocky smile. "What can I get you for a drink before you spill your guts to me." Even though I hate when bartenders do this—read customers and start small talk—I can't help but return the smile.

It must be the dimples.

"Aperol spritz," I say finally. The dimples disappear as he shakes his head.

"Sorry, babe. You're in a dive. Nothing fancy here. We've got hard liquor, beer, red or white wine."

I should have known, but it was worth a shot.

"White wine is fine," I say because after last night, hard liquor is absolutely the wrong choice, even if I could really use it. He shakes his head like he knows I secretly want something stronger but is willing to let me be. He taps a screen, putting in my order, I assume, before filling a large wine glass with wine.

"So, spill," he says when he clunks the glass in front of me.

"Spill?"

"What are you contemplating?" My eyebrows come together as I look left and right, trying to see if there's anyone watching. "Give me all of your issues."

"Uh, I just met you. Seems a little much, no?" I ask.

"The perk of a bartender—you can trauma-dump on me and then avoid this place for as long as you want. You never have to see me again *and* you'll probably feel a bit better."

"So you're, what, like, a trauma sponge?"

"I guess." The dimples come back.

"That sounds kind of . . . depressing." A chuckle comes from his lips, just loud enough to hear over the music in the bar which isn't as loud as it was last night, and the sound settles in my belly, sending warmth through my body.

"It's not. It's interesting. I like it, talking to people."

"So, you like drama?"

"I like to *listen* to *other* people's drama."

"Hmm," I say, not quite convinced.

"Okay, maybe I don't love the full-time therapist position—I really don't need to know why Mitchell's wife is making him sleep on the couch for the third time this week, especially when it's mostly because he's a fuckin' moron and can't figure out his wife doesn't want to hear his negative opinions on the dinner she made him. But the occasional info dump from a pretty girl? Yeah, I'd call it a perk of the job."

Now I lean on my arms, smiling at him. "Oh, so pretty girls are a perk to the job?" His eyes rove my body and a full-body burn starts.

Huh. That's new.

That does not happen, not to me at least.

To Kat, the hopeless romantic?

Yes.

To Abbie, who's boyfriend gives her the most unbearably hot looks?

Yeah . . . definitely.

But not me.

Not to say I don't like men or they don't affect me—they do.

But on *my* terms. Mostly, only when I know I want to get laid, when I leave my apartment with the distinct mindset of finding a man who piques my interest and get the urge out of the way before going right back to my mission of living string free.

And god, this man *screams* strings.

"Are you going to spill your issues, or do I have to wait until you've got a happy food high?"

"Shrimp basket's that good, huh?" I ask with a smile. But for some reason, I spill.

Maybe it's the wine, or the smell of the food, or the feeling of starting a new job, or knowing this is a bartender who has probably heard some wild shit.

Or maybe it's just the dimples.

Either way, I spill.

"My friends say I have trust issues." He stares at me, waiting for me to expand. "They say I need to stop making it so hard to let in new people. Apparently, I give people too many . . . tests. I just wait for them to fail them so I can further confirm my assumption people suck and shouldn't be trusted."

"Well, do you?"

"Do I what?"

"Test people."

I pause, trying to think about how to explain it.

Of course I do.

The problem is, if I say it out loud to anyone besides my best friends, I can't hide from it anymore. I can't continue to pretend I don't do that exact thing, that I'm not secretly still doing it despite my promise to Abbie and Kat.

But his eyes are kind and the wine is warm in my empty stomach and for those two reasons, I tell the truth. It's almost . . . freeing in a way, admitting it to a stranger.

"Yeah. I guess I do. But it's not my fault they fail." He raises an eyebrow and I sigh before expanding, justifying. "People give you the perfect version of themselves. They give you a hyper edited version, the one they *think* you want to see."

"Is that a bad thing?" he asks.

It's an unexpected response, and I mull on it.

I don't know if I've ever thought of that.

Is that a bad thing?

"I mean . . . yeah." That eyebrow raises like he doesn't quite believe me and I pause, thinking.

Is it a bad thing that people give me their best version of themselves instead of the flawed one?

"Let me reframe that," he says. "If everyone you met gave you their basest version of themselves, would you ever let them in?"

I answer instantly.

"No." His head tips a bit, like I've confirmed his thought. "But if everyone showed *you* their worst versions of themselves from the get-go, would *you* like them?"

"Of course I wouldn't." He gives me another look. *See?* it says.

"But wouldn't that make life easier, knowing what everyone's worst looks like before you invest time in them? We'd know right off the bat if we were going to be able to tolerate them at their worst."

The dimples come back as he crosses his arms across a wide chest, muscles flexing as he does, and *holy shit.*

I shouldn't be staring.

I'm here for a summer.

I'm here for *work.*

I *work* across the street.

"So, you're saying you only want to invest your time in people who you can *tolerate* at their worst?"

"You keep repeating what I say like it's supposed to change the meaning," I say, but even as I say the words, the meaning of his change.

With what I'm saying, I only *tolerate* people I love when they're at their worst.

When is Abbie at her worst?

When she's struggling. When she's in a bad place mentally. When she feels down on herself. When she needs me most.

When is Kat at her worst?

When she's questioning another relationship. When she's being flighty. When she can't focus on the conversation at hand. When her anxiety wins.

Do I solely *tolerate* them?

Of course not.

When Abbie and Kat are at their worst, I do what I can to help.

Unless I'm testing them, trying to push them away to see just how much they care for me.

Oh god.

Am I the problem?

Am I fucked up?

Am I the shitty friend?

The tiny voice in my head that's been nagging since December speaks.

Sometimes, yeah.

"What's brewing in there?" dimples asks.

"Hmm?" I say, not in this conversation anymore, so deep in my own thoughts and understandings.

"You stopped talking and started thinking. What conclusion did you come to?" I stare at him then at my nails, the pretty light-pink nails I did last night while Abbie hyped me up for me new job before going out.

"I'm thinking my friends are much better friends to me than I am to them."

He moves to a register, taps a few times, then walks back over to me.

"Why's that?"

"I'm at my worst way more than they are." It surprises me when I say it, despite it being the truth.

He gives me another strange look like he doesn't understand but doesn't speak so I keep going.

"The worst for my friends is when they need someone. My worst comes out a *lot* and they never blink an eye. I test them and I don't let them in on what's bothering me. I cut them off. I judge. And they never say anything negative."

"Except . . ."

"Except for when they were worried about me." He smiles like he's content with the conclusion I've come to. "They want me to make more friends while I'm here. To give people a chance. They gave me a whole ass intervention this morning, telling me I was self-sabotaging." I pause again, remembering the looks on their faces. "They're worried about me. I think . . . I think they have been for a while. I just didn't want to hear it."

"And you do now? Want to hear it?"

Again, I think before I answer.

"I mean, not really. But I'm alone here for the first time in a long time. My friends have never been farther than 15 minutes from me. It's jarring to have this insight and not know what to do with it." Someone sits at the bar and he leaves to go get an order and serve a drink, and I sit at my seat, sipping my wine and thinking about what I've revealed and what it means for me.

This morning was incredibly eye-opening, of course, but strangely enough, this conversation is helping me unpack everything even more.

"So, what are you gonna do about it?"

"I'm . . . I'm going to try and . . . give people a chance. Maybe."

"Maybe?" he says, dimples out and proud as he smiles.

My mind moves to Olivia who, apparently, is going to be my intern and seems . . . tolerable.

She might be worth giving a chance.

And Cici, the concierge who has been nothing but kind to me.

Maybe she would be someone to open up to.

I, then, think about the twins . . .

The twins who I've heard are the absolute worst. But even there —should I judge them and write them off based off one or two people's probably biased input?

God, this is much harder than I thought it would be, making friends and giving people *chances*.

"Maybe. Do you think everyone deserves a chance?"

Dimples sighs.

"I think some people deserve it more than others, but no. Not inherently. But you look like a smart girl. I bet you can weed the good ones from the bad."

I thought I had a good scale for people once.

I thought my mother taught me to gauge people well, to figure out their strengths and weaknesses and what they were hiding.

Until Jason. Then, I realized I was wrong.

"Here's an idea. How about you let me take you out on a date? We can celebrate your new chapter. I can show you around the island."

I sit there for a full thirty seconds, staring and slightly . . . confused.

"You want to take me out after I just dumped all of my baggage on you?" I raise an eyebrow at him.

"Yup."

"Yeah, not gonna lie, that doesn't make you seem the most mentally stable."

"Sounds like we're a good pair, then, no?" My mouth drops open with disbelief.

"You're going to have to try harder than that." He smiles and god, it almost makes me want to say yes.

"No problem. I can be patient," he says. A bell rings and the cook shouts something I barely can decipher before dimples leaves to grab a basket piled high with French fries and fried shrimp, sliding it in front of me with a smile. "Enjoy."

Later, I'm paying for my dinner after an hour of small talk that made me smile more than I'd like to admit. "Thanks," I say. "I needed this. And thanks for the advice."

"You have to come in again soon, keep me updated on your mission."

It must be the aforementioned happy food buzz that has me nodding. "Will do." I say, pushing my stool in and starting to head for the door before I'm stopped.

"Hey, Cami?" he says, and I turn back to look at him, partially confused by how he knows my name. "The brunette last night? She had her card on file. Signed the receipt before I walked you three over to the Beach Club." My mouth drops open and he starts laughing, but all I can think on the walk home is I so totally can't stand my friends.

And how much I fucking love them.

SEVEN

THURSDAY, MAY 18

CAMI

"Ahh, Camile! Thank you so much for coming to lunch with us!" Jefferson Kincaid says with a kind smile the next day when the hostess at the fancier of the two restaurants at the Beach Club walks me over to the table where he's sitting with Olivia and two blondes.

The twins, I presume.

I can't decide if I like this man. He's got sweet old-man vibes, but they also might just be rich old-man vibes, which are two totally different categories.

But I don't have time to think too much about that as I sit between Jefferson and Olivia, the blondes across from me and carefully taking me in, from my hair to my nail polish to the jewelry I chose to wear today.

And instantly, I know their type.

My father passed when I was young and my mother used his small life insurance to build an empire. He was the love of her life, she told me over and over, so what was the point in trying to find another love? Instead, she used her time and energy to build a well-known and respected business as well as a nonprofit helping widowed mothers get on their feet.

She is absolutely my idol.

But the opportunities she had meant I attended to one of the best prep schools on the East Coast growing up, brushing elbows with heirs to some of the largest companies in the U.S. People who never once in their lives wanted for anything and it very much showed.

I instantly know the twins fall into that category.

"You remember Olivia, of course," he says, and she gives me a tight smile before he continues on. "And this is Staceigh and Laceigh, my soon-to-be stepgranddaughters."

I smile at the blondes who are clearly twins, though not identical. Nearly, but not quite the same. They're gorgeous and the same age as Olivia (22, according to my internet searching), but they don't seem nearly as down-to-earth as my initial impression of the brunette.

One of them lifts her hand. "I'm Staceigh." I take her hand and shake it, giving her what I hope is a warm smile.

"And I'm Laceigh. E-I-G-H," the other says, mimicking her sister's moves almost to a T, and I try to hide my very much confused look when Olivia sighs before explaining under her breath.

"She's spelling their names for you. Stacy but spelled S-T-A-C-I-E-G-H."

"Oh," I say in a whisper, trying not to let my eyes go wide in shock.

So, the twins are a full-blown stereotype: blonde and gorgeous and uber rich with quirkily spelled names.

"I'm sure you'll also be working closely with the girls for Melanie's wedding and I figured this would be a fabulous time for you four to bond, as girls do." As *I* do, I watch as the twins give the most darling, angelic smiles. "Unfortunately, I won't be able to stay for lunch. I have a last-minute meeting I must run to." He turns to me with an apologetic smile. "This seems to be becoming a habit of mine, Camile, and I'm so sorry. Beginning of the season makes for extra craziness, you know?"

"Oh, it's no problem at all. I totally understand," I say and internally, I give a sigh of relief.

Now I can run off to my office and continue to work on digging into the mile-high stack of files left behind by whatever incredibly unorganized person *used* to run the events department at the Beach Club, as well as Melanie's ridiculous binder.

"But please, stay and have lunch on me with the girls. Girls, our Camile here is new to the Beach Club, so she doesn't know anyone here yet. Please, make her feel welcome."

"Of course, Mr. Kincaid," Staceigh says, batting long fake lashes.

"Oh, now, Staceigh. I told you to call me Grandpa."

It happens so quick, if you weren't looking you'd miss it—a momentary flash on Staceigh's perfect face of disgust or irritation or something similar.

"Yes, Grandpa. We'll make sure Camile feels right at home at the Beach Club," she says with a smile.

"Yeah," Laceigh says, her smile a little less practiced than her sister's.

"Perfect, well, I'll be off," he says, standing. "Camile, please remember, any question, Jeanne can answer any time."

"Great, thank you so much, Mr. Kincaid."

"Now, I won't make you call me Grandpa," he says, and I have to fight not to let my eyes go wide. "But you must call me by my first name at the very least."

"Of course, Jefferson."

"Alright, well, talk to you ladies later."

There is a chorus of goodbyes before the three of us watch Jefferson leave, tipping a chin at people he passes, smiling at others until he's out the doors. Then, I'm sitting at a lunch I don't really want to be at with Olivia and the Bitch Pack twins.

No, Cami. That's not fair. Just because Cici and Glen call them that doesn't mean you need to.

I need to give them a real chance.

With that thought, I straighten my shoulders, put on my kindest smile which is only a *touch* fake, and turn to my lunch mates.

Except the sweet smile plastered on Staceigh's face seems to have melted off as soon as Jefferson left the room. She takes a sip of her mimosa, scanning the room before her eyes roll into her head and she speaks.

"Ugh, there's Cara." There's utter *disdain* in her voice.

"Ugh," her twin says. Staceigh shakes her head, her voice dropping so only us at the table can hear.

"God, she thinks she's so fucking pretty because she goes to the same hair stylist as Rachel McAdams but she's so fugly." The vehemence with which she speaks is almost alarming, forcing me to remind myself to calm my facial features.

I'm not with Kat and Abbie.

I'm with the bitchy girls from high school and I need to remember how, in spaces like this, there is a hierarchy. One wrong move and you're at the bottom of the food chain.

They pick someone each summer to terrorize. Cici's words come back to me.

"So fugly," Laceigh echoes and for a moment, I wonder if she knows any real words or if she's a robot who can only repeat what her sister says. Just then, the woman they're talking about smiles and waves at our table, walking our way with a smile.

It shouldn't surprise me, considering I've dealt with their type so many times, but the complete change in the looks on the twins' faces throws me a bit. I glare over at Olivia, who widens her eyes at me like she, too, is confused at best.

"Cara!" Staceigh says, standing and leaning in to kiss the pretty brunette on each cheek. "So good to see you!"

"You too! I heard you guys would be here again this summer and I told Daddy we *had* to spend some time here as well." Her smile is genuine and I *genuinely* feel bad for her. She has no idea they were just talking shit about her.

"Well, we'll have to set something up. Maybe drinks tomorrow?" Staceigh says, her voice sugary sweet.

"Oh, I'd just love that!"

"Great. Call Kim, she'll set it up," Staceigh says with a wink before sitting and smiling at Cara. "Bye." There's a wiggle of her fingers and Cara's smile goes uneasy when she realizes she's very obviously being dismissed. The queen bee is over her presence.

"Okay, yeah. That would be great."

"Yup. Bye," Staceigh says, her smile gone, perfectly manicured hand moving to the straw of her iced tea and stirring.

"Bye," Laceigh says, blinking at the woman. Finally, she gets the hint, waving and walking off, clearly flustered. I watch her leave, both enamored and intrigued by the interaction before I'm pulled back into the table conversation.

"God, Cami, your makeup is just so pretty," Staceigh says with a sugary-sweet smile. The speed of which she once again turns is becoming less intriguing and more alarming. Possibly terrifying. No sane, levelheaded human can flip the switch that quickly. "You're just gorgeous, aren't you?"

"Uh, thank you. I appreciate it. A friend of mine is obsessed with makeup and skincare, so she's really helped me find what works for me," I say with an uneasy smile.

"So you agree? You think you're really pretty," she says, the genuineness of her smile melting, her head cocking to the side, and it's then I know.

Melanie is a bitch.

Olivia is a puzzle.

But the twins are the ones to look out for.

Thankfully, I'm a pro. I've played this game many times and I never fucking lose.

"Yeah. I do," I say, a small smirk on my lips, an eyebrow raised.

I watch it happen, then—a tiny fracture in the façade.

Her brain is melting, and she's unsure of how to respond.

It didn't go the way she thought it would. I didn't cower or get flustered. She didn't faze me the way she does everyone else.

I wait quietly, smiling, waiting to see how she'll recover from this hiccup.

But it doesn't happen because for the first time, Laceigh speaks without echoing her sister.

"He's coming," she whispers. "He's staring *right at us*, Stace!"

Staceigh's eyes flick over my head and her face magically goes from judgy bitch to calm, cool, collected, and maybe . . . sweet?

"Everyone shut up and act cool," she says, fluffing her hair. I give Olivia another wide-eyed, confused look and again, I'm pleasantly surprised when she returns it. Interesting.

Those perfectly manicured hands move to her hair, pushing perfect, straight blonde locks around until they lie even more perfectly as she adds a layer of lip gloss while her sister looks over my shoulder and continues her updates, whispering about how close this mystery man is.

I hope he actually is coming over because I would *love* to see what kind of man's got Staceigh's panties in such a twist. I'm sure it's some socialite, some rich man with a portfolio four inches thick.

"Who?" I ask, because apparently, I can't resist. Olivia shrugs, also looking over my shoulder, but she either doesn't know him or can't find him.

And then, Staceigh's sweet, serene look quickly flashes to one akin to someone who wants to murder someone—gritting her teeth and looking at me. "You stay quiet. This is a very important moment for me."

As if I would want to engage in whatever kind of weird rich-bitch mating ritual is about to happen.

"Got it," I say with a small smile.

I almost miss it as I move to look back at my food, but I think Olivia's lips tip in the tiniest smile. Warmth fills me as I think maybe I might have an ally in this chaos. The way her mother treated her, I can't imagine she's happy with this shit.

But the world comes crashing down with four words.

"Cami, is that you?"

EIGHT

CAMI

The blood in my veins turns into painful ice because I *know* that voice.

That voice convinced me love was real and then quickly reminded me it's all bullshit.

That voice ruined the pretty vision I had of happily ever afters.

That voice made all of my mother's musings my whole life come to reality.

Don't fall for love, Cami. It's nothing but heartbreak.

I spent my entire life rolling my eyes when she said that as I watched her mourn her one true love and build an empire. Rolled my eyes because my mom fell in love once and it was all-consuming. So much so that when my father passed away, she never recovered.

I wanted that once.

I wanted consuming love, something I would mourn for the rest of my life if I lost it. She warned me it wasn't worth the pain, wasn't worth the heartache she felt every day of her life.

But I didn't listen.

And I've spent ten years mourning what I gave to Jason Demartino.

Now, he's staring at me like he hasn't seen me in years and suddenly regrets that.

"Jason," is all I can say.

"Wow. It is you. God, I thought I was imagining something." He smiles then, and there are lines which weren't there ten years ago.

"Nope, it's me."

This has to be a joke. It *has* to be.

Some kind of sick, fucked-up joke.

Maybe Kat and Abbie set it up, payback for me being such a bitch or maybe a way to show me how he *clearly* wasn't worth all the mental hoops I've jumped through over the years.

God, just look at him.

"Wow. It's so good to see you," he says, taking me in.

I'm wearing a white button-up shirt tucked into dark high-waisted pants, the top few buttons undone and a pretty aqua necklace adding some color to the neutral outfit. I forever have the voice of Abbie in the back of my mind when I'm dressing.

"Uh," I say, unsure of how to respond.

It is *very much* not great to see him. I've spent years of my life wondering what it would be like to see Jason Demartino again, what I'd say to him, the mean words I'd spew, the looks I'd give. The way I'd tell him his dick is tiny and I definitely faked it the one, short time we fucked.

But staring at him now, I'm lost for words.

He looks . . . terrible.

Not terrible, terrible—he didn't grow a dozen warts or lose an arm or anything—but back then, he was *everything* to me.

I pictured a million times what he would age like, how we'd look together in my mind when I was young.

Now, his hair is clearly thinning—not enough to notice at first glance, maybe, but enough that if you stare long enough or if you, like me, have the image of how he used to look fresh in your mind, you'd see it.

And it wouldn't be a big deal—fuck, I'm the last one to body shame or set people to some impossible standard, and I've seen some men absolutely *rock* the bald look—but on him, the way he combs it, the way he keeps touching his hair but not moving it, it's clearly a sore spot.

He used to be built, running track in college and always chugging protein drinks, making fun of anyone, man or woman, whose physique wasn't societally perfect. Now, he's soft in the middle, the shirt not fitting right, like he refuses to size up.

But mostly, he looks tired and run down. Gaunt. He's got the look of someone who spent ten years thinking their misdeeds—both to their own body and to the mental state of others—wouldn't catch up to him but lo and behold, it absolutely has.

"You look great," he says then stares at me, clearly knowing I just gave him the once-over and waiting for his own compliment.

I don't respond.

I won't lie and say he looks great.

In fact, I'm fighting the overwhelming urge to spit in his face, a task which is occupying a huge chunk of my mental real estate.

"Cami, introduce us," a voice says, breaking into my battle of wills. Turning toward the noise, Staceigh is sitting pretty with an angelic smile, and if this were a cartoon, she'd have heart eyes and be making a-ooo-gah noises.

But then again, from what I know and the way she's got the subtlest look of hunger on her face, maybe she'd have Mr. Krabs's dollar signs in her eyes.

I'm frazzled when I look back at Jason, whose eyes are still on me.

On my tits actually.

And not even attempting to disguise it like the pig he is.

Jesus, what did I ever see in this man?

"Jason, this is Staceigh, Laceigh, and Olivia. Ladies, this is Jason Demartino."

Staceigh stands, pushing her hair being her shoulders in a curtain of perfect golden strands, and walks over to Jason, putting out a hand.

"Staceigh St. George. Of St. George Financial Incorporated," she says, relaying her pedigree with practice. Jason stares, long awkward seconds filling the air before he finally turns from me and shakes her hand. Staceigh lets out an uncomfortable giggle, her other hand moving to hold his as she leans in just a bit too much and laughs a bit too hard at a joke no one told.

While this happens, her sister stands as well, moving over to Jason before putting out her hand as well.

"I'm Laceigh," she says. "But not like the material. L-A-C-E-I-G-H," she says with a smile. Her sister glares at her with a venom I can feel from here.

"Jesus Christ, Lace, sit down and shut up," Staceigh says through gritted teeth.

Laceigh looks from her sister to Jason and back to her sister, confusion clearly clouding every molecule of her brain.

"Cami, are you free later for a drink or something? Catch up?" Jason asks while the twins bicker, moving his attention back to me unfortunately.

Hell fucking no, and I won't ever be free for anything with you ever again.

"Unfortunately, I'm all booked, sorry," I say, not giving him any details on *when* I'm booked or, more politely, when I'm free.

Mmm, never.

"Oh, I—" he starts, but then an older man comes over and puts a hand on his shoulder.

"Jason! I've been looking all over for you. Our table is this way," he says then guides my ex away from me and to a table with even more rich old men. I watch as he leaves, feeling the air clear and the weight, while not completely gone, begin to lift from my chest as he does.

I don't miss how Staceigh watches as well.

"How do you know Jason?" she asks finally, looking at me like there's a terrible taste in her mouth.

"Yeah, how?" Laceigh echoes. I stare, trying to decode her words and decide if it's worth the effort. Clearly, Staceigh has a thing for him, but should I warn her about Jason?

Give people a try.

Abbie's words echo in my mind and I make my decision.

If Staceigh is interested in Jason, she should know what a piece of shit he is.

It's the right thing to do.

I lean forward the way you would with friends when you have the good tea and speak just a bit quieter.

"Look, I see you're . . . interested in Jason," I start as soon as the twins and Olivia lean in. Laceigh's eyes move to her sister and they smirk.

She's interested in Jason.

Maybe not because she thinks he's hot or he's interesting or good partner material but . . . because of the power of him. The close proximity to wealth and influence and status that probably matches her own. That's what has piqued her interest.

"So, I met him when I was in college. He was a senior when I was a freshman." Silence and blank stares. "We met and we connected and everything was good. We started dating and he was sweet. Perfect boyfriend material, you know? Would take me out on fancy dates, bought me flowers, the whole nine, until . . ." A perfectly groomed and filled eyebrow rises. God, so I really want to tell everyone this?

But again.

I'm turning a new leaf. I'm being more open, trying to make true friendships.

And that's what friends do, right? Share their pasts stories of shitty men?

"So, I was a virgin. I was saving it for my first love, you know? I should have seen it coming, but . . ." I sigh, hating to bring this up at all.

Every time I remember this moment in my history, I cringe.

I was *so dumb*.

So naive.

And I really, truly thought he loved me.

"I slept with him and the next day, I found out it was all a bet. He'd been dating me to prove some point to his frat brothers. I was essentially blacklisted at all off campus events for the next four years of college because he had a long-term girlfriend at the time who transferred and tried to make my life a living hell."

It feels good to share this story with someone other than my friends who were around when it happened and also helped pick up the pieces.

Cathartic, almost.

Olivia looks at me with soft, empathetic eyes and I give her a smile.

"I'd just, you know, stay away. He's bad news. I heard he did it to more girls than just me back then."

Olivia's eyes go wide in shock, but then I look to the twins.

Laceigh looks bored.

Staceigh is uninterested.

"Oh wow, thanks *so much* for letting us know," Staceigh says, but her eyes remain locked on Jason's back as he sits at a table to the left of us. "What's his family like?"

And there it is.

She doesn't care if he's a piece of shit because he has a pedigree. And a pedigree means money and influence and a girl like this? That's what she wants.

"I don't know. I never met his family," I say, feeling defeat take over.

What was I thinking, that sharing some heartfelt story would win these women over, make them my friends? That we'd create some kind of bond over Niçoise salad and sparkling water?

"Hmm," she says, flipping her hair before going back to tearing apart every woman who is unfortunate enough to cross her eye's path.

As I leave the lunch an hour later, no closer to making friends or allies, the panic starts to creep in, the feeling that I'm set up for an impossible task taking over.

NINE

FRIDAY, MAY 19

CAMI

Friday morning is my first official day at the Beach Club without meetings and the relief is overwhelming. Being able to spend the day in my office mostly uninterrupted and going through all of the notes and files for upcoming events has eased so much of the anxiety I've felt. It doesn't hurt that my office is absolutely *gorgeous*. I don't know how Kincaid managed it, but it seems like nearly every window in this damn building has some kind of ocean view, and my office— another gorgeous room of white marble and dark wood—is no exception.

At about eleven, I jump in my seat when there's a small knock at the door, Olivia standing there, a small, nervous smile on her lips.

"Hey," she says then bites her lip. I stand, walking over to her, my hand out to shake hers.

"Hey, Olivia, how are you?" She shakes my hand and I'm impressed by how firm and self-assured it is, even though her entire body language screams *nervous*.

"I'm good. Uh, my grandfather sent me here to talk to you about the internship?"

"Oh, yes. Why don't you come sit down? We can talk about what you're hoping for and what I think I'll be needing and decide if this would be a good fit for you." Her smile is still nervous with a hint of warmth as she sits, smoothing her skirt over her legs and sitting prim and proper, as if she were trained to.

I bet she actually *was.*

"So why don't you tell me what you're hoping to get out of something like this?" I ask. "I know your grandfather mentioned a PR firm you're starting?"

"Yes. I majored in public relations and love that aspect of marketing and management. In a perfect world, I'd love to work on press and promotion for events, so I think being able to see how events like this work from the back end would really help me."

"That makes sense. Can I ask why you're not starting now? Why you're waiting for the fall if you're planning to work all summer regardless?" Olivia sighs and bites her lip.

"I know it probably sounds like I'm a spoiled brat, but I have a trust," she says and sighs. "It's not supposed to be available for me to use until I'm 30."

"But . . . ?"

"But my mother told me if the wedding goes smoothly, she will open access to it early." I furrow my brow, trying to figure out why the success of her mother's wedding would have anything to do with Olivia. "She does that. When I was younger, I spent a lot more of my time with my dad. I grew up on the island, spent my school years with him and then would spend the summers with my mom. Of course, I wasn't up to her . . . etiquette standards, so she'd bribe me to not embarrass her in front of her friends." Without my permission, my brows furrow, my face moving to a look of shock and disgust. "I know how it sounds. It wasn't . . . It wasn't terrible. But this wedding is important to her and her social circle, so she wants to make sure I don't . . . get in the way of that."

"I see," I say, unsure of how to feel about this. Olivia seems sweet, even if she was raised by someone who is clearly a horrible narcissist. In my own way, I feel bad for her, but there's also a kinship in a way. I was also taught to put on a different face for different people in my life. My mother, though she is the strongest, most amazing person I know, always pushed me to show people the curated, unswayable version of myself in order to get what I wanted. It's a trait I took to heart after I realized not everyone has the best intentions and the way to beat them is to join them.

Once again, I'm reminded of Abbie and Kat's push to be more open, to try and make friends, to stop testing people and give them an honest chance.

Maybe they're right. Maybe I should stop making people earn me before I give them even a fraction of myself.

And maybe I should start with Olivia.

"You know, I grew up in community like this. Not a beach club, obviously, but the same . . . concept."

"Rich people," Olivia says with a smile.

"Yes. It wasn't like that when I was really young, but once my dad passed away, my mom took the life insurance and . . . she made better for me. It was all she had left once he was gone—me and making something more, something better. She built her business and then used it to fund her charity, Moving Forward."

"Wow, that's amazing," Olivia says, and it's clear she means it.

"It is. I'm forever in awe of her. But what I'm telling you is we have that in common. Trying to find footing in this . . ." I wave a hand at the opulence around us. ". . . world regardless of whether we feel exactly at home in it." She smiles and nods.

"That . . . That actually is a really good way of putting it. I haven't been able to organize it in my mind before, how I feel when I'm here. It's like . . ." She sits back in the chair a bit, less uncomfortable and a little more at ease. "It's like I'm always expected to be *on* around these people, around my mom. When I'm out on the island or with my dad, I can turn it off."

"I have two friends," I say with a smile. "They're the only people I'm comfortable being the normal version of me around. They actually challenged me when I came here to try and be more . . . open." A laugh comes from her lips.

"They sound like my dad. He's always telling me that. He doesn't . . . He grew up normal. He isn't like my mom, doesn't have buckets of money, didn't grow up a socialite. He doesn't get it."

"It's hard to unless you've been inundated in it." She nods and it feels like progress. "Okay, so, full disclosure because you gave me yours, I want your mother's wedding to go well too. Not because it's my job but because I'm working toward my own event planning business and need the contacts the Beach Club and your mother's wedding could provide me. I also would love to be invited back to this position next year if things go well." She nods in understanding. "So this internship. Your grandfather wants you to take it?"

"Yeah. He said it's up to you, though. He doesn't want to . . . dump me on you."

I think about it for a moment.

Part of me—the version of me I've been told to put away for the summer—wants to scream *hell no* to having an intern.

She wants to do everything on her own terms and definitely not let this unknown person come into the business I've been creating, to get the chance to touch anything and potentially ruin something.

I think about my goal to be more open this summer.

I think of the thick ass binder from Melanie's wedding alone, as well as the dozen other folders for other parties I'm expected to plan.

And finally, I think about Leroy, the man who graciously gave me a shot when I needed a foothold into the world of party planning, despite my having no real prior experience, and inadvertently changed my life.

So, I nod with a smile.

"I think we could make it work. Once a week maybe? You can come, help me manage some of the details, and get some experience. You grew up here, right? So you know the ins and outs of most of these yearly events, I assume?" I ask, grabbing a stack of manilla envelopes and waving them a bit. She nods, already looking more at ease.

"Yes, I do. I also have big ears, so I know what everyone has liked and disliked about most of them. Many of the events are super outdated, benefitting the oldest members but not really catering to the younger ones, the new-money types. I've told my grandfather many times I think it's a huge missed opportunity." She bites her lip like she isn't sure

"Then I can *definitely* use your help," I say with a smile, and she smiles back.

And for the first time since arriving on this little island, I think I might take Abbie's advice.

TEN

ZACH

"Man, you gotta stop with that shit. You're never going to get laid if you keep on with the shitty fuckin' dad jokes," my best friend Nate says with a groan. I can't help but smile and remember the woman from the other night who *also* was unimpressed by my jokes.

"Had a couple girls in here last night, and they didn't seem to mind."

"Yeah, and where did they sleep?" he asks, an eyebrow raised. I roll my eyes.

"They were *customers,* man."

"Okay?"

"I don't sleep with customers. Much less customers so past the point of intoxication, I had to walk them back across the street to the Beach Club." My words pull another groan from him.

"There's your second issue. Getting caught up with *Beach Club* chicks."

"Fuck off, man."

"I'm saying. What has the Beach Club ever done for you besides given you a huge fuckin' headache?"

"Uh, keeps my business running?"

He grumbles, knowing that's very much the only way I can keep the doors to the bar open and my crew employed year-round. The Fishery survives on upping our prices in the summer months and serving tourists and whatever members of the Beach Club who deem it not a *complete* horror to have a meal or some drinks at a dive bar. Each summer the goal is to make enough to survive the slower moths without closing our doors for the winter or laying off any of my loyal employees.

It's the same structure started by my grandfather years and years ago, a man who prided himself on being one of the few businesses on the island that didn't close as soon as the season was over. I inherited the family business when he passed after spending nearly my entire life working here and vowed to keep up the tradition.

When I was 10, my first job was at the Fishery, drying glasses or running out orders from the kitchen to tables. When I was 17, I would clean the place before it opened, opting out of fun summer days of crabbing in the bay and drinking shit beer, instead earning minimum wage and learning the business from my grandfather. When I was 21, I became a bartender, and when I was 28, my grandfather passed, leaving the Fishery to me, his sole grandson.

"Fair enough," he says. "But those women over there are nothing but trouble."

"You never seem to have much of an issue with fucking them and moving on," I say, and he laughs before shrugging.

"That's because I know *how* to move on. Unlike some of us, I know how to have a nice little one-night stand, how to fuck a tourist and not get caught up in strings."

"You know, some people find my unwillingness to fuck anything with a pulse and a minor interest in me to be endearing."

"Not me. I think you're a fuckin' chump. You're not getting any younger, you know," he says, and any other moment, I'd give him some quip about him being a year older than me, but I don't.

I can't.

My eyes are stuck on the front door of the Fishery because despite the low lighting, I know who it is instantly.

Cami.

Camile, as her one friend called her.

To be totally honest, I had convinced myself after she was here, it was the last time I'd see her. For one, she doesn't seem the type to frequent dive bars. Luxurious, expensive wine bars in the city? Definitely. A little shack selling beer and fried fish?

Not her style.

But also, she doesn't seem the type to *enjoy* being vulnerable in the least, and last time she was here, intentionally or not, she was exactly that, revealing her own insecurities and nerves about her friendships and her new job.

Plus, she turned me down when I asked her out to dinner, so I assumed that would be her third reason for avoiding my place. Get away from the creepy old bartender who couldn't keep his eyes off her and clearly wanted more than casual conversation.

But here she is.

"Fuck, that's her," I say under my breath, Nate turning sharply in his chair.

"Who?"

"The girl who was here the other day."

"Fuck, the one in the heels?" he asks, and when I look to Cami's feet, she's wearing a pair of bright orange shoes playing off her dark skin in a way that looks really fucking good.

"Can you stop staring?" I say through gritted teeth, trying to make myself look busy by wiping the bar down as she slowly approaches.

"Ooh, does Zachary have a *crush*?" he asks in a sing-song voice, and really, I want to punch him in the face but I have no time. Cami is right here.

"Of all the gin joints in all the world, she walks into mine," I say, tipping my head to Nate who shakes his head and looks to the ceiling.

Cami stares at me like I'm insane.

To be honest, the number of times I've thought of her in the past couple of days?

I might be insane.

That's the only reason I can think of to explain why every time she's around, I say something stupid and cringy as fuck.

"Is that another dad joke?" she asks, one perfectly shaped eyebrow lifting, a mix of confusion and humor coming over her face.

I stare at her and then look to Nate, who sighs at the ceiling like he and God are communicating about what a fucking moron I am.

"*Casablanca?*"

"Oh. That's that old black-and-white movie, right? I've never seen it," she says, and I groan, moving a fist to my chest as if she stabbed me there.

"You've never seen *Casablanca?*"

"My mom loves it." It hits me then.

Dear god, I'm probably closer to her mom's age than I am to hers, and whether it makes me a scumbag or not, I've been picturing her naked for three nights.

"Sounds like your mom has taste."

"Or she's just old like you." There's a smile on her face that's so fucking adorable.

"Ohhh, burn," Nate says, and I glare at him. It's like we're 18 again and he's teasing me for some crush instead of in our goddamn 40s.

"Cami, this is my *former* best friend Nate. Nate, don't you have some kind of date to head out to?" I don't know if he *actually* has a date, but it's a fair assumption.

"Fuck off, man. Hi, I'm Nate," he says, his voice going from annoyed and joking to smooth and suave. "Are you new to the island?"

Cami smiles, her white teeth framed by red lipstick, and it's a good fucking look.

"I am, and I'm also so completely out of your league." She bats her eyes and I choke out a laugh and watch Nate's jaw drop.

He stutters, unsure of how to respond, seeing as I don't think he's ever experienced a woman not at the very least enduring his flirting.

It's refreshing.

It also makes Cami that much more appealing.

Finally, he speaks.

"Like her for you, man."

"I'm not for anyone but myself, but I'm so glad to get your approval," she says, eyebrow raised, and I'm enjoying watching them go back and forth.

"*Really* like her for you, man." I shake my head before turning to Cami again.

"He doesn't get turned down often. Clearly, he needs more practice."

"Aww, did I hurt your fragile ego?" she asks with a fake pout and this time, I laugh loud, my head tipping back. When my laugh slows, she's staring at me, wide-eyed and in awe and fuck, I like that.

I like it a lot, that look.

I smile at her which seems to knock her from her reverie, a smile forming on her lips.

"Alright, I'll leave you two to it. Hate to admit it, but you're not wrong—I do, in fact, have a hot date." I roll my eyes and shake my head. "You give this old man a chance, yeah?" he says, tipping his chin to Cami, and her smile widens, head shaking as he winks, waves at me, and walks out.

We both watch him leave before I look back to her and she sighs. "So, are you tired today?" I ask with a smile.

"What?" She bites her lip, looking nervous. "No. I mean, sort of. I'm still figuring out everything with my new job but I'm not . . . Why, do I look tired?"

Her hand moves to her hair, patting it like she thinks some kind of nonexistent disarray gave away her supposed exhaustion and goddammit. It's fucking cute.

"No, I just meant because you've been running through my mind all day." She rolls her eyes but can't quite hide the way her lips turn up.

"Oh my god, you really are the king of dad jokes, aren't you?"

"I did try to warn you," I say, and with the way she shakes head, a small smile spreading on her face, it's like she couldn't fight it. "So, you couldn't resist coming back to see me?"

Her smile grows as she grabs a paper menu on the bartop and tosses it at me. "Shut up. Yes, I'm back. But it's not because I wanted to see you; both grocery shopping and cooking for myself sounded absolutely miserable."

I move a hand to my chest and groan dramatically, like I'm in pain. "Really know how to cut a guy down, don't you? Here I thought you were coming in to see me again."

"Sorry to disappoint, just a hungry girl with zero motivation to cook and clean."

"What are you thinking tonight?"

"Surprise me."

"What about for a drink? Wine?" She sighs and shakes her head.

"A soda, please. I've got to work more tonight, catching up." Tapping the screen, I put her order in before adding dark soda to a cup of ice and walking it over to her.

"How were your first couple of days?" I lean on the bartop, genuinely interested.

She takes a sip before answering. "They were . . . interesting."

"Interesting?"

"Yes. I met some more of my clients."

"And . . . ?"

"Some were cool. Some were . . . exactly how I expected them to be." She smiles and I look over her head, tipping my head at regular as they walk in before moving to fill another glass with beer and sliding it to someone who waved for a refill.

The best part about this bar I've basically grown up in, is while the summer does bring tourists, I still have my group of regulars, people whose names and stories I know.

"Monday is the first day with my intern," she says when I move back in front of her between helping customers, once again leaning in on my forearms.

I don't miss how her eyes move there, lingering for a moment longer than necessary, and I fight a smile.

"Oh yeah? You decided to give her a chance?"

"I'm not in a position to turn down help," she says nearly begrudgingly. "I want to make a good impression so I'm invited back next season, but I also want the connections the place could give me. I'm just one person and . . ."

"And an intern would be a great help."

"Exactly. I have a feeling I'll be overworking myself for the next few weeks while I try and organize the calendar and set up contacts with vendors. What the previous person who had my job left behind is a fucking train wreck. Nothing makes sense." She sighs and this time, she genuinely sounds tired. "I should really still be in my office working."

"But you're here," I say with a knowing smirk.

She bites her lip again, and I'm clearly so totally fucked because my dick goes a little hard at the sight.

She turned you down, Zach. She's here temporarily. The Beach Club is nothing but trouble. This is what I try to remind myself over and over, but none of them seem to stick.

"Well, a girl needs to eat."

I can't help but smile as I shake my head, calling her out on her lie. How I know it's a lie, I'm not totally sure, but it definitely is.

"Nah, you're here because you wanted free counseling again, aren't you?"

"What, I brain-dump on you one time and now you won't let it go?"

"Babe, you can come in here every single night, drop your troubles on me for as long as you'd like so long as it means you come in and keep me company."

Her hair moves gently as she gives a small shake of her head. "God, you really are good at the flirty bartender thing, aren't you?"

Just then, the bell for the kitchen window dings and I move over to grab a red basket piled high with fried fish and French fries, sliding it in front of Cami before grabbing some ketchup and vinegar.

"Fish and chips?" she asks, staring at it. "But I didn't order."

"Shrimp basket is my favorite. Fish and chips is the most popular. You're a pseudo local now, so you need to decide your favorite menu item. We're gonna work through them one by one."

"What if I'm allergic?" she asks.

My gut drops.

"Fuck, are you? Sorry, I shouldn't have. I—" Her throaty laugh cuts me off.

"No, you're good. I love fish and chips."

"You're a pain, you know?"

"So I hear," she says with a wink, grabbing a fry and biting into it. I almost reply, probably about to say something that would scare her off more than I already have, but a group of six comes in and I take the opportunity to take orders and get some space from the pretty girl who keeps ending up in my bar and I can't stop staring at.

"You know, this is really, really good," she says when I walk back over, dipping her fish into tartar sauce and taking a bite.

"Told you."

"Do you guys ever do catering? I'm trying to build my list of vendors for events and this could be such a fun option." I shake my head.

"We haven't. Never really thought of it. Customers keep us pretty busy all summer, and fried food doesn't sit well."

"That makes sense. A bummer though," she says, dipping a fry into malt vinegar then ketchup. I grab a rag and start wiping down the bar in front of Cami for what feels like the tenth time since she walked in, my mind unintentionally trying to stay in front of her, to steal as much of her time as I can.

"So, you're contacting vendors?"

"Yes. Like I said, the person who held my job previously was kind of a mess. All of the numbers they scribbled are barely legible or clearly personal contacts, so I'm pretty much starting from scratch. Ideally, I'd love to work with businesses on the island, but I also know that's not always possible, with it being so small and me coming in so late in the season." She sighs, clearly stressed by the challenge.

"You know, I've lived here all my life. You ever need intel on a vendor or a contact, let me know. I'll see what I can do."

"Unfortunately, it looks like I'm going to be crazy busy the next couple of weeks. I don't know if I'll make it over here every time I need a contact or free therapy."

"You'll be missed," I say with a smile.

"How am I supposed to survive this without your sage advice?" she asks, clearly making fun of me, but I don't care.

I decide to try and shoot my shot one more time, reaching into my pocket to grab my wallet and pulling out a business card before replacing it. Grabbing a pen from the register, I cross out the number for the main line for the bar and scribble in my cell number. "If you feel yourself having another crisis, send me a text."

My stomach is in knots like I'm 15 and giving a girl my number for the first time, and I should be concerned considering this woman is so far out of my league and I've only met her 3 times and she clearly isn't planning to stay on the island past this summer.

But for some reason, none of that stops me from sliding the business card her way.

The smile that spreads on her face makes it worth the nerves. She looks down at the card, reading.

"Zach. That's your name? I had a feeling it wasn't actually dimples, which is what I've been calling you in my head."

"Yeah, dimples is definitely *not* my name," I say with a laugh. It's funny because most of my life, I've been teased about the deep indents in my cheeks I get with each smile, but with Cami? I don't think I mind it much.

"So, what is this? Are you offering to be my full-time therapist, available via phone 24/7?" Despite her teasing, she covers the card with her hand, moving it closer and adding my number into her phone.

"I mean, 24/7 might be a bit much, but if you need me, you send me an SOS text," I say.

"Be careful, dimples. I might think I'm your favorite customer after only three visits if you don't stop being so nice to me." I shake my head gently.

"You won't be for long if you call me dimples again," I say before Frank hits the bell and I use the opportunity to break the moment, turning away to grab the order.

But I don't think she misses how I didn't deny how she is quickly becoming my new favorite customer, whether it's smart or not.

Because the reality is, I should know better than to get tangled in a woman who isn't planning to be here long, a benny here for the summer. But I haven't stopped thinking of Camile since the moment she walked into my bar.

And now for the rest of the night and the following morning, I spend every free second glancing at my phone and waiting on a text from a new, unknown number to come through.

It never does.

ELEVEN

WEDNESDAY, MAY 24

CAMI

"So, how's it going so far? Working at the Beach Club?"

I'm in my office eating giant Caesar salad from the restaurant downstairs, Cici sitting across from me with a salad of her own on her lunch break.

Progress, you know?

This morning when I walked down to the front desk, I asked her when her lunch break was and if she'd like to eat in my office.

I'm not completely sure what it says about me when surprise took over me with her wholehearted "Yes," but either way, I'm enjoying her company.

"So far so good. My first event is on Monday, so we'll see."

"Ah, the Memorial Day brunch. How do you feel about it?" She stabs her fork into her salad and I follow suit, chewing to give myself time to think about my answer.

"Okay, I think?" I say, and Cici laughs, her head tipping back and a full bellied sound coming out.

This is what I think I'm going to like best about her. Unlike every other person I've met at the Beach Club so far, Cici doesn't put on an act around anyone. She doesn't opt for soft, polite laughter or tiptoe around the questions she wants to ask. She's just unapologetically herself, and if you don't like her, I'm pretty sure she wouldn't give a fuck.

It's similar to the version of Abbie post-Damien, and it's almost a comfort, having someone like that in my day-to-day. She might be five years younger than me, but she's more levelheaded than a lot of the women I know who *are* my own age.

"Wow, what a convincing statement," she says as her laugh dies out, and I grab a piece of my roll and toss it at her head.

"Stop. It's going well. The previous event manager left pretty decent notes despite being a total disaster and my intern knows a lot about the club, so I was able to get a lot done. But any event is nerve-racking in the planning stage. I'm much more of a day-of, trial by fire type of girl."

"Oh, yeah, I forgot Olivia was your intern."

"Yeah, she's coming in once a week for now, but she was such a big help yesterday, I might ask if she's available for more time each week." I pierce a tomato, popping it into my mouth and chewing. "I really like her. She's nothing like her mother."

Since last week, I've met with Melanie once more on Monday to go over what I had assembled thus far for her wedding. Unfortunately, the meeting went rougher than I had hoped, with Melanie shitting on two-thirds of my ideas, despite them coming straight from her own stupid fucking binder, and the twins giggling like they thought it was the most hilarious thing. Thankfully, Olivia was also a huge help with *that* on Tuesday, living up to our agreement to do what was necessary to make the wedding spectacular for both of our benefits. Before we left for the night, I sent a long email with updates and new ideas to Melanie, CCing her assistant. I was blissfully relieved when this morning, I received a reply with minimal updates and even a bit of praise for some of my out-of-the-box ideas.

But right now, I'm reading Cici's face that is . . . contemplative, like she wants to say something but won't.

"What's up?" I ask, my brow furrowing.

She doesn't reply for long moments, wasting time with eating, drinking, wiping her face, and pretty much anything she can to waste time.

Shit.

"It's nothing," she says finally.

"Tell me. This is a totally safe space, I promise."

"It's just . . ." She sighs again. "Just be careful with her, okay?"

"With who?"

"Olivia." I wait a beat instead of answering, giving her a chance to speak, one she does end up taking. "I told you we used to be friends, but we were best friends all through middle and high school."

I'm a bit taken aback by that, considering from what I understand, they are completely different. But then again, it's a small town and I know Olivia did go to public school here, *and* they're the same age.

"You were? But . . ."

"That first summer after her freshman year, the Bitch Pack came to the island."

Oh, I think. It's not hard to see where this is going.

"Okay . . ."

There's another beat before she speaks.

"Saying this as a . . . friend. I think you're cool and there aren't too many cool people who work here. Most everyone is either old as fuck or I've known them since I was three. It's in my best interest to keep you sane so you come back next season." A smile tips the edges of my lips with her words, and she returns the gesture. "And I've seen the twins giving you the *she's next* look."

"She's next?" My gut churns.

"I told you. They pick victims each year. It's like a game for them and their shitty friends. They pick someone and make their lives a living hell for fun." I don't say anything as her eyes drop, fingers occupied with moving food around on her plate. "That first summer, Olivia and I had a sleepover at my house and she told me all about them. How bitchy they were, how her mom was like, obsessed with their dad, and how her mom was basically begging her to make sure the twins had fun so they'd want to come back next summer." My gut churns and I fear where this is going. "We laughed about it, about how dumb the whole situation was. But a few weeks later, she stopped returning my texts, stopped calling to hang out, and then every time I saw her, she was with them, laughing at their bitchy jokes about people around them, whispering with them. She was so . . . different." Cici sighs and shakes her head and the disappointment, the hurt she still feels all these years later is palpable.

And relatable.

It's similar to how I've processed my history with Jason.

"I confronted her, asked her what was happening right before the big Fourth of July party. Every year, we used to stay in a suite her grandfather would set up for us, watch the fireworks over the water together, but I hadn't heard anything. I don't know. I was being dumb, thought maybe it was all a misunderstanding. Then the twins came over, laughed at me, and Olivia chimed in. The rest of the summer, the twins did everything in their power to make me miserable. Somehow, Mr. Kincaid didn't fire me, even though they tried to set me up a few times to make it look like shit they did was my fault." Finally, she puts her fork down and stares at me.

"I'm not saying this to scare you or because I don't want you to work with Olivia. It's good for you to work with her—she knows so much about the club and the customers and she has a lot of contacts. Just . . . be careful, okay? Especially with the wedding coming."

I think about how we agreed to work together to benefit our own needs—Olivia's being to survive the summer and keep her mother happy, mine to get contacts and build my business. For a small moment, a moment I feel guilty about almost instantly, I wonder if maybe that was a mistake, telling her that.

But then I remember just how stupid I was when I was 18, when I wanted to impress people and would do anything to win them over.

I think about Jason and what I gave up to try and keep him, and how much I've changed since then.

But still, it's clear her wound is still fresh, so I nod.

"Thanks for the heads-up," I say with a smile before moving to change the subject. "So, do you have any fun plans for Memorial Day weekend?" I stand, tossing my now empty salad container into the trash and grabbing my soda before sitting back down and grabbing my phone to check for messages.

"Not really. I'm working and then I thin—"

But I don't hear her words because my stomach drops to the floor with panic.

Because the first email in my inbox reads: CANCELLATION OF SERVICE

"What is it?" Cici asks, clearly reading my face, but I don't answer.

"No, no, no, no. Fuck. FUCK."

"What? What is it, Cami?" Her voice sounds more nervous by the moment, like she's worried I'm having a psychological break.

Honestly, I might be.

I just might be.

Finally, I look to her after rereading the very brief email.

"My bartenders dropped out."

"What?" She looks confused.

"My bartenders for the brunch. They dropped out. They aren't coming."

"And that's an issue because . . . ? The Beach Club has bartenders on staff."

"Yes, but they're limited in what hours they can take and there's an event in the cabana that I'm not in charge of that's utilizing all of them. Some are working in the normal bars for the day. I needed to hire two from a different company in order to have someone working the bar. Oh god. Fuck. *Fuck!*"

"Okay, okay. Let's think about this. I . . . I'm not working Monday. I can come in, work the bar."

"Kincaid requires all servers to be licensed. We can't just use anyone."

"Oh," Cici says, her face moving into a grimace.

"Yeah." *God, my first event and it's already fucked.*

"Why did they cancel? It's last minute and that can't look good for them."

"It just says a conflict of interest."

"A conflict of interest?"

"I have no idea." Cici bites her lip. "What?"

"I know it probably sounds like I'm grasping at straws but . . ." She takes a deep breath before answering. "Any chance it's the Bitch Pack?"

"No. There's no way," I answer quickly. "Why would they? That makes no sense. They've been nice enough to me." Cici takes a beat to answer before nodding.

"You're right. I'm probably projecting." Just then, her phone vibrates. "Shit. I hate to run right now, but I need to get back downstairs. My lunch is just about over." Shaking my head, I wave her off.

"No, you're fine. You have to work and I have to . . ." A deep sigh that doesn't help at all leaves my lips. "I have to deal with this mess." She stands, a pitying look on her face that I hate.

"Let me know if there is *anything* I can do to help. I can reach out to my friends, see if they know anyone . . ."

She trails off, probably thinking what I am.

What are the chances of someone being randomly free on one of the busiest weekends of the summer?

"It's fine. I've got this," I say, and with my words, my confidence returns just a bit.

Because I'm Camile fucking Thompson.

I can handle this.

It's six hours and an undisclosed amount of emails and calls to anyone and everyone I could think of before I send the text.

It turns out most good bartenders are booked on the first unofficial day of the beach season when you're at the Jersey Shore.

I'd successfully avoided the business card with the dark scrawl on it for four days, even avoiding the bar itself, but I'm now between a rock and a hard place with nowhere else to turn.

So, I send the text.

> Hey, it's Camile from the Beach Club.

I don't even take the time to send anything more, anything with context or something witty because I'm so beyond that mentally. It will have to do—I genuinely don't have the luxury of overthinking this, so I hit send and wait.

And wait.

And ten minutes pass before I allow the panic to start to settle in.

What now?

Do I clarify? Do I tell him I'm the girl he gave his number to on a Fishery business card?

What if that's not specific enough?

Maybe he knows a million Camiles. Maybe he gives his number to every half decent looking person that comes in and I'm not special at all.

But then again, I didn't leave my initial text open for much. Maybe he saw that, saved my number, and moved on with his night, thinking that's all I was doing: sharing my number. Should I just jump right in and ask my question?

And then my mind moves to even *worse* situations.

Like, what if he *gave me a fake fucking number?*

Oh my god.

I'm so dumb. Of *course* he did. Why would he give some random chick his real number?

Or maybe it was real, but he was hoping for a booty call and when I didn't text that night, he wrote me off.

Or maybe he *doesn't even fucking remember me*. God, how embarrassing would that be—

I don't get the chance to finish my thought spiral because my phone vibrates from my desk with an incoming text.

> Camile? Don't know her.

Oh god.

Oh fuck.

He doesn't remember me. This is traumatizing. I should leave the island now, never come back in case I run into him ag—

> You know, I gave my number to a pretty customer of mine named Cami, though that was almost a week ago.

My mouth drops when I read his second text, a mix of relief and irritation taking over me.

What an *asshole*.

> You're a dick, you know that?

> You're the one who didn't text me.

> You told me to text if I needed help with work stuff. I haven't needed help.

> Next time I'll be sure to clarify.

Next time. What could that mean? Does it mean the next time he gives his number to a random woman? Or the next time he gives me a demand? Or—

> So, what do you need help with?

Now I kind of feel like an ass because he's right. I didn't reach out to him until just now and only because I need something.

That makes me an asshole, right?

Asshole or not, though, I really need his help, so I'm not in a position to argue.

> Do you have a contact for a bartender or two I could hire for an event?

> When is the event?

Okay, not an outright no. That's good, right?

> Monday. A brunch at the Beach Club. I'll pay double their normal rate. I just need them to be properly licensed. Four hours.

I focus on deep breathing while I wait for his response.

To be honest, right before this, I was researching how to get a bartending and food handling license in case I needed to jump in and be a server.

Unfortunately, that would take longer than three days, and I only *have* three days.

> How many?

> Two. But I could make do with one.

Barely a minute passes before the next reply.

> And what do I get if I find someone for you?

My gut churns, the words sounding gross when I read them in my head, like he's expecting some kind of sexual favor in exchange for career help.

Fucking *men*.

> Uh, maybe this was a mistake.

> Ah, shit, I'm sorry. It's hard to be sarcastic in stupid fixing text messages.
>
> Fucking. Goddamn autocorrect.
>
> I was joking. You don't owe me anything for helping. I've got two bartenders that I can send on Monday.

I can't avoid the laugh I scoff out, nor can I deny the relief in knowing he's not a total scumbag *and* that I'll have bartenders for my event.

It won't be a *total* shit show.

At least not for that reason.

> Ahh yes. I forgot you're an old man who doesn't know how to work technology.
>
> Hey, I'm an old man who is saving your ass, aren't I?
>
> Fair. I do owe you one.
>
> How about a date?

My jaw drops and this time, it's not with the ick.

This is the second time he has asked me on a date and he second time I didn't feel vehement opposition to the idea.

You're here for work, Cami. Not to date some cute older bartender.

But also . . . my mind moves to way my stomach always churns with a bit of jealousy when Damien and Abbie are around, with how comfortable and happy and at ease she is anytime he is near.

Maybe a date wouldn't be the worst idea.

> I'm joking again. Technology, lack of seeing body clues, etc.

It wouldn't be the *best* idea, but I also don't think it would be the worst idea.

> Ask me again after Monday.

There.

That leaves it open for a *maybe*.

I know it was the right decision when he answers near instantly.

> Deal.

TWELVE

MONDAY, MAY 29

ZACH

The brunch starts at 10, but Rhonda and I get to the Beach Club at 9 as per the document Cami sent over Saturday morning. I've been here a few times over the years, so when the receptionist asks me if I can find it on my own or if she should call Cami down to take me up, I tell her not to worry, we'll make our way over.

When we walk in, I tip my head toward the makeshift bar in the corner. "Head over there, make a list of anything we might need before the party gets rolling while I go talk to the coordinator." Rhonda nods before heading that way and I scan the room for Cami.

I nearly stop in my tracks when I find her.

The few times she's been to the bar, she was either in casual clothes, like the time she came in with her friends, or business casual after work.

But today . . . Fuck.

She's gorgeous.

Her hair is in loose curls flowing down her back and she's wearing a light-blue sleeveless dress, fitted on top and loose when it hits her hips, ending just below her knees. When she turns her head, showing someone holding two large vases of flowers in their hands where to put them, she's wearing a dainty pearl necklace, small pearl earrings, and her makeup is soft and feminine.

She looks gorgeous, understated, and like she fits in in this room of utter luxury. Not like how some of the attention-seekers try, but in an effortless way they would be envious of. Somehow, she also gives the vibe that she can happily sit in your living room eating junk food and watching a shitty movie and be content.

I don't know for sure when I decided I was going to try and make this woman mine, but if it wasn't that first night, drunk off her ass and completely and totally unimpressed with me, it's right now. She's put together, utterly in charge, and fucking beautiful.

"Camile," I say, approaching her as the man she was talking to walks off. She turns quickly, a clipboard in hard, and it takes everything in me not to laugh at the look of shock and panic on her face.

"Zach," she says, her face confused. "I . . . What are you . . . Why—"

"Bartender. You needed one; I'm here."

She opens and closes her mouth three times before she finally speaks, and I can't resist the smile that breaks free onto my lips.

"You're . . . You're here."

"You needed a bartender. I'm a bartender. Rhonda's at the bar taking note of everything, making sure we don't need anything. If you don't have what we need, she can probably run across the street or to the store. We still have a bit of time."

She doesn't speak.

Multiple emotions cross her face.

Confusion.

Frustration.

Anger.

Relief.

Joy.

They all flash so quickly, I'm sure I miss a few in between, but I don't have time to continue deconstructing her features because she's grabbing my arms and dragging me through a door into a small empty room which must be used for storage when it isn't an event space.

"What are you doing here?" she asks, anger on her face, arms crossed over her chest, back to the door we just walked through. My face screws up in confusion as I look at her.

"I'm . . . You needed a bartender."

"Yes. Why are *you* here?"

"Cami . . . I don't understand."

"Neither do I!"

"I sent you over paperwork with licenses and food safety certificates." I faxed them over to the number she gave, not even insisting she walk across the street to get them despite the fact I really, really fuckin' wanted to see her face.

"Yes."

"One set for Rhonda, one for me." The anger melts into confusion before she moves to look at the clipboard in her hand, flipping papers before recognition and understanding dawn on her face.

Her head snaps up to look at me.

"Did you do this to see me or something?"

"Honestly?" I ask, looking at her but staying where I am, four or so feet between us. "Yes. But I also did it because you sounded desperate and I know how it can be to try and get people to work on Memorial Day. I'm licensed and so is Rhonda. Bar is slow on Memorial Day. I'm usually the only one who works and Rhonda could use the overtime." I stare at her for a few more moments, giving her the chance to speak, but she doesn't take it. "Is this . . . Is this a problem? I figured when I sent the paperwork over, you'd see . . ."

Finally, she sighs, her head tipping to the ceiling, her shoulders falling with defeat.

And then it happens.

The perfectly curated, perfectly in control version she wants everyone to see is gone, and in it's place is the nervous, anxious one.

"I should have. I saw Rhonda's name and scanned the rest. Didn't even notice your name. I . . . It's been a long week or so." She shakes her head, her dark hair shifting as she does. "I'm sorry. I shouldn't have snapped at you, accused you. You're doing a favor for me and I'm so very grateful. I just . . . I didn't expect it, and I'm under a microscope with this event and the bartender mishap wasn't the last of the bullshit I've been dealing with and I . . ." There's another deep sigh before she looks at me. "I'm sorry."

There's a shimmer in her eyes and it's clear she's on the brink of a total and complete freak out.

"Hey, hey, hey," I say, stepping closer, limiting the gap between us from four feet to one and leaning forward a bit to look in her eyes better. "Tell me what's going on." A second passes, her jaw going tight before she divests everything she's been clearly holding way too tight.

"The bartenders canceled last minute and you would be *shocked* how impossible it is to find a bartender on short notice. *Thank god* you were free, but I didn't think it would be *you* coming, and I totally should have looked at those contracts more closely but I didn't because I have eighteen million things happening at once and now I'm kind of panicking because what *other* shit did I miss? Like, did I remember to tell the kitchen Mrs. Sloane has a peanut allergy and Mr. Cosmo is going to come with his service dog who isn't even a real service dog but he pays a lot of money to the club so everyone let's it slide and Fido needs his own steak in a white bowl? And this is my first event here and if it fails, will I get fired immediately? If I get fired, where do I live because I sublet my apartment in the city and I refuse to shack up with Abbie and Damien, even though Damien totally has a bajillion rooms in his condo and it wouldn't be *that* big of a deal, but also it *would* because I refuse to burden them, especially after what a bitch I was last year, and I was up until midnight making a stupid fucking playlist for this event only to find out I didn't reserve the equipment ahead of time and it's being used for another event, which is *dumb* because I'm the fucking event coordinator! Shouldn't I get dibs?" She takes a deep breath in, like her brain is catching up to her mouth and remembered she needs air to survive. "And I feel like this is going to crash and burn and I'm in the wrong career." I smile at her, watching her chest rise and fall quickly, an outward clue of her panic.

"Can I?" I ask, my voice low as I lift my hand, hovering it over the strand of hair that has fallen into her face. Her dark eyes are wide and locked onto mine, her lips parted just slightly, and I don't miss how her breathing has quickened.

She nods and her quick breathing stops as I push the hair over her cheek, my hand moving around her ear and then down her neck before landing on her shoulder. Our bodies are so close now, barely six inches between us when I dip my head down, putting my fore-head on hers, my other hand moving to her other shoulder.

"Breathe, Cami," I say, and she finally takes in a breath. "You've got this. I've been to a few of these events, never seen it look like it was running so smooth. Everyone knows where they're going, what they're doing, and that's clearly because of the work *you* have put into this. It's going to be fabulous." I rub my thumb over the spot where her shoulder meets her neck. "You just gotta breathe, baby," I say in a whisper. A beat passes before she finally speaks.

"I don't know if I can," she whispers, and I can't help it. I smile at her. "I really like your smile," she says, then I watch her eyes go wide like she can't believe she said it but, finally, she also breathes.

"Good. When this is all over, go out with me. I promise I'll smile a lot." A smile of her own starts at the corner of her lips and she shakes her head gently. "No?" I ask, and fuck if my stomach didn't drop just a bit.

"Not a no. But not a yes, either," she says, and before I can answer, there's a knock at the door at her back, her eyes going wide with panic. "One minute!" I step back, rolling my lips between my teeth to fight an audible laugh. Her eyes go wide and she slaps my chest.

"Go. You've got an event to run, angel." Cami rolls her eyes and shakes her head again, but then the smile slowly melts from her lips.

"Thank you," she says, her voice low.

"Anytime. Now go. I'll wait for a minute so it doesn't looks suspicious," I say with a wink.

THIRTEEN

CAMI

The morning of my first official event at the Beach Club, the Memorial Day brunch, is upon me. I was unbearably nervous from the moment I woke, but there were also texts from my best friends, somehow sent without me hearing them.

> Good luck! You're going to KILL THIS EVENT!

That's Kat.

> Have the BEST day and don't let the bitches bring you down. You've got this!

There's a third message from Abbie in our group chat, a photo of all three of us at the beach last year.

> Can't wait to come down and recreate this for my birthday this year! We love and miss you, Cam! You're doing amazing and we're so proud.

Kat "loved" the image and the reply and when I saw it, I had to fight a lump in my throat.

Not for the first time, I found myself thanking whatever universe put Kat and Abbie in my path all those years ago.

But hours later, as I walk out of a storage closet, I thank whatever lucky stars seem to enjoy looking out for me because they also sent a handsome man who has a bartending license and knows how to quickly and concisely pull me from a panic spiral without even breaking a sweat.

Though, we will *not* be tackling the hurdle of the not quite almost kiss in the same storage room. I'll let myself do a girly happy dance and write a pros and cons list for accepting his offer of a date some other time.

Because right now, I have an event to slay and rich bitches to prove myself to.

And I'm doing that hours later when I'm standing in a corner, overseeing the success of the event and trying to get a quiet moment to myself.

I did it.

I *freaking did it.* Men and women are smiling, enjoying themselves. The cello player I begrudgingly hired was actually the better decision, since more people attended than RSVP'd so we needed a few extra tables to fit everyone, and the quartet would have made it feel cramped. The kitchen was even able to make the specialty diet meals looks spectacular without the guests feeling left out.

I've already had a few people come to me, tell me how fantastic this brunch is compared to previous years, and take my card.

And, of course, I've gotten the opportunity to let my eyes linger on the eye candy that is Zach and his dimples anytime he catches me staring.

I refuse to admit just how many times it has happened this morning.

But, of course, my luck never allows for peace and quiet to last for long, ever.

Which is why I jump when a hand lands on my shoulder unexpectedly.

I'm even more shaken when the hand doesn't leave and I realize it's Jason *fucking* Demartino.

"Oh, shoot, sorry, I didn't mean to scare you, Cams," he says, and the nickname takes me back to long study nights in his room in the frat house, of him smiling at me as I try and memorize facts for some class I would never use again but was a general education requirement.

"You good over there, Cams?"

The memory used to be soft and delicate despite our sour ending, but now it feels . . . cold and lifeless, tinged in stomach churning disgust. I can see it for what it was now—just another manipulation he executed, pretending to care, pretending to be kind and gentle and sweet.

His hand is still on my shoulder when I break free from the mental bubble of memory and step away from him, trying to distance myself.

"Is there something you need?" I ask pointedly. "Is something in the buffet empty, an issue with the men's room?"

I'm making it incredibly clear I am here to *work* and *not* here to talk to him.

In my mind, we don't even know each other.

There is no history here, no need for us to speak about anything other than work.

"I just wanted to catch up with you. It's been forever," he says, then his eyes move down my body, pupils dilating because he likes what he sees.

I have to work hard to fight a gag at the look.

When we were together, I was 18 and a late bloomer. I didn't grow into myself until I was in my early twenties, curves and, more importantly, appreciation for those curves blossoming.

Apparently, douchebag Jason likes the grown-up version of me as well.

"You look great," he says.

You look like shit, I force myself *not* to say.

But thankfully, I don't have to answer because a high-pitched voice speaks, a perfectly manicured hand moving to his elbow.

"Jason, there you are!"

Staceigh to the rescue, whether I asked for it or not.

I never thought I'd be happy to hear her voice.

Of course, her puppy dog of a twin sister is right behind her, wearing a purple version of her sister's pink outfit. I've heard of twins being color coded, but I never saw it in action until just now.

It's . . . interesting at best.

"Hi, Jason," Laceigh says

"Oh, hey, Stormy," he says, and I choke back a laugh.

A quick flash of pure anger runs in Staceigh's eyes before it settles back into her curated sweetness, perfected Stepford vibes flowing off her with ease. I'm surprised I haven't seen Olivia the whole event, though she did tell me last Tuesday her mother avoids these types of things like the plague. Maybe that means Olivia doesn't show up either?

"Staceigh. Remember?" Staceigh says, correcting Jason.

"C-E-I-G—" Laceigh starts spelling her name again and her sister hits her in the chest with the back of her hand. A tiny squeak leaves hers lips as Laceigh's hands hold herself there but her mouth shuts, like a dog who's been hit by its owner.

Honestly, the way she follows her around, it's not a bad comparison.

"What are you doing?" Staceigh asks Jason, moving around me to get closer to him like I don't exist. I don't to her, which is so totally fine by me.

It would be better if she could drag Jason off with her.

"Come to the balcony with me. I want to show you something," she says, not asking but instead insisting.

"Yeah, maybe later. I'm actually talking to my friend Cami right now," he says, and my stomach churns.

It's even worse when there's a quick flash of anger in her eyes.

"Oh," Staceigh says, jaw going tight. "Hi, Cami."

"Hi, Stace," I say, and I can instantly tell she does *not* like the shortened version of her name. "Lace." I turn to nod at her sister.

"I see you were able to find bartenders for the event," Staceigh says, and I stare for a minute, trying to decode her words. Did she . . . No way. "We had *such* a hard time finding some for our own party tonight. A busy night, you know?" Her smile is saccharine sweet and it makes me incredibly uneasy, like one of those creepy dolls in a horror movie you just *know* are going to murder the main character in their sleep.

"Yeah," I say, resisting the urge to show any kind of confusion or shock on my face. "We got really lucky." Her jaw goes tight and I spend another second trying to read her and coming up empty before I shake my head and turn to Jason. "You should go with them, Jason. I actually have to . . ." I look around, hoping for something—anything— to get out of this corner. "I have to go check on the buffet," I say and then step back, watching Staceigh's glare turn into a catty smile. "See you all later. Enjoy the party."

Staceigh's fingers wiggle in a little wave. "Bye, Cami. Talk to you soon!"

The words are too happy, too kind, and I can't help but think she's really putting her whole ass into winning Jason Demartino, pretending she's friends with the help, and he is so totally not worth a fraction of that.

The rest of the event flies by with so much praise and thanks, I'm floating on cloud nine by the end. I was so busy, I barely saw Zach and Rhonda leave when things wrapped up, instead getting a text from him ten minutes ago.

> You did great. Come to the bar tonight to celebrate.

I fully plan on doing just that.

Fuck, an event goes that well, I can absolutely reward myself by spending my evening chatting across a bar with the cute bartender who quite literally saved my ass.

But I don't have time to think too much about it because I'm cleaning up hours later when Olivia and the twins walk over to me.

"Hey ladies, did you enjoy yourself at the brunch?" I ask the same way I would any other guest. "Olivia, I didn't get a chance to see you around. I hope you had a good time."

"I came in late, caught the tail end, but I hear you did an amazing job, Cami," Olivia says, sincerity in her voice. "I've been coming to these Memorial Day brunches for as long as I can remember, and I've never heard such rave reviews."

"That means so much to me. Thank you, Olivia. I'm so grateful for your help on Tuesday as well."

"Yeah, it was lovely," Staceigh says, and the bloom of a job well done continues to grow.

I've been stopped at least a dozen times this morning, women and men asking for my card to set up meetings for some kind of planning this summer, both at the club and for private events.

"Olivia, ask her," Staceigh says, elbowing Olivia who suddenly looks . . . nervous.

"Yeah, Olivia, ask her," Laceigh demands. I truly am starting to wonder if Laceigh *actually* knows how to speak or if she can only mimic what her sister says.

Before I can ponder that much more, though, Olivia speaks.

"There's a, uh, party tonight. In the cabana area," she says.

"Oh, is there? I didn't see it on my calendar," I say, my brows furrowed, and I start to panic. *Was I supposed to plan that, too?*

"Oh, no, it's just something small my mom does. A Memorial Day party, exclusive invite only. That's where I was this morning, helping to make sure it goes well."

"That makes sense." It doesn't really, but what else is new with these people?

"We wanted to invite you to come, right, Olivia?" Staceigh says with a kind smile.

"Yes," she says.

"It would be *such* a good networking opportunity for you," Staceigh says. "Olivia told us one of your goals this summer is to make more contacts so you can grow your business independently."

"Uh . . . yes. It is."

"This would be such a great opportunity to mingle." Staceigh turns to her soon-to-be stepsister. "There's a theme, right?" There's a pause before Olivia speaks.

"Yeah. Americana. You know, to go with Memorial Day."

"So fun, right, Cami? I love a good kitschy, themed party." I nod even though the idea of a themed party gives me anxiety and I *know* I didn't bring anything in my wardrobe to work with that. I could go to the mall . . . I'd have to call Abbie . . .

"So, you'll be there?" Staceigh asks with a hopeful smile. For the first time since I met the twins, I wonder if maybe I've judged them wrong. Maybe they mean well but have no idea how to deal with outsiders.

Maybe I just need to give them a chance, like Abbie said.

Like Zach said.

Maybe I've built my wall too high, made my tests for friendship impenetrable so no mere human will succeed.

And with that realization, I smile and nod.

"I'll be there."

FOURTEEN

CAMI

I'm feeling on top of the world as I walk out of the Beach Club doors after cleaning up the event.

The brunch was executed fabulously, Jefferson Kincaid even pulling me aside after everyone finally left to tell me himself, *and* I landed an invite to an exclusive party.

Oh, and there was the little run-in in the storage closet I can't stop thinking about . . .

But now, I need to make a mall run and call my best friends to tell them they were right about letting people in and I officially need their help.

I get myself settled in the car and set my phone to handsfree before I hit send on a group call, listening to it ring less than three time before Abbie says hello, quickly followed by Kat.

"How did the event go?" Kat asks.

"You guys were right."

"Of course we were," Abbie says, a smile in her voice.

"How were we right *this* time?" Kat asks. And I'm glad it's not a video call so they can't see me roll my eyes.

"You were right, I should try to be more open, try to let people in."

"Oh, thank God," Kat says. "I thought you were going to say you're going to get bangs."

"She'd look so cute with a little fringe!" Abbie says, annoyed we are doubting her on *anything* style and beauty.

"I'm not getting bangs, Abbie, drop it." I just *know* she rolls her eyes dramatically before I keep talking. "I was invited to a party."

"Ooh! Yay!" they both say, and I'm pretty sure Abbie claps.

"It's a *beginning of the summer* Memorial Day party."

"So fun!" Abbie says, and the sound of her clapping her hands comes through my speakers.

"Who invited you?"

"Well . . . that's the catch. It's these rich girls who kind of seem bitchy. The one is interning with me—"

"Olivia? How has that been going?"

"Fine," I say, turning out of the Beach Club parking lot. "She's been nice and actually really helpful. She's the one who invited me, along with the twins."

"The bitchy ones?"

"Yeah, but I think they're just spoiled brats who aren't used to not getting what they want. I don't think they're *actually* that bitchy. I was raised around girls like them all the time. No one ever tells them no or that the way they're acting isn't right. It doesn't feel right to just . . . judge them based on something they don't necessarily understand."

"That's . . . huge, Cami," Kat says, her voice low and in awe, and I wonder if that's a testament to just how far I've gone in my testing and cutting off of people. If the fact I'm not using a shitty first impression against them impresses my *best friends,* I've really been a lot more closed off than I realized.

"It's not . . . I just . . . I heard what you guys said. When I went back to the bar to pay the tab—which was *paid for* by the way—I kind of trauma-dumped on the bartender and he said the same thing, that I should let people in and give them a chance before writing them off."

"Wait, what?" Abbie says. "Back up, back up. The bartender? You trauma-dumped to the hot bartender?!"

"Maybe not trauma-dumped, but I . . ." I sigh, realizing I've gotten myself stuck. "After that morning, I felt . . . It opened my eyes a lot, but I didn't know how to process it. Then, I met a few people who seemed nice enough and I went over to the bar and . . . I don't know. I was worried I would disappoint you guys and I needed someone to talk my thoughts out with."

"Oh, Cami, honey, no. We didn't—"

"I know. But it was necessary. I . . . I've gone too far lately in protecting myself. I was a bitch to Abbie when she was going through her shit with Damien because I wanted her to get revenge, but also, I wanted her to protect herself. I understand it's not normal for my gut instinct to be thinking people are inherently bad or they'll hurt me. I need to work on that. I'm going to while I'm here." I merge onto the parkway and speed up, incredibly happy again this call isn't video.

I don't need to see the looks they would be giving each other or the pity in their eyes.

"And I'm starting by going to this party," I say, the nerves still wrapping their tendrils around my stomach, but I'm fighting them.

You never grow if you never get uncomfortable.

And I'm starting to realize I have a *lot* of room for growth.

"I'm so proud of you for agreeing, Cam." Kat says, her voice quite.

"Jesus, don't act like I'm some kind of hermit who never says yes to anything."

Silence on the line.

"You guys!"

"Okay, you're not a hermit, but you don't, like, *enjoy* going out with new people. It's a big step, Cam," Abbie says. "I'd say I'm bummed we won't be there to support you but I'm not. I'm glad you're being forced to do this on your own *without* a security blanket."

"Well, I still need your support," I say. "I'm headed to the mall now." Abbie squeals and claps and I can picture her exuberance through the line.

"Why are you going to the mall?"

"It's a themed party. *Americana.*"

"Americana? What the fuck does that even mean?" Kat asks, echoing my thoughts.

But Abbie's reaction is exactly why I called her. She squeals on the other end and, again, the sound of her clapping her hands excitedly fills my car.

"Oh my god, perfect. I have a vision!"

"How do you have a vision after a single word?"

"Because I am Abigail Keller and I was *made* for themed parties."

I mean . . . she's not wrong.

"Can I get all of the required attire at the mall?" I ask.

"Absolutely," she says with a cat-like smile.

"Great. Now let me fill you in on what's been happening with the hot bartender," I say, and the squeals that fill my car are *exactly* what I expected.

I smile the entire drive to the mall.

FIFTEEN

CAMI

After spending way too much at the mall on clothes I'll probably never wear again, I decide the feeling in my stomach is most definitely *not* nervous butterflies and instead hunger pangs and the only way to soothe them is to head over to the Fishery.

It's definitely not because chatting with the hot, older bartender I spot as soon as I walk in calms me in a strange way.

Definitely not.

"You're early today," Zach says when I walk over to where he's standing with a smile on my face.

"I got out of work early. You know, a holiday, the event." He smiles and nods before speaking.

"So, how'd it go? Everyone seemed to be having a good time from where we were, but I was also serving liquor."

"Surprisingly well."

"Celebratory drink?" he asks.

"Not today, dimples," I say, and he cuts me off before I can continue, leaning into the counter of the bar in front of where I prop my ass onto a stool.

"I thought the agreement was if I told you my name, you wouldn't call me dimples?" The smile on my face widens and I'm reminded the true reason I came here was because he's way too fun to talk to.

And taunt, apparently.

"I think you misunderstood. All I said was I was pretty sure that wasn't your name, not that I wouldn't call you it."

"Something tells me you're not a *respect your elders* kind of girl." I let out a *pfft* noise and smile, leaning in.

God, why do I like bantering with this guy so much?

"Not even a little. How old are you, anyway, to think you qualify as an *elder?*" He smiles wider, those dimples deepening.

"Forty-five."

"*Forty-five?!*" I say, fully aghast. "Fuck, you really are an elder, aren't you?"

"How old are you?"

"Twenty-eight." I smile as I watch the shock cover his face.

"Jesus fucking Christ." He groans and something about it has my belly flipping in a way I *absolutely refuse* to speak on.

Refuse.

"I'm jailbait," I say with a small smile. "Much too young for you."

And then it happens.

Something flares in his eyes and *fuck, fuck, fuck.* I like it a *lot.*

"If you were too young for me, I wouldn't be making sure I was the one serving you every time you walked in here, angel."

Fuck, there's that heat in my belly again.

My tongue dips out, touching my bottom lip, and I don't miss the way his eyes watch it.

I need to change the goddamn subject.

"I can't have a drink because I got invited to a party," I say, and his eyebrow rises and he leans on the back wall, arms crossed on his chest.

A flame still licks in my belly though.

Goddamn.

"Did you now?"

"Yup," I say with a smile.

"How'd you score that?"

"Remember when I told you I would be working with a bunch of rich bitches and you told me to give them a chance?" He smiles. "Well, I got an intern and she's actually really nice and super helpful. We kind of came to an understanding about working together and it being mutually beneficial."

"And she invited you to a party?"

"Yeah, she came over with her sisters after everything was over and invited me to some fancy party tonight. It's going to be a really great networking opportunity for me."

"Well, look at that. Giving someone a chance really worked out for you, didn't it?"

"I guess it did." I smile for a moment, and then he says something I don't expect.

Not from a relative stranger, and definitely not from *this* man.

But what throws me off even more is how the words put a lump in my throat.

"I'm proud of you, Cami."

"What?"

"Proud of you for giving her a chance. I mean, I don't know you much except I've somehow become your unwitting therapist—"

"I don't—"

"Calm down, I'm not complaining. I'm just saying I know this isn't something you'd normally do. It's out of your comfort zone. Have you told your friends?" It takes a moment for me to swallow back the unexpected emotion before I answer.

"I did. They helped me pick out my outfit. I actually just came back from the Ocean County Mall."

"I'm glad. I'm shit at outfits, so I wouldn't be any help there," he says, and I can't help but let out a laugh, thankful for the comedic relief to break up my thoughts.

"So, you're telling me wearing the same outfit every time I'm here isn't just because it's the uniform?"

"Unfortunately, there is no real uniform here, so this is just my *style*."

"Ah, well, maybe that's why you're still single." I can't help but think of what a blast Abbie would have crafting a new wardrobe for him, and it makes me miss her just a little bit more.

"Yeah, well, you keep coming in to keep me company, so I must have *something* going for me."

"Maybe. I do have your number, though, so I don't even have to come in here anymore."

"You haven't used it yet, though."

Another flutter of butterflies.

"Yes I did. I texted you about the bartender issue." He smiles, leaning his tan forearms onto the bartop, lessening the gap between us, and my mind moves to the storage closet.

"But not again."

"You noticed," I say, my voice coming out in a shy whisper I don't intend.

"You give a pretty girl your number and she doesn't use it, you notice."

"Aww, did I hurt your feelings, Zachary?"

"Maybe. I do have a fragile male ego, you know?"

I roll my eyes and smile but still reach into my bag and pull out my phone, swiping to my texts to find the message I've started three times since I asked him for help.

> Hey, dimples.

Good enough.

I hit send before I look at him then watch his smile grow, watch those dimples appear, watch a tanned hand move to the front pocket of his worn jeans. Slipping his phone out, he stares at it and tips his head back in a quick laugh.

"Are you ever going to stop calling me that?"

I just shake my head then watch as a new customer waves him

down, and without my brain's permission, my eyes slide to his ass. It looks *really fucking good* in his jeans.

We spend the next hour laughing and chatting before I have to leave. I don't even realize until I'm doing my hair I didn't eat or drink anything at the Fishery.

Instead, I spent the full hour totally and completely distracted by Zach.

SIXTEEN

CAMI

I jinxed myself by sending Abbie and Kat a text before I got onto the elevator to head down to the cabana where the party was happening.

> Leaving now. I'm both nervous and cautiously excited!

I should have known being nervous to go to a dumbass rich-kid party was a sign from some higher being to back out.

I should have known even more when there was a fucking *bouncer* outside of the cabanas, and again when he gave me a look like *what the actual fuck?*

I'm in a pair of high-waisted red shorts with a loose blue tank with white stars. Abbie convinced me to go full red, white, and blue with my makeup, with bright-red lips and dark-blue eye shadow, her cautiously coaching me over FaceTime how to slick a white eyeliner line overtop.

I even added little white star face stickers to my temples.

I'll admit it: I look cute. Really fucking cute.

But it doesn't take long after I smile at Cici, who is manning the reception area when I walk through the huge front doors, to I know I fucked up.

"Hey, Cami! How are you!"

"I'm good," I say, playing with the strap of my bag and looking around, trying to see if I can spot anyone I know or, at the very least, anyone dressed for the event.

Through the glass double doors, the twins are staring at me with wide, knowing smiles spreading on their lips.

Acid churns in my gut with the look. That kind of look *never* means anything good. Behind them sits Olivia, her eyes wide, her face pale. I don't have much time to try and interpret the looks, though, because Cici is staring at me, looking more and more confused by the second.

"I'm here for the Memorial Day party? Is it . . . Is it through that door?" I ask with a tip of my chin, the acid and panic building.

Something is off, and it's not because of anything explicit that I think this, but because my gut is telling me so.

And despite everyone trying to get me to trust more freely, I *never* go against my gut.

"The . . . Memorial Day party. The one Melanie is hosting?" she asks, her eyes narrowing.

Oh fuck. Shit.

The confusion on her face, the grins on the twins'.

No, no, no.

"Yes . . . ," I say, and her eyes widen.

"You're wearing . . . that?"

I close my eyes and breathe in.

"Yes. Olivia and the twins told me it was *Americana* themed." Her eyes widen.

"Fucking Bitch Pack," she whispers under her breath. "It's an all-white party, Cami." Her eyes roam my body as the blood leaves my face. "You've been set up."

"No. No, it can't—"

But it can.

It *is*.

In fact, it all makes sense.

The invitation, the cruel look in Staceigh's eyes when I walked in.

"Why would Olivia . . . ?" My mind moves to the conversation we had where I thought we had a truce, a shared goal to survive this summer.

Was *that* all a game, too?

"Go before any potential clients see you, Cami," she says in a hushed voice, knowing the reason I'm on the island this summer is to build connections and the type of connection I need would see this as a *major* faux pas.

"I can't," I say with panic but also determination filling me.

"You can't?"

"I can't. The twins already saw me."

"Fuck," she says. "Okay. Okay, no worries. We've got this."

"I most definitely do *not* got this, Cici."

"I know. But I do." She moves around the front desk, grabbing my hand gently but firmly before tugging me back behind it. She leans forward, digging in her bag before lifting a white dress.

"Here. You're a little taller than me and your ass is better than mine, but it's stretch fabric. It should still work. It's a little wrinkled because it's been in there for two weeks when I went to a Mother's Day brunch before work, but it's clean."

"What? I can't—"

"Backroom. Go change now."

"I don't—" Her hands go to my face and she stares at me. In my heels, I tower over her.

"We cannot let those bitches win, Cami. You let them win, your entire summer is fucked because you become an easy target. I know how they work."

I don't want to ask how she knows because she told me she was once their target. But even if I didn't know her history with the Bitch Pack, I don't *need* to ask when the shadows cross her eyes.

"Cici—"

"I've been watching everyone arrive. You want to build an event business for rich bitches? You want exposure? They're all in there. They thought they could beat you, but you're stronger than they are. They are spoiled brats who throw tantrums when things don't go their way. You are a grown ass woman. Show them how a grown ass woman acts, Cami."

I let her words sink in and remember what my mother told me the first of many times when I came home crying after dealing with mean girls.

The best revenge, Cami, is letting them see you thrive when they wanted to watch you fail spectacularly.

With that, I grab the fabric, nod, and head to the back of the employee room to change.

SEVENTEEN

CAMI

It takes ten minutes to change into Cici's dress, and when I look at myself in the mirror in the employee backroom, I'm happy with what's reflected at me.

The dress fits in all the right places, hugging curves and showing off my deep brown skin in a way which makes me think I just might have to buy this dress from her when all is said and done because I definitely want to wear it again.

When I walk out of the room to the front desk, Glenn is there with CiCi, a hand on her hip which he pulls away as soon as he spots me.

They are so totally fucking.

"Dammmmmnnn, Cami!" he says, and Cici rolls her eyes, slapping him in the chest. "What, she looks good!"

"You do look great, Cami. Shit, it totally fits you better than it fits me. You have to keep that dress now. You know that, right?"

"I was totally thinking I need to buy it off you," I say with a smile, and she shakes her head.

"Absolutely not. Consider it your *welcome to the island* gift from me. We're not all rich bitches here."

I smile again.

I like Cici. A lot.

"You took the stars off your eyes?" she asks.

"Yes. I can't do too much about blue shadow, but I think it still looks cute so I'm keeping it."

"Definitely do. It's still Memorial Day, after all." I nod before staring at the glass doors again, my stomach in knots. Instead of leaning into my anxiety, though, I'm focusing on my need to prove the Bitch Pack wrong.

If I focus on that, I can't focus on the disappointment coursing through me.

"You gonna be okay?" Cici asks, and I take a deep breath before putting on my smile.

It's one I've perfected over the years, the one I give everyone to reassure them I'm good, I've got things under control, and they don't need to worry about me.

When I was younger, I sat in front of a mirror for hours on ends practicing different versions until my eyes blurred. I was making sure it looked natural, not forced. Making sure my smile didn't pull at the corners of my eyes too much, that it wouldn't leave laugh lines.

I worked to make sure the smile I shared with the world looked genuine so no one could question the validity of it.

When I see it in pictures, though, I know.

I know it's fake.

I always wonder how no one else does.

"I'm great. Thank you so much, Cici. You totally saved my ass. Let's do lunch or breakfast sometime soon, yes?" I ask, bending to grab my bag.

"Definitely," she says. "And you're welcome. I know what they're like. Us girls have to stick together, you know?" she says with a smile.

I don't remind her it was other women who put me in this position, but instead nod and head toward the glass doors.

It's clear what a setup the *themed outfit* was when I walk in. The entire room is dressed in white shirts, white pants, white dresses.

The staff walking around serving trays of hors d'oeuvres and expensive champagne are also in white, and all of the decor matches the theme—white rugs, white twinkle lights, white explosions of feathers, and white satin draped over railings and chandeliers.

It's a goddamn white party and I was dressed like I was going to a fucking Fourth of July frat kegger.

When I was changing, I realized how dumb I was. In the new light, the smiles of Olivia and the twins now look different—less kind and welcoming and more manipulative and conniving.

Of course, their eyes burn on me as I walk straight toward where they're sitting with their group of other perfect bottle blondes, all with perfect tans and trainer-sculpted figures, all with tiny smirks on their lips.

Except for the twins. Laceigh looks utterly confused and Staceigh looks . . . furious.

That makes me happy, vengeful joy filling my veins.

But the most confusing is Olivia.

Olivia, whose face is mostly neutral, but her eyes shine with something close to . . . pride, maybe?

Regardless, each gaze is a reminder of why the fuck I am the way I am.

Be nice to them! Make friends! Give people a chance!

My best friends think I'm insane for shutting people out until they give me a reason to let them in.

This is why I do it.

This right here. The humiliation is churning in my gut, telling me to fucking run away and never look back. To leave the island, apologize to Damien for ruining this opportunity, and say *fuck it* and let the twins win this game I never wanted to play.

To let them have Jason, who is standing with the group as well, his hand on Staceigh's waist. I don't miss how her eyes flick from me to him and back again. There's a fire that burns brighter when she realizes he was staring at me not with humor, but intrigue.

Is this why she did this? Why I was set up to fail?

Over this fucking shitty ass man?

A man who has his arm around another woman's waist as his eyes are locked on my tits?

God, these really are the worst kind of women. The type who would throw another under the bus because of a fucking *man*.

A man with a receding hairline probably still living off Daddy's money just like he was ten years ago.

Or maybe it's just all a game and she hates to lose. I've come across the type more times than I can count—the mean girl who plays games with people's lives because she wants the power that comes with it, a high she can't buy.

Does she want control?

Does she want power?

Finally, my eyes move to Olivia as I step closer to the group. Olivia, who I thought was on my side, someone who had the same goals, the mutual need for the summer to move smoothly, only for her to be the one to invite me here.

What's Olivia's motive? I can't help but think as I close the gap.

Does she want to impress her shitty fucking friends, friends we both know would throw her under the bus just as easily?

Is she trying to win over her soon-to-be stepsisters?

Or maybe she's really just like this. Cici did warn me, after all. Was I tricked into thinking she might be more, be better or different?

Maybe this island and the "intervention" have me so twisted, it's throwing my normal detection off.

I should have seen this a mile away.

Either way, I knew when I realized what happened, I had two options.

Option A, I could run the fuck out of this place and hide in my apartment until I'm forced to leave, only coming out this summer to do my job and never returning to this island.

It would be a sound choice—normal, semi-safe.

Absolutely *sane*.

It would cut any benefit of working here this summer, greatly reduce the networking I was planning to take advantage of, and would generally be a waste.

Or, I could choose option B.

I could straighten my shoulders, put on my bitchiest, rich-girl smile I perfected back when my mom would take me to similar events, and I could walk right up to them.

I can make them question whether their plan to embarrass me worked.

I can smile at the boyfriends, watch as their eyes graze over my tits and ass, and know in some fantasy, they're dreaming of fucking me, not their boring, bitchy girlfriends.

I put a smile on my lips and gently cock an eyebrow as I stare right at Staceigh, adding extra sway to my hips as all three men sitting in their little group stare at me.

Because I choose option B.

I can mourn another failed friendship in my apartment later, but right now, this is vital to being able to show my face on the island ever again.

And I *will*. I will show my face on this island.

I won't hole up and let them win.

I won't run. I refuse to let them think they got away with their bullshit mean-girls trick which they are way too fucking old to be pulling off.

It's becoming more and more clear no one has ever put them in their place, has never played them at their own game. Maybe no one was brave enough or strong enough or they haven't found anyone who gave as little of a fuck as I do right now.

But they've met their match.

They fucked up when they fucked with Camile Thompson.

All eyes are on me now as I near their little group.

But I'm only focusing on three sets of eyes.

Olivia's and the twins'.

Staceigh elbows Olivia with a bitchy smile on her lips, tipping her chin to where I stand as if no one noticed me.

As if they didn't see me enter the cabana in a completely different outfit, as if I missed the disappointment flashing over her face when she saw me enter the party in a stunning white dress.

Olivia's head moves to look at me, the same mean smile on her face, but I'm almost caught off guard when I watch it falter.

When there's a flash of guilt there.

But when I've been burned, when the scent of revenge is in the air, I never falter.

As she watches me step closer, my own bitchy smile takes over my face, confidence radiating even if the pit of my stomach is still full of the acid and self-doubt I felt when I realized I was set up.

I'm winning, I tell myself as I take a few steps closer to them. But I can't help but hear the tiny voice in my head telling me to run, saying I should have ignored Abbie and Kat when they told me to give people a chance.

That I should prioritize my mental health over all of this—the mean girls and the rich-bitch games and Jason, the reminder of my poor decisions when I was younger, the reminder of what happens when you're weak and let people in.

But then I remember *who I am.*

And I remember I love two things more than saving my mental health.

The first is proving people wrong.

It's why when they held an intervention, I felt attacked. It's why, when they told me I don't let people in, I instantly let in Olivia, trying to prove to them I'm not that closed off person.

"Hey, ladies," I say with a sugary sweet smile.

The friendliness in my words makes Staceigh's jaw tick, like she can't believe I'm not losing it on her, like she's disappointed I'm not giving her the reaction she expected. But she doesn't know this is now just the beginning, and I love to play the long game.

Because the second thing I love is a good revenge storyline.

"Nice dress," Staceigh says, and the sneer on her face tells me she's waiting for me to crack.

"Thank you so much," I say, keeping my words kind and genuine. "I'm so lucky my friend had it. I got the invite confused and thought this was a themed party. Goodness, that would have been embarrassing, huh?" My eyes look over the room of perfect white outfits and I give a dramatic cringe.

"Your shoes are red," Laceigh says with a smile.

"Great job, Lace. They *are* red," I say, fighting the urge to give a passive aggressive little clap. "Love *your* shoes, Stace. I have those Choos in black. I just love how classy they look in a neutral," I say, tipping my chin down to her blue, scrappy heels.

Her cheeks go nearly as red as my shoes as I call her out for her own alleged faux pas, watching her dig a sharp elbow into her sister's ribcage.

Finally, I move to look at Olivia, a strange mix of fear and frustration in her eyes.

"Thanks for the invite, Liv. It really looks like we're going to have a great summer together. You remember our conversation, right? About helping each other and whatnot?"

She doesn't say anything, but it's clear in her eyes she understands the quiet reminder I gave her.

She is in control of how the summer goes—whether we're friendly and have a good time, treating each other as equals, or whether I make her my bitch.

"Remember, two pumps of caramel in my iced latte on Tuesday, kay?" Her jaw goes tight and her cheeks go red.

"Iced latte?" Jason asks, finally speaking and looking confused.

It's still strange to hear his voice after years of remembering him laughing at me and telling me what an idiot I was for deigning to believe *he* would want a piece of trash like *me*.

In my mind, the mind of a woman who was so heartbroken, so taken aback, and so unbearably in love with this man child, his voice was smooth and deep, refined and expensive sounding.

In the current reality, it's nasally and a full octave higher than I thought. I look him over head to toe and smile.

His shirt fits just a bit too tight—he was on the track team in college but obviously didn't continue the sport after, instead moving to work for his daddy's Fortune 500 company. It shows.

Even the mustache he's *attempting* to grow is pathetic looking, not full but patchy and embarrassing.

Then, I remember how I looked in the mirror of the backroom— tits on display, rounded in all the right places, the dress hugging my curves, especially my ass. He always told me he loved my ass and would grab it anytime I was near.

My eyes roam his . . . date, Staceigh.

Gaunt and thin, not in the svelte way where it fits her body because that's how she's naturally built, but thin in a way where I know her day starts with not enough calories and way too much exercise.

And then I smile.

I smile because they might think they won.

The twins, Olivia, god, even Jason.

They might think they won, that they're better than me, but somehow, in this moment meant to degrade me, I'm feeling like I've come out on top.

In a way, it's also confirming the fact I *should* prioritize me, not being nice or making friends or giving people multiple chances like my friends think I should.

I'm doing *just fine* on my own, *thank you very much.*

"Oh, you didn't know, Jason?" I ask, blinking innocently. From the corner of my eye, I notice both Olivia's and Staceigh's expressions are full of concern. "Olivia here is my intern for the summer." The smile of pure fucking satisfaction spreads on my lips as her cheeks go from pink to red.

"Wow. Guess there's a lot I missed. You have your own intern now, Cams," he says and again, the nickname tugs at something childish and hurt in my heart.

"It's been a long time," I say, my voice firm and empty, clearly no invitation in the words.

Jason, of course, is stupid and doesn't notice.

"We should get a drink, catch up. What do you drink?" he asks, standing even though his hand was just on Staceigh's knee.

God, he's still a piece of shit. Some things never change.

But it sure is funny to watch Staceigh grab his wrist and tug so he can't move away from her.

"I drink red, Jason," she says, eyes wide, a clear directive in them. He doesn't even look at her, like he can't hear her, his eyes locked on me, waiting for an answer I don't intend to give. "Jason, you're here with me, remember?" Staceigh says through gritted teeth. His jaw goes tight but he doesn't argue.

God, they were made for each other really.

It makes me wonder what she has on him to make him so incredibly bought by her already when just a few days ago, he had no idea who she was and didn't even look her way.

"Oh, don't worry, Stace. Jason and I are old friends. We go way back, don't we?" I ask with a smile. "God, it was almost ten years ago now, right?" He opens his mouth to interrupt and I wonder if he can see the malice, the game in my eyes. "I will say, I really hope he got that issue in check." I finish with a faux concerned sigh and I have to fight a laugh at my own dramatics.

"Condition?" Olivia asks, and her face has changed again, going from embarrassed to interested.

Her eyes move from mine to Staceigh, like she's looking to check if she's in the clear for deigning to entertain what I said, before looking back to Jason.

"What *condition?*" Staceigh asks, voice lowered.

I fight a gag when Jason reaches over to grab the blonde's hand and lifts it, pressing his lips there.

"Nothing to worry about," he says, and she bats her eye lashes at him, clearly sold by the gesture.

Again, *gag.*

"It's just, you know," I say with a shrug. "It was always so . . .

quick. But then again, I'm sure it has . . . improved with age." I make a little face, feigning sympathy, then lift my hands, crossing my fingers.

"She's lying," Jason says, but his cheeks turn an interesting shade of pink and Staceigh's face goes a bit white.

I can't help but smile.

"Your secret's safe with me, Jay," I say with a wink. "Well, anyway, great seeing your guys. I'm gonna go check out the hors d'oeuvres. Thanks for the invite, girls," I say with a wiggle of my fingers, and I soak in the reality that all three women have faces like they sucked on something sour while Jason's jaw is tight.

A small victory.

One I really fucking need because now that I've faced them, the panic, humiliation, and anger is brewing in my veins.

But still, I walk slowly, smiling at guests but also looking for an out.

EIGHTEEN

CAMI

I walk away with my shoulders back, nodding at some people and smiling at others as if I'm not having an internal crisis.

I somehow survived—and may have even won—the challenge, but the overwhelming adrenaline rush is still there, still flooding my veins and making my hands shake as I reach for the doorknob of the bathroom.

My eyes drift closed and I let out a small breath as I realize not only is the bathroom unoccupied, but it's a single. I can lock the door and not worry about anyone entering after me while I have my meltdown in peace.

This might just be the worst day ever.

How the fuck has everything spiraled so quickly?

From my almost kiss with Zach to this morning's rush of a successful event to the invite I thought was an olive branch to now *this?*

I huddle in the bathroom in a borrowed dress, contemplating if this is even worth it.

Should I stay, endure the mean girls in hope of getting enough contacts to build an entire business? Sure, it's the smart decision, and it's the one that would help me grow the quickest, but is it *worth* it?

I have an *entire summer* ahead of me.

An entire summer of Olivia as my intern, of planning a wedding for the father of the twins, of running into Jason De-fucking-martino.

Is it worth it?

The panic starts to build, the aching inability to get fresh air to the bottom of my lungs taking over.

What am I doing here?

I stare at my phone while I sit in the bathroom, unsure of what to do.

But suddenly, I remember I'm Camile fucking Thompson.

Fuck that. Fuck them making choices about *my life* for me just because they're immature and spoiled.

They don't deserve this panic I'm feeling.

They don't deserve to win when I've worked my whole life to get here, to get an opportunity like this.

Taking a deep breath, I run through my options, my normal grounding routine.

Option one: I could run back out there and tell the twins and Olivia just how I feel.

Tell them what terrible humans they are, how they're spoiled and so bored with their seemingly perfect lives, they need to play with other humans for entertainment and just how fucked that is. What miserable lives they must lead.

Outcome: I would probably get fired. At the very least, I would be the laughingstock of this party.

I would be my own downfall.

The people here don't care if my feelings are hurt or if a rich girl was mean to me.

I mentally cross this option out because that means they win.

Option two: I sneak out and call my friends and whine about how they were wrong about giving people chances and I was right.

Outcome: the Bitch Pack wins because I would be leaving with my tail between my legs which is what they want, isn't it?

I cross that one out.

No, thank you.

Option three: I stay, pretend to enjoy myself, and hate every moment

Outcome: I'm miserable all night and potentially give them even more ammunition to fuck with me later.

Again, no.

I'm at a loss.

How the fuck do I get out of this?

The panic starts to build, overtaking me, the space in my lungs seeming to sting with each breath.

A panic attack is coming.

I'm about to have a panic attack in a cabana bathroom.

No, no, no. That won't do.

I need to get myself in check because if I don't, they win. I need to use the methods I learned in therapy.

What do I see?

An expensive marble bathroom.

What can I smell?

Cleaning products and some kind of jasmine air freshener.

My blood pressure dips as the anxiety loosens it's grasp, as I grab back onto reality and out of the panic.

What can I hear?

People laughing.

The panic comes back with a vengeance as my mind tells me they're laughing at my expense, that there's an entire group of people right outside the door that knows I'm having an anxiety attack.

My mind starts to win, picturing an entire room of finely dressed people all laughing and pointing at the bathroom door.

The thing about anxiety is, it's not always reasonable.

In fact, it's *rarely* reasonable.

And in this moment, mine is winning. My pulse starts to rise and

I'm beginning to think escaping out the backdoor is a solid option.

But then my phone vibrates in my hand and I look down to see it.

> DIMPLES
> How did the party go?

The text is simple if not unexpected. He's checking in on me.

The panic lessens as I think of the damn dips in his cheeks and the way his neck looks when his head tips back with a laugh. My chest loosens and the edges of my lips start to tip as I tap at the screen of my phone and reply.

> You checking in on me, dimples?

> Maybe.

> Stop calling me dimples.

I laugh, the sound echoing around the marble, and the panic lifts further. Strange how ten typed words can change my mood.

> So how is it? More fun than you anticipated?

I stare at the words, typing a few of my own before deleting, rethinking.

Do I want to let him know what a train wreck this is? How I fell for the oldest trick in the book, how I'm mortified and locked in a bathroom? I wouldn't want to admit this to my best friends in the moment. Instead, I'd wait until it was over and I'd made my way out of this embarrassing situation, my mind spinning the story enough to make myself seem strong and in control.

Not weak and emotional.

But before I can think of a better response, my fingers move on the screen, nails tapping as they do.

> Terrible. It was an all-white party and no one told me.

His response is near instant.

> What is it, a bachelorette party or something? Are you uncomfortable with all of the dick paraphernalia?

Again, I laugh and the soft sound echoes off the tile. How on earth am I laughing right now?

> I love dick paraphernalia, thank you very much.

His response is quick and makes me snort out a sound.

> Noted.

> But this isn't a bachelorette party, just a run of the mill rich-bitch party. No dicks to be seen. The problem is, I came in a red, white, and blue outfit."

> And . . . ?

> And it was a trick.

> Sorry, angel. I'm sure you look stunning no matter what. They're probably jealous.

God, he's good at this.

This stranger who I've been venting to for two weeks is handling this better than my friends would. It's like somehow, he knows I don't need a solution or righteous anger or a reason for how it might have just been a simple miscommunication.

I need commiseration.

> I was able to get a new dress, but now I'm hiding in the bathroom.

My stomach growls, making me remember I haven't eaten since

breakfast, surviving on nothing but the bagel I had this morning and copious amounts of coffee. Now that the adrenaline rush has worn off, I'm starving.

> And I'm hangry because I haven't eaten all day and all there is to eat here is like, little crackers and shit.

It's a throwaway text as I try and decide how to escape this hell and what I need to feel a bit better once I leave.

But his reply is both unexpected and shockingly welcome.

> Come back to the bar. I'll feed you and give you a beer and you can trauma-dump on me.

> Are you offering me more free therapy, dimples?

> Always.

His response puts butterflies into my belly.

> But if you keep calling me dimples, I'm turning you over my knee and spanking your ass.

A rush of heat runs through me, burning the butterflies and leaving a molten warmth in my lower belly.

This is a terrible idea.

Such a shitty, horrible fucking idea.

But . . . maybe it's not.

Maybe it could be exactly what I need.

I go through my options in my mind. I could say no. Hell, I probably *should* say no because he works at the bar across from where I'm working and living and this town is tiny from what I can tell.

And I'm here to *work.* I'm here to network and build my business.

But . . .

I could go to the bar.

I could go and let him feed me and flirt with me and . . . see where the night goes.

I could *let it* go somewhere.

A fun summer fling while I stress all summer working with these fucking women sounds nice. Maybe that's what I need.

I could handle that, I think. And I could surely use a friend.

So, potentially against my better judgement, I stand from the toilet with the closed lid, straighten my shoulders, and head out the door to make my formal exit.

But before I do, I send one last text.

Be there in ten, dimples.

Walking around a corner with a smile on my face, the angry, annoyed glares from women dressed in expensive designers burn my skin, as do the hot gazes of men.

When I was getting ready, I worried my original outfit was too much for a girl with curves—my cleavage out, my ass barely covered, the softness of my belly not hidden—but Kat told me to shut the fuck up because, in her words, I looked stellar.

Kat, of course, has never had the . . . pleasure of having to attend uptight events like this.

Abbie has the experience, both from stupid asshole Richard and now with Damien, but her opinions are also skewed. Not just because we're friends, but because she's with Damien Martinez, a man who, even if Abbie walked into an all-white party wearing hot pink and feathers, would tell her people were staring because she's so fucking beautiful, she takes his breath away, not because she's a sore thumb.

The dress I borrowed from Cici is even tighter, revealing even more.

I should feel the panic and embarrassment washing over me.

In any other situation, I would of course, surrounded by all of these prim and proper attendees.

But right now, I've decided my exposed assets work in my favor, making me stick out but also garner the attention that will make all the uptight bitches mad and all the poor, unfulfilled prep boys fight a tent in their pants,

I've told Kat and Abbie this more times than I can count, but sometimes, all it takes is a hint of confidence and a Marilyn Monroe smile to win the battle.

From my childhood, I know there is only one way to win with women like this, and that is to never ever fucking crumble in their presence.

Ever.

Because when you have more money than God and none of your friends like you because of your personality, your only valuable currency is social *wins*.

And I fully plan to cash in today, not pay out.

Instead, I walk with my head held high, moving to the main room where Melanie is now sitting, the Bitch Pack all around on white couches (Who the fuck buys a white couch anyway?) probably bragging about some trip or some bag they just bought.

But I couldn't tell you because when I walk in, the conversation stops, all eyes on me.

"It's been so very real," I say, standing in front of the bride-to-be. "I wish I could stay longer, but I have a date tonight. I just wanted to come in after work to say hello."

"Oh no!" Melanie says. "We barely got to talk. You truly did such an amazing job on the brunch today from what I saw of it. Unfortunately, I was here"—her hand moves around the room, indicating the white party—"so I didn't catch the whole thing, but Olivia told me it was absolutely phenomenal." I fight the scrunch of my brow, fight showing my confusion, instead leaving a soft, kind smile on my lips.

Now, why would Olivia do that, tell her mother I did a good job?

I look at her and her face is completely blank, showing nothing at all.

"That truly means the world. I can't wait to continue working on your wedding." Her smile widens before she speaks.

"You know, after planning this little party, I have just *so much more respect* for event planners." Staceigh lets out a choked laugh, but Melanie doesn't catch it. "I didn't even think of half the things I'd need, like bartenders." My blood chills and my eyes move to Staceigh.

It's there, in her eyes.

I know before Melanie even continues talking.

"Thankfully, Staceigh was able to make a few calls and get two for tonight! Heck, maybe she should start working with you too, Camile!" Staceigh's shrewd eyes smile even if it never touches her lips and I know.

She is the reason my bartenders backed out.

"Actually, while you're here, I have a few friends who are looking to plan some events this summer and in the fall. I'd love to introduce them to you if you have a few moments before you leave for your hot date." She wiggles her shoulders and gives me a wink like we're close friends rather than her being my employer's daughter, and it very much gives Amy Poehler in *Mean Girls* vibes.

Either way, there is no way in hell I'm saying no to this.

"Oh my goodness, absolutely. I would so appreciate that," I say with a smile. "Let me just say goodbye to the girls." My eyes move to the twins, Staceigh's jaw tight, her face pure fury.

Perfect.

Just fucking perfect.

I just love when a plan backfires.

And then it comes, the cherry on top.

A whisper, maybe not even loud enough for Melanie to hear, but

I do. "I thought you said this would work," Staceigh says, glaring at her soon-to-be stepsister.

And it's then I know.

Staceigh might be the ringleader, but she keeps her hands clean.

That's why Olivia invited me rather than the twins themselves, why Staceigh had that gleeful look in her eyes and Olivia looked just a tiny bit hesitant.

But what's her motivation? What's her reasoning for joining in on the bitchiness? I thought we had some kind of agreement, but I guess not. The thought is confirmed when Olivia turns to Staceigh, a small smile on her face before she speaks.

"This is just the start, girls. Don't worry."

And it's then I know for sure I'll have to watch my back the whole summer.

But that's fine.

It's not like I haven't done that before.

So, I smile sweetly at the Bitch Pack, tip my head to them, and wish each a goodbye, leaning in to kiss Staceigh on the cheek in an unexpected move.

"You have to try harder than that," I whisper into her ear, loud enough for her sister and Olivia to hear before I stand straight, wiggle my fingers in a wave, and turn back to Melanie, acting like I have not a care in the world.

And while in the morning, I might over examine this entire exchange, might tear it apart and regret it all and how it might impact my job this summer, the rush of a well-executed revenge runs through my veins

And that rush continues as I get glowing reviews for the brunch I organized and three potential clients into my calendar for consultation to see how we could work together.

I ride it as I leave, waving to Cici and planning lunch for later that week, before I make my way across the street so the hot bartender to feed me and let me vent about my chaotic day.

NINETEEN

CAMI

It's not too busy when I walk into the Fishery about ten minutes after I told Zach I'd be there, more tea than expected since I spent the time chatting with Melanie's friends and collecting new contacts. I doubt he even noticed, though. It's not like he was watching the clock, waiting for me to show up or anything.

"There she is," he says, eyes on me as I step up to the bar. "Took you long enough." Well, there goes the theory that he didn't notice. Why does that put butterflies into my belly? "Nice dress."

"Yeah, I got it from a . . . friend," I say, thinking of Cici and the kindness she showed me tonight.

"Why do I feel like that word is a surprise for you?"

Because it is.

Because I have two friends and I'm fine with that. In fact, I prefer it to be that way. Too many friends opens up complications and the opportunity for disappointment.

My mind moves to Olivia and how I held some hope for friendship there only to be tricked by her.

I was so stupid.

I shake my head subtly before I smile.

"I've only been here two weeks. Having a friend is a . . . nice surprise."

"You? Cami, the girl who won me over in a single night sitting at my bar?"

"I won you over?" I say, putting a hand to my chest and giving him an exaggerated smile, leaning onto the bar.

His eyes dip to my cleavage that is out and proud in the too small dress, my skin a sharp constant to the white fabric in a way even I know looks fucking fantastic.

"Oh yeah," he says with a smile. "Big time."

Our eyes lock for a moment longer than necessary and that tug in my belly happens again.

No way.

No fucking way.

Do I . . . *like* this guy?

No, no, no.

Absolutely not.

I'm just . . .

I'm just hungry.

Hungry and in a terrible dry spell.

Yes. That's it.

"I believe I was told you'd feed me?" I ask with a smile.

"Got maybe three minutes before Frank rings the bell. Already put in your order," he says with a smile.

"How'd you know what I want?"

"Because you never know what you want when you come in here. You just stare at the menu until I give you a suggestion and you agree to eat that."

"Fair," I say. "And a drink?"

It's then he flat out shocks me.

I didn't think I could be shocked again tonight, but I should really get used to the motto of *expect the unexpected* when I'm on this island, it seems.

Because Zachary *whatever his last name is* grabs a wine glass and fills it with ice before reaching behind him to grab a bottle of amber liquid and a familiar blue label, pouring it on top.

Then, he reaches under again, grabbing a bottle of Prosecco, pouring it into the glass before using the soda dispenser to top the glass with club soda.

"What the—" I say under my breath, thoroughly confused.

"Fuck, almost forgot." He reaches over to a cutting board, grabbing an orange slice already sitting there and putting it on the edge of the drink. "An Aperol spritz."

"An Aperol spritz." He pushes it closer to me, but my eyes are locked on his thick fingers, manly and utilitarian, a small, healing cut on the thumb, calluses on his pointer finger.

It seems so out of place on the delicate wine glass, on the stem of the fancy drink.

Out of place in this bar, really.

"You like them, right?" he asks, and when I look at his face, he looks . . . nervous.

Nervous.

It also looks out of place.

"Uhm. Yeah, but . . ." I look around, trying to see if customers are listening, but it's slow. "You didn't have the stuff."

"Yup."

"But now you do."

"Yup," is all he says again, his nervous look melting into a familiar, easy smile.

"Did you—" I start, ready to ask what I'm pretty sure is a dumb question, but just then, a bell dings and a grimacing Frank appears in the window.

"That's your dinner," Zach says, dimples out as he winks and heads to grab it off the counter.

I'm still sitting at the bar at ten.

My clam basket is gone, as is the basket of fries Frank brought me with a surprising smile and an elbow at Zach. He left not long after, Zach telling him he could handle any other food orders as needed.

"Wow, it really *is* slow tonight," I observe, looking around the bar, noting I'm the only one here.

A wide smile—and, is that a light blush?—crawls over Zach's face.

"We, uh—" A hand moves to the back of his neck and he rubs there. "We closed at nine."

My eyes widen.

My mouth drops.

"What?"

A low laugh leaves his lips and a mix of panic and embarrassment and something warm runs through me.

"It's a holiday. Not much happens here on Memorial Day, parties all over the island. We close early."

"Oh my god. I'm so sorry. This is so embarrassing!" I scramble to stand, not thinking about the two Aperol spritzes I downed in the last two hours.

I start to trip as I grab my purse while trying to stand from the stool, digging through my bag to find my wallet to pay and leave before this humiliation takes over me completely.

Yet another unbearably embarrassing moment.

But before I come face-first with the ground, Zach is moving around the bar, somehow making it to me before I'm even fully off the stool, catching me with a firm arm on my waist.

"Woah, you good there?" He holds me as I steady myself on my feet, barely even tipsy since I drank on a full stomach but more than flustered.

The flustered feeling only gets worse when I register his arm on my lower back, when I move a hand up and touch his firm chest without thinking.

"I'm sorry. I didn't mean to—I mean, I thought—" The panic and anxiety rise, words not coming easily through the fog of my brain.

This is how I get.

It's also why I don't like getting close to people. No one needs to know self-assured Camile Thompson who plans parties for a living has crippling social anxiety and second-guesses every single interaction.

I'll probably replay this night on my goddamn deathbed, wondering how I didn't see the signs.

The entire bar emptied out, Cami. How dumb could you be?

"Hey, hey, stop," Zach says.

He's still holding me, an arm wrapped around me, my hand still on his chest, no longer because I'm steadying myself but because the heat under my hand is somehow grounding.

The fog of panic starts to recede.

"If I wanted you to leave, I would have told you the bar was closing, Cami," he says in a whisper, his free hand moving to push a strand of hair behind my ear.

He's touching me.

He's *touching* me.

His fingers are warm, and they burn a path past my cheek, around my ear, down my neck.

"Oh," I say because my brain has stopped working.

"I think I like you, Cami," he whispers, and the words move through me like warmed honey, thick and sweet and heavy.

"Oh," I repeat, and then the dimples come out.

"Would it be okay . . ." He pauses, staring at me, his hazel eyes meeting mine before he pulls his bottom lip between his teeth like he's nervous.

This man is nervous.

"Can I kiss you?" he asks.

Oh.

Oh.

I don't . . .

I don't think anyone has ever asked me that, if they could kiss me.

Actually, if we're being honest, I kind of always thought it would be weird, it would break the moment if someone *asked* to kiss me instead of just grabbing me by the back of the neck, pulling me close, and planting their lips on mine.

Isn't that what all the movies and shows we watched as kids told us was unbearably romantic?

But I've never had a full-body heated reaction to being kissed before, not in the way five words are impacting me at least.

Because Zachary *still don't know his last name* is staring at me, a hand on my waist after catching me from falling, after texting me to check in when I had a shit night, after making sure his bar had the ingredients to make the drink I asked for, and he just asked me if he could kiss me.

As if my body language, the way my fingers are now gripped in his shirt, the way my chin is tipped to stare at him isn't enough.

He wanted to be *sure*.

And there has never been a hotter moment in my life.

My head moves in the tiniest nod, so small I worry he might not see it and I'll have to break this moment that has me enraptured by speaking, but that worry is gone in a heartbeat.

"Thank fuck," he whispers against my lips before his are on mine and, *finally*, we're kissing.

His lips press against mine and the room goes silent.

The music—the only other sound in the empty bar—goes quiet in my head and there is only this man and his lips and the heat of his body. His lips are soft on mine, tentative, simple and beautiful and everything a first, unexpected kiss should be.

The hand on his shirt unfurls, moving to the back of his neck as his arm on my waist tightens, pulling me closer as his other moves the side of my body in the too tight white dress before landing on my jaw, tipping my head to get better access.

And then teeth nip at my lip.

And my mouth opens just a bit.

And he takes that opportunity to slide his tongue along my teeth gently, requesting access almost as kindly and gentlemanly as he asked to kiss me.

I say a silent yes to that as well, opening my mouth, and that's when it happens.

Another snap of electricity courses and his rough hand on my jaw slips, sliding to the back of my head, holding me in place, and then we're *kissing*.

Tongues and teeth and the inherent need to get his body as close as humanly possible to mine.

Both of my hands are on his neck and I try to use it as leverage, to get more, to get closer despite my heels evening out our heights a bit.

Because Zach is *tall*.

At least six feet and towering over me as his tongue twines with mine, tasting of the soda I've noticed he sips behind the bar and orange from the slice he stole out of my drink, and it's absolutely everything.

Or, I think it is until his hand on my waist trails down to my ass, gripping it tight and pulling me into him so I can feel he's hard against my belly. The movement comes as a surprise, as does the rush of heat it sends through me, the feeling of both drawing the tiniest of moans from my throat.

The sound has Zach freezing and I think, *That's it. I fucked up, scared him off, broke the moment.*

I can't have one good fucking thing tonight, can I?

This handsome man is kissing me and it's sweet and beautiful and I can't even keep a stupid *moan* in—

But my thoughts are cut off when his hands move until both are on my waist and then *I'm* moving, turning so my back is to the bar. Then, he's lifting me with strong arms until my ass is sitting on the bartop, my feet swinging a good two feet off the ground.

A scratch of metal chair leg on concrete floor fills the bar as he haphazardly moves the chair to the side then uses a hand to spread my legs to make space. One warm hand stays on the bare skin of my thigh, and I would focus on how nice it feels, except then he's *standing between my legs* and one hand is back to my neck and he's moving so his lips are on mine again.

And gone is the sweetness of our first kiss.

In its place is pure heat and unadulterated bliss and longing and *yearning.*

The hand on my thigh keeps moving, thumb swiping down to my inner thigh then back up, not sliding upwards but still, the move feels . . . intoxicating.

My hands move to his stomach and suddenly, I'm bold.

I trail over the black bar tee he wears every day, sliding and smirking into the kiss as my nails scratch at soft abs through fabric, the hand on my thigh tightening and a small groan leaving Zach's chest.

And holy fuck, my pussy tightens with the sound.

I've never had a *thing* for vocal men.

I've never had a thing for being vocal *myself.*

That being said, on a few drunken girls' nights with Abbie, she's unloaded her sexcapades with Damien, telling us he has a filthy mouth in bed, how the uptight and proper lawyer tells her all the filthy things and groans in her ear and . . . I'd be lying if I said I wasn't interested.

But the idea of any of the men I've dated over the years *groaning in my ear* never sounded hot.

Until it was Zachary *I really need to figure out his last name* groaning simply because my nails scraped his skin through a shirt.

Yeah.

I want to hear that again.

I also want *more.*

One hand moves back down, down to where his hand is on my thigh, and in a move I didn't think I was capable of, I push his hand up.

Just a bit.

Just an inch, maybe not even that.

But he gets the hint, his thumb brushing with each centimeter it moves, the feeling exquisite torture as I try to figure out when his thumb will hit somewhere better. His tongue continues to touch mine, and his lips continue to slide over mine, my free hand moving to grip his hair.

Then, for the second time tonight, Zach surprises me.

Right before he reaches where I really, really want him to go, he stops kissing me, pressing his forehead to mine. Both of our breaths are ragged as his thumb grazes right under where I need it.

"Come home with me," he whispers, that thumb swiping left and right along the line of my panties as I resist the unbearable urge to tip my hips, to reduce the space between his thumb and where I'm dying for him to be.

"What?" I ask, my brain in a haze.

"Come home with me. I'm not far from here. Come home with me."

"I—"

"We don't have to do anything. I just like you, Cami. I like you a lot. And I don't want to be making out with you on my bar, and I sure as fuck won't be touching this pussy for the first time on my bar." My tongue comes out to lick my lips, my mind trying to think of the right answer, trying to remember the way letters form to say the words *yes, please*.

He takes my hesitance as nerves or second-guessing though, and because he truly is a fucking gentleman, he moves his hand lower, back to my knee. I can't help but mewl in protest.

That makes the dimples come back out before he speaks again. "We don't have to. I just . . . Fuck, Cami. I haven't stopped thinking of you since you walked in. I don't do this, kiss women who come in and get their numbers or ask them to come back home with me, but I—"

I don't need his speech.

I don't need him to convince me he's a good guy or that I'm different.

I already think he's a good guy.

And I don't really need to be different, not when I'll only be here for the summer.

Maybe *this* is what I need.

Not to let in some girl to be my new bestie, but to let in a man for the summer.

A fun fling with a nice guy.

So, my hand moves to his mouth, a finger touching his lips to stop him before I speak, a smile on my lips.

"Can you drive?" I ask. His smile widens in response and I know that was the right answer.

TWENTY

ZACH

Cami smiles sheepishly as I wipe the spot on the counter where her ass sat so I don't forget in the morning—as if I won't stare at that spot for the rest of my life and think about the way her hand moved mine up her thigh. Then, she follows me out the door, standing beside me as I look around the empty parking lot.

"How'd you get here?" I ask, brows furrowed as I take her hand in mine.

"I'm parked across the way in the residents' lot." She tips her head to the Beach Club. "Walked over." She looks around the lot, not seeing any cars. "Uh . . . should we just go to my place? We can walk . . . ," she says, clearly unsure.

"Nope, we'll take my ride."

"Your . . . ride?" she asks and it's cute, the low confusion in her voice, but that clears as I tug her to the side of the building where my bike is. "Oh. Oh, no. No, no."

"Get on, Cam," I say, my hand on her lower back.

"No."

"No?"

"I don't do motorcycles." She glares at it like it might bite but then her hand reaches out, touching the leather of the seat.

She's intrigued, at the very least.

I move behind her, our bodies lining up.

"You ever been on the back of a bike?" My hand goes to her hip, pulling her back against me.

"I, uh . . . no, I—"

"We'll drive along the water. It'll be nice, then we'll be at my place."

"Your place."

"My place," I say, a hand moving to her lower belly and pressing there. A light breath leaves her lips and even though the hardness of my cock lessened as I locked up the bar, it's coming back with a vengeance at her tiny breath alone.

"I don't . . . ," she whispers, voice shaking as her body seems to melt backwards into mine further. "Helmet."

"I've got an extra," I whisper, matching her voice, pushing her hair behind her shoulder and pressing a kiss below her ear.

But instead of a shiver or a sigh, though, I get stiffness. Her body goes still and she moves from me.

Not far—my hand is still on her stomach—but the gap between her back and my chest increases by a single millimeter.

"What?" I ask, my voice no longer a whisper.

"What?" she echoes, and I move my hand on her, letting her step forward before I turn her to face me so I can read her better.

"What just happened?"

"What do you mean?"

"No, no. You play that game with your friends who you want to think you're okay or your clients who you put your mask on for, but you won't fool me, Camile." Her tongue comes out, nervously wetting her lips. My hand moves until I'm cradling her jaw in my hand, forcing her eyes to meet mine.

Nerves are there.

Or second-guessing.

That won't do.

Camile came into my bar like a fucking tornado and for the two weeks since, I haven't been able to think of anything but her.

Every evening, my eye is on the door, hoping she'll walk through and make me smile. When I gave her my number last week under the guise of *therapeutic mental-dumping*, every chirp of my phone made my stomach flip as I waited for some unknown number to show on the screen. It's like I'm fifteen and I have my first crush instead of nearly forty-five and way too fucking old for this shit.

And fuck if I'm going to let her overthink this, if I'm going to let whatever intrusive thought just jumped into her mind ruin tonight.

"What just happened, Cami?" I ask, my voice lower and softer.

"I . . ." I raise an eyebrow at her hesitance, reminding her without words to tell me her truth.

"You've got an extra helmet?" she asks low, and then I get it.

I shake my head, the nerves in my stomach melting into something warmer, something sweeter at the thought that Cami is bothered by the idea of me and some other fictional women. My arm goes back around her waist, pulling her in tighter and speaking against her lips now.

"I don't do this," I reiterate. A beat passes as we share breaths, as I hold her close to me, her hands locked between us.

"Do what?" she finally asks in a whisper, and I call that a win.

She's not running.

She's not pushing.

She's listening.

For a woman who has told me herself she drops people in her life as soon as they fail some test, as soon as they show the tiniest hint that something isn't perfect, I think this is a win.

"Play with the women who live here. I don't flirt with the women who come into the bar. I don't spend all day staring at my door, waiting to see if she'll come in. I don't get fancy fuckin' wine just so I can see the smile on her face when I tell her I stocked it. I sure as *fuck* don't give out my number in case she needs emotional support, and I *definitely* don't stare at my phone for a week waiting for someone to text me." Again, her tongue dips out to wet her lips as I watch a million thoughts and emotions cross her eyes, as I watch understanding unfold.

But I'm so close, the tip of her tongue touches my lips, her breath hitching in a way I find so unbearably sexy. I can't help but lean forward a quarter inch and press a small kiss there.

A gentle brush that leaves me dying for more.

"And Cami? I never take a woman on my bike."

"The helmet—"

"My daughter's."

"Oh."

Her little ohs have me smiling against her lips.

"What do you say?" I ask. "Wanna come home with me?"

I watch as my words move through her mind, warring with what I assume is her common sense and her desire to go.

But then it happens.

I watch a smile grow on her own lips before she speaks.

"Let's go."

TWENTY-ONE

CAMI

"Swing off but watch your leg," he says, his hand moving behind him to run up my thigh in a simple gesture, setting my skin on fire. He uses the hand to hold me in place, the toes of my heels on the foot pegs still as he points to a metal pipe. "That gets crazy hot. You put your bare leg on it, you'll get a nasty scar." My eyes widen in slight panic and he laughs, his hand on my thigh tightening.

"Do you know from experience?" I ask and watch as he takes off his own helmet before turning to me and giving me what might be my new addiction.

His easy, simple smile.

"More times than I can count. I've learned to wear boots and jeans anytime I'm riding." He puts a hand out to give me something to hold onto while I swing my leg over and hop off the bike, eyes roaming my body and I tug my dress down with one hand.

He doesn't let go.

"Might want to keep that in mind for next time," he says, and I quirk an eyebrow at him even though I'm not totally sure if he can see it through the visor of the helmet I'm still wearing.

"Next time?" I ask.

His hand moves to the little clip under my chin before helping to slide the helmet off my head, placing it down on the bike, and smoothing my hair down.

I refuse to even let the thought of helmet hair grace my mind.

"Next time," he says, moving my hair behind my neck and pulling me closer, pressing his lips to mine in a soft, sweet touch which leaves me wanting more before he steps back, still holding my hand and leading me up a little winding path.

The house in front of us is tiny.

Not tiny in an *oh god, it's a weird, creepy hole in the wall* way, but tiny in a cute Jersey Shore beach cottage way. It's on the water and even though it's dark, a dock can be seen going out onto the bay. There are little pots here and there in the front yard where I assume flowers once were, but the front porch light shows they're all filled with weeds.

He smiles when he catches me staring at them, shaking his head.

"My daughter went through a flower phase. Forced me to get a million pots and dig her flower beds, the whole nine."

"And you did," I say.

"I did. And the fascination was replaced by something else the next summer. Some years, I remember to pull the weeds and pop something in there from the nursery, but I also never remember to water the little shits so . . ." He shrugs, broad shoulders moving under the black bar tee he wears, and it reminds me of how warm and muscled his back felt as I held him on the short drive from the bar to his place.

I'd never seen the appeal of a motorcycle before, hearing nothing but loud engines at annoying hours and terrible, horribly tragic stories on the news, but five minutes on the back of Zach's and I get it.

The salty ocean air on my arms and legs, his warm body in front of mine, my body wrapped around his was heaven. Then, when we hit a red light, his hand left the handlebars and moved back to my knee, squeezing then sliding up farther, his thumb brushing my inner thigh and reminding me where we were going and, more importantly, what we were going to do there.

Yeah.

I get it now.

But motorcycles and ocean air fly out of my head once he unlocks the door with one hand then tugs me inside, slamming the door and pressing me to it without even deigning to turn on the lights in the house.

"God, I've been thinking about this for weeks," he murmurs, head dipping to my neck to kiss me there.

Instantly, there is no air in my lungs anymore; it leaves in a huff of lust and need. My hands go to his hair, nails scraping his scalp and digging in as his tongue moves along my neck. He continues to move, licking and kissing until I'm squirming, his lips at the sensitive place where my jaw meets my neck. And then they're back on mine.

And he's not kissing me sweet anymore.

It's not even the heat level from the bar, sexy and sweet. No, this time it's just fire and lust and *need*. His lips move against mine like he can't get enough of me, like he thinks if he stops, I'll disappear or I'll come to my senses and stop this.

As if that would happen.

As if I *could* stop this.

This is all I want right now. My body is on fire, my mind blank of common sense as his tongue moves against mine, as he groans into my mouth, as his hips move to mine, grinding so I can feel how much this kiss is impacting him as well.

I think I could do this forever, kiss Zach and groan and moan into his mouth as he keeps me pinned against his door.

When he finally breaks the kiss, his hands leaving my body to support himself against the door and look at me, I mewl in protest, the sound bringing the dimples out just a hint.

"I want you, Cami," he says, staring me down, hands on either side of my face. "Want you really fuckin' bad. I think you can tell."

"Uh-huh," is all I can say because *yes*, I can tell.

"I want you, but I also don't want to fuck this up." My chest is heaving, brushing his with each gasped breath.

"Fuck this up?"

"I told you. I don't *do this*. Don't flirt with tourists, don't take women on my bike, and I sure as fuck don't take them back to my place and fuck them until they're hoarse."

I'm panting, mind spinning, but I can't resist speaking. "Is that a promise?" A single dimple comes out and I lean in, letting my tongue touch his skin there then kissing down his neck. It's a compulsion, like my lips can't leave his skin, like if they do, I'll combust or the world will stop spinning or something equally dire will happen.

"Seriously, Cam," he says finally, a hand moving to my jaw and tipping it so I look at him. "I like you, Cami. I like you and I don't want to rush this." My brow furrows, but he keeps speaking. "If that means we make out all night and you wake in my bed fully clothed and I make you eggs, great. If that means I take you home right now and we make a plan for me to take you out on a real date before we even get past the front door, I'm fine with that. What I'm not fine with is taking you inside, getting my fill, and you thinking that's all we are."

"Zach, I—"

"Know that shit scares you. That's fine. We've got all summer to explore things. But I'm telling you right now—I want that. To explore with you. Explore *us*."

My heart is racing now and it's not from lust or attraction.

It's from *panic*.

He sees it of course. He seems to have this strange ability to see *me*, to see past the façade to who I really am. When he sees it, when his eyes go soft, I expect him to ease it. I expect him to treat me with kid gloves and kindness and back off from the topic. Maybe to say fuck it and kiss me again and throw caution to the wind.

But he doesn't.

Instead, the grip on my chin tightens.

"Don't. Don't go in that shell of yours, overthinking everything and trying to forecast the future."

How does he *know*?

"I want you. I want to make you moan my name as I slide into you, Camile, but I want it knowing you won't regret it. You've had a crazy night. I don't want to mess up something that could be really fuckin' beautiful because I'm thinking with my cock and taking advantage of you."

Thoughts tumble in my mind.

Thoughts of how distraught I was a few hours ago and how Zach eased it.

Thoughts of how he's spent the last couple weeks listening to my shit for literally no reason other than he might . . . like me.

How every test I've thrown at him so far, he passes with flying fucking colors.

It makes no sense.

It could all be a trap.

I could leave the summer destroyed.

But then my mind stumbles on Kat and Abbie, on them telling me I need to take chances, live less calculated and safe. Stop protecting myself from being hurt.

Life is about getting your heart broken. When you die, do you want to remember all the times you avoided getting hurt, or the experiences and the people you met despite the pain the world can dish out?

And I decide right then.

I don't want to live a life of outsmarting my emotions, of being too smart to get hurt by others.

I want to live a life that's memorable, pain and all.

And that starts by taking chances.

"I want to keep things simple, Zach. I'm not in a place where strings and commitment are something I can promise you. I won't... I won't be with anyone else, but I can't promise you more than something physical."

"I can work with that. We can take it day by day, but know I don't share. I won't share, Cami."

I bite my lip because despite telling myself over and over I don't want a relationship, I do want exclusivity, to know there's no one else he'd be spending his nights with.

It's what has me nodding in agreement, what has me moving to my toes despite Zach's hand on my jaw. Then gently, so gently I would question if he could feel it if his fingers didn't tighten on my hip at that exact moment, I press my lips to his.

"Okay. Now show me your place, Zach," I say in a whisper.

TWENTY-TWO

CAMI

"Showing me his place" turns out to be smiling, taking my hand, and dragging me to his room while I giggle the whole way, feeling freer than I have in years.

I stop giggling when he pulls me into his room and tosses me onto his bed, though, his eyes burning with heat that singes through me.

"Take off the dress," he says in a growl.

"What?"

"The dress. I need to see you. Take it off."

I'm not in a position to argue, especially not when his hand moves behind his neck, grabbing the back of his tee and tugging it over his head. It's then I get to see his chest, which is broad and strong and dotted with a dusting of dark hair I really can't fucking wait to touch. He's stocky and broad and everything I never knew I was unbearably attracted to, including when I notice the V leading to his hard cock still hidden by jeans is soft, not sculpted and defined.

He leans down to take off his boots before he speaks.

"Now, Cami," he says, not even bothering to look at me as he undoes the laces of his boots.

I don't waste any more time, wiggling to get the stretchy white dress over my hips and tugging it over my head, leaving me in a brown bra and underwear set and my heels by the time he's standing in just his jeans.

"God, you're fucking beautiful, aren't you?" he asks, standing there and staring at me, his eyes filled with fire. I can't fight the urge to bite my lip and cross my legs, covering just a small part of me. "No, no, no. No, you don't. Legs wide, Camile." I chew on the lip nervously as he shakes his head, eyes stern. "What are you nervous about?"

The words come easy, his arms crossing his chest as he leans on a wall and stares at me.

He's looking at me like I'm not sitting in just my underwear and he's not in just his jeans, his hard cock bulging. It's like this is a normal Tuesday and he's asking me what the weather is like.

"What?"

"You think you're so hard to read, angel, that you hide everything so well. And you might—the idiots you've dated before might not have known you, and your friends might not fully get it. But me? You can't hide from me. The look on your face, the way you crossed your legs. You're uneasy. Tell me why."

I stare at him, unsure of what to say.

"Can't we just . . . you know, do what we were doing?" I ask.

"If you're going to be in my bed, you need to know just how fucking beautiful you are. The shit I'm going to do to you, your head can't get in the way." Heat rolls through me with his words, with the images that run through my head. "So tell me. What's going on in that pretty head of yours?" I roll my lips between my teeth, contemplating which is stronger—my ego or the throbbing between my legs. Throbbing I'm pretty sure he will be the only one to ease right now.

The throbbing wins.

"I'm a woman, Zach. There are aspects I'm not wild about concerning my body. I've never been naked in front of you, in case you don't remember." He nods then, uncrossing his arms as he takes a single step closer, and I breathe a sigh of relief that this uncomfortable section of our night is over.

Onto the fun stuff.

"Show me," he says, his face firm, his thumbs hooking in the loops of his jeans.

What?

"What?"

"Show me."

"Show you?"

"Show you what you think I won't like. Show me what you're not wild about."

"I don't—"

"Show me the parts of you you don't like because I swear to fuck, Cami, I've been staring at you for weeks. Now that I've got you half naked in my bed, I can't find a single fucking flaw."

"Zach, this—"

"*Show me, Camile.*" He says it so firmly that I don't know how to argue.

But I also don't quite understand how to comply.

"I don't know how," I say in a strained whisper. He smiles then, the dimples appearing and somehow putting me at ease.

"I can work with that. Let's start with your legs. Uncross them." I take a deep break and do as he says, leaving them still closed, thighs touching. "Spread." The word makes my belly flutter, my pussy tighten, but I do it either way. "Good girl. Now tell me what you don't like about your legs," he says, stepping forward and kneeling between them.

My breath hitches, but somehow, with his eyes locked to mine, I don't have the option to lie or avoid. So, I answer.

"They're too thick," I whisper. "They're hard to dress."

His hands move to them, thumbs brushing the area I'm talking about whisper soft, his eyes moving to them as he glides callused fingers over my mahogany skin. "What else? What else don't you like?"

I expected him to give the requisite *you're beautiful* which wouldn't mean much to me, so I'm surprised when he just asks for what's next. I clear my throat before speaking.

"My hips. Too wide and they have stretch marks."

I watch one think finger move along the light lines there, lines I've been self-conscious about since high school when some bitchy girl pointed it out at a pool party.

"What else?"

I'm prepared to answer this time, my next sore spot ready.

"My belly. It's too soft." No amount of dieting or working out helped so eventually, I stopped doing what didn't bring me joy. "I love my body," I say, feeling the need to clarify.

"Good," he says, hands trailing along my belly.

"I love my body but the world doesn't."

It's a truth I don't know if I've ever said out loud.

"Good thing I'm not the world, right?" is all he says on the topic before his fingers hook beneath the waistband of my underwear, tugging them down and leaving me in just a bra. "Spread so I can show you just how much I like this."

I do and my breath hitches as his hands move up my thighs again, thumbs sliding to either side of where I'm throbbing, full of need and desire.

"Yeah, this is really fuckin' pretty," he whispers, the knuckle of one finger gliding through the wet there. "And you're fucking drenched." He swipes back down then slowly slides that finger inside me, then back out, repeating the torturous cycle.

"Zach!" I moan, my hips lifting as the pleasure builds so slowly and painfully, I don't know how to function, how to breathe. There is only Zach and his fingers and the way his eyes burn on me.

"You need more, angel?" I nod and he chuckles.

"*Zach! Please!*" I moan as his wet knuckle grazes over my clit again, making my hips buck.

"Be good and you'll get what you want."

A finger slides in, grazing my G-spot for a millisecond and then repeating the circuit.

But still, I stay there, watching him play with me, hoping that will get me what I want.

"So good," he says finally then thrusts three fingers into me, my back arching off the bed as I scream his name. His thumb goes to my clit as those three fingers move inside, pressing on my G-spot over and over, pleasure building with each pass.

"Oh god."

"That's it, baby, let go. Don't think, just feel." His fingers leave and I mewl in protest before those three fingers move to my clit, swiping left and right.

I might explode.

It's everything and it's nothing and I need more and less at the same time.

"Zach!" I shout.

"You're not going to take long, are you? Fuck, I think you were made for me," he says under his breath, his face so close to my pussy as he does, his breath plays along sensitive flesh as he moves those three fingers back inside, stroking the spot inside of me again as that same pleasure builds, starts to crest, so fucking close—

And then they're back at my clit, left and right, the pace quick and predictable, making the feeling in my belly build again, bigger than anything I've felt before. My head tips back as I lean on my arms, and I moan loud, the orgasm right in reach. I just—

And it's gone again as he thrusts those fingers back in, teasing. Each time, he gets me so close before switching and it's pure torture.

"One more, Cami. One more then you let go," he says, and when I look down at him, his hazel eyes are on me, his face between my legs as he kneels on the floor.

"Please," I beg, feeling it start again.

He smiles.

I decide I hate those dimples as he once again removes those fingers, going back to my clit, and I scream in frustration.

But what happens next is what sets my blood on *fire*.

The hand he hasn't used moves, pressing gently right above my pubic bone, and I scream. It adds a pressure I don't know what to do with, adding to the pleasure as he continues to rub my clit near furiously now.

"Oh god, oh god. Fuck! Zach, I can't—"

"You can, baby. Give into it. Let go," he murmurs, an edge to his words, and they have me falling, my arms collapsing as I scream, a rush of liquid coming from between my legs as I come.

And come.

And *come*, his fingers still manipulating me as my hips rock, liquid coming in bursts alongside the pleasure. It's like a never-ending orgasm, each one building and building quicker than the last, each just barely taking the edge off.

"Fucking *beautiful*," he says as his fingers leave me, as he leans forward and flattens his tongue along me before standing and moving to his jeans.

I'm still teetering on an edge I jumped off already, watching him as he pulls his cock out of his underwear, lost in the image, lost in the pleasure.

"Bra off," he says, reaching over to grab a foil packet and already halfway through rolling it on before I come to my senses, able to break my eyes from watching Zach palm his thick cock, and undo my bra. "God, look at how *pretty* you are," he says, then he takes his cock in hand, sliding it up and down my swollen pussy. He's teasing me incessantly but *finally*, he notches the head, and I groan at the way he's already stretching me.

It's been way too fucking long.

Then, slowly, torturously slowly, he slides into me.

"Zach," I groan as he stops when he's deep inside of me.

"I know."

"*Zach*," I repeat, my hips lifting a bit as I try and get something, anything.

"What do you need?" he asks, one hand on my hip, the other

letting a thumb gently, *so gently,* swipe against my clit before moving up my body to my breast, tweaking a nipple and forcing a low moan from my lips.

"I need you."

"You have me."

He's out to kill me, clearly.

"I need more."

"Tell me exactly what you need, then. I can't read minds, Cami," he says and *goddammit,* the man is smiling.

He knows exactly what he's doing.

Fine.

I can play.

I can *take* what I need.

My hand moves down my body, stopping at my clit and moving quickly, circling and building it again, this time full of him, the pleasure unbearable.

And he watches.

He watches, planted deep inside, eyes locked to mine as I rub my clit, as I take myself closer and closer to orgasm.

"Fall," he whispers as I moan. And I have no option, my eyes still on his as I scream, making myself come again while planted on his cock.

It's glorious.

All-consuming.

Something I've never experienced in my life—a mix of the intimacy of his eyes on mine and the unbearable feeling of another orgasm. I want to bask in it forever and ever and never leave.

But clearly, he doesn't have it in him to wait for me to come down to earth because then he's pulling out and slamming in rough.

A scream bubbles in my throat, my eyes rolling back as he repeats the motion, his cock brushing soft, swollen tissues with each thrust in.

"Let me take a picture," he says, his voice a groan as he stares down at where he's disappearing into me.

"What?"

"A picture, fuck, the way you look right now. They way you're taking me. Fuck." I stare down between us, no longer looking at his face, which is a mask of pain and pleasure and desperation, but to where his cock is sliding into me slowly before sliding back out, a torture in and of itself.

"I don't understand," I whisper, words barely working. The hand holding my thigh open tightens and I groan at the feeling before I speak. "A picture for what?"

"I need a picture of this to fucking jack off to until I die, Cami."

That sounds hot.

That sounds so fucking hot, I clamp down on him, pulling another groan from his lips.

"Only if you say yes, angel." I lick my lips, moving my eyes from where we're joined to his face. It's then I notice he's staring at me, eyes fixated like he's reading every thought and waiting for my answer.

The look there takes every sane thought from my brain, the heat there, the fucking *obsession* burning in his eyes.

Obsession with me.

With my body.

Fuck.

"Yes," I breath. "No face."

Well, at least I have a shred of common sense left.

"No face. *Fuck.*" He reaches over, grabbing his phone and opening it, staring at the screen and positioning it above us, another moan falling from him because he clearly likes what he sees.

My pussy clenches again.

Well, let's add this to shit I never thought I'd be into.

And because I'm so far gone from who my mind tells me I am, my hand moves down, down, down until I land on my clit.

"Fuck yes, play with your clit."

The phone hovers over as he continues to slowly fuck me, pulling out and sliding in effortlessly, one rough hand on my hip.

"Make a pretty movie for me, baby."

Shit, if that's not hot. I do as he asks.

Slowly, my hand moves, circling my clit, driving myself higher, higher, and higher until—

"I'm gonna come, Zach," I whisper, my voice breathless.

"That's it, fall for me," he says, and that's all it takes.

My neck arches as I come, panting as wave after wave of pleasure takes over me, my hips moving to push him deeper into me as he groans a noise that has me moaning louder.

"Fuck, that's it, angel," he says through a nearly pained growl as I rock on his cock, my feet planted in the bed as he hovers over me, dragging my orgasm out. "Fuck yourself on my cock and take me with you."

But it's *building again.*

"I can't," I whisper, my face to the side to look back at him in the dimly lit room, phone in his hand directed at where he's disappearing in me, but his eyes are on mine. "It's too much."

"You can take it, Cami. Fuck, give me another. That's it, baby. Rub your clit again." My fingers keep going at my swollen, sensitive clit as the pressure rises once more, my hips moving to take him, to take myself over the hill again.

I barely even realize he's no longer doing anything, just letting me take what I need.

"Fucking beautiful," he says, his voice in genuine awe, one hand loose on my hip like he wants to do whatever I feel like, the other holding his phone above where we're joined.

The thought of what's being saved has me clenching around him again, the crest so, so close, so big and all-consuming, it terrifies me just a bit.

"I can't . . . It's too . . ." The words are panted and panicked as I feel the pleasure in my belly, in my lower back, heat everywhere, so much fucking pressure building I think when I fall, it might destroy me.

"I know, I know. Me too. Keep going. Make me come, Camile," he says in a hushed, pained voice and something about it—maybe the confirmation he feels it too, or the fact his voice is strained with the need to come, or maybe it's the challenge for me to finish him off . . .

It has me moaning, has my voice hoarse as my back arches off the bed and I scream his name as I come again. He collapses on top of me, thrusting once more before planting deep and coming in me, and although the world spins around me, although I'm floating in clouds of pleasure, he's there. And he's real.

And for now, at least, I somehow know he's mine.

TWENTY-THREE

TUESDAY, MAY 30

CAMI

Hours later, I'm still in Zach's big bed, white blankets pooled around us, a midnight snack of cheese and crackers decimated on the bedside table.

So much better than hanging out at some stuffy rich-bitch party.

"Look," he says, phone in hand once again. My body heats remembering what's saved on his phone, what he did.

What *we* did.

I never thought I'd like that—photos being taken of me, home videos for his pleasure.

But the idea of Zach having this token of me?

Fuck.

"I want you to look at it. If you're not comfortable with this, I'll delete it. You can't consent to this kind of shit in the moment, but I was so fucking lost in you . . . We should have talked about it."

Something about that feels like he's passing a test I didn't realize I was giving him.

"Oh," I whisper, looking at him.

His lips tip like he can read my mind, read how I like that.

"Yeah." Fingers brush back my hair, trailing down to my bare shoulder before his thumb brushes there.

It's not sexual, just like . . . like he wants to keep touching me, to keep putting his hands on me.

"So, is this your thing? Pictures and whatnot?" I ask.

"I have lots of *things*. Sometimes it's taking filthy pictures while I fuck you. More recently, my thing has been beautiful girls with a wall ten feet high who come into my bar and flirt endlessly and dump their worries on me. Bonus if she calls me dimples even after I tell her my name."

I smile when he gives me those dimples, and he just shakes his head at me.

"Speaking of your name, what's your last name?"

"My last name?"

"Yeah, for my records in case you turn out to be a serial killer or something." His smile widens but he gives it to me all the same.

"Anderson." The name triggers something in my memories, something buried under exhaustion and adrenaline and good sex and I can't quite dig it out.

"Zachary Anderson," I say, liking the sound of it. He presses his lips to mine once with a smile before scrolling on his phone again.

"Okay, look," he says and gives me the phone.

Glancing at the screen in his hand, I grab it to get a better glimpse.

Because it's graphic.

It's sexual.

It's absolutely *feral*.

And fuck, is it hot.

His skin on mine, his cock deep in me, my fingers on my clit.

I swipe and there's more. Some are almost artistic angles, sexy snapshots of a hip or the softness of my belly and the curls of my pubic hair.

Some are raunchy, his cock pulling out to the tip, my legs wide, my perfect French tips circling my clit.

And then there's a short video—a clip of him sliding in then pulling out, of my fingers moving chaotically.

I know if I hit the button on the side of the phone, increasing the volume, I'll hear us both moaning.

My pussy clenches, wanting more.

But I don't miss how my face is missing in all of them.

I don't miss how he kept his word, how nothing shows *me*.

"You can delete and I won't be offended," he says, thumb a metronome on my shoulder blade.

I pause, unsure how to tell him I don't *want* to delete this.

Fuck, I want to send them to myself, a sexy moment of a summer fling.

"This is what does it for you?" I ask with a smile.

"Does it for me?"

"Home movies." He bursts out laughing, his head tipping back, and the sound fills me with warmth.

"I mean, if you're asking if I like to watch myself fucking a beautiful woman, yeah."

My gut drops, my mind going to the immediate thought that he probably has an entire drive of women he fucks, saved images and videos of all the times he's done exactly this.

My brain tells me to hit delete.

"No," he says, and I look at him confused. "No, I don't have some kind of stockpile of filthy shit. A relationship ends, I delete anything I have. If you're not mine, neither are these photos."

My gut drops again for a different reason.

"Zach, I—"

"I know we're not anything right now, but I like spending time with you. You're fun. You're sweet. I really like fucking you."

I close my eyes and breathe.

Tonight was a reminder of everything I've worked to avoid.

New friendships. New relationships. Ties and tangles and anything that could maybe, possibly, get too close and destroy my heart again.

"I don't . . ." I sigh. "I don't date."

"Funny because I'm pretty sure most people would call this a date." He rolls over until he's hovering on top of me and again, my mind tumbles with confusion.

The truth is, I like Zach.

I like his smile and I like his laugh and I like how he gave me a safe space but didn't ask too many questions. I like how he's not chiseled and he's real and he has dimples and he likes to eat junk food but can also whip together a fucking charcuterie board in ten minutes.

But I don't like anyone for more than a few weeks.

They always show their true colors eventually.

"It doesn't have to be serious, but I'm telling you right now, I'm not letting you go easily. I'm not having you for just one night, at the very least. So those pictures . . . I can delete them now. I can get rid of them and we'll never talk about them and I'll never ask that of you again," he says, and my mind, my sick, twisted, traitorous mind thinks it would be a shame.

A shame to lose those photos and that video forever but also, a shame to lose that option with him forever.

Fuck, what is wrong with me?

"But if we don't—if I don't delete them, I can send you those on a night we can't see each other." His face dips, his mouth going to my ear. "You can watch me fuck you, and I can listen to you come while you do."

Oh my fucking god.

A smile creeps across his lips.

"Fuck, you like that," he murmurs.

I do.

I like that a lot.

"I don't know if there will be a next time, Zach," I say. "I mean it when I say I don't date. I have a job to do up here and it's not . . . this. I want to make sure you don't have the wrong impression."

"That's fine. I know there will be a next time. I'll believe in next time enough for the both of us." His words are low and growly and again, my pussy clenches with desire. "But before I fuck you again, before I muddle your brain more with sex, I need your answer. And I'll ask again in the morning, when you're in my shirt and I'm making you breakfast. But what are your thoughts right now?"

Making you breakfast.

God.

That sounds nice.

"Breakfast?"

"I'm gonna feed you in the morning, Camile." My brow furrows.

"I can't stay the night. None of my stuff is here."

"What kind of stuff?"

"Toothbrush, face wash, my bonnet, pillowcase, pajamas . . ." I could go on and on, but it's starting to feel and sound like an excuse. His hand goes to my face, and he looks at me with his warm eyes and I almost forget what I was saying.

"Can you go a night without it? Just one. I have a spare toothbrush." I stare at him for a few heartbeats, reading him, seeing he *wants* that—me to spend the night. So I nod, agreeing.

I can handle one night, right? What's the worst that could happen?

"Good," he says, and the smile taking over his face confirms the thought he *wanted* that. How could I say no? "So, what are you thinking?"

"Thinking?"

He reaches over to the forgotten phone, the obscene images still there on the screen.

"Delete?"

I stare at the shot of his cock halfway in me and my body heats.

I definitely don't want him to delete them.

"Are they . . . Do you have somewhere safe to save them?" I remember he told me he has a daughter—what a nightmare it would be for her to be trying to play fucking Candy Crush and then stumbling upon her father fucking some woman.

The poor girl would need therapy for decades.

"Password protected album," he says.

I stare at him, my trust detector so finely tuned, trying to decode him.

I don't know why, but I trust him.

I trust this man.

Maybe this is what I was being pushed to—not Olivia and the Bitch Pack, but this man.

"Keep them," I whisper, the words alone sending heat down my spine, another wave of flames chasing it when his eyes go dark with lust and he smiles a carnal look.

"I think you were made to be mine, angel," he says, and then he rolls over me, showing me just how much he liked my answer and leaving zero space for me to overthink his words.

TWENTY-FOUR

CAMI

I'm sitting in an oversized tee shirt from Zach's closet and a pair of panties at a kitchen island, scrolling my phone mindlessly, monitoring the socials for the Beach Club events page as well as my own.

Meanwhile, Zach is at the stove, cooking me eggs.

I think I've entered a twilight zone.

Maybe *this* is why Abbie instantly started to fall for Damien.

I could see it happening. It really wouldn't be hard.

Maybe the key to finding a good man is getting an older one—fuck these young guys who barely remember to wash their sheets.

I might be forever changed after last night, after finding a man who can blow my back out and who willingly ate me out until my fingers were sore from tugging at his hair during round two.

A man who cleaned me up and cuddled into me all night long.

And a man who is now making me *breakfast* instead of urging me to leave as soon as the sun started to creep into his bedroom.

Who walked me into the kitchen, made me a cup of coffee, then lifted me until my ass was planted on the small island in his kitchen where he kissed me breathless and told me to sit still while he made me food.

I take a sip of said coffee while I think on it.

An older man.

Huh.

Never saw that coming, did I?

But it seems a lot of things I didn't see coming are headed my way when the knob to the front door twists, pausing for a moment when it's locked. The person on the other side must have a key, though, because there's the click of metal on metal, the lock twisting undone, then the knob moves again.

My eyes snap to where Zach stands at the stove, his broad shoulders bare and stiff.

The world slows and my thoughts rush in.

He has a wife.

She was out for the weekend and he thought he was safe to have a fling, a one-night stand with the idiot who fell for his kind words and hot looks.

The taut muscles of his back and the panic hovering in the air tell me everything I need to know.

And so does the dark head of hair walking through the door, turning quickly to close it behind her before she speaks.

It must be his wife.

Or his girlfriend.

Someone he doesn't want me to know exists at the very least.

I'm sure of it.

At least, I am until she speaks.

"Dad, Mom is driving me insane . . . ," she starts, her voice trailing off in a hushed whisper.

But it isn't panic filling me.

It's also not shame.

Not even some almighty brand of feminine rage over the fact we've both been betrayed.

Nope, none of that happens.

Instead, pleasure and karma flow through my veins when Olivia's shocked face stares back at me.

Her long hair which was curled perfectly last night is straight now, the ends barely curving in, and she's wearing a loose tee and a pair of jean shorts.

She looks almost normal, like an all-American girl down the Shore for the holiday weekend instead of a socialite with an extensive trust fund.

And even through her fake tan, her face has gone pale.

It's then I know, signs I didn't recognize before clicking into place.

Olivia is Zach's daughter.

And the way he described her—sweet and silly and a daddy's girl torn between parents who were never supposed to be together—is true. With the way panic is taking over her face, I can tell she is afraid of her father finding out the truth of who she is outside of the safe bubble he created of her.

God, the universe really had my back on this one, didn't it?

Because Zachary's daughter isn't a young girl, a tiny princess who has him wrapped around his finger like I assumed.

No, his daughter is the spoiled princess of the Beach Club.

Olivia is his *daughter*.

Zach's daughter.

Oh my fucking god.

And now I'm sitting at his island in nothing but her father's tee shirt after letting her dad feed and fuck me after she made my night a living hell.

God. Sometimes, karma really is so fucking sweet, isn't it?

I take her in, her frozen body barely having stepped into the small kitchen, and smile a sweet smile.

"Hey there, Liv," I say, breaking the silence and twisting my body until I'm facing her, the oversized tee covering everything but leaving absolutely nothing to the imagination.

Her face goes a bit paler and Zach's confused gaze burns on me.

"Do you . . . Do you know each other?" he asks.

He told me at the bar once his daughter is sweet, the kindest soul he's ever met.

When I look back at the woman who pretended to be just that before laughing when I made a fool of myself, panic spreads across her face.

I've always prided myself on being able to read people.

It's why I don't *trust* people.

Rarely have I found someone who has *purely* good intentions. In fact, the only one I've ever found is our sweet Kat.

Even Abbie has her moments.

But right now, I'm reading Olivia and it's all so clear.

She's terrified I'm going to tell her father about the trick she played with the twins. That I'm going to tell him she's not the angel he thinks she is, wrecking the way he sees her, or something along those lines.

Her mother is a rich benny, met her at a party at the Beach Club when we were kids. I've spent Livi's whole life working to make sure she didn't turn out like her. Making her learn the value of a dollar, how to treat people with kindness.

I remember him telling me that at one of my dinners at the bar.

My dad is a local. Hates my mom and everything she stands for. I need to play the game this summer to get my trust.

Oh, she's playing the game alright.

God, what a chaos this is.

Good thing I fucking *love* chaos. A smile spreads across my lips.

If Abbie were here, she'd kick me under the chair, tell me to *be nice* through gritted teeth and wide eyes. She would remind me being unkind doesn't get you anything, doesn't win you favors.

But where has being nice and trusting people got me?

Humiliated in front of the wealthiest people in this fucking town?

In front of the man who destroyed me years ago?

You know what?

Fuck being nice.

I'm going to be *me*.

"Oh yeah, I know Olivia," I say and watch the color drain from her face even more. Her mouth opens and closes once, twice, three times before I break eye contact and look over at Zach, my voice going sugary sweet. "She's my intern."

When I turn my face back to her, she looks . . . confused.

"Intern?" he asks

"Yeah. Olivia is the one who gave me the invite to the party last night." I'm fighting a smile. It's so hard not to just laugh at the absolute absurdity of this situation. I was fucked into oblivion in an effort to cope with the embarrassment his *daughter* dished out last night.

And now his daughter is staring at me with wide eyes, begging.

Begging . . .

Begging for *what?*

"You . . . You went to Mel's party?"

It hits me then.

It hits me *Melanie* is Zach's ex. I can't decide if *this* is a sign the universe hates me or if it's just poetic, dumping this interesting bit into my lap.

I slide off the island, making sure not to flash my intern before leaning against it, my body turned toward Zach but my face toward Olivia.

"I'm planning her wedding," I say with a smile.

The smile isn't because I'm happy I'm planning the wedding of my summer fling's ex.

It's because the whole situation is truly laughable.

"You're planning my ex's wedding?" Zach asks, and I can see it there. It's in the way his eyes roam my body as I sit in his kitchen wearing his tee and a pair of panties he tore off me last night before he fucked me until my voice was hoarse, the way his eyes burn with the same memories fresh in my own mind, and, most importantly, the way he doesn't smile per se but there's a hint of a fucking dimple . . .

He finds this *funny*.

He finds the situation entertaining at the very least.

Until he doesn't.

Until I watch something click in his mind. I can assume it's exactly what Olivia was hoping he wouldn't find out.

"Wait, Livi invited you?" he asks, his brows coming together with confusion.

Ding ding ding.

Olivia's face goes a shade paler, but something must be wrong with me because instead of basking in the sweet revenge of her father figuring out what a bitch she is, I'm stuck on the way he says her name.

Livi. It's cute, sweet even. I like Livi better than fucking *Olivia.*

Livi sounds like a girl I could be friends with.

She sounds like a down-to-earth chick who I would invite for a night out with Abbie and Kat.

Olivia sounds like a privileged rich bitch who pranks the help in order to appease the fancier, richer, bitchier girls.

Olivia's mouth opens as she looks from me to her father and back again, and I decide to throw her a bone.

Revenge isn't very fun if it's quick and easy.

"Yeah. Big misunderstanding. It's all good. All's well that ends well, you know? The whole catastrophe led me . . . here." I move to my toes and kiss Zach on the cheek.

"We'll talk about this later," Zach says in a low, warning tone, and I widen my eyes at his daughter, rolling my lips into my mouth and biting on them. I just know my face screams what I'm thinking— *ooooh, Olivia's in troOoOouble*—before finally speaking and giving the illusion of helping her dig herself out of the hole.

"I *thought* she said Americana, but she said *American, Memorial Day.*" Her brow furrows, making her look confused and possibly like she thinks I'm stupid, which annoys me more. *Hello, my girl, I'm giving you a life vest. Take it.* "I was so excited for the invite, I totally missed the part about all-white party. It was my bad really."

Zach doesn't look like he's buying it but finally, *finally*, Olivia gets the hint.

"Yeah, I uhm." She clears her throat, finally moving her body as she steps into the kitchen farther. "I should have called you. Made sure you understood. That's . . ." Then, she stops moving, her eyes sincere for a quick flash of time. "I'm sorry, Cami."

And again, in a way seeming to be uniquely Olivia, I can't fully read it.

Or at least, I don't trust my *ability* to read it.

Is she telling the ruth or is it another game? Is it her telling me what she thinks I want to hear in order to win this round?

Does she *actually* feel bad?

"All good, Liv," I say, keeping my words light.

"Well, this is . . . a surprise. I was, uh . . . We were . . ."

"You fucked her," Olivia says deadpan, and my eyes go wide with her words because I did *not* expect that from her.

Clearly, neither did Zach, whose body whips toward his daughter.

"What the fuck, Livi?"

"Well, you did, didn't you? It's a Tuesday morning and you're in shorts and she's in *your* shirt. Math wasn't my *best* subject, but I'm not stupid."

"You're not stupid, but you're acting like it." Zach has a look I haven't yet seen on his face, one of true . . . indignation? Confusion, maybe?

I speak, trying to break the conversation before it goes further.

"You know, I think . . ." But I stop there because suddenly, I'm unsure of myself.

Suddenly, I feel like I'm intruding.

And suddenly, it feels like yet another sweet moment of this summer goes up in flames because of Olivia.

First, this job, which felt absolutely like a dream when I arrived, has quickly devolved into a unique nightmare.

Then, the stupid party I thought could be a turning point.

"I think I'll head on out of here. I have . . ." I bite my lip and tug at the hem of the shirt, trying to cover my legs, no longer feeling like playing this game.

"No, you don't."

"What?"

"You don't have anything," Zach says, abandoning the stove and walking over to me, an arm wrapping my waist and tugging me into his side. "You told me this morning you don't have to go into your office today, you're working from your apartment and you can make your own hours."

Fuck. I did say that, didn't I?

"Livi, I have no idea what's going on, but you better drop your attitude. I'm telling you right now, I like Cami. This has nothing to do with you." My belly flips at his outright announcement of how he feels about me.

Of course, I thought he *liked* me—he told me a few times last night and, you know, *last night happened*—but for some reason, there's a difference between when a person tells you in private they like you and when they tell someone *else* they like you.

It means something different. It means more.

To me it does at least.

Should it scare me how he's so free with admitting he likes me?

Should I be embarrassed I'm acting like a little schoolgirl with a crush?

Should I be nervous I might *also* like him?

I don't have time to dwell on it because Olivia replies to her dad reluctantly.

"Okay, Dad," she says under her breath. He nods, sighs, and runs a hand through his hair.

"Okay. Now, come on. I'm gonna take you both out to breakfast. Livi, you can tell me about your internship you happened to forget to tell me about." She rolls her lips between her teeth.

"That's not necessary," I say, my gut dropping. Truth be told, with this new revelation, I need space to understand what happened last night at the party, what happened at the bar and then here at

Zach's place, and then what happened this morning. "I should get back to my place, attempt at least a little work. And I don't have anything to wear other than the white dress . . . ," I say, my voice trailing off.

"Are you trying to get out of this breakfast?" Something about the way Zach rarely beats around the bush continues to both surprise and elate me. I nod with a wide smile, not even bothering to lie. I'm totally going to do that. He returns it, shaking his head and pulling me close. "Fine, you go dump on your girls, but you come to the bar tonight, give me the downlow on what they decided, okay?"

I should agree just to get out of here and delete his number. I should avoid the bar until kingdom come, pretend this never happened because this? This is *messy*. And I don't do *messy*.

But his smile, the look he's giving me, the way his warm arm wraps around my waist . . .

I can't do it.

I can't give him a smile and lie and then avoid him for all eternity.

So instead, I let out a small laugh and nod. "It's a deal."

I get his dimples in return.

Those dimples might be my downfall, that's for sure.

"Dear god," Olivia whispers from behind us, and I don't know if Zach hears it but if he does, he ignores it.

"We're gonna have to drive Cam back to the Beach Club on the way though," he says, his hand still gripping my hip in a way I really like.

"What? Why? Can't Cami drive herself?" The snotty tone is back in her voice and I don't miss the way Zach's face goes hard, like he wants to give her a talking to but doesn't think in front of me is the right place.

It probably isn't.

I would absolutely find it way too entertaining.

"We took my bike here from the Fishery."

Silence takes over the room.

"You took your bike?" Olivia asks. Zach nods, and I find the exchange interesting to say the least. "But you never put girls on the back of your bike." Her voice is low and confused and it's interesting to know Zach wasn't lying when he said he didn't take women on his motorcycle.

"That should tell you what you need to know, Livi. Come on, Cam. I'll help you get your stuff together so we can get you back to your place," Zach says, a hand to my lower back, and he guides me out of the kitchen before his daughter argues.

"I'm driving," Zach says ten minutes later, after I got my things together, brushed my teeth with what he declared to now be *my* toothbrush, and threw a way too oversized tee of his over my dress. There was also a minor make-out session against his bedroom door which left me winded and dying for more.

Olivia sends a sneer my way before shouting, "I get shotgun!"

"Olivia, Camile is a guest—" Zach starts.

"She's my *boss*, Dad."

"She's a *guest*, now drop the fucking attitude, Olivia Samantha, or we're going to have a problem." I have to fight an *ooh, full name* taunt.

"It's fine, Zach," I say, my voice low. "I'll sit in the back. I'm the shortest anyway."

I really want to say, *It's fine. I'll get a cab back to the club and then leave the Shore. Maybe leave the entire fucking state of New Jersey.*

But I don't.

Because I *won't*—it would mean the Bitch Pack and Olivia win and that will not do.

"Are you sure?" he asks, his eyes soft, and fuck.

I am *not allowed to like this guy.*

I'm definitely not allowed to like how his eyes get soft when he looks at me.

But of course, Olivia sees it, too, and audibly gags.

Her father whips his head to her.

"Swear to fuck, Olivia, get it together. You're being a spoiled brat, and that's not who I raised. You know my rule." She stares at him and he stares back and it's clear this is a common occurrence.

It's even more obvious when she rolls her eyes and mumbles, "Check my attitude at the door."

I fight the laugh I really want to let out, instead moving to grab the handle for the back seat.

"It's fine. I have some emails to answer," I lie.

And then it happens.

Zach laughs, stepping toward me, wrapping an arm around me, and pressing his lips into my hair before stepping back again, Olivia's keys dangling from a finger when he speaks.

"Are gonna go text your girls and tell them about this mess before you even get home?" he asks.

And even though I'm a great fucking liar, I can't deny it.

I don't think anyone could deny that after this shit show, they need to info-dump on their best friends.

So instead, I just smile and nod.

He shakes his head. "Tell them I say hi," he says before opening the car door and watching me slide in.

TWENTY-FIVE

ZACH

Livi was silent the entire drive to drop off Cami. I stepped out of the car to walk her to her apartment, where I kissed her against the door and prayed to whoever was listening she wouldn't take it as goodbye because I most definitely haven't had enough of her yet.

She was silent as I hopped back into the car and drove to the diner on the island *and* through the first ten minutes as Lori took our order, even though both of us have had the same exact thing for the past fifteen years.

Finally, once our coffee is delivered and I'm able to take a sip, I lean forward and stare at her, breaking the silence.

"Are you gonna tell me what that shit was?" For the first time since we got in the car to leave my place, she looks at me, and not for the first time, I see her mother.

The bitchiness I spent her entire childhood working to beat back is right on the surface. I'm not sure if a spoiled attitude is something one can *inherit*, but if it is, Olivia got it. Thankfully, she keeps it chained up for the most part, except when her mother is in town or when she's spent too much time with those bitches at the Beach Club.

Melanie was never supposed to be someone who spent more than a night in my life.

The rich girl who came down the Shore for the summer to spend her daddy's money.

The woman I met in a crowded bar when I was too drunk to make good decisions, not invested enough to want to even have breakfast with her, sneaking out before the sun rose.

My best move?

No, I was a dick.

But I guess karma always wins because I got a call the week before Labor Day from an unknown number.

Melanie was pregnant. And I was tied to her forever.

"I don't know what you're talking about," Livi says, fingers holding the spoon as she continues to stir her coffee as if it's taking a full ten minutes for a teaspoon of sugar to melt in the hot liquid.

"Is this the game we're playing? The game where you pretend not to know what I'm talking about, where I have to lay it out for you like I did when you were ten instead of you acting like a twenty-three-year-old woman with a fuckin' college degree?" There's silence as she continues to stir her drink, and it takes everything in me not to grab the spoon and toss it across the diner.

"I really thought you'd grow out of this shit by now, Livi. Your mom and those bitches come to the island and you become a different person."

"I don't."

"You do and we both know it. You go from the kind woman I raised to this . . . fake person. Trying to ruin other people, to embarrass them. That's not you, Livi." She doesn't reply. "Or maybe it is and the version you give me is the fake one. Maybe you pretend to be a decent human to keep me out of your hair and really your mother won all those years ago, turning you into a tiny version of herself. Someone who doesn't care, doesn't work hard because she knows she'll always have anything she wants."

That snaps her out of her silence as I thought it might.

She's always hated being compared to Melanie.

"Aren't you the one who told me to *play the game?*" she asks, her jaw tight.

She's right.

I did.

"I told you to play the game to keep your mother out of your hair and to get your trust. Not play the shitty games those bitches play. You're better than that."

"Am I?"

"Yes, Livi. You are. Why would you even say that?"

"Because I don't think I am, Dad. I know *you* think I am, but I'm not. I'm just like them, aren't I? Doing what it takes to get what I want? I want my trust early, Mom said I need to make the summer go smooth, keep the twins happy, and I'm *doing it.*" I sigh.

I hate this for her, how she's constantly in an internal struggle of trying to please her mother and trying to live the life she wants to.

She might complain about Melanie until she's blue in the face but since she was little, all she ever wanted was praise from her, to make her happy. When she was younger, spending her school year with me, her mother off jet-setting, it was easy. All Melanie wanted was to be able to live her life string free but be able to play with her little, living Barbie doll when she came to the Beach Club in the summer.

But as Livi got older, it became harder for her to please her mother and balance the rest of her life. I tried my best to step in when I could, when I thought I could help, but more often than not, any intrusion from me made things worse for Livi. Instead of helping the situation, her mother would take her irritation with me out on our daughter.

"There's a huge difference between keeping spoiled brats happy for a summer and trying to sabotage someone who did nothing against you."

"How do you know Cami didn't do anything against me? What, you fucked her once and now she's some kind of saint?"

"First off, you need to quit this shit. What I do in my personal life, who I spend my time with has fucking nothing to do with you."

"If you're fucking my boss for the summer, then yeah, it does have something to do with me."

"If you spent five minutes with me since you came back to the island after school and told me about the internship I had no fucking clue about, I might have been able to put the pieces together, been able to avoid an awkward fucking situation."

She doesn't have anything to say about that.

To be fair, even if I had known, I don't know if it would have stopped me, considering it's only been two weeks and Cami is already so far under my skin.

But I absolutely would have warned both of them.

"Can you at least tell me what happened? I know Cami was covering your ass when she said it was a misunderstanding. I'm not stupid, Olivia." She sighs, probably knowing from years and years of being my daughter, my request isn't really a *request* but a demand.

There's a moment when Lori brings our food, placing it in front of us, but once she walks away again, Livi finally answers.

"Staceigh's into some guy. Some old money douche, I don't know. But he used to date Cami or something and he's clearly still into her." I fight the way that bristles, the way my hackles rise, the way the thought of Cami being with another man, a man who probably has a lot more to offer than a bar owner who rarely breaks even each year, makes me want to punch something. "Staceigh isn't used to not getting what she wants. She wanted to get her out of the picture." She goes quiet again, grabbing a fork and picking at her hash browns.

"And?"

"And I guess at the brunch, the guy ignored Staceigh and tried to talk to Cami instead. It made her mad." I roll my eyes, knowing how these women can be. "She decided the best way to get her way was to embarrass Cami in front of everyone, invite her to Mom's party and tell her it was themed. You know the rest." She never lifts her face, like her breakfast is the most interesting thing she's ever seen.

"How did you get involved, Livi?" She gives an exasperated sigh before looking at me and answering.

"She doesn't actually *do* anything. She's used to having all these minions so eager to be her friend, to get the perks of being in her little group, that they'll do anything. But she likes fucking with people. I need to survive this summer, Dad. I need my trust. You know as well as I do starting my business is the best way to get out from under Mom's thumb. If I wasn't on Staceigh's side, I'd be her target this summer and it would definitely fuck with Mom's wedding. I needed to play the game."

"There's a difference between playing the game and trying to destroy someone's career."

"Her career wasn't destroyed, Dad. God. You're so fucking pussy-whipped. She found out, came in a white dress, and got contacts she wanted. It was a win-win all around."

"It's days like this I wish I fought harder for full custody. Sometimes you're so lost in that world, you can't see common sense. I saw her, Livi. Before the party. The woman was excited. Thought she made new friends. That's hard for her; she doesn't trust easy. You and those girls proved she was right not to." I remember the way she looked so excited and hopeful in the bar before she headed to the party, the way she was wavering on letting people in just a few weeks ago, how she saw this as her first step toward being more open.

And the way *my daughter* was the catalyst to prove she was right all along to be closed off for fear of others letting her down.

"So what, you fuck her one time and flirt with her at your bar and you're suddenly on her side?" Livi asks, her voice angry and annoyed, her own wall up.

I wonder if that's why I know how to handle Cami and her fears how she needs to let things out and talk them through out loud. She might take the advice of others, but she won't act on anything until she works through it in her own mind.

They're so similar. The fact they're so at odds is almost comical.

I also know just like Cami, she's saying this shit to get a reaction, to piss me off and force me to back down.

"I love you, Livi, more than anything, but you're an adult. I'm an adult. You don't get to tell me who I can and cannot date. I like her. We spent the night together. If this shit didn't scare her off, I'm planning to spend more with her." I watch my daughter's face go slightly green. "I'm not going to tell you what to do, but I think if you gave her a chance, apologized and tried to make it work, you'd get along."

She puts her fork down and stares at me, very clearly over this conversation. "Can we please change the subject?" she asks, desperation in her voice.

I know from years of experience this means she's done. Nothing more I say will penetrate her wall and anything else I say will just *add* to it.

"Fine," I say with a smile. "Why don't you tell me why your mother is driving you insane this time?" I ask, biting into a piece of bacon with a smile, knowing that's why she came to my house in the first place even though this topic isn't much more enjoyable for her.

But still, she rolls her eyes, sighs, and starts her own version of a verbal dump, getting her complains about her mother out so she can go on enduring her for another week without exploding on her.

TWENTY-SIX

THURSDAY, JUNE 1

CAMI

> What did the cucumber say to the pickle?

> No idea.

> You mean a great DILL to me.

> Wowwwww.

> Have a great day, angel.

> You too, Zach.

It seems to be Zach's new thing to send me a terrible dad joke in the morning, and even though I will never stop making fun of him for it, I can't say they don't put a smile on my face.

Which I most definitely need as I walk into work Thursday morning with a literal mountain of work to do and enough anxiety to last a lifetime.

Especially when at nine, Olivia doesn't show up for her internship despite having confirmed the day and time with her via texts yesterday and the giant stack of work I set aside for her to do: a stack of details which need ironed out for her mother's wedding, some outreach I need her to do for vendors, and mockups for new clients who are being onboarded this week.

They're things I specifically set aside because either she'd be a great help or they would be things she should have experience with before starting her own business. Despite the trick she and her soon-to-be stepsisters played on me, I want her to leave this internship with knowledge she can use.

But she's not *here*.

By 9:30, it's pretty clear she's not just late, and I start to panic, trying to figure out what to do.

Do I write her off, go about my day like she wasn't supposed to be here? Do I get mad?

Do I tell Jefferson?

He *is* paying her for her time here, and he told me to let me know if there were any issues with Olivia. As my boss, isn't it my job to tell him if she's pulling a no call, no show? Still, something about tattling on her feels . . . unnecessarily catty, despite us not being on great terms.

My mind moves back to the conversation we had her first day, about her trust and her mother and just needing to make it through this summer and prove herself. I remember her telling me how her grandfather really wants her to excel at this internship in order to feel comfortable with sending business her way and how I identified with that, how I also am using this summer to prove myself and pull in contacts to build my business.

Maybe it's the salty air of LBI.

Maybe it's the challenge to give people more space to mess up and to prove themselves instead of just writing them off, even if their other advice on giving people chances backfired spectacularly.

Or maybe it's the fact I woke to a stupid dad joke this morning that has me deciding to say fuck it and go on my day without telling Jefferson.

To give her some grace and just get the job done myself.

But still, at ten, when she hasn't shown her face at the office, I send her a message.

> Hey, are you still planning on working today?

The reply comes almost instantly, which is a surprise.

> I can't come in today. I'm helping my mom with her wedding dress. I'm so sorry. I sent an email at eight.

I check my email for the third or fourth time this morning and don't see anything until I check my spam where, just like she said, there's an email from her.

HI, CAMI,

I'M SO TERRIBLY SORRY, BUT I CAN'T COME IN TODAY. I'LL BE IN THE CITY DRESS SHOPPING WITH MY MOTHER. I KNOW I WAS GOING TO BE WORKING ON SOME OF THE WEDDING PREP TODAY, SO PLEASE FIND BELOW A COLLECTION OF COLOR SCHEMES, THEMES, AND VENDORS WHO WOULD BE AVAILABLE ON THE DAY OF THE WEDDING.

THE ONES HIGHLIGHTED IN GREEN HAVE ALREADY BEEN REACHED OUT TO AND YOU SHOULD RECEIVE A PROPOSAL FROM THEM EARLY NEXT WEEK.

AGAIN, I APOLOGIZE ABOUT THE LATE NOTICE AND . . . EVERYTHING ELSE.

SINCERELY, OLIVIA.

Attached is an extensive document filled with everything she told me would be there—food and entertainment vendors, color schemes that are close to what Melanie picked out in her giant binder but just a hair different, more sophisticated looking. There are links for favor ideas and the contact info for a surprise live painter to have at the reception.

It's not something she could have pulled together in an hour—she must have worked all night on this. But why?

Why would she put all this effort into helping me when just a few days ago, she was working with the twins to ruin me.

Either way, I don't have the time or energy to overthink it, deciding to trust her one more time and using this document to knock out most of the wedding tasks at hand. I stay late working through Melanie's binder, trying to iron out as much as I can before our meeting on Monday, knowing I won't have much time this weekend with a Beach Club luncheon on Saturday and a baby shower I coordinated in the cabana on Sunday.

I just have to hope she isn't trying to fuck me over again.

Friday, June 2

Are you a loan?

Can't say I am.

Because you sure have my interest.

Back at ya, dimples.

Stop calling me dimples!

Talk to you later, Daddy.

I'm wondering if I made the wrong decision in trusting Olivia the next morning, though, when I walk into my office to find Olivia, the twins, and Melanie sitting at my desk, all with coffee cups from downstairs in hand.

"Uhm, hello," I say, confused.

"So nice of you to show up," Staceigh says with a smug look like she caught me in something.

"Yeah, it's—" Laceigh looks at her wristwatch and spends just a few moments too long staring at it before moving to look at her phone and answering with a smug smile. "Nine oh one." I have to roll my lips into my mouth and bite in order not to scoff out a laugh.

"Yes, well, sometimes the elevator takes a minute and I wasn't anticipating any meetings so early this morning. I'm lucky enough Jefferson allows me to make my own hours, so I don't actually have to be here at nine on the dot." I give Melanie a smile, praying she isn't *also* in the mood to give me shit about not being here at nine on the dot when I didn't have a meeting with her on my calendar.

I've emailed her and her assistant a few times since our first meeting.

"Oh, it's no problem. I just have so many ideas and I didn't want to wait until Monday to meet up. This wedding *has* to be perfect. Staceigh had the great idea of trying to get in here as soon as possible in order to see you before any other clients came in." I give Staceigh, who has an evil smirk on her face, a tight smile. "Thankfully, Jeanne was downstairs and told me you didn't have any guests on your calendar today and I could just scurry on up here!"

I need to add talking to Jeanne to my to-do list today apparently.

"Thank goodness for Jeanne. I will most definitely do my utmost to give you the best day ever, Melanie," I say, putting my bag down and grabbing a stack of files off my desk.

Yesterday, despite not having Olivia's help like I had planned, I was able to make mockups for the entire event proceedings using the documents she sent me in conjunction with Melanie's binder from hell, and I even thought ahead to create extra copies for each of the women sitting at my desk.

We'll call it my *ass-saving intuition.*

I start to hand the manila folders out and watch Staceigh's jaw go tight with irritation.

"I put together these files based off of what you handed me at our last meeting and took the liberty to contact some vendors to see what would be feasible with the timeline we're working with. Why don't you ladies go through it while I make myself a quick coffee, yes?" I don't bother to give Olivia any kind of props because at the end of the day, I need to protect my own business and brand. Melanie nods, taking her folder, and the twins exchange nearly demonic smiles before I hand the final folder to Olivia.

"Olivia, so lovely to see you," I say and watch as she bites her lip and grabs the folder before I turn to where the coffee station is in my office.

"This is amazing, Cami. I don't know *why* my previous planners weren't able to capture my vision like this," Melanie says as I begin making my coffee, noting I have to hit the grocery store since I'm officially out of coffee pods, which is weird because I thought I had bought a bunch. I *have* done a ton of long nights, though, the past week, so maybe I just drank more than I realized.

I *don't* say, "Well, it's because you handed me a hot pile of shit in that file and nothing made sense. I spent a full day last week researching comparative weddings to understand your vision and low and behold, little to none of it matched what you *thought* you wanted."

Instead, I say, "Being able to take a few ideas and understand what you want is my gift!" I'm playing it like it's no big but secretly, a weight is leaving my shoulders at her words.

If I can win over Melanie Kincaid, then I'm in.

If I can not only *handle* the ultimate bridezilla, but give her the event of the year, I don't need to worry about the networking and ass-kissing.

This type of high-profile client will come to *me*.

I'm smiling as I pour creamer into my coffee, stir it in, then add some sugar.

When I take a sip to test for sweetness, though, I gag, spitting it in to the cup.

Why the *fuck* does my coffee taste like salty asshole?

I grab the creamer container, checking the expiration date when the smug smiles on the twins, sitting at my desk, just in my line of sight, make everything click.

The sugar.

I spill some into my hand, pressing a finger into the granules and tasting it, understanding instantly.

The bitches changed out the sugar for salt. Then, my garbage catches my eye and there are a dozen little coffee pods opened and spilled in the can.

And they made it so I can't make a new cup.

God, what are they, ten?

The smile on Staceigh's face makes me want to let her win. To walk over to her and throw a fit and ask why she's such a raging fucking cunt.

But that's what she wants.

If I do that, the twins win.

So instead, I raise a single dark eyebrow and lift my cup in their direction, taking a long sip even though it tastes horrible.

I can get a new coffee later.

But the look of annoyance and anger on Staceigh's face?

That I can't recreate.

TWENTY-SEVEN

FRIDAY, JUNE 2

CAMI

It's a full hour later when I'm finally able to shoo the women out of my office and take a sigh of relief. Melanie loved most of everything I laid out for her, giving me the go ahead to book vendors *at any cost*. But that wasn't what surprised me the most.

It was when Melanie told me it was the *twins'* idea both to go dress shopping last minute yesterday, taking Olivia away from me, *and* to show up first thing in the morning with no warning. My mind instantly drifted to the email Olivia sent me, the email that, if I hadn't received it yesterday, I would not have been *nearly* as prepared for this meeting this morning.

It could have gone a totally different direction.

And I don't miss the way Olivia's eyes watch me when her mother shares that information as if to say, *See? I wasn't lying and I didn't totally fuck you over.*

I still can't quite figure out Olivia and whether she's on my side or not. Whether to trust her or keep her at arm's length. At first glance, with her inviting me to the party and setting me up, I'd say absolutely not. She's enemy number one. But when I dig into my gut, I can't quite believe she's as horrible as she seems—or maybe as she *wants* to seem.

Either way, after I walk them to the elevators, making sure the twins have no chance to mess with anything else while they're on this floor, I walk back to my office and slump into my chair.

There's no way it's only 10 in the morning.

My mind travels to spending yet another late night eating at the Fishery and flirting with Zach, this time stealing the occasional kiss before I headed back to my place way, way past my bedtime, and I can't regret it.

But I do need to sleep more in order to survive this summer.

And coffee.

I need coffee.

My thoughts are interrupted when my phone vibrates on my desk. I can't fight the smile spreading on my face.

> How's your morning going?

>> I just spent an hour with your ex.

Barely thirty seconds pass before he replies.

> Ah, so your morning's that bad, huh?

>> It wasn't actually terrible. She likes my ideas. I'm just utterly exhausted now and I have no coffee.

> No coffee? Isn't that basically your life blood?

>> Yes, so I'll be miserable until I can make it to a grocery store.

> You still haven't gone to a grocery store?

> I keep meaning to, you see, but a hot bartender keeps convincing me to just come see him at work every night when it's time for me to eat dinner.

> What a bastard.

I laugh out loud, shaking my head and marveling at how suddenly, I'm not exhausted and worn out.

> Yeah, but he's really good in bed so I'm letting it slide.

> Though, it could have been a fluke. It was only one night.

I add that one on without thinking and regret being so forward the second I hit send, but as seems to be his way, Zach is on the same page as me.

> I bet he wants a redo.

> Soon.

> Very fucking soon.

The speed of his messages has me laughing as I push my phone aside to open my emails for the first time today and send out replies to anything immediate before starting the day's to-do list. A few minutes later, my phone buzzes on my desk again.

> Do you have a minute?

> What for?

> Come out front.

> Out front?

> Of the Beach Club?

> Jesus, Cam, just come down.

I stare at my phone for thirty full seconds before the butterflies start pinging in my belly, and with a speed I didn't know my uncaffeinated body could manage, I race down the stairs, bypassing the elevator all together before waving at CiCi who gives me a funny look, but I keep going.

And there, in the front of the building, leaning against a column in a black shirt and blue jeans, is Zachary Anderson.

"Hey," I say. "What are you doing here?"

He lifts a paper cup, tipping it my way. "Coffee."

"Coffee?"

"You don't have any, right?"

I keep staring, lost in this moment and trying not to read into what it means.

Reading into things like this is a recipe for attachment.

Attachment is a recipe for getting hurt.

And this is a fun summer fling. Nothing more, nothing less.

"Right...?"

"I own the restaurant across the way. Made you a coffee."

"But you don't go in until later," I say, taking the coffee he hands me, ignoring the fact I know his work schedule better than I know my own.

"Yeah, well," he says in a whisper, but I can't concentrate on his lack of an answer because he's tugging me into him until my front is flush with his and his forehead is against mine.

"Is it cool if I kiss you here, in front of your work?" he asks in a whisper.

"I'll riot if you don't," I reply before he kisses me through a smile, long and slow and sweet and tasting of black coffee and mint toothpaste and everything good in the world.

He tastes like *Zach*.

Finally, the kiss breaks and he rests his forehead on mine.

"What the fuck are you doing to me, Cami?" he whispers.

I don't answer.

I can't.

Because I think if I do, I'll reveal too much.

"Go back to work, angel," he says, breaking my panic, and I push on his chest with the hand not holding my coffee, rolling my eyes.

"You gotta stop that angel shit."

"Are you gonna stop calling me dimples?"

"I can call you Daddy instead?" He shakes his head, those dimples coming out.

"You're a pain, you know?"

"What? You *are* a daddy after all."

"Go to work before I spank you like I *am* your daddy," he says, and goddammit if it doesn't have me fighting the urge to rub my legs together.

He notices still, somehow.

"Noted," he says, leaning in once more to press his lips to mine softly before walking away without another word.

"Was that Mr. Anderson?" CiCi says with wide eyes as I walk back into the building, wearing a completely goofy smile on my face, I'm sure.

"Yeah, he brought me coffee from the Fishery."

A beat passes before she speaks again.

"The Fishery doesn't open until three."

"I know."

"How did he bring you coffee from there? And why? And *how*?" The smile on my face spreads without my permission until it nearly hurts, but I don't reply. "Oh my fucking god. Are you fucking Mr. Anderson?"

"Can we please stop calling him that?" I ask, lowering my voice. "And can you please be a bit quieter?"

"Sorry," she says. "Are you fucking Olivia's dad?"

Okay, that's not much better.

"I'm . . ."

"Holy shit, you are. Oh my god. *Oh my god!* When!? How!?"

Looking around, I don't see anyone nearby, but I know this place even if I haven't been here long.

I know nothing said in open air stays a secret for long.

"When's your lunch?" I ask, and she smiles then comes to my office at noon to hear all the details of the last week. Of my first drunken night at the bar, of the flirting, of the stage room the day of the brunch, of him making my night all better after the white party . . . and of Olivia walking in the next morning.

And I can't lie.

It feels good.

It feels really good to have another friend, another person to lean on and tell my story to.

And I have my two best friends to thank for it.

It's not until I'm leaving my office for the night and lift the empty paper coffee cup that the brown sleeve slips down.

That's when I grab the cup and see dark, manly handwriting on the white paper once hidden beneath the brown coffee sleeve.

You drive me to distraction.

Well, that makes two of us.

TWENTY-EIGHT

CAMI

Saturday, June 3

It's a good thing I have a library card.

Are libraries open on Saturdays?

Because I'm totally checking you out.

You're a mess.

Let me feed you tonight.

At the Fishery? I have work in the morning....

I'll get you back in my bed soon, but if the best I can get is feeding you in my bar, I'll take it.

Sunday, June 4

Are you a banana?

Good morning, Zach.

Because I find you a-PEEL-ing.

Back at you, handsome.

Good luck with your event.

Thank you. I'll miss you tonight.

Glad to hear it, angel. Me too.

Monday, June 5

Are you religious?

Not especially.

Because I think you're the answer to all my prayers.

Ooof.

Not my best work. Have a good day.

Tuesday. June 6

Are you a parking ticket?

Do motorcycles even get parking tickets?

Cause you've got fine written all over you.

You haven't even seen me in a few days.

Whose fault is that?

Capitalism's, I guess.

Fair. Let me feed you tonight.

Deal.

Wednesday, June 7

You know what's beautiful?

No, what?

Read the first word of my text.

Wow, that was actually a pretty good one.

They're all good ones.

Sure they are.

Thursday, June 8

If you were a president, you'd be BABEraham Lincoln.

JAIL.

Fair. That was a bad one.

Admitting it is the first step, I hear.

Have a good day, Cami.

. . .

Friday, June 9

Come downstairs.

Is that today's joke?

No, come downstairs.

The text comes after the longest week of my life, filled with executing events, setting up new client consultations, and hanging out at the Fishery any night I'm not too tired to do much more than crawl into my bed. The nights I've gone to the bar, I stayed until close even though I didn't stay at his place and he didn't stay at mine mostly because as much as I don't want to look too closely at it, I *like* being around Zach.

I also don't hate the hot and heavy make-out session we have every night when he walks me to my apartment, pinning me to the door before heading to his own place like a gentleman. I never thought I'd get tired of the gentleman act, but I wouldn't hate it if he cavemaned his way into my apartment and insisted on spending the night.

All that to say when his morning text comes through, I stare at it confused and still drowsy.

Downstairs?

Yes, Cam. Come downstairs. I'm right past reception.

Oh. Downstairs.

Warmth runs through me and I can't fight the smile on my lips or the way I nearly run for the stairs to see Zach quicker. When I walk past CiCi, she smiles at me, shaking her head, but I don't do more than share her smile.

As I walk out the glass doors, the late spring heat warming my air conditioning-chilled arms, my smile grows when he comes into view.

Zach leans against one of the decorative columns, his motorcycle boots beneath his jeans, ankles crossed, and a white paper cup in his hand.

"You don't have to do this, you know," I say, smiling at him before taking the cup from him.

"Yeah, but it's the only time I'm getting to see you outside of the bar and for some reason, all I want right now is to see you."

I don't tell him the same overwhelming need to see him has been overtaking me as well.

I don't tell him last night I had to *force* myself not to go to the Fishery after my event.

I don't tell him the way I can't stop thinking about him has me panicking just a bit.

But somehow, he knows.

"It's all good, Cam. Just bringing you coffee."

"Yeah," I say in a whisper. "I, uhm. I was thinking about coming to the Fishery tonight. Maybe seeing if . . ." I let my words trail off, wait for him to fill in the gaps, but instead he groans aloud and not in the good, sexy way.

"I gotta go to a wedding up north this weekend. I won't be back until Sunday."

I try not to pout.

I try not to let my mind travel to what happens when shitty men go away.

I try not to focus on the fact we aren't *anything* more than dad jokes and coffee and one amazing night.

"Oh. Okay."

"I wish I weren't, angel. Or I wish you were going with or literally anything that would mean I get to spend more than a few minutes with you."

"You don't owe me—"

"Stop. We already talked about this. I like you. I think you like me, even though it scares the fuck out of you. We don't need to play these games, okay?" I don't answer but his hand moves to my chin, tipping it and forcing me to look at him. "Okay?"

"Okay," I whisper.

"Now, you go on up to work. Tonight, I'll be in a dumb fuckin' hotel room. Do you have plans?" I shake my head. "I'll call you."

"You'll call me?"

"Yeah. We'll go back to high school, chat all night on the phone."

The idea blooms warm in my belly, and I work to fight a smile.

"You like that," he whispers against my lips, his thumb brushing gently against my jaw. I don't answer.

But I don't have to.

Because Zachary Anderson has only known me for three weeks and somehow, he can read me better than most anyone can.

And I don't know how to take that.

I wave at CiCi, who gives me wide eyes, but I don't check the paper cup until I'm in the elevator alone. I don't know if last time it was a fluke or if he even knows I saw it, but I have to know if it's there again.

My heartbeat races when I check, though.

```
If I had a star for every time I thought of
you, I'd have a whole galaxy.
```

TWENTY-NINE

FRIDAY, JUNE 9

CAMI

> How was your day?

The text comes in as I walk through the door of my apartment, absolutely drained from said day. I'm actually grateful I won't be going across the street to see Zach. If I did, he would inevitably read my face, a skill I've learned he is a master at, and demand I tell him about every last thing that's getting to me.

Of all days, I really would not want to do that today.

For one, the people I'm venting about are *his daughter* and his ex's future stepdaughters. Zach sees the best in Olivia, and I know I'm annoyed because the side *I* see isn't the side *he* sees. And as much as I'm enjoying our back and forth digs and battles whenever I'm around Olivia and the Bitch Pack, it's . . . immature.

I don't like being that person.

And I *really* don't want Zach to see me as that person.

Two, I'm so fucking tired, I just want to collapse in my bed and scroll on my phone until I pass out.

Maybe make myself come before I do, but garnering the energy might be beyond the scope of what I can handle right now.

And three . . . I like venting to this man way, way too much.

Long.

Too long to talk tonight?

Butterflies flutter in my belly and I bite my lip, weighing my options.

I don't want to vent or have a brain dump.

But something else...

And you should know, by talk I mean chatting for thirty seconds so I know you're good before I convince you to have phone sex with me.

Well.

That's straightforward.

But also . . . appreciated.

And totally what I need right now.

Instead of replying, I quickly change into my pajamas of an oversized sleep shirt and a pair of panties, forgoing a bra because I wore one all day and no thank you, before I settle into my bed and hit send, the phone ringing just twice before Zach's deep voice answers.

"I didn't actually think that would work."

"I've had a long day. It was an easy sell."

"All good?" I sigh because I should have known kind, considerate Zach wouldn't just get right into the good stuff.

"Yes. Just a lot of events and a lot of voices and ideas."

"Got it," he says, and silence fills the line.

"What about you? How's wedding things?" A smile is in his voice when he answers.

"Good. Uneventful."

"Who is it, getting married?"

"Friend of mine in Ocean View. Friend of mine's little sister is getting married, and they're from the kind of family where if you're friends with one of them, you're friends with everyone from the grandmother to the dog." I laugh.

"Abbie's from a family like that, kind of. Well, her sister married into one. It's a small town and everyone knows everyone. You should see them at Thanksgiving. It's wild."

"So you get it then," he says, and the smile in his voice strangely tugs something in my belly, makes me miss him.

"I do." The line goes quiet, not an uncomfortable silence, but the kind where neither of us knows who is going to go first.

It shouldn't surprise anyone when it's Zach who breaks it.

"So, what are you wearing?" he asks, and I genuinely laugh out loud.

"Jumping right into it, are we?"

"Cami, I don't think you know how long I've been thinking about this." Heat rolls through me.

"About phone sex with me?"

"Fuck yes. The noises you make when you're turned on amplified? Yes. I've been thinking about it for a while."

"Oh," I blurt, unsure of what else to say. "Well. I'm wearing a sleep shirt. And underwear." He groans. "It's not sexy, I promise."

"When are you going to understand everything you do is sexy, Cami?" I shrug and feel silly when I realize he can't see it. "I need to clarify. Do you really want to?" he asks, and I'm learning this is his way, making sure whatever we do, I'm fully comfortable with it.

I like it more than I care to admit. "If you don't, we can sit on the phone like we're in high school and flirt until you're too tired to talk."

I bite my lip, thinking for just a moment before I answer.

"I do, Zach."

"Fuck yes. Do you have a tablet? A laptop?" I bite my lip before answering.

"Yes." The word is barely a whisper but again, he hears it all the same.

"Good. Go get it. I'm going to email you a video." My entire body goes warm.

"A video?" Again, the word is barely a whisper.

"From when you came to my place."

My body ceases the warmth, full-blown heat ricocheting through me, starting in my belly and leaking through my veins.

From when I came to his place.

It's the only time I've been there but I remember it well.

"The second round," he says, voice low and gravelly.

Again, heat runs through me.

The second round.

It was after our conversation about the photos and videos, after we had cleaned up and had a snack.

After he set up his phone across from the bed to catch the whole thing.

My hands shake as I grab my laptop, getting the password wrong twice while trying to balance my phone on my ear before I finally get in, clicking to my email.

"Have you . . . Have you watched it?"

"Fuck yes."

Why is that even hotter than whatever we're about to do?

"I'm sending you the edited one," he says. "Don't open it until I say, okay?"

"Okay," I say in a whisper.

"Good girl. Now take off your sleep shirt."

Licking my lips, I set my phone down, tugging the shirt over my head before tossing it into the corner and grabbing my cell again. "All done."

"I'm going to request a FaceTime."

"A FaceTime?"

"You're going to watch us, Cami, and I'm going to watch you."

Oh dear god, why is that the hottest thing I've ever heard? I don't have time to overthink because then my phone is beeping, the video call request coming through, and I hit the button to answer.

Funny how all of my nerves evaporate with his face, eyes hot but wearing a smile. He moves, situating the phone on something before leaning back on the hotel bed, white pillows and blankets all around him. He's so fucking handsome, his hair cropped short, his skin tan on his arms, the tan lines from the bar tees he wears exclusively making a smile come to my own face. His chest is bare and even through the phone I can see his cock is hard beneath his white boxer briefs.

God.

He's so fucking handsome.

"Look at you, baby. So pretty," he says, and I shake my head and roll my eyes.

"All you can see is my face."

"That's all I need, Cami." Heat isn't in the words, instead a comforting warmth. "But for this purpose, put your phone on your laptop so it doesn't block the screen but I can see you."

I bit my lip, unsure of how to feel about being so exposed to him, but then his hand moves, palming his cock, and fuck. I can't not give him whatever he desires.

"Fuck, look at you," he says and heat floods my veins all over. "Panties off, Cami." Licking my lips, I do as he demands, feeling awkward and clumsy as I move my underwear down my legs until they're forgotten on the floor. "Spread, let me see you."

Again, I abide, spreading my thighs.

"You look so fucking pretty, angel. Wish I were there. I'd eat that until you couldn't breath if I were." His words seem to float in the air around us as I enter some kind of hormone and adrenaline driven dream state.

That's the only excuse I can think of for why my hands move up my thighs, fingers spreading myself open so he can see just how wet I am with nothing more than his words and a promise.

"God, look at you. Touch your clit, Cami."

I thought he'd never ask.

One orange-painted nail moves from my entrance, gathering wet as it moves until it's hovering over my clit where I then circle it gently. A heated breath leaves my lips as I continue the same path. Down, over, up, circle.

"Rub your clit. Just your clit," he demands, and I moan as two fingers touch me now, rubbing in small circles. My head tips back, my eyes drifting shut as I moan, my pussy clenching as the sound of Zach groaning reaches my ears, forcing my eyes to open.

On the small screen of my phone, Zach has his cock out, his hand wrapped around it, slowly moving as he watches me play with myself.

"Oh fuck, that's hot," I say, my eyes now fixated on him, on what he's doing, on how his hand is moving, on the way his eyes drift shut for just a moment.

"Email. Now. Open the attachment, Camile."

Camile.

When did my name get so fucking sexy?

I don't have time to ponder that, though, because I have a video to watch. I move, clicking the attachment, checking the sound, and hitting play.

It's not the first time we got together, all hands and lips and frantic need, not him overtop of me, holding the phone above me, but the second time, late, late into the night when we took our time, more controlled but no less earth-shattering.

It doesn't start at the beginning with Zach setting up the camera or us kissing or Zach eating me out.

No, it starts with me on my hands and knees, my back arching deep, Zach behind me, his hand closest to the camera on my hip, his other wrapped in my hair, tugging until I'm staring at the ceiling.

And his cock buried in me.

Actually, that's a lie. It's not buried in me. It's fucking me, his hips moving fiercely, my breasts swaying with each movement, my ass moving back in a way I distinctively remember was to try and get him as deep as humanly possible.

I feel empty, seeing it, remembering it. Knowing how good he feels inside me.

A low moan leaves my lips when the video version of Zach

groans, his hand moving back before landing on my ass. I watch my jaw drop, a scream leaving my chest.

My heart is beating, my blood made of fire as I watch.

"Fuck, I wish you could see yourself right now. Fucking gorgeous, mouth open, eyes wide. Do you like it, Cami? Do you like what you see?" I can't answer.

I can't move.

I can't pull my eyes from the vision before me, from the way Zach is fucking me, the way we look so fucking good together.

God, it's magnificent.

"Touch your pussy, Cami. Watch it and put on a show for me," Zach says, voice low as if he, too, is lost in another world.

But his world is me right now.

So I do as he asks, my eyes never leaving his as I play with myself, fingering my pussy, rubbing my clit, moaning as I watch the video we made together. It's interesting, like I'm feeling the pleasure from both now and then, and after just a few minutes of it, it starts to build into something big.

"I'm close," I whisper, two fingers pumping inside me.

"Not yet."

"Zach," I moan.

"Not yet, Cami." My eyes move from my computer to my phone, watching him jack himself off, his mouth open as he pants, eyes hooded and locked on me. Even through the screen I can feel the burn. "What's happening?" he asks, and I remember my assignment, looking back at the video and moaning.

It's strange watching something I experienced once, even though it seems like another person.

"I'm on my knees," I say, my voice full of lust even to my own ears. "Oh fuck." I crook the fingers in myself, pinching my nipple to replicate what I know I felt then.

"What else?"

"Oh god, Zach. Your hands are on my breasts, and your lips are on my neck." I can almost feel the scruff of his five o'clock shadow there, the way it was just a little raw the next morning.

"Fuck, yeah, I remember. My cock is in you; you're rubbing your clit?" I groan at his words and the visual and my fingers and it's all melding and overwhelming me. I can't separate his words from reality, from what I'm seeing.

Complete sensory overload.

"Hold on another minute, Cami. I remember, you made yourself come on my cock and then I filled you. That's when you'll come."

"Jesus, god, it's so close," I moan, my eyes drifting shut.

"Eyes on me." They pop back open. "Keep your eyes on me. I can hear it. You're so close. You're being such a good girl, Cami. I'm gonna make myself come and that's when you come, baby." I moan, but my eyes stay locked on his hand on his cock, working faster now, chasing his own orgasm.

I want that.

I want to watch him come, want to listen to the sounds he makes.

I'm usually so lost in what happening, in how he's getting me there when he comes, I haven't gotten the utter *pleasure* of watching it.

So I watch.

I continue to work myself with my fingers, my legs spread so Zach can watch his own show, but I get the pleasure of watching *him*.

As the moans of Zach and me on my computer ratchet, I watch Zach's hand quicken.

And then it happens.

My moans on the computer turn to screams as past-me comes and his eyes drift shut.

His grip tightens and the growl the man on my phone lets out is all-consuming.

The hottest things I've ever heard, especially when it's followed by a deep, groaning, "Fuck, Cami."

It's then I fall, the orgasm starting in my belly, radiating in a band to my back and tingling down to my toes, leaving me lightheaded and floating. It seems to last forever, waves and waves of pleasure crashing over me as I buck my hips into my hand, and I wonder if it's Zach or if this is just the new way I come, full body and never-ending.

Either way, I'm not complaining.

I'm cleaned up in my bed, cuddled into a stack of pillows, my phone precariously perched on my ear, a happy orgasm daze taking over when we talk about our plans for the next week or so.

"I'll be back on Sunday."

"Mmm," I say, my eyes closed, my body warm and happy.

"I want to see you. Bar is closed on Monday."

"Mmmm," I repeat, a smile on my lips.

"Can't tell if that's an affirmation or you ignoring me."

"I have an event on Sunday. Starts at five, goes to eight," I say of the anniversary party I'm coordinating. "I should be done by . . ." I try and do some math in my head. "Nine? Nine thirty?" He's quiet for a moment before speaking.

"If I come at eight, can I help you close up? Stay the night at your place? Rhonda and Frank have the bar covered for the weekend."

He sounds nervous.

He sounds like he's worried I'll say no, that I won't want to spend as much time as humanly possible with him.

He sounds so fucking sweet.

"Yes, but I won't let you work. Just come hang until I'm done."

"I help you close up, I get you to myself quicker." I shake my head and smile even though he can't see it.

"No, you can't help work, but you can absolutely come spend the night, Zach." He laughs and it's contagious.

"We'll see how that works out. But okay. Good. I, uh. I can't wait to see you," he says, his voice low, and again, there's nerves twisted in his words and it's so fucking sweet, I can't help it.

I can't help but give him my own offer.

"What are you doing on the Fourth?"

"Besides working?"

"Besides working," I say with a smile.

"Nothing."

"Any chance you could go in late?"

"What for?"

"To come to the Beach Club party." Silence fills the line and I get nervous.

Of course he wouldn't want to go to a Beach Club party. It's his ex's father's business. It's weird. It was such a dumb thing to even say. "You don't have to. It was just an idea. My best friend and her boyfriend are coming. I think you'll like him. I can't hang out, so maybe I'll just head to the Fishery after. We can hang out then, and I—"

"Cami, shut up." My mouth closes, but indignation fills me. "Now don't get all angry because I told you to shut up." There's a laugh in his words. Is it normal for him to know me so well already?

"Yes. I'll come to the party for a bit. Walk you in, meet your friends. I won't be able to stay long, have to go to the bar. But you'll come to me after." I don't speak. I take that in. *Walk you in, meet your friends.*

I think somehow, he knows that is what I wanted: his presence, to introduce him to Abbie outside of a drunken night and for him to meet Damien, since I really do think they'll like each other.

"Does that work?"

Another beat passes before I answer, a sleepy smile I can't fight on my face.

"Yeah. That works."

"Good, angel. Now tell me about your day."

THIRTY

TUESDAY, JUNE 13

CAMI

Olivia is staring me down on Tuesday morning when she comes for work, but I can't even bother to give her a single care in the world.

Because for the second time in a row, Zach spent the night at my place and he woke me with kisses on my neck and between my breasts and down my belly and really, how can you have a bad day when you wake up that way?

> I had a really, really good night last night.
>
> And a really good morning.

> What, no jokes today?

> Nope. I'm hoping you already have a smile on your face. I know I do.
>
> Just wanted you to know I really like spending time with you.

His text has me smiling so wide, I can feel the pull in my cheeks as I try to decide how to reply.

"God, can you please stop?" Olivia says, her voice low and filled with malice.

"What?"

"You're texting my dad, aren't you?" I furrow my brow, looking at her and turning my phone over so it's facedown on my desk.

"I don't see how that matters at all."

"You spent the night with him, didn't you?"

"Again, Olivia, I don't see how that has anything to do with you." She huffs and rolls her eyes before crossing her arms over her chest and staring at me, daggers in her eyes.

"Look. I get it. You don't like me. I pulled a trick on you and now you're sleeping with my dad to get back at me, but—"

"Let's back this right the fuck up so I can clarify a few things. I don't dislike you, Olivia. I think you're actually a good person caught between a rock and a hard place, but it does not excuse how you treat me. How you give me attitude every damn day you're in *my* office. Yes, you do great work and I am so thankful for that, but it would make my life a fuck of a lot easier if you and your stepsisters weren't such spoiled brats and didn't keep trying to pull petty shit on me."

She continues to stare at me, but instead of that same malice as before, there is . . . conflict in her eyes.

"I get you don't like me because I'm with your dad or whatever, and I pretty much understand inviting me to the white party wasn't your idea. You are being used as a pawn to keep Staceigh's hands clean." I take careful note of Olivia's face, watching her roll her lips between her teeth, guilt written all over her.

But also, it's confirmation.

"From our conversation when we first started working together, I understand. I understand your sole goal is to make it through the summer and the twins play a big part of that. What I don't get is why am *I* the target? I thought it was Jason, which, please relay to Staceigh she can have my trash, but they're tied at the hip now, so I just don't get it."

They are, too. Every time we cross   paths around the Beach

Club, Staceigh is touching Jason, making sure his full attention is on her, and Jason seems to be eating it up.

But she also continues to stare me down and make any and every attempt to make me miserable, whispering in Melanie's ear new ideas for the wedding she *knows* are impossible, like hiring Harry fucking Styles to sing at the reception, as if the man just makes house calls.

I don't expect Olivia to tell me anything, so I'm surprised when she opens her mouth to speak.

"She wants you to fail."

"Yeah, I got that." She shakes her head like I'm not getting it, not understanding something.

"It *started* as Jason. She was annoyed his attention was on you when she had her eye on him." That's what I thought, but . . . "But then you didn't fall for her shit at the party. She had told all of her little minions how funny it was going to be to watch you walk in and humiliate yourself. You didn't. She saw that as a personal hit."

"Jesus fucking Christ. Are you kidding me? I stopped *her* from humiliating *me* and it's *my fault*?" Olivia shrugs.

"She's never gone head-to-head with someone and not had them back down. She's also mad people like your work and you are actually doing well here at the Beach Club."

"So why are you getting dragged in?" Olivia bites her lip.

"Because of my trust. I have to keep them happy. And no offense, Cami, my trust and being able to have the capital to start a business without having to keep my mom happy for the next eight years? It's more important than whatever woman is keeping my dad's bed warm." I roll my eyes and shake my head, but I get it in a fucked-up way. As a woman who has lived a good chunk of my life putting myself first and cutting ties when things got too messy, I get it.

I don't like it, but I get it.

Still, I sigh.

"Thank you," I say.

"Thank you?" Olivia asks, clearly confused.

"Thank you for letting me know her motive. It helps. And it

might help me avoid any bullshit she pulls in the future. Or any bull-shit you try to pull to keep her content." A wicked smile spreads on Olivia's lips.

"Just remember, I'm in this for myself, Cami. If I have to drag you down to keep myself standing, I'll do it."

And you know what?

I can't be mad at her for that. At least she's being honest.

That, I can work with.

"I wouldn't expect anything less," I say with a smile before going back to work.

THIRTY-ONE

WEDNESDAY, JUNE 21

CAMI

> Are you a campfire?

> Smoky and keeping bugs away?

> Because you're hot and I want s'more.

> I don't know the last time I had a s'more.

> We should fix that sometime soon.

> Promises, promises.

I'm working at my desk when my phone beeps with a new text and I stare at it, seeing my client's number on the screen. Her birthday party is in two weeks and I've been working closely with her to plan the event.

HOLLY MCADAMS

Hi, Camile. Just wanted to let you know I'll be canceling our meeting tomorrow morning and will no longer need your services. I've spoken with a friend who agrees the vision isn't being executed properly. I'll be reaching out to other event coordinators today to find something that works better. xxHolly

What in the . . .

Holly. Holly McAdams.

Not a member of the Bitch Pack, but at parties, she does hang in their vicinity. She's turning 24 and Olivia and I have gone back and forth multiple times about her event, trying to make it work in a way that isn't a total train wreck. Her vision is so incredibly particular, she refuses any other insight. I told Olivia I actually hated how it was turning out and wished she were more amendable to my ideas.

In theory, I should be happy she's taking her business elsewhere. She wasn't having her event through the Beach Club, so it's no loss of revenue for them, but it was a personal event under my name.

An opportunity to show the island elite what I could do, even with her strict boundaries.

I need this client.

I need this event and the exposure.

And even more, I'm fucking confused as to why she's canceling so last minute. Holly McAdams is Type A, which makes her a pain as a client, but she's also a ridiculous people pleaser. Half of her "ideas" are just things her mother or her friends *insisted* she have at the party, and then she told me she *needed* to have it.

Something feels so incredibly off, so I grab my phone and dial her number.

I head down to the casual restaurant, Turf, which offers basics like burgers, salads, and sandwiches, midday to grab some sustenance as I continue my work hustle, my head pounding from staring at my computer for the past four hours.

The day feels sour and gloomy despite the sunny afternoon, and it's fully my mood that's causing it.

And as if by kismet, the Bitch Pack walks past me in too-dark fake tans and teeny tiny neon bikinis, matching sarongs tied around their waists, and the storm cloud hovering over me breaks a bit.

This should be entertaining.

"Hey, Cami," Staceigh says with an obnoxious wiggle to her fingers.

"Yeah, hi, Cami," Laceigh says with a giggle.

Olivia follows behind, cautiously averting her eyes from looking at me, and that's when I know.

But it's Staceigh my eyes are locked on.

They have fire in them. Pure, unadulterated anger.

I think this girl *actually* hates me. And when she speaks, it all makes sense.

"I spoke with Holly McAdams this morning," she says, a slight, evil tilt to her lips. "I told her how you feel about her vision for her birthday party and she informed me she's pulling out from using your services."

I don't show my cards. I don't reveal anything.

Instead, I tip my head to the side and look at Olivia but address my question to Staceigh.

"How'd you know I was working with Holly?" I ask, adding a bit of her own dumb blonde into my tone.

"Olivia told me."

My eyes move to Olivia and a tiny hint of betrayal runs though me. I knew, of course, that's where they got the heads-up, but I think a part of me was hoping otherwise. A part of me was hoping that despite the turmoil, like we originally agreed upon, we were on the same page.

"Guess you're gonna have to fill your calendar again, won't you?" Staceigh asks, clearly proud of herself.

There it is. Olivia was telling the truth about that at the very least. The twins are annoyed I'm actually succeeding at my job and frustrated whatever tricks Staceigh is pulling aren't working. They aren't stopping me.

Clearly, she has underestimated me.

It's not the first time it's happened and surely won't be the last. That's fine.

"Actually, I was coming down to find Olivia," I say, the feeling of success and victory creeping into my veins.

"You were?" she asks, her voice full of caution.

Good. She has no idea.

"Yeah. I think I might need to hire you on for more than just the one day a week." The twins make a confused face, part not understanding my words and part, I think, at the idea of *actually working a job.*

God, can you imagine? Insert eye roll here.

"I don't—" Olivia starts, but I turn, grabbing my to-go order the hostess is walking over my way with a smile before turning back to them.

"Yeah, you see, I explained to Holly about all of the ways I really think her event could shine and the things I think she should exclude. She was really receptive, said she appreciated how I wasn't just going to blow smoke up her ass like some of her . . ." My eyes roam the three girls in front of me. ". . . friends. I told her I wanted her party to be the event of the summer. She appreciated it *so much,* she asked me to also plan her engagement party," I say with a sugary sweet smile.

"Her . . . engagement party?" Laceigh says, eyes wide.

"Oh, shoot, they haven't announced it yet," I say with a fake cringe, going in for the kill. "Don't tell anyone I told you, but Connor asked Holly to marry him. He'll be off the market soon!" I add extra enthusiasm into my voice until it sounds fake even to my ears.

Laceigh's face falls.

Ah, the rumors were right.

She has her eyes on Connor Gomez.

Her sister's jaw is tight and I give her the sugariest smile I can muster, as if I don't even notice the daggers she's throwing me.

"Isn't it just so great, Staceigh?"

She doesn't reply, and I take a deep sip of my soda before looking at my phone.

"Well, I have another consultation for a new client in about ten minutes, so I gotta blast, but Liv, I'll let your grandfather know I have extended the invite for additional work to you!"

Or really, *you have no option but to sacrifice even more of your summer and work with me, sucker.*

I leave the three girls with a fun little wiggle of my fingers and turn, basking in the fact I most definitely won another round.

Friday June 23

> Are you a camera?
>
> Nope.
>
> Because every time I look at you, I smile.
>
> Aww, that's cute. I like that one.
>
> Finally.

On Friday, I walk into my office and Olivia is already there waiting for me, albeit begrudgingly.

"Good morning, Olivia," I say, a smile on my face and dropping a coffee on her desk.

She looks at it like it's poisoned.

"Your fave. Sugar-free vanilla, nonfat iced latte."

I stopped at the little café downstairs on my way in to work this morning to get Olivia a coffee. Even though she's been awful to me and has been conspiring with the twins to try and tear me down, she still works for me and I did ruin her Fridays for the foreseeable future by forcing her to accept additional intern hours.

She looks at it then back at my where I'm putting my own cup on my desk and dropping my bag on the hook.

When I was first given this setup with her little desk in the same office as mine, I hated it.

But really, it just feeds into my plans to annoy the fuck out of this girl until she quits.

"How do you know what I drink?" she asks, staring at it.

"I'm not an idiot. I pay attention."

"God, you're like, obsessed with me," she says under her breath, and I let it slide as I watch her take a cautious sip before declaring it safe, I assume.

"You ready to have a great day? I sent over some files for you to work on first thing this morning last night. If you could get those to me as soon as possible, that would be fabulous." She stops and stares at me.

"Why are you so chipper?" she asks, caution in her words.

"Oh, you know. The sun's shining, we have a new client to interview today, and your dad ate me out before I got to work."

Her face goes green and the bloom of a fresh win fills my chest.

"It really is the little things in life sometimes, you know?"

THIRTY-TWO

TUESDAY, JULY 4

CAMI

> Are you a fireworks show?

> > Fireworks are set for 10:30 on the dot.

> Because you make my heart go boom boom.

> > Are you coming tonight?

> For a bit, yes.

> > Can't wait to see you.

The Fourth of July party is set to be . . . well . . . everything.

If I can somehow make it go off without a hitch, that is.

Thankfully, the staff of the event, I've learned, are incredibly capable of pulling literally any idea I have off seemingly flawlessly, so when Abbie told me she and Damien would be attending the party, I knew I'd be able to spend some time with her without stressing about the ins and outs.

And I'd also get yet another opportunity to network.

And, possibly most importantly, keep an eye out on the twins and Olivia.

Damien insisted I invite Zach to the party so he would have someone to spend time with while Abbie and I inevitably gossiped, which is why I'm now standing with Abbie, Damien, and Zach early in the night before the true chaos of any event starts.

It's also when Olivia and the twins walk by, right as Zach has his arm looped around my waist and Abbie is filling me in on Kat's most recent boyfriend she just dumped. Staceigh catches my eyes, stopping dead in her tracks, her sister not noticing and walking right into her back.

"Ow!" Laceigh yells.

"God, Laceigh, you can't even function as a human," her sister whispers under her breath before turning to her soon-to-be stepsister. "Olivia, isn't that your dad?"

It's so interesting how her voice goes from bitchy and annoyed to siren-like and husky.

Jesus Christ, please tell me she's not—

"It is," Olivia says, her jaw tight.

But even I am not prepared for the brash confidence Staceigh displays next when she walks ups to my man and her soon-to-be step-sister's father, puts her hand on the shoulder of the arm not wrapped around me, and bats her eyes at him.

She doesn't even bother to acknowledge my existence.

"I've heard so much about you, Zach," she says, her voice a sultry tone that has my jaw dropping and my eyes widening. Abbie's face isn't much different than mine, shock and incredulity written there.

Zach stares at her hand, then at her, then at his daughter, and finally at me.

I can't fight the way my lips tip despite the way my jaw is nearly on the floor with her blatant move.

"Nice to meet you . . ."

He knows who she is, but he's playing the game.

It makes me fall for him just a tiny, minuscule amount and

Abbie's smile grows. When I glance at Damien, he looks as entertained as I feel.

Because this can't be real life, right?

"Staceigh," she says.

"And I'm Laceigh. E-I-G—" she starts before her twin cuts her off.

"Jesus, Lace, stop it. You're a fucking idiot with that shit. No one needs to know how to spell your damn name."

Well.

It looks like no one is free from Staceigh's bite when she has her eye on a prize.

"We should get a drink," she says to Zach and once again, I'm not annoyed by her words. I'm mostly impressed—it takes a lot of ego to be that blatant.

"I'm sorry?" Zach asks, and it's so fucking cute how genuinely confused he is.

But her hand is still on his arm and she's still too fucking close to him and I genuinely cannot tame my inner psycho any longer. It's getting less funny by the moment.

In the corner of my eye, Abbie closes her eyes, shakes her head, and takes a deep breath, knowing I'm about to do something unhinged.

"609-295-1555," I say, leaning in and staring right at Staceigh as I do. I watch her face form confusion—not enough to furrow a brow which might leave a line, God forbid, but enough I know she's lost as fuck.

"What?" she asks in a bitchy, whiney voice I'm starting to realize is just her normal voice.

The sultry voice is for men.

The catty voice is when she's trying to prove herself or win some kind of fight.

This is how she actually talks naturally.

But even though I'm focused on her dumb, bitchy face, I don't miss the way Olivia's neck goes back in confusion.

She, of course, knows that string of digits.

"That's his number," I say, staring at her. "609-295-1555. You want him, shoot your shot." Staceigh's jaw drops just a little. "If he takes you up on it, he's yours. What do I care?" I ask then stare at my nails like I couldn't give two fucks about what's going on. I refuse to admit to anyone, much less myself, I'm incredibly interested in whether Zach would take this younger, wealthier girl up on her offer.

"You're giving me your boyfriend's number?"

"Honey, I know you don't get this because everything is a damned competition of who can be a bigger bitch in your world, but if a man is on my arm, he's got eyes for me and me alone. He wants a little thing, no ass, and even fewer brain cells when he could have . . ." I tip my upper body back just a hair before I continue, swiping a manicured hand down my body. ". . . this? Let him."

She doesn't answer but I don't miss how Zach steps back out of her reach and rolls his lips between his teeth.

"Do you want me to write it down for you?" I ask. "Or I could text it to you?" She keeps blinking before answering.

"What?"

"His number, Stace. She'll write his number down for you," Laceigh says, bless her soul.

"I understand what she's saying. I'm not a fucking moron." Another long beat passes as I tip my head as if to say, *Aren't you, though?* before she rolls her eyes and stomps off, her sister close behind.

"Later, Dad," Olivia says quietly with a wave of her fingers before following the twins.

It's then Abbie finally lets out a guffaw of a laugh.

"Oh my god, did you see her face?" I just smile, basking in the moment as Zach wraps his thick arm around my belly, pulling me back into him.

"So you memorized my number, did you?" His lips move to right below my ear.

"I . . . I mean . . . I—" The panic starts to build at the idea of him knowing that telling fact.

"201-555-7656," he whispers there, and it makes a shiver run down my spine.

Not because of his breath against the back of my neck or from the feel of his warm body against mine or the way his thumb swipes over my belly and makes heat build there.

No, it's because he just recited my phone number.

"Memorized it as soon as you texted me," he whispers for my ears only.

"Why?" I ask, even though I shouldn't.

Questions like this often require reciprocation and I don't want to answer that question.

But it's worth the potential flush that will crawl over me if I have to when he speaks quiet and low, for my ears only.

"Seemed important."

My phone number seemed important.

And it's a testament both to where I've been mentally and emotionally over the past ten years when that—an adult memorizing ten numbers in a time of cell phones and saved contacts—affects me so profoundly.

Because what it really means is he thought I seemed important.

And *that* means something to me.

THIRTY-THREE

ZACH

"She a handful?" the man Cami introduced as Damien asks, his girlfriend chatting a few feet away with my girl excitedly. I haven't seen this side of Cami, not really, other than that very first drunken night, and it's nice to see her open with someone other than me.

She still refuses to admit that, convincing even herself she's her closed-off ice queen when we're together.

That's fine.

If she keeps spending time with me, I'll treat her like whatever kind of queen she wants to be.

"She thinks she is," I answer after thinking about his question. Cami told me the man is incredibly protective, so I'm surprised when he tips his head back and lets out a deep laugh. I thought there was a fifty-fifty chance of him deeming me being anything but glowing about Cami as some kind insult against his own girl.

"Sounds about right. She tell you about their little scheme when Abigail and I first started dating?" I smile.

"Glitter in the vents of her ex?"

"Fuckin' genius and psychotic, those three are. Abbie's sweet, but she's got a righteous streak. Cami doesn't hide hers, but that's kind of the appeal of her, you know?" I nod because I do know. The way Cami doesn't play games, doesn't hide who she is from anyone except for clients is part of the reason I'm so into her.

I grew up on the island and here there tend to be two groups of people come summer. There are the locals who are burnt out and frustrated over the bennies and tourists coming and thinking they run the place but needing to present a hospitable face in order to succeed. Then, there are the tourists, who all play some kind of game for whatever reason—business or to climb a social ladder or whatever they're trying to get.

Sure, Cami plays nice with her clients, but she's always been Cami.

And that? That's what I'm falling for.

"Yeah. I know," I say, and Damien smiles like he understands the conversation going on in my mind.

"Tell you now, Kat's the one you gotta watch out for," he says, lifting a glass of dark liquid to his lips, and that shocks me.

"Kat?"

"Oh yeah. The girls think she's cotton-candy sweet and she is, but I can see it. Her own little psychopath is brewing beneath the surface, waiting for someone to fuck her over enough to pop out." I widen my eyes at him. Cami has told me of the three of them, Kat is the sweet one, the one with no red flags, the people pleaser.

"Interesting."

"You'll see," he says. "When all three of them are together, it's more obvious. Those two are loud about it. The quiet ones are the ones you need to look out for."

"Fair enough," I say, knowing my daughter herself fits that mold. I sigh then run a hand over my close-cropped hair, staring at Cami whispering to Abbie and watching as they both instantly start laughing. "Hopefully, I'll get the chance to see it," I say almost too quietly to hear over the noise of the party, but clearly, Damien didn't miss it.

"Don't fuck it up and you will," he says then takes a step closer to me, tipping his head to me so our conversation stays between us.

"She's closed off for a good reason, some asshole when they were in college. Been with Abbie for about eight months and the girls are close, so I spend a lot of time with Cami. She's a good one, means well. Wants what's best for her girls. Has the biggest heart of all of them, really, and that's saying a lot. It took Abbie a while to get over her inserting her foot in her mouth a while ago, but not me." I look at him, taken aback. From what I understand, Cami pushed Abbie to continue some scheme at the expense of Damien in order to get revenge on some ex.

If I were Damien, I think it would take a while to get over that.

"I get it. I get her, in a way. She's good, but she's scared. She doesn't want to get hurt, doesn't want the people she loves to get hurt. But once she lets you in?" He looks over at my girl then at me and shakes his head gently. "Game over. You're in. She'll protect you until death."

His words ring true with the image I've created of Cami in my head—a woman who is terrified to let people in after watching her mother become closed off after her father's death, then being tricked by a man she thought she trusted.

Damien's words make sense, the advice something I'll be revisiting often throughout the summer as I try and prove myself to her. As I try to convince her to give me a chance.

She still thinks this is some fun summer fling, that once Labor Day rolls around, she'll go back to the city or wherever and start her new life without me.

It's going to take a lot of work.

That's fine by me though.

I'm a patient man.

THIRTY-FOUR

CAMI

I don't get much time with Abbie, Damien, and Zach before I'm pulled away to go put out a fire in the kitchen, and then I'm called from location to location to double-check things here and there.

The entire time I'm walking on air, completely in my zone.

I've heard of people finding their purpose, finding something they were always meant to do and how it just becomes . . . easy. It seems that's finally starting to happen for me, now that I'm out of sweet sixteens and working on higher profile events.

And I'm thriving.

That is, I am until I head to a bathroom with Abbie, trying to steal even a small moment with my best friend and, of course, to get the gossip she's inevitably been collecting throughout the night.

Life hack: get a friend who loves to eavesdrop. Bonus if she does it at an event you're working so you can get the dish on what people are thinking before the end of the night.

"Everyone is so impressed, Cami," she says as we walk through the bathroom doors.

"I'm sure they're just drunk."

Abbie rolls her eyes and shakes her head as we walk into the spacious bathroom. At the entrance, there's a powder room with sinks and large mirrors and a small divider leading to stalls Abbie runs off to while I stand and check in with the bathroom attendant.

"Hey, Sonja. How are you doing in here?" The older women's face explodes in a kind smile before she responds.

"Just fine, Cami."

"Did Cici come in and give you your schedule for the night?" I ask. I stole Cici from the Beach Club, making her my assistant during events after Jefferson approved my request. Her main job is to be the primary contact for all employees working events.

"Yes, and Val relieved me for my break half an hour ago. I just got back."

"Okay, perfect. Do you need anything in here? More supplies, food or drink for yourself?"

"I'm good, Cami. Been doing this a long time," she says, her smile kind with a hint of humor, like she finds me entertaining.

"What about a chair? You're on your feet all day in here!"

"I promise, I'm fine, Cami."

"It's her job, isn't it?" a low bitchy voice asks, just loud enough for me to hear intentionally but quiet enough she could play it off like it wasn't meant to be heard.

Staceigh.

And her crew, it seems. Her sister, Olivia, and her Bitch Pack are all following behind the Queen Bee herself.

"I'm sorry, did you say something, Staceigh?" I ask loudly, turning to face her.

"Oh, me? No, I didn't say anything. Must be losing your hearing, Cami. You are pretty old." Her smile is catty and her little friends all giggle at her joke as if it were actually funny, and for a split second, I actually pity Staceigh St. George.

Imagine going through life with not a single person genuinely liking you beyond being terrified you'll tear them down or wanting to use you for the social status you'll bring them.

I shake my head and let my small moment of empathy go, watching Abbie roll her eyes. The girls all go to separate stalls.

"I'll have Glenn bring you a chair, okay?" I say once they're gone, and even though she shakes her head like it's unnecessary, Sonja smiles and thanks me before I go to the mirror to check my makeup, slicking a fresh layer of red lipstick on.

Olivia comes up next to me, moving to wash her hands but staring at me in the mirror all the same.

"How are you enjoying the party, Olivia?" I ask, being careful not to move my mouth much.

She doesn't respond instantly, watching me rub my lips together, put the lid on my lipstick, and put it back in my little bag before using my nail to fix the edge.

"That shade makes you look like a hooker," she says eventually, continuing to stare at me in the mirror.

I smile a wicked, bitchy smile, and since she grew up in this life and with these people, she knows what kind of smile it is. It's the category of smile that looks kind and sweet, but there's venom beneath it.

I've practiced a lot of looks in the mirror, from the best way to smile without causing lines to the signature Tyra Banks smolder, but this one? I never had to practice it.

I think I was just born with the skill.

"You should really be nice to me, Olivia. You never know, I could be your new stepmommy someday."

She stutters at my response and I just keep smiling in the mirror.

"God, you're such a bitch, aren't you?" she asks, her words low.

"Takes one to know one, babe," I say, but her words send her breath my way and the incredibly strong scent of liquor follows it. It's then I notice the wobble of her legs as she straightens and reaches for a towel to dry her hands.

Fuck.

"Olivia, are you drunk?"

"What are you going to do, tattle on me to my dad?" she asks and it's confirmed.

Olivia is drunk off her ass.

"Olivia, why don't we," I say, pausing, trying to think of an answer because even if she's a spoiled brat, she is, for lack of a better word, my employee and my . . . boyfriend's . . . Sure. My boyfriend's daughter and my boss's granddaughter.

There's some level of responsibility here I can't deny.

"Why don't I take you to my room, help you sober up?"

"I'm not drunk, Cami. God." But her eyes are hazy and off as she says it. "I only had like, two, three drinks."

"What have you eaten, Olivia?" I ask, now getting more and more nervous. Sonja is also eyeing us with concern but Olivia is moving past her, heading for the exit quickly. I have no option but to follow her before something terrible happens.

"Hey, Sonja, can you please tell my friend Abbie I had to run?" I ask over my shoulder but continue walking out of the bathroom without getting her response.

"Olivia!" I say, following her out. "Olivia!"

"Jesus, why are you so obsessed with me?" she asks, walking away, and I smile awkwardly at a few women I recognize, trying to avoid a scene, but continue following Olivia. Finally, I catch up to her, grab her wrist, and tug her into a hall.

"Olivia, you're drunk."

"And?"

"And you're at a Beach Club event as my intern and your grand-father is . . . somewhere."

"What do you care?"

"Look. I know you aren't a big fan of mine and I know we have some . . . weird—"

"You're fucking my dad."

"Jesus Christ, Olivia, he's an adult. And so are you! Stop this. You sound like a spoiled child." That shut her up and I wonder if anyone other than Zach ever speaks firmly with her or if she's spent her life like the twins, never being told no. "You want—you need your trust released early. The best way to do that is to prove yourself. Getting hammered at a party isn't the way—"

Somewhere along the way, I said something wrong, or maybe I was never going in the right direction, but either way, she tugs her hand out of mine.

"You don't know anything. For all you know, this is all part of my plan. Stop trying to be friends with me, Cami. Go do your job or whatever."

And then she's stomping off, a little wobbly on her heels, toward the twins who have a shockingly kind look on their faces as she approaches.

Maybe all this time, I've been reading both the twins and Olivia wrong.

Maybe they're friends and Olivia isn't annoyed as fuck by them.

Maybe Olivia really is just a spoiled brat who doesn't care about anything or anyone.

Unfortunately, I don't have time to contemplate much more or make an attempt to step in once again because just then, an employee working the event is next to me and I'm off to put out yet another fire.

THIRTY-FIVE

CAMI

"We need to talk," Abbie says, coming behind me less than thirty minutes later. "We *need to talk*," she repeats in a more serious tone then starts walking, her hand on my wrist so I have no option but to follow her, and she moves toward a door I know leads to a small, unoccupied room.

"Abbie, what the hell?" The door closes behind us and my hand reaches for the light, making us both blink a bit before she speaks.

"You need to go help out Olivia."

"What?"

"You need to help Olivia. Save her before they fuck her over."

"What are you talking about?"

"Olivia? Your boyfriend's daughter? She's completely hammered."

"I know. I talked to her in the bathroom and followed her out and tried to talk some sense into her. She didn't want it."

"You need to force it on her then. She's going to get hurt."

"Abbie, I know you have a soft spot for literally everyone on Earth, but—"

"Those bitches are getting her drunk and are trying to humiliate her."

Silence fills the little broom closet we're in and Abbie crosses her arms on her chest.

"What?"

"I overheard them in the bathroom."

"I need more info, Abbie." She sighs like I'm annoying and she can't believe I'm making her take the time to tell the full details.

"I was in the bathroom, heard you leave, and I was going to follow but then I heard those bitches talking about Olivia."

"And?"

"They're getting her drunk. Apparently, the girl, though she grew up in a bar, doesn't drink much. The poor thing is a lightweight, and from the little I gathered, doesn't know her limits." That makes sense, seeing how she was acting. "They're being nice, getting her drunk, and then want to humiliate her."

"How?"

"I'm not totally sure, but I did hear the bitchiest one say they're going to make sure the grandfather and the mother sees."

"Jefferson?"

"I guess. Something about her getting a trust?"

Well, fuck.

I hadn't told that part of Olivia's story to Abbie. It didn't feel like my place. But if the twins know . . .

"Fuck." I say, my fingers moving to my temples as I try to sort my thoughts out.

"Yup. Like I said, you need to save her. No one else is going to. Grab her, force her into a room where she can't get into trouble. Let her sober up."

"Abbie, I can't just force a drunk girl into a room."

"Normally, I would agree, but in this case? You have to, Cami." I let out a groan, looking at the ceiling. Why does it feel like every moment at this godforsaken club is a disaster?

"She's not going to believe me. She hates me, Abbie. She thinks

I'm fucking Zach to get back at her for that night with the party."
Abbie rolls her eyes.

"God, seriously? Is everyone here really that full of themselves?"
I don't respond, but I don't have to. It's obvious. A moment passes as I
try to figure out how to get Olivia out of this mess.

"I don't want to drag Zach into this. He . . . She values how he
sees her. I think if he found out she got drunk, he'd drag her out by
her hair and she'd be embarrassed and it would impact their relationship."

A long beat passes while Abbie looks at me and she's smiling
through it.

Why is she smiling?

"He's good for you, you know."

"What?"

"Zach. He's good for you."

"Abbie, this is not the time—"

"I know. Just want it on the record that I like him. A month ago,
no way in hell you'd try to protect a girl who was an utter bitch to
you, no matter the circumstances. But now you're with Zach and . . ."
Her voice trails off, but she doesn't have to finish. I know where she's
going.

"I'm not with Zach—"

"No time to argue semantics, Cam. We've got a reputation to save
and an ally to make."

"An ally?" I ask as I follow her out of the broom closet, her heels
clicking on marble with purpose.

"These bitches have to go down and I think she might be the best
way to do it."

And even though this night is going up in flames, I can't help but
smile because Abigail Keller on a mission of petty revenge will
always and forever be my favorite version of her.

THIRTY-SIX

CAMI

> What do you call a cow with no legs?

What?

> Ground beef.

You're really bad at this.

> I know. I wanted to soften the blow. I hate to do this last minute but Liv, Abbie, and I are doing a last-minute girls' night in Abbie's room!

Girls' night?

> You know, decompressing from a night of work, drinks, junk food, gossip.

With my daughter?

> With my assistant and best friend, Mr. Anderson.

> Do you hate me? I know we were planning to spend the night at your place...

> You think I would hate you for spending time with my daughter, who I've been telling you for weeks I'm concerned has no real, good friends?

> We had plans.

> Plans change. Have fun with Livi, baby.

> I'll miss you.

> I'll make up for it by eating your pussy for hours tomorrow.

Wednesday, July 5

Olivia wakes in the giant bed of Damien's condo at the Beach Club and it reminds me very much of where Kat, Abbie, and I were barely two months ago, hungover in this same bed.

Except when Olivia wakes, I'm not hungover next to her like I was last time. Instead, I'm sitting in the love seat in sweats, waiting for her to come back to the land of living.

I've been here, wide awake all night, worried she'd get sick or wake up alone in a strange bed and freak out. By the time Abbie and I got to Olivia, she was in even worse shape than she had been less than an hour before and it was clear the twins weren't planning to do anything to stop it.

Stealing Olivia and keeping her safe meant I also bailed on Zach. Instead of meeting him at the Fishery after the event like we had originally planned, I had to lie, telling him I was bonding with her and having a fun little girls' night.

Will I have a lot of explaining to do when I finally talk to him?

Yes, probably.

Will I be so totally caught if Olivia decides not to go with the lie?

Absolutely.

But I heard her when she told me in her moment of clarity she doesn't want her dad to think differently of her.

I heard Zach when he told me how much he hates the person Olivia becomes around the Bitch Pack and how over the years, that's hurt their relationship.

I heard her when she told me she plays the game so the twins don't fuck with her, so her mother can get married and ride off into the sunset, leaving Olivia alone.

And I heard her when she drunkenly told me not to tell her father last night.

So, I spent the night sober and totally wired on panic and adrenaline and scheming, watching Olivia toss and turn in her sleep. But finally, it seems she's awake as she groans aloud.

"Oh god," she murmurs under her breath, eyes still closed but head tipped to the ceiling.

"Are you okay?" I ask, and instantly her eyes pop open. "Shit, I didn't mean to scare you."

"What the fuck?" she asks, sitting slowly. "What are you doing here?"

"It's my friend Abbie's room."

"What?"

"Well, technically, it's Damien's room, but he's of the *what's mine is yours* mindset, so it's Abbie's."

"*What?*"

"Don't worry, they stayed in my room for the night. I would suggest sending them a nice little thank you note for making it so you could hide out here and not make an absolute fool of yourself."

"What the fuck are you *talking about?*" she asks, voice still quiet and croaky, and finally, I give her the answer she's looking for.

"I brought you back here to Damien's room last night."

"What the *fuck? Why would you do that?*" she asks but then puts a hand to hear head like she's trying to hold it together,

I'm sure it's throbbing unbearably at the very least.

"What did you do to me?" she groans.

"Are you going to be sick?" Olivia shakes her head, instead accusing me again.

"What did you do to me?"

"I saved you," I say with an eyebrow raised in her direction. "You're welcome."

"Why would I thank you for *kidnapping me* and bringing me to some random person's condo?"

"Do you drink often, Liv?" I ask, and she shakes her head. The shake is quick and ends with her closing her eyes tightly and turning just slightly green. "Drink this," I say, handing her a bottle of electrolyte-doused water. She sips it slowly and we sit in silence. After a few minutes, I'm pleased to watch some of the green leave her face before I hand her two pain pills.

"The twins got you unbearably drunk."

"I don't—"

"They gave you drinks. They were way stronger than you thought, I'm sure. They were pure sugar and alcohol." Her eyes close and she sighs.

"I had three drinks."

"That you *remember*. You'd had a few drinks when I talked to you in the bathroom—"

"You were being a bitch then—"

"And *you* were already slurring your words." She takes that in for a bit and the thoughts twist in her mind like she wants to argue, to tell a different version of the truth, but she can't.

"I don't drink very often," she finally says, resigned.

"That makes sense. That would explain why you had no real idea how to handle your liquor."

"Wait, so how did I get here?" She's starting to come to, the cast of pain over her eyes lessening and the green color dulling even more.

"I brought you here. Well, Abbie and I did."

"Why? What's your grand, evil plan?" Her eyes go wide. "Shit, my dad. You told my dad, didn't you? God, I can't believe you—"

"Your dad thinks we have finally bonded and had a girls' night."

Olivia goes silent. "I texted him and said we had a come to Jesus moment in the woman's bathroom and we were having a fun little night in Abbie's room. You'll have to call him later to confirm you're alive and if you want, then you can tell him the truth. I won't stop you." Her eyes go wider somehow. "But you don't have to. My lips are sealed."

She stares for long, long moments but I wait for her answer.

"I don't understand." I sigh.

"Abbie was still in the bathroom when I left to follow you and overheard the twins planning some scheme. They were giving you too-strong drinks and were planning to humiliate you."

"What? I—"

"They know about your trust."

Silence. The silence is deafening.

"That doesn't make sense."

"Doesn't it?"

"They've been . . ." A pause and she bites her lip. "They've been nicer." I tip my head in a *uh, red flag, babe* way. "I'm serious. It's like they came to their senses about us being stepsisters soon and they've been nicer."

"Olivia . . ."

"Look, just because they hate you doesn't mean they have to hate me." She bites out the words and in another world, I'd probably be annoyed. Instead, I just feel sad for her.

"Of course not. They don't *have to* hate you, but they do because you're gorgeous and, when you want to be, you're kind and people like you and you take the spotlight off of Staceigh."

More silence.

"How do I know this isn't some kind of setup? Like, are you the one trying to get at me?" I roll my eyes and sigh, walking back over to the love seat I spent the entire night on and trying not to scream.

"Jesus, Olivia. Look. I know you think I hate you. I don't. Am I happy you tried to fuck me over with the twins and gave me that lame fucking invite? No. Am I ecstatic you three have spent the last month trying to make me miserable? Absolutely not. Am I happy you have a fucking shitty attitude every time I'm around? Nope. Am I happy when I'm with your dad, you do literally anything in your power to make him hate me as much as you hate me for seemingly no reason? No. But I don't *fucking hate you*. Believe it or not, I see a lot of myself in you: a girl who is trapped in this petty bullshit with no easy way out. I told you I attended to a prep school and I had to play the game to survive. I get it. But I *don't* get why you fucking think I'm the devil incarnate for no reason."

Once again, silence fills the room.

Eventually, I sigh.

"But if you need it, Abbie has a recording. The twins talking to each other about your trust, about getting you drunk, about humiliating you." With that, her eyes go wide. "If you need that proof, I'll give it to you."

A small part of me I refuse to admit exists will be bummed out. A small part will be sad she won't take my word for it, will need that evidence, but still . . . I understand. I would want the proof.

It feels like an eternity before she speaks, one where I tiredly watch thoughts and emotions pass over her eyes and face, waiting for her answer.

But when she finally does, she surprises me.

"They need to be stopped," she says quietly.

"Stopped?"

"They can't keep living life like this. Like bitches who get whatever they want. They don't like you because of Jason. That's really it. And the fact you don't fall for their bullshit and everyone actually *likes* you because you're not a total cunt."

"I figured as much." I didn't necessarily know about the *not a total cunt* part, but the rest? I got that much.

"Last summer they were so horrid to a lifelong member of the Beach Club, she left by July. I haven't heard from her since and we used to talk pretty regularly." Then, her eyes go far off. "Cici used to be my best friend. We grew up together on the island; our dads are friends. I introduced her to the twins the first summer they were here. I'm an only child and the idea of having sisters was . . . exciting. I thought all four of us could have a fun summer together."

I don't say anything when she pauses, her eyes drifting to the window. Instead, I wait for her to continue. "I don't know why they do it. They have everything they could ever want. I'm assuming it's because Staceigh can't deign to let anyone have any attention other than her. It was the summer after my freshman year." She sighs and there's *pain* there. "My mom told me they needed to have a good summer, if something happened to ruin her going after their father, she wouldn't pay my tuition." My mouth drops open and finally her eyes move to me. There's a sad smile on her lips. "I didn't know what to do. I didn't have much of a choice, though, when they started to go for CiCi. So, I was a bitch and I cut her off so they wouldn't go after her." She shrugs, moving to look out the window again.

"It seemed like the right thing to do, to let her live her life. She's from here, likes working hospitality, and I know working at the Beach Club was the only way she could afford to go to college."

"So you let her think you were a bitch and you hate her because of the twins?" She doesn't say anything but I know the truth. "You should tell her, Olivia."

"Why?" Her head swings to me again, a firmness to her that wasn't there moments before. "So she can tell me I'm a shitty human? I know I am. I know I've spent four years putting my own survival first, letting the twins tear people down in order to keep myself safe. God, look what they've been doing to you. I never stepped in." Olivia shakes her head, a small, sad smile on her lips. "No, it's better this way."

"Were you serious? About stopping them?" I ask a few minutes later, breaking the silence of both of us lost in our thoughts.

"Yes." She means that, too. I can tell. I get up, putting a hand out to help her stand.

"Okay. Then come on. Let's get some toast and more water in you and we can talk."

"Talk?"

"Oh, Liv. Women like Abbie and me? We don't let this kind of shit fly." A smile is spreading over my face and my body is filling with a joy and excitement I haven't felt since I got to the island.

"What?" Olivia says, moving her feet to the edge of the bed gingerly then standing. "What do you mean, women like you?"

"A few months ago, Abbie's ex dumped her. He was a piece of shit. We got drunk, made a list, and made his life a living hell. Cancelled orders, glitter in his vents, Abbie fucked his boss and made him take her to the company holiday party . . ." I sigh, thinking back on those months fondly. "It was glorious."

We're headed toward the living room where Abbie is waiting for us.

"That's amazing."

"Tip of the iceberg, my friend. Petty revenge is kind of our thing," Abbie says with a smile, looking impeccable in a pink workout set, sipping a coffee with a platter of fruit and bagels in front of her Damien sent up.

"God, I want to be you guys when I grow up."

"Stick with us, kid, and we'll make it happen," I say, popping a bottle of champagne and pouring it over orange juice because putting this feud on hold for the greater good deserves a goddamn celebration.

THIRTY-SEVEN

CAMI

"So we're going to make their lives living hell?" Olivia asks, staring at the list Abbie has written in her signature pretty pink handwriting.

"Yes, but in a subtle way. Little things to make them miserable, but nothing big enough for, say, the tabloids."

"Or prison," I say with a glare at Abbie.

"Or prison," she agrees with a roll of her eyes.

"I can't decide if you guys are awesome or fucking unhinged," Olivia whispers, and Abbie smiles.

"Both, babe. We're both." I move my glass to clink with my best friend's before we look back at the list.

"So, we've got the basics here, and none of it should really be able to be pointed back to either of you," Abbie says, reading over the list. That was important to me—there's no reason for Olivia or me to risk our reputations or jobs in order to get back at the twins.

"It feels . . . lacking," Olivia says.

"Lacking how?" She waits a heartbeat before she answers.

"I want to do something bigger." There's a gleam in her eyes, and I decide trusting my gut in the very beginning and thinking she might be cool was probably a good idea.

She is, in fact, very cool.

"I love it. What do you have in mind?" Abbie asks.

"Hold up, let's think about this." It's weird being the voice of reason in this situation.

"They're bitches, Cami. They've been making my life a misery for four years and I'm *over it*."

"Yes, but let's remember why you've been letting them do it." I stare at Olivia with sympathetic eyes.

"I didn't get this memo. Why have we been putting up with *The Shining* twins' torture?" Olivia laughs but I'm the one who answers.

"Olivia has a trust. She wants to start her own PR business, but her trust doesn't open until she's 30. Her mother told her if she didn't make any waves, the fall after she graduates from college, she'd get it." There's no need to add how Melanie has used this tactic before, threatening to not pay her tuition unless she played the game.

"Let me guess, that's this fall."

"Ding, ding, ding. I won't let you put your career in jeopardy, Olivia."

"What about yours?" she counters. "My mother's wedding could be huge for your career."

"And it still will be. When I say subtle, we mean it. Mental warfare with zero tracks left behind."

"It *is* our specialty."

"Okay, but making them look dumb in front of their shitty friends won't put a dent in their reputation. It needs to be big."

"Olivia—"

"I don't care, not really. I'll get my trust when I turn thirty. Until then, I bootstrap my shit and hustle it out. I'll . . . I'll apply for grants, loans, whatever. I can't let this shit go. Worst case, I work a corporate PR job for a few years and start on my own when I have the capital."

"I like her," Abbie says with a smile.

"Me too," I say. "But why now? Why this?" Olivia sighs.

"It's a culmination. Do you really think I haven't daydreamed about putting them in their place? God, what I would give to punch Staceigh in the face, ruin that nose job—"

"I knew no one had a nose like that in real life," Abbie says under her breath, and I can't help but laugh.

"And if she's turning her tricks to making *me* miserable, my dad is probably next." My stomach feels sick with her saying something I've thought out loud.

"Do you think she would?"

"I wouldn't want to put it to a test." A beat passes. "But yes. I think they would. They'd mess with his business, probably. It's an easy target, relying too heavily on tourists and the Beach Club for customers in the summer."

I sigh. "Okay. You're right. But we need to be careful. I don't want him to know what we're doing. He wouldn't like it, even if it's what brought us together." Olivia stares at me for a long moment.

"You really like him, don't you?" she asks, her voice low.

"Yes, I do." I don't hesitate before answering, and I don't miss the happy smile on Abbie's face. "I know it isn't great timing and I know it probably seems like I did it on purpose, but I promise I didn't know you two were related at all. If I did, I probably would have avoided the Fishery all together. I like him, and I'm sorry if that makes you uncomfortable, but unless he wants to end things, I won't stop seeing him." She stares at me before giving a small shake of her head.

"I'm sorry, Cami. Really, I am. I'm sorry I was such a bitch to you and I'm sorry for thinking you'd only be with my dad to get back at me. It wasn't right. I've been so focused on myself, on surviving this summer, I didn't think about anyone else." I smile, grabbing her hand.

"Thank you, Olivia. I appreciate it, really."

And just like that, Liv and I are on the same team and it feels really fucking good.

THIRTY-EIGHT

FRIDAY, JULY 7

CAMI

> Do you have a pencil?

> I'm more of a pen girl myself.

> Cause I want to erase your past and write our future.

> I can probably pencil you in for dinner tonight.

> I'll have the fries waiting for you.

There are a multitude of papers and notebooks in front of me as I work at the table in the corner, organizing everything for a first birthday party for Mrs. Thomas's grandson, Weston. But if we're being honest, I haven't truly seen any of the words or numbers or figures on the pages in close to an hour.

Instead, I've watched the Bitch Pack make the lives of the staff at the Beach Club's casual restaurant a complete misery.

First, the air conditioning on the outdoor patio wasn't cold enough, the Jersey Shore humidity messing up a fresh blowout.

Then, Staceigh wanted the dressing on the *side* but also wanted the salad tossed and then she decided the salad should come with soup, but, god, it's too *hot* for soup in the middle of July, *you idiot.*

One of the Bitch Pack girls wanted sweet tea *unsweetened,* then complained it just didn't taste sweet enough.

Laceigh was incredibly disappointed the selection for sugar free, dairy free, gluten free, vegan entrees did not, in fact, include chicken as an option for an add-on.

To be fair, I'm pretty sure that last one was just Laceigh being . . . Laceigh.

But each request, each scorn, each complaint was accompanied by quiet laughter as soon as the staff member left. Just another example of how making other people's lives miserable is just a *game* for these women. It further cements my theory everyone should have to work in some kind of customer service industry with the public for at least a year when they turn 18 to learn some humility and compassion.

Like the draft, but better.

Though, these kind of people would probably fake something like bone spurs in order to get out of it.

And, of course, Olivia is sitting with them, sharing fake smiles that look genuine, laughing along and, when no one is looking, giving apologetic looks to whoever they're messing with this time.

It's when the Bitch Pack is all giggling, a sweet server running off to escape their cruelty, when my phone buzzes.

> OLIVIA
> They're paying.

> Got it.

I lean over to the table next to me with a kind smile.

"Hi, I'm so sorry. I have to use the bathroom. Can you just keep an eye on my things? I don't want them to think I just left them here and throw any of it out," I say to the older woman with a laugh.

"Oh, no problem, Camile! I'd be happy to." It's so interesting, the people who have started to learn my name here.

I've found there are two camps at the Beach Club.

The group that, like Gloria here, are kind and welcoming and excited for the change and new events I've brought to the club.

And then there are numerous generations of Bitch Packs who like things the way they are, who don't understand why I'm here and will do anything to ignore me as I walk past.

I like the Glorias, to be clear.

"When you come back, could you spare a few minutes to chat about an event my family is having over in Hoboken this October? I'm in charge of planning my son's fiancée's bridal shower and really want to welcome her into the family in style."

And this is why working here, despite having to deal with the Staceighs and Laceighs of the Beach Club, has been invaluable. Because my name is slowly leaking into the minds of the wealthy here and I'm slowing booking more and more events outside of the club and into the fall and winter.

Finally, after years and years of trying to find my place in this industry, it's happening. And I have the Beach Club (okay, and Damien Martinez) to thank for it.

"Of course! I'd love to," I say, grabbing my bag as I head not to the bathroom, but inside of the restaurant to find . . .

"Jessica!" I say, grabbing the arm of the poor server who got the short straw and was forced to serve the Bitch Pack today.

"Hey, Cami, how's it going? Do you need a refill?" she asks, and god, she looks worn the fuck out and there is a single group of humans to blame for that.

I hate them more each day, I swear it.

"No, no, hey, you're serving the twins, right?" An exhausted sigh leaves her and she nods.

"Yes, and they have me running ragged for what I just *know* will be the world's tiniest tip."

"Look, can I ask a favor?" I ask right before diving into my scheme.

It's another thirty minutes after my chat with Jessica before the Bitch Pack stop trash-talking everyone in the vicinity and Staceigh asks for the bill with a flippant wave of her wrist. Thirty minutes in which I successfully book a consultation with Gloria and hand her a stack of my non-Beach Club business cards to share with any friends.

It takes another five minutes after she takes the check and Staceigh's card before she's walking toward them, biting her lip. Her eyes scan the room and find me just a few tables over, not in eyesight of the twins. She gives me a subtle thumbs-up.

"Are we done, here? God, if you thought you would get a tip for fucking around in the back all day, you're sorely mistaken," Staceigh says, a hand out to grab the checkbook to sign.

"Yeah," Laceigh says like an idiot bully sidekick in some 90s kid's movie.

I don't know how she actually functions in the real world.

"Uhm, Ms. St. George, the card was actually declined."

Silences takes over the Bitch Pack's table and I have to roll my lips into my mouth to fight the laugh which is dying to escape. The fact a card declining is the ultimate *oh fuck* in this group, and not in a concerned friend way, is so fucking wild to me.

"What do you mean it was *declined?*" Staceigh asks in a hushed whisper.

"Well, I ran it and it wouldn't process the charge, which means the bank—"

"Jesus, I know what *declined* means, but my cards *do not decline.* Do you know who I am? *Run it again.*" Her voice is an angry growl, fury running in the words, and it's clear she truly thinks this is *Jessica's* fault, that it couldn't be her card.

Which is true, but she doesn't need to know that.

"I did, Ms. St. George. I ran it four times."

The Bitch Pack side-eyes one another, having an unspoken conversation of *Can you believe that?* and *God, how embarrassing for her.*

"Run it *again.*"

"If I run it again, it will get locked out."

"Run. It. Again."

Jessica shrugs and nods, walking back into the restaurant, winking as she passes me.

"Can you fucking believe her? Does she even know who I am?"

"I'm so sorry you're going through this, Staceigh," one of the Bitch Pack girls says. Rebecca? Candice? I can't keep them straight anymore.

"Shut up, Peyton," she snaps at her supposed friend, also reminding me of the blonde's name.

All eyes are on the door as a silence takes over the table, no one sure what to say, Staceigh's jaw stiff.

And then Jessica is returning and this time, though she has an apologetic look on her face, it's obvious to me it's fake.

God, she's loving this.

If there's one thing I learned working at a restaurant through college because my mother refused to let me become, well, a Staceigh, it was never to fuck with the wait staff.

"Declined. Sorry, Ms. St. George. Do you have another I can process?" Her jaw goes tight.

"It's a fucking black AMEX. Why the *fuck* would I need another?"

"Well, in case this one gets declined," Jessica says.

"Get your manager."

"I'm sorry?"

"I said"—Staceigh leans forward, her face getting redder by the moment—"get your goddamn manager so I can have him fucking *fire you* for this bullshit."

"Okay," Jessica says with a smile then practically skips off. A minute later, Jessica walks back with an older blonde, maybe mid-forties, with a take-no-shit look on her face.

This could be the end of my scheme but thankfully, Lauren is also a friend of mine, helping me manage most of the internal catering orders for events on the property.

"What seems to be the problem here?"

"Your idiot of an employee says my card is being declined but it's a fucking *black card*."

"Ah, I see. So, unfortunately, black cards can, in fact, be declined. It doesn't happen . . . often, but it does happen."

God, I love this.

I love this so much.

The longer I work here, the more relationships I form with the staff, all of whom are incredibly hardworking and kind, and none of them deserve the shit some of the clients at the Beach Club pull. But most importantly, I've learned everyone here has had a run-in with the Bitch Pack and the twins and never have they left a good impression.

"Do you even *know who I am?*" Staceigh shouts, and now eyes throughout the restaurant are moving to their table, necks craning to try and get a better look at the circus.

"I do, but the rule at the Beach Club has always been and will always be everyone pays their tabs, no matter what. That's an order direct from the owner, Jefferson Kincaid."

"His daughter is going to be my *stepmother*."

"Yes, I understand that. Do you have another card I can run?"

"I already told *that* idiot this is my only card."

Silence takes over the entirety of the restaurant and god, it's so sweet.

"Is she broke?" a woman to my left whispers. I don't look at who it is, knowing that's where Quinn Carter was sitting.

"I hear she was cut off," another voice behind me says.

A third voice comes from somewhere else in the restaurant, seemingly making a call. "Oh my god, you're never going to believe what's happening right now. No, no, *Staceigh St. George is broke.*"

Perfect.

So fucking perfect.

And when the red starts to crawl farther up Staceigh's neck, I know she hears the whispers, the humiliation is hitting its mark.

Only in this world is a card declining something to be *ashamed* of. In a world of endless wealth, even the insinuation that you don't have money is social suicide.

Now is my signal.

I stand from my table, grabbing my bag once more and walking over to the table, my heels clicking in the quiet, the only other sound being low smooth jazz. Olivia, who has remained silent this whole time, looks at me.

I give the table a soft, apologetic smile I practiced in the mirror before turning to Jessica and Lauren.

"I'll cover it, Jessica," I say, handing her my own black card with a smile.

"That's not necessary," Staceigh says through gritted teeth.

"You have another way to pay?" Lauren asks, her Bronx accent coming out a bit.

God, she really hates Staceigh.

Can't say I blame her.

Staceigh doesn't reply.

"Put their bill on my card and bring the receipt to my table to sign, okay?" I say, my voice sweet as cotton candy.

"How the fuck can you afford this?" Staceigh says, her arm waving at the table. "You're a fucking party planner."

"Yes, I'm a very sought after event planner at an exclusive country club. Heck, I've got you to thank for some of my current clients. The Memorial Day party you so graciously invited me to?" I raise an eyebrow at her, never breaking eye contact and letting her know *I* know she was behind it all. "Got me so many leads. You were right. It was a great networking opportunity."

I smile at all the women at this table, some with wide eyes, some annoyed, some sitting with a faint smile, and I have to wonder what the twins have done to *them* to make them happy to see the twins put in their place.

"Actually, another round. On me." Jessica curls her lips in, fighting a laugh. "Can you do that, Jess?"

"Absolutely," she says, grabbing my card.

As I walk away, all eyes in the room on me, all kind smiles, I cross off the first item on our burn list.

THIRTY-NINE

MONDAY, JULY 10

ZACH

> Are you the package I ordered?

I don't think so.

> Because I want you at my house in the next 24 hours.

God, they get cheesier and cheesier.

> Did it make you smile?

Maybe.

> Good. Now you owe me.

I owe you because you made me smile with a crappy dad joke?

> You owe me because you like me and want to make me happy.

Keep thinking that, dimples.

> I will. Now tell me you'll spend the night at my place tonight. I have off tonight.

I can't. I have to walk my turtle.

Oof, really twisting the knife today, aren't you?

There's a pause before she answers and for a moment, I almost jump in and tell her I'm joking as I watch those little dots pop up, go away, and pop up again. Each time, my heart jumps and Jesus fuck, when did I become 16 again, worried about what a girl thinks?

Sorry. I'm in a shitty mood today.

Bitch Pack shit?

Thankfully, no. It's something personal.

Consider my interest piqued. I also refuse to take note of how worry bubbles in my gut—worry for her and the need to find a way to make it better, whatever it is.

Everything okay?

Another long pause and instead of continuing to stare at my phone, I set it down on the wood of the table out behind my house, staring off at the water and drinking my coffee. It takes everything in me to fight the instinct to build a list of shit that could be going wrong for Cami and counter it with a list of ways I could help fix any of them to make her life easier.

Again, *when did this happen?* It's not that I haven't had women in my life.

But never in my 45 years have I been unable to think of anything but a single woman.

I wake early to send her a text before she heads off to work with the sole intent of making her smile.

Count down the hours until she gets out and comes to the bar for a few hours while she jokes with Frank and drinks stupid fuckin' Aperol spritzes which taste like fruity asshole but make her smile.

Hold her hand as I walk her back to the Beach Club each night and make out against her door like fucking teenagers.

And now we can add scrambling to grab my phone when she texts me back, watching it slip from my hands and just barely saving it before it skitters off the dock and into the bay.

> I'm fine just... girl stuff.

Girl stuff.
Girl stuff?
Oh.
Oh.
That's an easy fix.

> Ahh, girl stuff. Come to my place and I'll make you feel better.

> God, you're a pig, Zach. For future reference, I don't do period sex and I don't do blow jobs.

> You don't do blow jobs?

> No. I don't like them and I don't do things I don't like. You can write me off now, if that's a deal breaker.

I know this is going nowhere good, both because I've known Cami for a bit and because I raised a daughter. In this case, texting leaves way too much room for tone interpretation and I refuse to try and defuse his potential bomb with written words.

Instead, I hit send on my cell, bringing my phone to my ear and listening to it ring barely three times before she answers.

"What?"

Fuck.

Well, I guess it's good I called because she's definitely not happy with me.

"Angel."

"I'm busy, Zach. What's up?"

"Come over tonight."

"I told you—"

"I don't care about that, Cami." There's a beat before she answers. Anytime that happens, I get a strange rush of pride knowing I knocked her off her normally sure footing.

"All men care about that."

It's then I know.

This is one of those tests she loves to give. She told me about this that first sober night in my bar—she gives tests to see if people like her, if they can endure her. Clearly, she hasn't figured out how fucking gone I am for her, for every one of those "flaws" she has a carefully curated list of. She sees those insecurities as reasons for people to abandon her, to betray her.

I wonder who helped her make that list?

Was it just that douchebag Jason?

Was it her mother, well-meaning or otherwise?

Was it society and its unending pressure to make her conform to a hyper-specific mold of how women should be, how they should act, and what they should want?

Or was it all Cami, slowly tearing herself apart and then purposely showing whatever she declared to be ugly to scare off anyone who might get too close and hurt her?

I've known since the first time she started to open up to me I'll take whatever time she deigns I deserve to hold in her life and use it to show her those flaws are in fact strengths. To show her she doesn't have to perform for anyone, much less me. To prove the person she is is more than enough and anyone who can't see it isn't worthy of her, of her time, her energy.

"I don't."

Silence fills the line but I don't work to fill it.

"I'm cranky."

"I know." She sighs and I know if I could see her, she'd be rolling those big, beautiful brown eyes of hers.

"I'm bitchy when I'm on my period."

"Doubtful, but that's fine either way."

"I'll make you watch sappy girl movies and probably cry."

"I'll make sure I have tissues." She continues going through her mental list, trying to scare me off, to prove herself right.

"It won't be a cute cry. It'll be an ugly, Kim K type of cry."

"Not sure what that means, but I'm gonna go with a *that's fine* for that as well." Another beat passes before she makes a resigned sigh but somehow, I know it's not a *fine, whatever* kind of sigh.

She's still ready to battle.

"Zach—"

"I have a daughter, Cami. I *raised* a daughter. I bought her tampons and chocolate and listened to her yell at me because we didn't have the right kind of ice cream. I get it. I don't care. I don't mind. Men who care about that shit are fucking dickwads and I'm telling you right now, I'm a lot of things but I'm not that. I miss you, okay? I want to spend the night with you, want you to sleep in my bed, and I want a fucking redo of our first morning. I want you in my shirt while I make you eggs or pancakes or bacon or whatever the fuck you're craving tomorrow morning."

She doesn't reply and I stay quiet for a moment before I try again.

"So, what do you say, Cami? Are you gonna stay the night with me?"

And I wait. I wait for what feels like an eternity because I'm man enough to admit if she says no, my ego will in fact be a bit bruised.

Finally, she sighs.

This is a resigned sigh, in the way I know means I won.

"The right ice cream answer is cookie dough," she says, her voice low.

"Got it." I can't fight the smile that definitely leaks into my voice with my words, and I can almost hear her shaking her head, a smile of her own on her lips.

"Why do I just know your dimples are out?"

"Because they never go away when I'm talking to you, Camile."

"God, I think that was my favorite one yet," she says, her voice wistful.

"Favorite what?"

"Dad joke. That was my favorite one."

I don't have it in me to tell her it wasn't a joke.

Not in the least.

When the bell chimes above the door, panic fills me because I have no clue what I'm doing here. Everything in the store is completely foreign to me, signs displaying curl patterns and oils and cremes and care products.

There's an entire fucking wall of combs and brushes, some of which look like fucking torture devices. I don't know the last time I brushed my hair, keeping it short enough on the regular so I barely have to do much more than use my fingers to make myself presentable.

You're here for Cami, I tell myself as I head straight for the register. No point in pretending I know what I'm doing when I can go to the expert and have them point me in the right direction.

"Hey, how can I help you?" she asks, a kind but slightly confused smile on her face.

"I need . . . things," I say then fight the unbearable desire to smack myself.

I'm in a store.

Of course I need *things.*

"Hair things."

Jesus, Zach. Hair things? You're in a fucking hair store.

The middle-aged woman rolls her lips in, trying to fight a laugh.

I can't be annoyed—it's probably hilarious seeing me struggle and being uncomfortable.

I shake my head, feeling a smile grow on my own lips before I try a third time.

"I've got a girl. A woman. My girlfriend?" I shake my head again and Jesus fucking Christ.

I'm *forty-five.*

I'm forty-five and I have no idea how to handle this situation. I don't even know how to *explain* Cami. When this started, she told me this was for the summer, but it's quickly becoming so much more than that. We both know it, but I also know in my gut that if I told her she was my girlfriend, she'd argue and say we were just fuck buddies. That would undoubtedly turn into a heated argument when I told her there was no fucking *way* that's all we were.

But I don't have time to dwell on the complicated definition because the woman smiles and nods. "Got it. You're here for her?" I sigh in relief.

"Yes. I need things for her." Glancing around the store again, I'm confused but determined all the same. "Last time she stayed at my place, she told me she didn't have her *stuff.* I want to make sure she has what she needs." The woman's face softens, but I don't tell her I want Cami to have things at my place to remove as many arguments against her spending the night with me as humanly possible. "I think she said a bonnet? And a pillowcase?"

I probably shouldn't be spending money on things Cami has at her place, the bar not performing the way it should at peak season, but I'll do whatever I have to to make her feel comfortable.

To show her she means *more* to me.

To try and convince her to give me a shot.

"Got it. Don't worry, I know exactly what you need," she says, stepping out from behind the register and waving for me to allow her. "Tell me about her hair."

I do as she asks and within twenty minutes, I'm leaving with a heavy bag, my wallet lighter but a smile on my face all the same.

FORTY

MONDAY, JULY 10

CAMI

I've only just walked into Zach's house when he stares at me with what might be his goofiest smile yet, both dimples out and proud, holding a greasy bag in one hand and a tub of cookie dough ice cream in the other. I stop, the door clicking shut behind me and my bag slipping off my shoulder before he speaks.

"Alright, I've got ice cream and I stopped at three different places to get you French fries. Figured you can find a backup for when you don't want to eat at the Fishery." I continue staring at him as he puts both down. "I've got that air fryer thing going; Livi says that's the best way to reheat French fries. No promises, though. If this brand of cookie dough isn't what you're into"—he moves to the fridge, opening the freezer where there are not one, not two, but four other containers of ice cream—"I got more. I also got this sweet cream one and a tube of cookie dough, though you're not technically supposed to eat it out of the tube." He closes the freezer and smiles at me again, a hint of nerves there.

"I've been doing it for the better part of 45 years, though, and I'm still standing, so there's that." He shrugs before moving to another bag on the island. I cross my arms on my chest, watching him move around his kitchen, warmth filling me with each word.

"This bag has girl essentials. Not sure what you use, got a few different kinds of tampons and pads, with and without wings. Also grabbed some different pain killers and one of those heating pads." He moves to another bag. "And there's candy and chips in this bag. That's what Livi always wanted, but I can run out for anything else."

"What's the last bag?" I ask, tipping my chin to it, and he bites his lip.

"Last time you spent the night you said you needed things. I uh . . ." He moves the bag then lifts a few things out. "I wasn't sure if you were going to bring them, and I wanted to make it easier in the future. You know, if you wanted to spend the night without bringing all of your things. So I went to the hair store and got some. I'm not sure if this is even what you wanted or needed, but the lady was really nice and helped me so I just . . . got it all." His voice trails off as I stare at his hand, two silk-lined bonnets in one hand, a package of silk pillowcases in the other.

My tongue comes out to wet my lips as I try and figure how to answer, how to respond to what equates to a few hundred dollars in things Zach bought to make me feel comfortable in his home.

"Shit, did I— Did I overstep? I promise I wasn't trying to. I just wanted to make you feel—"

"It's perfect," I say through the lump in my throat that has its own throbbing pulse.

"No, you look . . . Fuck. What is it, Cam?" he asks delicately, walking toward me where I haven't moved since I stepped in. I can't do more than shake my head and fight the tears.

He wraps me in his arms and I lose it, crying over ice cream and tampons and pillowcases, but it's not that.

It is, but it isn't.

This. This is what Abbie has.

This is what Kat is always chasing.

A partner.

Someone in your corner who wants to take care of you.

I never thought it was something I wanted or needed but having it in front of me . . . having Zach in front of me, driving all over the island on his lone day off to grab me everything and anything I might need to make my day better because I told him I was cranky and had my period . . . shit.

This is it. This is what everyone wants, isn't it? It's not the sex or the romance people ache for when they say they want someone in their life. It's not the fun date nights and couple's vacations driving people to face the torture of dating apps.

It's *companionship*. It's finding someone who wants you to be your happiest and doing whatever it takes to get you that not because it benefits them, but because they like you and care for you enough to want you to have it.

Shit.

Shit, shit, shit.

"You didn't have to do this," is all I can say as I sniffle into his shirt, his hand stroking up and down my back.

"I know," he whispers. "But I wanted to. I want to take care of you, Cami."

And that? That means more than any grand gesture ever could.

We're on Zach's couch watching *Casablanca* when it happens.

Yes, *Casablanca* because he decided I needed some *cinematic schooling* and apparently, he still hasn't forgotten I've never actually seen the movie.

I threatened to make him watch all of Abbie's favorite girly rom-coms, like *Legally Blonde* and *Mean Girls* and *Miss Congeniality* in exchange, but he patiently reminded me he once lived with a preteen girl so he's seen them all already.

So, we're watching the old black and white movie when my phone rings.

"Shit, I should get that. It might be work," I say in a murmur.

Last week, I had to put a spam filter on my email when *someone* put my work email on a marketplace ad for *free pedigree kittens*, my inbox overflowing and hiding my actually important emails.

The next day, I thought I was having an incredibly peaceful day of minimal intrusions.

Until I left for the day and realized *someone* had turned the ringer on my phone off, meaning I had a completely full voicemail and had missed every call to my office. As a result, *all* of my clients now have my cell number, which is an experience in and of itself.

To be clear, the twins had been in my office that morning for another wedding meeting, furthering their mission to ruin my career.

"All good," he murmurs in my ear as I sit in his lap wearing comfy pajamas.

But I don't see a client's name on my screen when I lean forward to grab it from the coffee table splayed with junk food.

"What?" Zach asks, probably reading the way my body goes still.

"It's . . . It's my ex." He straightens, looking at me and at my phone.

"Your ex? The one from college?" Of course he knows the story of Jason and how he's at the Beach Club.

"Yeah," I say, my voice low.

"Is he a client? What does he want?" I shake my head.

"No. I have no idea. I didn't even think he still had this number."

"Answer it," he says, sitting straighter and moving me in his lap so I'm sitting between his legs.

"What?"

But I don't have to ask a second time when he grabs my phone, tapping the green answer button and putting it on speakerphone. I look over my shoulder, eyes wide, and he's *smiling*. I have no choice but to speak.

"Uh, hello?" Zach reaches over for the remote control, hitting pause so there's no noise in the room.

"Hey, Cami. It's Jason."

"Uh, yeah. I know. Caller ID and all." There's a smile in his voice when he replies.

"Aw man, you kept my number?"

I don't answer right away as Zach's hand moves my hair from my neck and he presses his lips there, the thumb on the hand on my hip swiping in a slow rhythm against the skin where my tee has ridden up.

"Uh." I clear my throat. "I just keep moving my contacts from phone to phone."

"Sure," he says like he doesn't believe me.

"What is he doing?" Zach asks, his breath running along my ear, and I shrug.

"How are you?" Jason asks.

What the fuck is going on?

"Uh, I'm fine. Is there something you need? An event or something for Staceigh?"

"Who?"

A small part of me finds that hilarious, and I know Zach does too as he huffs a laugh against my neck before pressing a kiss there again.

This is weird.

This is so weird, and not just because my ex is calling me.

I'm sitting on the lap of my . . . boyfriend, his hand sliding under my shirt now until the entire thing is on my lower belly. It's warm and even though aspirin has eased the ache of my cramps, it still feels better than any heating pad I've ever used.

And even more, my breathing is slowing getting quicker.

"Staceigh. The twins? Last I saw you, you two were dating." The pinky finger of Zach's hand moves below the waistband of my shorts and I whip my head back to look at him, but he smiles.

"Shhhh," he whispers.

"Oh, yeah. I mean, we're not serious or anything," Jason says, then he asks me a question but I can't hear because Zach's hand is moving lower.

"Zach, my period," I whisper.

"I know. Let me take care of you, angel," he says, the words so quiet, only I can hear.

Maybe it's the way he uses that silly nickname based off a shitty pickup line.

Maybe it's Jason on the phone that has my mind scrambled.

Maybe it's the plea to *let him take care of me*, something I haven't had in forever.

Or maybe I'm just horny.

But either way, I nod.

His free hand moves, wrapping my throat, his mouth moving to my ear where he whispers, "Stay quiet."

"You know, Cams?" Jason says.

I don't answer.

I can't answer because Zach's callused finger is gently circling my clit and words don't work.

"Answer him," he whispers in my ear.

I clear my throat.

"Sorry, what?"

"I said, we should meet up soon. Get dinner. Talk about . . . us."

"Absolutely fucking not," Zach murmurs, pulling my earlobe into his mouth and biting while the hand on my throat moves my legs until they're each on the outside of his, spread wide.

"I think that's a . . ." I take a shaky breath as he presses harder on my clit, my mind short-circuiting for a moment. "A bad idea."

"Aww, come on. I miss you."

In another world, I think that would hurt, Jason missing me ten years after he callously broke me for fun then disappeared from my life.

But I can't find it in me to care right now.

Especially not when Zach's fingers pinch my clit, causing me to yelp in shock and pleasure and Zach to chuckle into my neck.

"Are you okay, Cami?" Jason asks. Zach's finger continues to circle my clit, his legs ensuring mine stay completely spread as his other hand moves under my shirt to my breasts. I have no bra on since I'm in pajamas, which gives him immediate access to my nipple.

Access he takes advantage of as he pinches and rolls it, my body involuntarily arching into his touch.

"Shit," I whisper.

"Mmm, are these sensitive, Cami?" His voice is a low growl in my ear and I nod because they are—my breasts are always sensitive and sore at the beginning of my period, something I usually gripe about.

But right now . . .

"Should I stop?"

"No, no, no," I reply, my hips moving to get more from his finger still circling my clit slowly.

"Cami, is everything okay?" I almost forgot Jason was there on the other line. Zach's fingers tighten on my other nipple, making it impossible to answer, but Zach does instead.

"Look, man. It's after hours. If you have a work question, call her office in the morning." Looking over my shoulder, I give him wide eyes but all I get in return is a heated gaze and fucking dimples.

"Who the fuck is that, Cami?" Jason asks, but just then, Zach rolls my clit harder, making a small moan come from me finally. I'm shocked I lasted this long, to be honest.

"Her man. Now, I've got plans with her. Do you have anything important to say, or are you just calling to catch up? Because telling you now, she wants nothing to do with you." My hand holding the phone shakes as he continues to play with me, continues to drag me higher with his fingers and his mouth and his *words*.

Something about the way he's speaking to Jason, the way he's claiming me as his heals something I didn't realize was broken still.

"This is absolutely ridiculous—"

"Suit yourself, man. Gonna make her come. You wanna listen, have at it," Zach says then tosses my phone across the couch into a pillow. I don't know if Jason can hear anything or if it's muffled or if he just hangs up, but I don't have the ability to care.

Because now Zach is working with a goal, rubbing my clit, his teeth scraping the sensitive spot beneath my ear, his fingers tightening on my nipple.

"You're so fucking beautiful, Camile. Always, but especially like this, writhing on my lap, at my mercy." I moan again and this time, it's not quiet or masked. "That's it, be loud for me, baby. Let everyone know who makes you feel this way."

"Fuck, Zach!" I shout, the crest coming faster than anticipated.

"Who owns your body, Cami?"

"You do."

"Whose are you?"

"I'm yours."

"Who takes care of you?" he asks, slowing his roll of my clit just as I hit the edge, gently taunting me.

"Oh god, fuck, Zach. You do! You do and I fucking love it. Please, god, let me come!" I'm shouting, pleading now, and his chuckle reverberates through me but then his fingers are back with a vengeance.

"Good girl. Now do as I say and come in my lap."

With his permission, I do.

I come hard, screaming his name, my voice breaking halfway through, leaving my mouth open, my head tipped back on his shoulder, his teeth nipping my neck and my ear as he eventually slows his fingers and lets me come down from the all-consuming high of being his.

"Was that necessary?" I ask when my mind begins to function once more. Zach moves then, removing his hand from my shorts and using both hands to turn me until I'm straddling him. I don't miss how he's hard beneath me.

"Yes. Absolutely yes. That was me telling him you're mine."

I should argue.

I should tell him that was unprofessional and childish, even though Jason clearly wasn't calling for anything work related.

There are a million things I should say, but I don't speak any of them.

Instead, I shake my head and let my lips tip a bit. "You're crazy, you know that?" I ask, my hand moving behind his neck.

"Crazy for you," he says, and it's cheesy and cliché and kind of lame, but it's not the words that have my heart stopping, have warmth filling me, and have me pressing my lips to his.

It's the look in his eyes telling me he 1000% feels that to his bones.

It should scare me, but like everything else when it comes to Zachary Anderson, I push past that and live in the now.

And the now is really, really good.

FORTY-ONE

CAMI

"When you plan weddings, do you think about yours one day?" Zack asks hours after the call with Jason as we lie in his bed, and my heart stutters.

Even in casual relationships, I hate this question.

This topic, generally.

"No."

"No?"

I'm reminded of what my mother told me when she got remarried years after my dad died. It was a marriage of convenience, a simple merging of corporations to strengthen her ties, a chance to support her nonprofit further. She likes Carlson, my current stepfather, well enough, but it was never about love.

Only a fool marries for love, Camile.

Love breaks you.

Love leaves you with bruises that never heal the same.

She told me that one night, reminding me how my father was her one true love and she'd never have that again, so why not form mutually advantageous pairings.

To this day, I can't help but wonder if maybe she wishes she never met my dad, never fell for him, never experienced that heart-break. Was it worth it, at the end of the day?

I used to pair the argument with my experience with Jason, convinced the answer was *absolutely* not. No amount of glorious love was worth the emotional baggage I left with, the tear which never healed smoothly, instead leaving a bumpy, calloused scar.

Damaged.

I didn't think anyone could convince me the potential damage that comes with letting someone in was worth the high.

Now I'm . . . conflicted, at best.

A long moment passes as I try and figure out how to respond, as I sift through all of my thoughts and emotions and ways to tackle this conversation.

Because while I might not hold my mother's dreary vision of marriage, my own is unconventional at best.

"You're not gonna scare me off, Cami," he whispers, his hand playing with the tips of my hair.

Something about that.

Something about the words and the promise has me speaking, throwing caution to the wind.

Or maybe it's the challenge, him telling me I can't scare him off. Maybe my subconscious just wants to test that statement, see how far we can push him before I'm *too much* for him. Before I'm not worth the headache.

It wouldn't be the first time.

"I don't want that," I whisper under my breath, tracing the line of his sternum and refusing to look anywhere but at my finger.

He knows what I'm doing, of course—distracting myself, trying to distance myself from the conversation at hand. But it's Zach, so he lets me sit in the silence of my words and treats me with all of the patience in the world.

"I don't want the white wedding and the big dress or the cake."

"So, you want something simple?" I shake my head again.

"I don't want any of it. I don't want the ceremony. I don't want the *wedding*."

"So . . ." He waits a beat before guessing.

I know he's going to get it wrong before he even speaks.

Most people do.

No one gets it.

"A courthouse thing?"

"I don't want to get married," I whisper, and it feels like a dirty confession. It's filling the room with noxious gas I'm afraid to breath in because if I do, it will ruin this precious, delicate thing I have with Zach.

God, I know he wants that.

Just fucking *look* at him.

He's perfect. He loves commitment, loves family. Of course he would want to get married one day when he finds the right person.

Shit, he probably wants another kid. I could see it, Zach cradling a little baby in his arms, doing late-night diaper chances. Unfortunately, this . . . this I will not bend on.

Never.

This could spell the end.

It was beautiful while it lasted.

"You don't want to get married," he says, the words blunt and heavy in the quiet room.

"No. I don't like the idea of it. It's silly. We don't live in a time when women are used as negotiation to strengthen alliances or get dowries. Generally speaking, we don't live in a reality where the wife stays and tends to the home, raising the children and doing all the cooking and cleaning, while the man goes out and supports the family. But we do live in a world where marriage is used to make it harder for a woman to leave. Where marriage means a woman takes the man's last name and he gets more of a say in things. Where if things aren't going well, you need the government to allow you to dissolve the relationship." I shake my head and sigh. "I don't trust it.

If I love someone, if we're so perfect together, why does it need to be put through some certification? What does that change?"

He's silent and I can't tell if it's a judging silence or the kind where he's waiting for me to fill in the gaps.

I go with the latter.

"It just seems unnecessary. If I love someone, I don't need a piece of paper or some wild party to let the world know. Love . . . I think love is sacred and quiet and beautiful. Sometimes it gets corrupted along the way, turned into something ugly in order to fit some kind of norm. I don't like that. And I don't want the white picket fence and the two point five kids, so I really don't see the purpose."

Might as well give him it all.

"And my dad passed away when I was ten. All I have left of him is his name. I wouldn't give that up for anyone. Life . . . it's unpredictable. I love my mom and think she's amazing but we suffered. Even if it wasn't financially because his life insurance saved us, we suffered. My mom lost the love of her life and I grew up with no father. I wouldn't want to put a child through that. So, you should know, I don't want that either. Kids."

The silence in the room is deafening and I wonder if he can hear the way my heart pounds.

I also refuse to think too much about why I care what Zach thinks, why I just know it will crush me when he says no, this won't work.

Or worse, when he tells me he'll change my mind.

He doesn't leave me in misery for too long, thankfully. "One of the biggest points of contention between Melanie and me was I didn't want to marry her. Her father—to her father it was a big deal. An unwed mother and all that. And to Melanie, it was a social status, being a wife and being a single mom at 20 was a death sentence in her world. Especially when the father was some poor local instead of some kind of heir." He gives a small huff, a laugh devoid of humor. "They offered me anything and everything. A house, a car. Money.

But all I wanted was Livi. And I wanted her to have my last name."
His fingers twist the tips of my hair again.

"I'll never know if they didn't think to threaten to take her from
me because they didn't see the value or if Jefferson thought it would
be too cruel. I like to think it's the second. But I stuck to my guns,
refused to marry Mel, and once Livi was born, she was mine. Mel
was sent to some retreat to lose the baby weight and would come to
the island for the summers. That first summer after she was born, I
was grateful I never made the mistake of marrying her. I saw the
misery it would have put us all through. I didn't want to be chained to
her. I still don't want it, not with anyone."

The panic that had settled in my gut starts to calm.

"You don't . . . You don't want to get married?"

"Don't see a reason why. I don't want more kids—Livi is enough
for me. And I agree. Marriage has become less important in the past
fifty years or so. I don't need the government to tell me if someone is
mine. That's none of their business."

"Oh," I whisper.

"I only asked because I figured . . . a job planning weddings. You
must love them." I lift my head, looking at him for the first time since
this conversation started, and smile.

"I actually hate parties," I say quietly and revel in the feeling of
his chest rumbling with a deep laugh.

"You hate parties?" I nod.

"I have ridiculous social anxiety. Can't stand small talk. I can do
it when I'm thinking of it as a business transaction or work or wherever. But if it's a party for me?" I cringe. "Nope."

"Noted. So anniversaries will be vacations, just the two of us,
deal? You in a bikini is much more enticing than you in a party
dress."

"Deal," I say, and then he kisses me and the remnants of my panic
dissipate.

I don't realize until the next morning it's just another test of mine
Zachary Anderson passed.

FORTY-TWO

FRIDAY, JULY 16

CAMI

"Good to see you two enduring each other," Zach says to me with a smile, his eyes drifting to where Olivia sits chatting with Cici. "And that those two are on good terms again."

The week following the Fourth of July party, I forced Olivia and Cici to have lunch together in my office. Neither was happy to be there, Olivia nervous nothing she said would convince Cici to give her another chance and Cici still hurt by what happened four years ago. But with me moderating the conversation, we were able to not only begin to mend their friendship, but get Cici on the side of our revenge plan.

The latter wasn't hard, to be fair, but the friendship mending is also not taking nearly as long as I feared. It seems what Cici really needed was for Olivia to explain and apologize genuinely. I wasn't around when they were friends so I can't confirm or deny, but I think they're almost back to normal, the friendship bouncing back quickly.

It reminds me of how Kat, Abbie, and I are—kind of like sisters who might fight and argue, but always love each other to death underneath it all.

"I'm just glad I was able to help," I say, taking a sip of my Aperol spritz. Zach tells me every time I come in they taste like ass and he hates making them, but he always has Prosecco for me and I've caught him taking sneaky sips more than a few times. He wipes down the bar before leaning in on his elbows.

"I know you did that. Not sure how, and I'm not sure how Livi got the Bitch Pack to leave her alone, but thank you." I wink at him then take another sip of my drink, watching the twins and their pack of rich girls walk out of the bathroom, Staceigh in the lead, then shifting my eyes to Olivia. She instantly winks at Cici, who nods and turns away from her as if nothing happened.

"They're good girls," I say.

"And them?" Zach asks, tipping his head subtly to where Staceigh is looking around like she fears if she touches a thing, she'll catch an incurable disease.

"I don't know what you're talking about," I say, using the cocktail straw to stir my drink.

"Doesn't seem like their type of place, but Livi walked in with them like it was a completely normal thing to do."

"I think they just wanted to check out the local spots, you know? Liv talks about you and the bar all the time, probably just... interested." He stares at me, so very much not buying it, but I just smile and shrug.

I definitely don't tell him Livi *may* have mentioned to them she sees Jason here pretty regularly and Staceigh will do anything to *bump into him.* Thankfully, he doesn't have any more time to cross-examine me as the twins walk up to the bar, a look of determination on Staceigh's face as she moves right next to me, leaning on the dark wood bartop.

That's the exact spot where, on Memorial Day, Zach lifted me while he kissed me, his hand sliding up my thigh before he asked me to come home with him.

When I look from that spot to Zach, I know he remembers the moment at the same time, the glint in his eyes making my belly warm.

The warmth cools when Staceigh speaks.

"So, Zach, what are you doing after this?" Her eyes are wide, eyelashes fluttering, and I'm embarrassed for her.

She's literally the age of his *daughter*, who is sitting three seats down, and is almost his daughter's *stepsister*. I can't tell if she really can't put together how weird that would be or if she's just playing her game and doesn't care.

At this rate, it could be either.

"Going home," he says bluntly, moving to the beer tap and pulling a glass for a customer, sliding it to him.

"Maybe we could hang out, you know? I've tried texting you a few times. It must not be going through though." She gives him a little pout and with her words, my eyes go wide and my jaw drops.

There's no fucking way.

"Probably because I'm ignoring them," Zach says, his eyes moving to me, and even though a real smile doesn't cross his lips, I watch a dimple pop up like he can't resist finding my face hilarious.

When I gave Staceigh Zach's number, there was no universe where I thought she would *actually* write it down and reach out to him. Because *why would she?*

My eyes move to Olivia and Cici, both who have similar looks of shock on their faces, though Cici's eyes keep moving to the front window like she's waiting for something.

"Well, that's not very nice," she says with a full pout and a whiney voice.

"I'm in a relationship and you are much too young for me, Staceigh. Flattered, but I hoped you would get the hint when I didn't reply."

The switch flips and she goes from sweet to annoyed in a heart-beat, cruelty leaking into her eyes like poison.

"What, so you'll take Cami's old ass, but you don't want this?" She tilts her body as if to show off and it's so sad to see, I can't fight the scoff of a laugh escaping my throat. "Fuck you, Cami. You know I'm hotter than you." I lift my hands in a placating gesture, so very much not wanting to get involved in her superiority complex. "You're just jealous."

"I told you, Staceigh. Shoot your shot. If he took you up on it, Zach was yours. I'm not interested in a man who isn't unbearably crazy about me."

"And I am," he says under his breath, just loud enough to reach my ears over the music, and I smile.

"God, I'm so turned on right now," I whisper to him, leaning into the bar and pretending the twins and the Bitch Pack aren't there.

"Yeah?" His dimples deepen as he smiles full out now.

"Yeah."

"I mean, if you want, I bet Frank could watch for a bit. I'll take you behind the bar—"

"Zachary Anderson!"

"Just saying, offer is *always* on the table," he says, and I roll my eyes.

I look to Cici again and raise an eyebrow, and she nods. My head moves toward the front windows where a tow truck is moving, Laceigh's car hooked to the back, waiting to merge onto the road.

"Oof, Lace, did you forget to pay your car payment?" I ask with a cringe. Heads turn my way and I give a sympathetic smile to her and her sister. "I know you had that issue with your black card, Stace."

"What are you taking about?" Staceigh says with a roll of her eyes. But already, her "friends" are following where I was looking, seeing her sister's car pulled away into the road.

"What!? Oh my god, someone is stealing my car!" Laceigh shouts, standing.

"Looks like you're getting towed, not robbed," Zach says, wiping his hands on a towel and staring at me with a knowing look. "Know anything about this?" he asks quieter. I shrug and smile.

"Is everything okay with you lately? Did your dad . . ." I pause for dramatic effect. "Cut you off?" The eyes of the Bitch Pack go wide, like it's the most embarrassing thing that could possibly happen, and Staceigh and Laceigh sputter.

"No! That would never happen!" Staceigh says then looks at her crew of judgmental friends who aren't quite buying another hit to her reputation. "That would *never* happen."

She's trying to reassure them, to maintain her spot at the top of the hierarchy, and for a very quick moment, I'm sympathetic. Imagine spending your entire life trying to prove your fake self to your fake friends and for what? Power? Prestige? It's not true friendship, that's for sure. She has more money than any one person could ever need, but she's still not happy.

But then I remember how she treats everyone around her and my momentary sympathy vanishes.

"I don't know. You should probably try to go talk to them before they're gone," I say, tipping my chin to the parking lot, watching as the truck makes a right and drives off into the night. "Oops."

"Shit, let's go," Staceigh says, the Bitch Pack following behind her begrudgingly as her sister runs in front, yelling, "My car! Stop stealing my car!" as if the tow truck driver will hear her. All eyes in the bar are on the girls as they leave.

As the door closes on them, I look to Cici and Olivia, both completely failing at any attempt not to laugh.

"What the fuck was that?" Zach asks, looking from me to Olivia to Cici, and all three of us smile but don't reply. "Livi?" She shrugs but doesn't speak. "Cici?"

"No idea, Mr. Anderson." His eyes move to mine.

"Cam? I know for a fact there is no way that girl's car was just repossessed." I roll my lips and fail at fighting a laugh.

"I mean . . . it could just be that she parked in the handicap spot and . . . I don't know. Maybe someone dropped an anonymous tip and it was towed away. Maybe. Possibly. But I don't know." Cici and Olivia instantly start laughing and I smile as I watch Zach tip his head to the sky and shake it while sighing.

"And you didn't tell them because . . ." My head cocks back with a look of confusion.

"Like they told me it wasn't a themed party?" Zach gives me a *touché* look.

"Wait," Zach says, looking to his daughter. "Livi, didn't you come in Laceigh's car? You didn't warn her?" Olivia rolls her lips and then Cici, Olivia, and I all burst out in laughter as Zach figures it out, shaking his head like he doesn't know what to do with us.

Another off the list, I think.

FORTY-THREE

CAMI

Monday August 21

Are you a magician?

I do love a good surprise.

Because when I'm looking at you, you make everyone else disappear.

I like that one.

My place tonight?

Yes please.

See you soon, angel.

Tuesday August 22

If you were a fruit, you'd be a "fine-apple."

It's too early for this shit, Zachary.

Morning, angel.

Morning, Daddy.

I thought we agreed you'd stop with the Daddy?

Dinner later, dimples?

Wednesday August 23

Morning, beautiful.

Are you bringing me caffeine?

How'd you know?

The only time I don't get a dad joke is when I get coffee.

Waiting downstairs already.

I don't get coffee from Zach every single morning, mostly because he tried it and I yelled at him.

"*There's no need to wake up early after every late night just to bring me coffee, Zachary,*" *I said, my hands on his chest one morning when he looked extra tired.*

"*I like to. I like seeing your face in the morning. And the way you smile when you see me.*" *I rolled my eyes and shook my head.*

"*How about coffee is restricted to mornings you don't wake up with me?" He didn't answer for a moment. "Please? You're old. I need you well rested if you're going to keep me up all night."*

That was all he needed.

"Fine."

And since last night I had a late event, and we slept in our own beds, he's leaning against the marble column with that paper cup, holding my coffee exactly how I like it.

It's not until after he kisses me winded and smacks my ass as I walk off, not until I'm alone in the elevator, that I check under the paper sleeve of the cup, looking for his thick, dark handwriting.

`Even in zero gravity, I would still fall for you.`

Thursday, August 24

> Is your name Google?

> I think we both know by now it's not. Can you imagine moaning that in my ear?

The thought makes me snort out a laugh while I wait for his response.

> Because you're everything I've been searching for.

Butterflies erupt in my belly.

> Your place tonight?

> Come to the Fishery first and I'll feed you.

> See you then.

Friday, August 25

Are you an electrician?

Good morning, dimples.

Because you're definitely lighting up my night.

Speaking of night

I've got a late event tonight and one in the morning.

You owe me double on Saturday, then.

Double?

Orgasms. I expect twice as many to make up for it.

Deal.

FORTY-FOUR

SATURDAY, SEPTEMBER 2

CAMI

> Good luck today. I know you'll kill it.

>> What, no dad joke? If there was ever a day I needed some levity, I think it would be today.

> Got time for coffee?

>> From you? Always.

> I'm outside.

"Is everything okay in here?" I ask, holding my clipboard and cup of coffee Zach brought me as I walk into the bridal suite. Bridesmaids in a rainbow of pastel colors stand around, hair and makeup perfect.

"You cannot wear that, Staceigh. I absolutely forbid it," Melanie says as she stands in front of Staceigh, her hair in curlers still, wearing a robe with her arms crossed on her chest. Both have firm jaws and angry faces and it's interesting to experience. Like some kind of battle of the Barbies.

"What the *fuck* am I supposed to wear then, Melanie?" Seems the artificial sweetness has melted.

"I don't give a shit, but you can't wear that. It's three sizes too big and looks horrific. It's bright fucking orange. The theme is *pastel*, not neon. What were you *thinking*?"

I know exactly what Staceigh was thinking.

I know because Olivia gave her the idea just a week ago.

"What about the day of the wedding?" Livi asked as we sat in my office eating Chinese out of the containers.

"We've got the slideshow. Isn't that enough?"

"I mean, there's no reason not to try and do more, don't you think?" Her smile was nearly evil.

"What are you thinking?"

"Bridesmaid dress?"

Melanie assigned each of her ten bridesmaids a different pastel color and allowed them to pick from three different styles of dresses in order to make sure each of them looked their best on her big day. To be honest, I was kind of shocked she did such a thoughtful thing, but Melanie also told us she needed everyone to look their best in her wedding photos so as not to detract from her.

So not completely selfless.

"Aren't they already picked out and tailored and everything?"

"Cam, you forget how if you have enough money, you can do just about anything."

With that, Olivia planted the seed in Staceigh's mind a neon version of her assigned pastel orange would look better on her and also make her stand out from the other bridesmaids and, of course, Staceigh fell for it.

And, wouldn't you know it, when she went to the seamstress who works with the Beach Club, her dress and mine for the event got mixed up, and her measurements were used on my dress and mine on hers.

Oops.

"What seems to be the issue?" I ask as I walk in, still wearing my casual pre-event outfit of leggings and a loose tank top.

"Fucking Staceigh is messing up my entire vision," Melanie says with a pout.

It's so incredibly unsettling to witness a grown woman acting like a toddler.

"I'm not fucking anything up. It was the seamstress!"

"The *seamstress* didn't pick this hideous color!"

"Okay, okay. Is it just the color? Or . . ."

"It's way too big."

"I can pin it," Staceigh offers.

"Absolutely not. You just won't be in the wedding."

"But—"

"Actually, I might have a solution," I say. "The dress I was planning to wear today was being tailored as well and looking at that dress, I'm wondering if they didn't swap our sizes."

Staceigh sends daggers my way but I ignore it and give Melanie a kind smile.

"I was going to have to go back to my place and grab something different, but maybe it will work for Staceigh? It fits with the color scheme."

"Absolutely not—"

"I trust your opinion, Cami," Melanie says. "If it fits her, she can walk in the wedding."

"Perfect, I'll go grab it."

"Oh, and Cami, might as well wear Staceigh's if it fits you." The bridezilla has melted off her face as she sits back in the makeup chair and sips her champagne. "Might as well get use out of it."

I smile as I nod and head toward where I tucked the dress away, but not before I give a subtle wink to Livi's thumbs-up.

As I step into the elevator, finally alone for the first time all morning, I slide down the paper sleeve and stare at the note Zach left.

I still haven't figured out if he's aware I've ever seen a single one of them, but each time I look forward to seeing what sweet nothing he's left me.

Today's makes my heart skip a beat.

Is summer over? Because I'm ready to fall for you.

FORTY-FIVE

CAMI

"Cami." As I walk toward where the ceremony is being held, I turn, surprised to see Zach in a white shirt and black slacks walking my way.

"Hey, you," I say with a smile. "I didn't know you would be here."

"Melanie invited me and I think Livi wanted me here as extra support. It's going to be a long day for her, her mother, and the twins and . . . well, everything." He pauses, his eyes roaming my body as he does. "Fuck, you look gorgeous."

The dress fits perfectly, just like I knew it would. With a knee-length hem and a bodycon style, the thick tank top straps and the flattering V in the front accentuating my curves without being indecent, the bright orange color plays off my skin perfectly. Paired with hot pink and orange heels, the outfit is everything I hoped it would be.

Staceigh can't say the same about the beige dress with the tea-length hemline, high neck, and capped sleeves. Its unfitted shape was the cherry on top of the hideous dress and she threatened to not walk before Melanie threatened to tell her father.

"Thank you. There was a dress mishap so I . . . had to swap with one of the bridesmaids. It was mostly good luck, ya know?"

"Good luck . . . ," he says his eyes narrowing on me. When he speaks, he's staring at me like he's trying to read me and panic fills me.

No one can read me like Zach can, and in this moment, that's not a good thing.

Thankfully, my cell rings, Melanie's number on the screen.

"Love seeing you here, but I gotta run. It's game time, ya know?" I reach up on my toes, pressing my lips to his gently before stepping away. "I'll see you after the ceremony. We can make out in a storage closet or something," I say with a wink.

"Hey." Before I can walk off, Zach's fingers grabbing my wrist. "One sec, yeah?" I nod, confused and panicking, a million reasons for his quite tone and concerned face running through my mind.

"What's up?" I ask, hitting the silence button on my phone, and he pulls me into a corner.

"What are you two planning?"

The anxiety and guilt swirl in my stomach, making me nauseous.

"What are you talking about?"

"Too many whispers with you two, too many looks. What are you guys planning?"

"A wedding, obviously," I say, trying to brush him off.

He doesn't buy it.

I absolutely *hate* how much he's grown to know and understand me.

Why do people want a partner who understands them?

It's fucking overrated, if you ask me.

"Camile."

I don't reply because in all reality, this has nothing to do with him.

This is for Livi.

He sighs.

"I don't know what you two are planning, but please, Cam. Be reasonable. Livi needs her trust, and if this wedding doesn't go perfectly, she won't be getting it." I should just say yes, lie, anything to get away from his piercing gaze.

But I don't, of course.

"She doesn't need that trust, Zach. She's brilliant at what she does and she'll succeed no matter what." His jaw goes tight with my words.

"So you are doing something, aren't you?" Again, I don't reply. "God, Cami. Are you kidding me?"

"It's not a big deal, Zach. Livi is just . . . She needs to do this. She doesn't want her trust if it means her mother constantly has it to hold over her head. She's tired of catering to all of them at the expense of herself."

"Jesus, Cami. Can you at least admit life would be easier if she had that money? She wants to build a business."

"At what cost?" I ask quietly.

"What?"

"At what cost? What will unlocking that trust early cost her?" He opens his mouth but doesn't speak. "It will cost her dignity, for one. And her morals. And probably friendships. God, it's already cost her that, hasn't it? Getting that trust comes with ties, Zach. I know you keep telling her it's important, and I get it. I do. Life is just *easier* with money. But getting it means her mother gets a hand in that business. She's finally out from under the carrot of Melanie paying her tuition if she behaves the way she wants. She's done with it. It's toxic."

Now, it's Zach who doesn't respond.

"She needs to do this for her," I say, pleading in my voice, begging for him to understand.

"She's putting her future at risk. She needs to just deal with her mother."

"How has that worked out for her so far, Zach? Twenty-three years of *dealing* with Melanie and what has that gotten her besides stress and anxiety? She has no friends, not really. She started this summer with *zero* confidence, and I've watched that grow. That? That's what she gets if she does whatever she wants and stops catering to Melanie and the twins." I shake my head, stepping back so his hand isn't on me anymore.

What's the point? Why torture myself with how good his skin feels on mine when this is all about to go up in flames?

Nothing good lasts long, after all. Not once people get a glimpse of who I really am.

"What did catering to Melanie get you, Zach? 18 years of arguing over what was best for a kid Melanie barely even knew? Stress and anxiety?"

"It got me Livi."

"And now Livi is an adult who can make her own decisions. Let her."

He opens his mouth but doesn't have time to answer as someone comes over.

"There you are, Cami. We need your help with the florals," they say, and I nod before turning back to Zach.

"I have to go. I'm sorry."

He doesn't respond again, his jaw tight, and I really never thought this decision would hurt. It feels like I'm choosing revenge over a man I could very well fall for, if I haven't fallen already.

But I'm not choosing revenge, not really.

I'm choosing Livi.

My *friend.*

Last time, I chose revenge, letting it threaten a ten-year friendship. I was willing to sacrifice everything to get what I thought we *needed* to reap.

This time. I'm fighting for my friend. And that makes all the difference. This time, I'm choosing to help Livi find the confidence and freedom she needs, and you know what?

If Zach doesn't understand that, if he can't handle that part of me, then he's not the one for me.

Even if each step I take away from him breaks a small part of me.

FORTY-SIX

CAMI

It doesn't happen until late in the night. That's by design, after all. No need to make the twins the center of Melanie's wedding.

It's long after the early sparkler send-off which happened barely an hour into the reception because Huxley had to get on a red-eye back to California for work, long after most of Mr. and Mrs. St. George's friends and colleagues have left when I give the sign to start the show.

The only people who are left, really, are the friends Staceigh and Laceigh invited to enjoy the expensive spectacle so they could show off. The Bitch Pack that's been here most of the summer plus friends from school and California.

All doting on the twins like they are some kind of deities instead of just unbearably spoiled brats.

It's when Staceigh steps up to the podium with a microphone and a fake smile of subdued kindness on her face that the final plan goes into action.

Weeks ago, I asked the twins and Olivia if they waned to do some kind of speech at the wedding to commemorate their parents. Olivia instantly declined, stating she'd rather say a few words during the rehearsal, which she did and it was lovely.

When Staceigh heard that, though, of course, she couldn't resist the opportunity to have the spotlight.

"I want to give a speech. With a presentation," she had said, her eyes sparkling with opportunity. *"A slideshow of all the fun things I did this summer."* I had furrowed my brow in confusion, not quite understanding.

"A slideshow about . . . you?"

"Well, yeah. I, of course, am my father's greatest accomplishment." I stared at her thinking surely, there had to be some kind of punchline I didn't understand.

There had to be, right?

But she just stared at me like I was stupid.

"I mean . . ." I looked from her to her sister to Olivia then to Melanie, who was scrolling her phone like she couldn't be bothered. *"We only have an hour between the bridal party walking into the reception and the sparkler send off so Huxley can get onto his jet in time. I don't know how we could fit a slideshow in . . ."*

"Oh, he doesn't have to be there. It can be later."

I sat there with my mouth open for a beat before Melanie looked up from her phone and waved at the twins. *"I don't care, that's fine. Ten. Everyone will be gone by then anyway,"* she said, and fire burned in Staceigh's eyes.

I just *know* the two of them are going to butt heads once Melanie is *actually* in the family.

Initially, I thought her "speech" was going to be a train wreck and mess up the entire vibe of my carefully curated event. But later, Olivia and I realized what a gift this truly would be, slowly collecting everything we'd need to put the twins in their place once and for all.

"I'm so excited to be here with all of you today," Staceigh says with a serene smile. She changed her dress as soon as the ceremony was over, much to Melanie's chagrin, and is now wearing a sparkly silver mini dress. It's clear she sees this wedding less as an event for her father and stepmother, and more of a social event for *herself*. "Thank you all for coming. As many of you know, I've been gracing the Beach Club for four summers now."

I snort out a laugh and I don't miss a few staff members who do the same. When my eyes meet Olivia's, they're wide and as shocked as mine.

God, the woman genuinely has no concept of *anything*.

But, of course, Laceigh in the front row claps for her sister like she won a goddamn Nobel Peace Prize.

Music starts as Staceigh steps aside, her slideshow starting, and honestly, it's *embarrassing* to watch. Her smile is serene like she's waiting for the oohs and ahhs, for the world to confirm once again just how wonderful she is.

The first photos are of her outside the Beach Club doing classic sorority girl poses, then they trickle into others—her in the cabanas, her at the beach. Literally a dozen photos of Staceigh doing... nothing.

Not a photo of her father or of Melanie. There's not even an image of her twin sister, as if she feared it would take the spot light off her too much.

She's watching the room, too excited to see her minions praise her to keep an eye on the screen when it happens. I'm in the corner watching everything—the crowd, the screen, Staceigh, the Bitch Pack —so I see when it moves from another picture of her posing on a lounge chair to a screenshot of text messages.

Of her calling her closest minion, Violet, an idiotic bitch who is too dumb to function.

The next slide is her telling Laceigh and Olivia Jason really needs to contact her father's doctor and get hair plugs because he *looks so ugly, it's embarrassing*.

Murmurs start on the third where she's bragging about sleeping with a man who is engaged to another Bitch Pack member, but it's not until the next photo where she circled all of the places on a woman's body which, in her words, "needed work," that she finally turns and sees what's on the screen.

Dozens of messages highlighting what a horrible person Staceigh St. George is.

The idea came about when Olivia groaned about another message sent into the group chat between her, Staceigh, and Laceigh. It was a new idea for how to make *my* life miserable, but we quickly learned with a little pushing from Olivia, Staceigh would happily dump all of her thoughts about anyone in her inner circle. Confessions and secrets and mean, horrible thoughts about people who think she's a genuine friend.

We catalogued each one, not sure what to do with them at the time, but as soon as Staceigh said she wanted a slideshow speech, the idea bloomed in Olivia's mind.

She might be more revenge-driven than even I am, and that's impressive.

And now, the group of everyone Staceigh has worked so hard to convince to put her on a pedestal is getting a front-row seat to just how rotten she is, inside and out.

"What!? What is this?" she shouts, standing in front of the screen and holding her arms up like it will hide anything.

It was her, after all, who insisted on the largest screen the Beach Club could get its hands on.

My eyes shift to Olivia on the other side of the room, the same stealth smile on her lips.

"Someone stop it!" Staceigh shouts, but no one moves.

The issue with being a bitch to every single employee and staff member is no one wants to jump in to save you when your reputation is falling apart.

The quiet whispers have turned into angry words, fingers are pointing, phones are recording the meltdown of Staceigh St. George, and honestly?

It's better than anticipated.

When I look back to where Olivia was, she's giving Cici a fist bump and I wonder if this is healing for them, for their friendship, to see the woman who tore them apart torn down herself.

"You!" Staceigh shouts, pointing to me. "You! Turn this OFF!"

"I don't understand. You said you wanted to show off your father's greatest accomplishment—you?" A few snickers happen in the crowd of the twins' friends.

"Not like *this!*"

"Oh, alright, let me see if I can find the right person," I say, slowly pulling out my phone and pretending to scroll.

"Ugh!" She shouts, "Laceigh, *do something!*" Her sister stands up, stumbling as she tries to get to her feet.

"What should I do?!" poor Laceigh says, not used to being asked to do something without explicit instructions.

"Jesus Christ, I'll do it myself!" Then, she stomps over to the laptop, lifting it and smashing it to the ground. The screen goes dark and I point to the DJ, giving him the thumbs-up.

"Alright, ladies, that was an . . . interesting presentation. Let's get back to dancing!" The music starts again, and Staceigh runs from the room, her sister trailing close behind.

Mission accomplished.

FORTY-SEVEN

CAMI

"You *fucking bitch!*" The words ring in the humid air as Olivia and I stand just outside the exit of the Beach Club later that night, making sure guests grab their party favors and anyone who needs it gets a town car home.

"Stace, I don't know—"

"I don't give a *fuck* what you know, Laceigh. You don't know anything, you're so fucking stupid," Staceigh says, her face full of fury as she approaches us. "You two *ruined my life.*"

"I have no idea what you're talking about," Livi says, a smile on her lips.

"The fuck you don't. That slideshow? What *was* that, Olivia?!"

"It was a mistake. Oops," Livi says, her voice completely devoid of any guilt.

"Why did you *do that*?! Now everyone hates me! And it's your fault! I can't believe this." I can't fight my laugh, the humor of Staceigh fully blaming Livi for the messages *she sent* trash-talking everyone in her inner circle delighting me. "And then no one would *turn it off!*"

Or how it was somehow her fault when not a single staff member was willing to turn off the slideshow because through the *entire summer,* the Bitch Pack has repeatedly treated them all like trash.

The fact she can't even get *close* to taking accountability for her actions says *everything.*

"You're never getting that precious trust of yours, Olivia. No fucking way. I know your mom said if this wedding went well, then you would get it. Well, looks like you're fucked, aren't you?" There's cruelty on her face I've never seen but always knew laid not far under her false smiles and pounds of makeup. "And *you!* You're next, you know that, right?" she says, turning her venom to me. "This wedding was a fucking *flop* and it's all your fault. You'll never work on the entire freaking East Coast *again.*"

I think about that. I think, in theory, she could have that power if we hadn't just ruined her reputation. But even if that wasn't the case, if she could make it so I never get another event planning contract, I would be okay with it.

Some things are worth it, I'm learning. Friendship and relationships and the people around me? They are worth it.

"You know what they say, Stace. You play stupid games, you win stupid prizes, and you've made it your mission to play games with other people's lives," Livi says. "Eventually that shit comes back to bite you in the ass."

"I have no idea what you're talking about." I shake my head at her then decide it's my turn to speak.

"The second I came here, you decided you hated me because what? My ex wasn't into you? Jesus, get a grip. You're a disgusting human, Staceigh. It's obvious to *everyone.* You use people, talk shit about them, and then expect them to kiss your feet, but what the *fuck* do you bring to the table?"

"My father—"

"*Your father isn't you.* You need to understand that."

"You *ruined my life.*"

"We did no such thing, Staceigh," Olivia says. "You willingly put all that shit into a group chat, laughing about people's insecurities because it makes you feel better about your own. If you didn't want people to see how nasty you are, maybe just don't be *nasty*. Maybe if you want people on your side, don't treat them like trash. No one turned it off because you treat everyone who works here like they *owe you something*."

"They're *employees*."

"And?"

"They *work for me*."

"No. That's where you're wrong. You think because you have money and your daddy has some power that you, what? You deserve everyone to bow down to you? Newsflash, Staceigh, most people at this place have money and some kind of tie to power. You are not special. But not everyone decides to treat everyone around them like trash."

"Fuck you, Cami."

"Just because she's telling you something you don't want to hear doesn't mean you get to be nasty to her, Staceigh," Livi says, and warmth fills me at her sticking up for me.

"You're just as much trash as she is, Olivia. You're a nobody."

"I'm fine with that. I don't need everyone to kiss my ass like you do. But sorry to tell you, babe, you are *also* a nobody now." Olivia looks around like she's trying to find something or someone. "Where is your posse, Stace? Gone. You treated them like trash and not even your daddy's money could keep them around." Staceigh's face gets redder and redder before her head tips to the dark sky, a growl of anger leaving her.

"God, I could just . . . I could just *hit* you right now," she says, fury in her eyes directed at Olivia.

"Do it," Livi says, putting her hand out to her sides.

"What?"

"I said *do it*. What do I care?" She takes a step closer to her new stepsister and I fight a laugh as Staceigh steps backward.

"Your mom isn't going to give you your trust early after all of this shit."

"You already told me. I don't care. Fine," Olivia says, and pride flushes through me.

Is it weird to feel so proud when Olivia is potentially making her entire life unbearably difficult?

"Fine?" Laceigh asks, her face screwed in confusion.

"I'll get it eventually, just not right now. In the meantime, I'll work my ass off to build my business. And I'll be proud as it grows on my own merit. You wouldn't know what that's like since you've never worked a millisecond in your life."

"You're such a fucking waste, Olivia. You could have really been something." She says it like it's an insult, but I can see it now—it's a compliment to Olivia.

"I don't want to be *something* if it puts me in the same category as you. Women like you make me sick. You're catty bitches who judge others while having no concept of what the real world is like. Mean women who will destroy others to get what they want. It's embarrassing, actually, Staceigh."

"Like your mother?" she says with a smile, and it's clear she wanted her words to hit, to hurt Liv. "Isn't that what she does? Boss people around, climb the social ladder, care only about herself?"

"Sure. Like my mother. My mother who watched your entire slideshow, had the ability to stop it, I'm sure, and let it go. You think you've won my mother over? Try again. You can't *win over* Melanie. She's just like you, out for herself."

"I'm going to hit you," she says, clearly annoyed her words aren't making the impact she wants them to, and the way she steps forward, ready to strike, makes me laugh.

This woman clearly has never done anything physical other than fancy gym classes and Pilates in her life, much less get into a fight.

"I fucking dare you," Olivia says.

And then it happens.

I watch as Staceigh of the French manicures and zero-calorie drinks moves her hand back and slaps Olivia across the face.

"God, I was hoping you'd do that," she says under her breath, then she moves to hit Staceigh back, gripping her hand in her hair and tugging her to the ground.

I watch as they topple over, a scream ripping from Staceigh and a literal *giggle* coming from Olivia, like she's living for this moment.

"You fucking *cunt*!"

"Takes one to know one, Stacy," Olivia says as she sits on Staceigh's chest and slaps her across her face.

"Ahh!" Staceigh yells, her hands moving to try and cover her nose. When her sister screams, Laceigh moves slowly my way, like she thinks she's going to fight *me*.

I smile and shake my head, lifting one hand in a "stop" sign.

"Uh, uh, uh, Laceigh. You wait your turn. I'm sure Olivia will have enough energy for you next."

She, unfortunately, doesn't get the chance to argue, though.

Because when she opens her mouth, a police siren blares, red and blue lights flashing against the marble columns of the Beach Club, and all four of us freeze.

Except for Staceigh who yells, "Arrest her! She attacked me!"

Well, fuck.

Less than thirty minutes later, the brawlers are placed into separate police cars to be driven to the station. I should be horrified, but when I take in the happy smile on Olivia's face and the small trickle of blood on Staceigh's lip, a very strange big-sister-type pride starts to fill me.

But that doesn't last long when Zach comes up behind me. I'm not sure where he came from or where he was during the fight, but now he's . . . here, watching his daughter get driven away in a police car.

Fuck.

For a moment, I forgot about him. Forgot Livi was his daughter and he had asked to me keep an eye on her. I forgot how he told me he was nervous she would lose her trust, how he asked me to keep her shit under wraps so this exact situation wouldn't happen.

At the same moment, Jefferson Kincaid is looking my way, Melanie Kincaid, now St. George, standing next to him in her white dress, arms crossed on her chest and murmuring something to him.

There it is.

I think I just watched it in real time. Olivia just officially lost her trust.

"What the fuck just happened?" Zach asks, fury in his words.

And I just lost Zach.

FORTY-EIGHT

ZACH

The drive to the police station is quiet, Cami in her orange dress, not a hair out of place as she stares out the window of her car. She insisted she come when I asked to take her car to go get Olivia, and I wasn't going to argue.

She's lost in her thoughts and so am I, so there's no point in filling the car with small talk.

Plus, what am I going to say?

Great job on my ex's wedding?

That slideshow tearing down the Bitch Pack was kind of funny, but you probably fucked yourself over with it?

Why didn't you stop Olivia from slamming her fist into her new stepsister's face?

Or maybe we could joke about the fact Melanie's husband left before all of the chaos erupted and whether or not the twins will ever admit what happened to their father.

We walk into the station together, Cami crossing her arms on her chest as soon as she exits the car so holding her hand and walking in together isn't even an option.

God, what a fucking *mess*.

"Can I help you?" the woman at the reception asks.

"I'm here for Olivia Anderson?"

"Ah, the brawler. Yeah, eyewitness reports say she wasn't the instigator so she can be released, but she will be called into court. Are you putting the bail up?" she asks, and I sigh, nodding.

"No, I am," Cami says, and I look to her, ready to argue, but it's there again.

That fucking wall.

That wall I spent *months* tearing down.

There's also clear evidence she's ready for a fight if I try and argue with her.

"Cami," I say, letting her name hang between us.

"I've got it." She digs in her bag and pulls out her wallet before looking at the receptionist. "Where can I go to get cash?" She points her in the direction of the proper window and Cami walks off.

"I'll call it in so we can get her out of here, okay?" I nod and she lifts a phone, making a call to another desk to send the message to release my daughter.

From jail.

For a fistfight.

Jesus, what is my life right now?

Ten minutes later, heels click on the tile floor frantically.

In walks Laceigh St. George, her dress a mess, her hair all over the place, and mascara running down her cheeks.

"Where is my sister!" she shouts at the receptionist.

"Excuse me?"

"My sister! You have her!" The receptionist looks from Laceigh to me and I raise my hands in a *not touching that one* kind of way before she sighs and turns toward the twin. Just then, Cami walks out, her own heels clicking rhythmically on the floor as she tucks her wallet into her little bag.

"Ma'am, I'm going to need you to calm down."

"I can't calm down. I need my sister!" For a moment, I wonder if she knows how to function outside of her twin. From what Cami and Olivia have told me, I don't think so.

"Who is your sister?"

"Staceigh Annette St. George. S-T-A-C-E-I-G-H!" The receptionist takes a deep breath before nodding.

"Okay, I understand. Your sister initiated a fight. Unfortunately, we can't just *let her out*. Do you have cash to meet bail?"

"I don't have *anything!* I came right here! Who even uses cash anymore!?" The receptionist's brows furrow as she looks at the frazzled blonde.

"Ma'am, do you have your wallet? An ID?"

"I just *told* you! I drove right here! I didn't bring anything."

"Are you telling me you drove here with no license?" God, this girl isn't the brightest bulb, to walk into a police station and tell them she drove here with no license. She probably also had a few drinks while she was at the wedding too. Just then, an officer walks out with Olivia in tow.

"I don't need an ID! Don't you know who I am?" Cami sighs and when I look at her, despite her sour mood, I can see her fighting a smile.

"Sorry, ma'am. I don't."

"I'm *Laceigh! L-A-C-E-I-G-H!*" The officer steps forward and Olivia walks to us

"How can I help you today, Miss Laceigh?"

"I need you to let my sister go!"

"Has she posted bail?"

"Where would she post it?! Instagram? Snapchat?" She lifts her hand, holding a phone. "She can't! I have her phone!" This time, both the officer and the receptionist can't fight a laugh, which makes Laceigh's face go red with frustration. "My daddy is *not* going to like this."

"Yeah, well, when your daddy is ready, he can call me. No offense, princess, but I'm not too worried about your father. Your sister assaulted a woman with multiple witnesses," the officer says.

"Olivia started it!"

"Multiple sources confirm your sister hit her first and Ms. Anderson was fighting in self-defense."

"But Staceigh was defenseless! She's just a girl!"

I watch the officer blink a few times before she nods, clearly at a loss for words.

"I demand to speak to your manager!"

God, it just keeps getting worse.

But also, it's late, it's been a disastrously long night, and I need to get my girls home.

"Come on," I say, looking at my daughter who is clearly ruffled from a fight. "Let's get home."

"You can't let her leave and not let Staceigh!" Laceigh yells. "She *attacked my sister!*"

"You and your sister can press charges, but reports at the scene say your sister threw the first punch."

"It was less of a punch and more of a bitch slap," Olivia murmurs under her breath, and my hand on her shoulder tightens in a *don't press your fucking luck* way.

"So?"

"So Ms. Anderson was responding in self-defense."

"Are you *kidding me?* Did you see what she did to Staceigh? She was the one who needed to defend herself!"

"Not by law," the officer says, and the confusion flickering in Laceigh's face is humorous.

"My dad always told me never to start a fight, just end it," Olivia says with a smug smile.

Part of me wants to smack her upside her head and remind her where the fuck she is and how she's 100% testing her luck. But also, part of me wants to give her a high five, the same way I did when she got suspended in first grade for kicking a little boy who made fun of her and touched her ponytail.

I took her to ice cream that time.

I don't think ice cream is in the cards tonight unfortunately.

At least, not right away.

"Let's get out of here before you get into more trouble," I say, directing my daughter out of the room, Cami following behind silently.

And it's not the rich twin yelling, "I'm going to sue!" at my daughter twisting my stomach in knots.

It's Cami's silence.

FORTY-NINE

CAMI

I'm in Zach's room when his voice comes from behind me.

He dropped Olivia off at the Beach Club, where I'm hoping she runs straight to her room and locks the door in order to avoid any more issues, then drove us to his place. Part of me wishes I could have gotten out at the Beach Club, too, but I know that's not how this is going to work.

"What are you doing?" he asks, and when I look over my shoulder, he's standing there in the doorway, an adorably confused look on his face that actually hurts my soul.

God, I hate this.

I *never* should have listened to Abbie and Kat.

Sure, I made friends—I was able to really *get* Livi and help her find her way, I hope, and I was able to repair her friendship with Cici, but look where it lead me.

Inevitable heartache.

It's my own fault, of course, my own stubborn love of revenge and my desire to help Livi pull off the payback of the century, but along the way, I fell for Zach.

I fell without warning and I fell hard and now I'm trying to avoid the dramatic goodbye, to grab my few things I left here and leave.

Do I take the pillowcases and bonnets?

Or maybe . . . maybe I leave them for the next girl, so he doesn't have to go through the process again. That twists the knife a bit, the thought of a next girl.

I hope she's better than me. Kinder, smarter. I hope she makes Zach happy and does everything in her power to hold on tight to him. He deserves that.

I already hate her.

God, I'm fucked up, aren't I?

"What are you doing?" he asks, and the lump in my throat I've been dutifully ignoring starts to throb and ache with unshed emotion.

"Getting my things together," I say, reaching for a shirt I left here a few weeks ago, a shirt he washed and folded and put into a drawer neither of us have gone through the process of acknowledging. The drawer which, at some point over the summer, became "my drawer."

I expect him to step in front of me, to give me a gentle letdown, the easy, kind ending to our relationship.

It's his style, after all, cotton candy sweetness and kid gloves that made me fall hard.

He doesn't though.

As also seems to be his way, he knows what I need or maybe just what I'd prefer.

Room. Space. Distance.

I definitely *don't* want his touch. I don't want one last reminder of what I'm losing out on—of how I walked into this expecting a summer fling and zero strings and I'll leave with my first broken heart in ten years.

Even if I'm the one who broke my own heart this time.

"Why are you doing that?"

It was worth it, though, breaking my heart. Worth it if it meant Livi got to win at the end of the day, if I got to, somehow, against all odds, forge a friendship with her. If I got to help her find her feet, find a bit of who she is.

"So you don't have to deal with it later," I say, then my hand brushes the silky bonnets he picked out for me. "Do you mind if I take these? I can leave them. I just . . ." My mind trails off once again to the idea of someone else using what he bought for me.

"You're not taking those anywhere."

God.

God, god, god.

I should have known he would do the knight in shining armor thing.

"I really, really don't want to do this, Zach. Please. Let me get my stuff and go. If you need me to, I can drive you to the Fishery, to your bike since we took my car here."

"Unnecessary." A mix of relief I won't have to prolong this and panic that I *won't be prolonging this* fills me. "Unnecessary because you aren't going anywhere." I sigh and close my eyes, hands still in the drawers, before he moves farther into the room.

Abbie once told me about this.

How Damien is silent most of the time, but she can *feel him* when he's near. Like a tingle of her skin and she knows to open her eyes, to look around because he'll be there.

I thought she was fucking insane, but I get it now. The side of my body closest to Zach prickles with recognition, like even the hairs on my arms want to get nearer to him.

"Please don't do this, Zach."

He stops a few feet from me, leaning on a wall this time, arms crossed on his chest.

"Why? Why are you grabbing your shit?" I sigh and look at the ceiling, wishing three months ago, I hadn't taken Abbie and Kat's advice to be more open.

Wishing I'd stayed closed off and put my head down and worked.

I wouldn't be dealing with this if I had.

"I fucked up. I abused your trust. You asked me to do one thing, to help keep Livi safe, to get her through this event without her getting into trouble. I didn't. And I did it intentionally. I'm leaving to give you space. It's not fair for me to be here while you process that, muddling your thoughts."

"The very last thing I need is space, especially when it's from you."

"What?" The word is half panicked and half exasperated.

He takes a step closer, still not touching me but barely a foot from me now.

"You stuck up for my girl. You might not have done it the way I wanted you to, Cami, but you went down swinging for her. Do you think I don't understand what you two did tonight put your own career at risk?" I bite my lip. "That? That's what she needs. Not a fucking trust fund, not a fuckin' posse of Staceighs. She needs friends, real ones. She needs to be shown she doesn't need all of"—his hand moves in the general direction of where the Beach Club is miles away—"that in order to succeed. But she does need good people on her side. And that, she's never had. That confidence, the ability to stand up for herself. Her mom turned her into a quiet dormouse full of insecurities. What you gave her? God. That was everything."

I stare at my hands still in the drawer, trying to understand what he's saying.

He . . . doesn't want me to pack my shit and leave.

He doesn't want me to get the few items I left here for convenience and extricate myself from his life forever.

He isn't mad for what happened with the Bitch Pack.

And slowly, my world crumbles.

Or, at the very least, my understanding of the world does.

Because I thought . . . No, I knew this would be it.

The final test.

There was no way he wouldn't fail.

Olivia was *arrested* for fighting.

There's a huge chance Staceigh will be pressing charges. She absolutely won't be getting her trust early, her hopes of starting her business easier crashing and burning on the marble entryway of the Beach Club.

And it's all my fault.

After all, it was my plan I egged on.

I'm sure Melanie St. George is absolutely mortified, calling everyone she can think of to try and mend fences in her delicate social circle, to make excuses for Olivia and make sure she doesn't lose her invites to any of the high-profile parties her social standing relies on.

I just *know* Staceigh is in the ears of anyone who will listen, telling them not to hire Livi no matter what.

Let's not even *think* about how the network *I* so carefully built this summer is decimated as well.

But despite all of that, Zach is telling me to stay.

In fact, I think there's a chance if I try to leave, *that* will infuriate him more than anything that happened in the last 48 hours.

"Olivia's going to lose her trust."

"No, she won't," he says, shaking his head. The world stops moving.

"What?"

"Nothing Olivia does short of committing murder would keep her from collecting that trust when the time is right."

"I don't understand. She . . . She had to work with me all summer. She was proving herself to Jefferson and she had to keep her mom happy—"

"Yeah, I didn't fight that because I hate to admit it, but Olivia is spoiled as fuck. She has no concept of how the world works, how much things cost, how a real job functions. She needed that, to be an intern for a ballbreaker like you." He says the words and my jaw drops right before those dimples pop out again. "So, I could have stepped in, reminded her even if she didn't get her trust early, her grandfather would never let her fail, her business would thrive on her name alone, but Livi was doing well with you. She was learning a lot, liking the work even if she didn't want to admit it, and I knew all along you two would eventually work it out, become friends."

"You . . . knew we'd work it out?"

"Do you think I would date a woman my daughter hates?" I scrunch my nose.

I had, in fact, wondered that. Wondered why this man was so gung ho to create and maintain this relationship with me, knowing his daughter and I were fully at odds for so long.

"Never—and I mean *never*, Camile—would I be with a woman who I knew in my soul would always be a point of contention between my daughter and me. Love you, love you like crazy, but I will always choose her."

Love you like crazy.

I have no time to dwell on those words because he keeps talking.

"I knew you two were giving each other shit, too. Knew she was probably making work miserable before you two figured your shit out and you were probably doing the same, but honest to God, Cam—I think it was meant to be. You two are so fucking similar, whether you admit it or not."

"We so are not—"

The dimples come out as he smiles and shakes his head.

"Told you. You're the same. You both fight anyone who fights *you*. You both have a chip on your shoulder. You both have some trauma that has to do with your past and rich assholes. Yours is that jackass, and Livi grew up with a flighty mother who cared more about money and status than her own daughter. You both have a wall a mile high, both refuse to let people in. Both hide the real you under layers and layers and I truly think you both really needed each other to see that."

My heart thumps a little harder with each of his words and his hands move out, grabbing mine from where they have been stuck in the drawer the whole time.

My skin and my soul calm when I finally have his skin on mine.

"You both needed this summer, this chance to take back what was taken from you by these assholes, to prove something to yourselves. I think you did that." A beat passes before a smile crosses his lips yet again. "Though I'm dying to know what the catalyst was, what made the two of you throw aside your differences and work as a united front." I think of the night I forced a drunk Livi into my room. "And what else you were doing to those girls over the summer. I know it wasn't just the wedding."

"We had Laceigh's car towed and let a rumor fly it had been repoed," I blurt without thinking, my voice low, and a chuckle leaves Zach's lips. "We made friends with the staff and someone in the restaurant pretended all of Staceigh's credit cards were declined."

"Oof, that had to hurt her ego," he says, and a smile crosses my lips too.

"I came over and saved the day, paying her bill."

His head tips back and an arm goes around my waist and he tugs me closer as his body jolts with laughter against mine.

"God, you two really are meant to be friends." I continue to stare at him in confusion and panic and longing as he continues to let his laughs die down before finally tipping his head down and moving his hand to brush a hair behind my ear, twisting the ends in a familiar, comforting way.

"You are beautiful, Cami. You're beautiful and you're kind and you fight for what's right, even if you do it in a bit of an unhinged way. You work hard and you don't let anything stop you from what you want. So what if Livi loses her trust for now? She gained a friend. An *ally*. Someone who is in her corner when I'm not around, and that, baby? That means more than anything."

And in that moment, the panic takes over.

I really hate this about myself. How I can hear these wonderful, beautiful words being said, how he can be telling me everything I want or need to hear, and all my mind can think is *this can't be real*.

Men don't do this.

Men don't see an incredibly flawed woman, a woman with so

much baggage she regularly goes on revenge missions just to feel something, and tell them they *love them like crazy.*

When my brand of truth comes out, men get wide-eyed and call her a psychopath.

They tell her she's crazy and ask her not to slit their tires.

When a woman like me shows her true colors to a man, shows the darkness hiding between the sweet, curated version of herself, she loses him.

"I don't want to see that, Camile."

I don't answer.

The anxiety in my chest is too big, my heart racing too fast, the thoughts in my mind too intrusive.

"I don't want to look at your gorgeous face and see you questioning things, see you battling your demons alone. What's going on in there, in your head?"

I still don't answer, but as always, Zach is patient.

He's patient and kind and the thumb rubbing on my waist turns into a soothing point, something I can focus on just enough to get words to work once again.

"You can't . . . You can't pass this test, Zach," I say, my words barely audible. His thick eyebrows come together in confusion.

"What?" Taking a deep breath, I force myself to move, to step back out of his grasp that's confusing and muddling what I know is right and true with what I *want* to be true.

"You can't pass this test. You passed the others and it was a fluke. But this one . . . it's bad, Zach. I did something . . . bad and I did it on purpose. And it impacted your *daughter.* You should know—I don't feel bad about it. I'd do it again."

He takes a step closer but I back up.

"This is who I am. I am the person who doesn't let shit go, the one who wants to dish out just desserts to everyone who I think deserves it. And sometimes, I take shit too far. I am not kind words and dad jokes and thoughtful gestures. I'm revenge and scorn and retribution."

"What was the test, Cami?" he asks, ignoring my words.

"What?"

"What was the test? What test did I pass?"

He takes another step closer to me, and I can't do this.

I can't have him closer. He muddles my mind and makes me think there might be hope in the world, there might not be just a universe of people who want to destroy my heart.

I might have found a man who wants to mend it.

Or even more terrifying and consuming, I've found the man who's okay with the shattered pieces, who likes watching the light reflect off them. A man who is happy to take me as I am—broken and unfinished—so long as I'm his.

"I'm broken," I whisper.

"I know." His answer sends a chill down my spine.

"I push people away."

"I got that."

"I can be mean and cruel and I say shit to hurt people, testing them to push them away."

"Know that too, Cami." I can't breathe. I can't *function*.

"I'm never going to change. I'll keep testing you. I'll keep trying to find your flaws."

"I'll keep passing them. Tell me, angel. What were the tests? What did I do right?"

And because I don't know what else to do, I tell him.

"I messed with Olivia because she played a trick on me and you didn't leave."

"She deserved it. She was raised to treat people with kindness, from me at least." I rub my lips together. "And it brought you to me, so all's well that ends well."

"I spent weeks purposely making your daughter miserable and rubbing our relationship in her face."

He smirks at that one.

"She deserved that, too."

"I teamed up with your daughter to take down her stepsisters."

"You expect me to be mad you gave my daughter her first true friend in that godforsaken Beach Club?" My heart skips a beat. "Not just a friend, but a confidante? Someone she can trust, she can tell secrets and worries to? Someone she can hang out with and who she doesn't have to have her guard up with? Fuck, watching you with my girl? Might have made me fall harder, Cami."

"Zach—"

"What else?"

I panic, trying to think of more, trying to prove to him he is so much better than the mess I am.

"I . . . I . . . I don't give blow jobs. I hate it."

"I can live without blow jobs if it means I get your tight pussy, Cami."

Fuck.

Now I'm confused, panicked, *and* turned on.

He steps closer but the backs of my legs bump into the bed so I can't go any farther, can't run when he wraps his arms around my waist and presses his forehead to mine before speaking quietly.

"You know, you passed all of my tests too."

"Your tests?

"Oh yeah." His smile spreads.

"Livi walked in, you were in my shirt and panties, and you didn't even bat an eye."

"I was planning my revenge," I say. Clearly, he doesn't get it, doesn't get how deep my brokenness goes.

"Either way. Then the bitches of the Beach Club gave you their all and your backbone was never stronger. Look what you did."

"I caused a riot."

"I told you I was done with kids and you didn't blink," he says as if this is some kind of tit for tat.

"I don't want kids," I say.

"Neither do I. I told you I don't want to get married again, and you didn't try and convince me otherwise."

"I don't want to give anyone power over me, much less make it legally binding. In fact, that technically could be a test, too. You should run, Zach."

"I'm not running from you, Cami. I told you. And baby, I know that's what you want to do right now, but I'll go where you go. If you run, I'm chasing you."

An eternity passes, Zach patiently standing in front of me, waiting for me to speak.

"You didn't leave," I say finally, revealing everything whether he knows it or not.

"*That* was my test," he says in a whisper.

"You didn't leave. I gave you so many chances, so many reasons to run."

"I only want to run to you. To run after you, if I have to."

"I don't understand. I don't get how," I confess, and it feels freeing to say. To admit to him, to anyone, really, I'm unsure of a situation.

I've spent my entire life calculated and cruel, trying to make sure everything matches the image I want people to see. *Confused* is never in the equation.

"I know."

"You know?"

"I know you don't understand. That's okay." I continue to stare at him, lost and so very confused, before he turns everything upside down again.

"Angel, I love you. I love you and the chaos you bring and your vigilante sense of justice. I love how you love Livi enough to fight for her. I love how you're loyal to a fault. I love how you're beautiful inside and out." Silence.

"And I know you love me too."

There's silence because I don't know how to respond.

Panic build and builds, my throat closing with what I think are tears, but I don't give in to the urge to break eye contact.

And I'm so incredibly glad I don't because it means I get to watch his face when he speaks again.

"I know those words aren't ones you like. You don't like to say them. They mean too much, and that's too scary. I'm telling you right now, Cami, I don't care. I don't care if you spend the rest of your life never saying you love me, so long as you endure hearing it from me and you spend the rest of your life by my side."

Finally, he stops speaking, the quiet in the room nearly suffocating.

I don't know how long we stand there, staring at each other in silence, before I open my dry mouth and speak.

"I'm scared."

"I know, Cami. That's okay."

It's not a grand gesture, not some big declaration, but it means more than anything else he's said in the last ten minutes.

More than he's said in the last hour, the last day.

Maybe all summer.

And it washes all the panic from me like the tide rising, a wave crashing and destroying the wall I built over all these years.

"Okay," I whisper.

It's not much, but somehow, he knows it's more.

A wide smile pulls on his lips, those dimples coming out.

"Okay."

And then we're kissing and all is right in my world.

"Move in with me."

The world stops again.

"What?"

"You don't have to say yes now. A lot just happened, but I want it in your head. Move in with me."

"Move in with you," I echo.

"Yes. Move in with me. Move down to the island."

"Permanently?"

"I mean, I'm pretty well stuck here." He leans forward, resting his forehead on mine. "And I'm pretty well stuck on you." My breathing goes uneasy, panic filling me. "I know it's too much right now. This is a lot. But I want you to keep it in your mind. I want you here. I want to wake up with you, want you sleeping in my shirts and sitting on my counter while I make you breakfasts. I don't want to send you texts to tell you I made it home from the bar on my bike. I want you to know I'm safe because I pull the covers back and kiss you while you're sleepy."

In that moment, I realize *I want that, too.*

I never wanted that, except maybe when I was young and stupid.

But I want it, the partnership. The comfort, the day-to-day.

A long moment passes before he speaks again.

"You don't have to answer now. I just want you to think about it. I want you here."

I stare at him, my body warm in a way I don't think I've ever experienced, before I ask a question of my own.

"If I do, will you still text me your dad jokes every day?"

And then he laughs.

It's a full-body laugh that reverberates through me, and he tugs me in closer to him.

"You're never escaping that, Cami."

Thank God.

FIFTY

SUNDAY, SEPTEMBER 3

ZACH

Livi has a small scratch on her elbow but that's the sole proof of her quarrel on Sunday morning when she comes over for breakfast.

"So, I hear she made bail eventually."

"Laceigh had to wait until the morning before she could get her out," Livi says with a small smile.

"Don't you laugh at that, Livi. She might be a bitch, but the girl spent the night in a jail cell because of you."

That's when Cami snaps, a choked laugh coming from her mouth.

"You too, Cami. This was your fault, too." She just rolls her eyes and I give her a look that tells her exactly what I'm thinking.

Keep it up and you'll be in trouble later.

I know she knows when she bites her lip and then raises her eyebrow.

Promise?

I can't help but smile and shake my head.

"Ew, gross. Glad you guys are happy but also, please stop." Cami's smile grows and my own lips follow suit. Now it's Livi's turn to shake her head. "Anyway, Dad, you should totally let Cami plan the end of summer party at the bar." My gut drops with my daughter's words and I try to ignore them both as I use my fork, pushing eggs around on my plate.

"What's that?" Cami asks.

"Oh, it's this party my dad throws for the locals and the staff on Labor Day. Like a last hurrah for the summer. It's a blast. Music, drinks, food, all the good stuff."

"No way!" She elbows me and I can feel her eyes on me. "I can't believe you didn't tell me! I can't believe you'd deprive me of an opportunity to plan a party for you!" She takes a sip of her coffee before speaking again. "Of course, I wouldn't charge you, if that was what you were worried about. I mean, we don't have too much time, but I'm pretty awesome, so Livi and I can definitely whip something together."

"With the wedding chaos, I totally didn't even think to tell you about it," Livi says. I sigh, not wanting to say what I have to, but . . .

"Yeah, I'm not sure what's going to happen with that. Going to have to play it by ear." I know, though. There will be no party this year, at least nothing big enough to require Cami's touch. Maybe something small for the employees, the college kids who work for the summer.

"What do you mean?" Livi asks, confused.

"Not in the budget." I still don't look up from my plate but the room goes quiet. "Things are tight this year. I still don't know what my plan is for the offseason. I can probably keep everyone on until December then hire back in April, but I don't think I'll make it the whole season."

Silence covers the table, and I use the opportunity to look at my plate, pushing the eggs I no longer have an appetite for around and vigilantly ignoring both of my girls' eyes burning on me.

"Dad—"

"Zach—" they both start, but I don't answer and they don't finish their sentences.

There's not much to say, after all.

The Fishery has proudly remained open all year for as long as I can remember, my grandfather starting the tradition well before I was born, keeping overhead low and creating spiked summer pricing which lowers again in the winter for locals. The goal every summer when all of the tourists come in to the island is to get as much business as humanly possible in order to fund the slow months, to keep the full-time staff employed all winter.

"What happened?" Livi asks, her face a mix of shock and horror and sadness.

I know the feeling.

I knew by the end of July something was off when my daily totals started falling well below my normal numbers for that time of year. I couldn't figure it out, thinking maybe it was just *time,* but then Nate told me about the rumor.

"It doesn't matter, Livi. It's all good."

"Dad, what *happened?*"

Cami stays calm which, to be quite honest, is more nerve-wracking than Livi's kind, empathetic look.

"*Who* happened?" she asks, her jaw set, her arms crossing on her chest, and I know in my bones Cami already knows.

The vengeful angel she warned me of when she was trying to convince me she was no good for me comes out, as if I haven't seen that version of her simmering beneath the surface near daily and love her more for it.

"Put the claws away, Cami."

"I'm right, aren't I?" she asks, her jaw tight, and fuck. Even now, admitting to them I failed with my business for the first time, I can't help but smile. That hint of a smile goes full blown when she tries to fight a smile of her own.

"What's happening? Why do I feel like you two are having some kind of a conversation I'm not a part of?"

"We are," Cami says.

"But you don't have to worry about it, Livi," I say, my eyes remaining locked with Cami's.

"Oh god, is it sexual?" Her face goes a bit green. "Look, I can handle you two being together because I think you're perfect for each other, but I can *not handle* you two being loud about your sex life. Fuck no."

"Calm down, Livi, it's not that," Cami says with an eye roll.

I love that, too.

Her calling Olivia *Livi* just because I do.

"Then what *is* it?"

"It was them, wasn't it?" Cami asks.

I don't speak, but I don't have to.

She knows.

Somehow, Cami always knows.

"It was *who*? Jesus Christ, maybe I take back being okay with you two being together if this is what it's going to be like. This is annoying as fuck."

"Livi," I say, a warning in my voice, and she rolls her eyes but there's no time to break in and chastise her because Cami speaks.

"Your darling new stepsisters." My jaw goes tight. I didn't want this, didn't want to stir the pot further between the four of them, but it seems inevitable.

"No," Livi whispers.

"Looks like it."

"What did they do?! I'm going to kick their asses." There's a pause before she smiles, the same smile she had when she was a kid and would do something bad she was very much not apologetic for doing. "Again."

"Jesus, Livi. Let's not do that again, please."

"My best friend is in love with a really good lawyer. I've got you covered, babe," Cami says to my daughter with a wink and goddamn.

I'm really fucking in for it, aren't I?

Forever.

I look to the ceiling and shake my head, though I can't find it in me to be mad with whatever higher power put both of them in my life.

"So, what was it, dimples?" Cami asks, and I glare at her. I don't even hate the nickname anymore, but I'll keep up the act forever.

"Nothing specific. Nate told me he heard a rumor, some nasty things about the Fishery. Then, a few smaller parties were cancelled last minute." I look to Cami, knowing she's probably already panicking she had a hand in it. "Nothing you were in charge of." Relief fills her momentarily. "But all of that combined . . . it just wasn't a great year. It's fine. There's a first time for everything."

I've more or less resigned to this fact.

"No," Cami says with a shake of her head. "Fuck no. This will not happen."

"Cam, angel, I—"

"Nope." She stands, her chair scraping against the tile as she does, and then she looks down at Livi.

"Come on."

"What?" she asks, but my daughter is already standing, moving her plate away from her and reaching for her bag on the kitchen island.

"Come on. We have to go into the office."

"Girls, it's a Sunday—"

"It's a Sunday and I'm not letting those bitches fucking win." She's beautiful like this, angry and vengeful and on a warpath, especially when I know the outrage comes from her feeling like I've been wronged.

"Camile—" I reach for her wrist to stop her as she grabs her own bag and keys.

"No. No way, Zach. You told me yesterday you were okay with me and my revenge. You were *fine* with me fighting for Livi. Well, newsflash, babe. You won me fighting for you, too."

"That's not—" I start, shaking my head.

"I know it's not. But I'm going to anyway."

I sigh, resigned, knowing there's nothing I can do to stop her.

I wouldn't really want her to be mine, not the real Cami, if I tried.

"Come, Livi. We've got work to do."

"Don't get arrested," I say as she comes closer to where I'm now standing, moves to her tiptoes, and presses her lips to mine.

"No promises," she says, and I groan. "Come on, Livi!"

And then they both run out the door, giggling and on a mission.

I just shake my head.

This is the life, I suppose.

FIFTY-ONE

MONDAY, SEPTEMBER 4

CAMI

> Are you Italian?
>
> Because I want a pizza you
>
>> Not now, I'm trying to save your bar.

We work quickly, Olivia crafting the cutest fliers and hanging them all over the island, the Beach Club, and handing them out to anyone who would take it while I called in every single favor I had acquired over the summer. By Monday morning, we even have a plane pulling a sky banner to promote the party.

ANTI-B*TCH PACK PARTY! SEPT 4, 6 PM @ THE FISHERY!

According to Nate, Zach's friend who works at the airstrip, using the entire word *bitch* could get all of us in trouble and to be honest, we've had enough trouble in the past few days.

And we'll have even more when the twins realize we're in direct competition with their *End of Summer Bash* they're throwing at the Beach Club in order to try and save their reputation and image. Livi and I have spoken to at least fifteen employees, inviting them to ditch working the event and head to the party at the Fishery. I thought for sure no one would be onboard but, as seems to be the way, this little town continues to shock me.

Livi had to explain to me most everyone who works at the Beach Club is incredibly tired of how the twins treat everyone and wouldn't mind sticking to to the Bitch Pack. The island locals are a tight-knit community and when they hear one of them is suffering—like, say your business is going to have to close because of bitchy tourists—they all band together.

I think Zach is still pretty much in denial of everything and is humoring Livi and me, moving forward with the mindset this is *one last hurrah* rather than a save the bar type of event.

There is not a single doubt in my mind, though, that we'll do just that.

Which brings us to now, standing in front of the mirror at Zach's house and waiting for him to come in and see my outfit. Livi and I decided sparkly and fun was the vibe, something that was only further sparked when she called Abbie and Kat, inviting them down for the party.

Of course, there is no universe where Abbie Keller can resist a party, so she, Kat, and Damien are already down in Damien's condo at the Beach Club, ready to spend the night with us.

"Don't be mad, okay?" I say to Zach in the other room, tugging the short hem of the sparkly champagne-colored dress down a bit, knowing as soon as I take a few steps, it's going to pop back up. The top plunges to my sternum, showing ample cleavage.

I won't lie. I look *good*.

Really fucking good. I'm showing way too much of my mahogany skin and not hiding nearly enough and I love it.

Here's the thing: I love my curves. I think they're sexy and I wouldn't change them for anything. And I like to dress in a way that shows them off because, again, I love my curves and I don't give a fuck what anyone else thinks.

The issue is, I've dated enough men to know while they love the *look* of women wearing revealing clothes, they very rarely like actually having *their* woman on their arm *in* revealing clothes. Far too many men see women as property, and once they acquire said property, it should be for their eyes only.

So as I wait in front of the bed in the tight dress and high heels, I'm anticipating an argument with Zach.

"Mad?" he asks, and when he walks in, his eyes roam me slowly, heat burning there and my belly going warm from the close proximity of *Zachary Anderson* looking at me like *that*. But then his face morphs into confusion. "I don't get it."

"This is my outfit for the party," I tell him, biting my lip.

"Got that." He moves farther into the room, stepping until he's just a few feet from me, crossing his arms on his chest.

"Aren't you . . . mad?" Again, confusion covers his face, his brow furrowing as if he's trying to understand my words.

"Why would I be mad?"

"Because of this dress."

"That dress is gorgeous," he says simply.

"I agree. But it's . . . it's tiny." I do a slow spin so he can see all angles.

"Got that. Your ass is barely covered in it." I bite my lip but he shakes his head. "Why would that be an issue?"

I sigh, feeling ridiculous even explaining this. "Because men like you don't want to show off what's theirs. They want it to be for their eyes only." He continues to stare at me, clearly not understanding, so I continue speaking to explain. "Men like the *idea* of a woman wearing a tight, tiny dress out in public, until they realize other people will see her like that."

"Come here," he says, opening his arms.

I don't move.

I'm too nervous, waiting for the other shoe to drop.

"Camile, come here," he says, and this time, I do because he uses that firm voice he also uses in bed and my body can't help but obey.

He takes a step closer and moves the chunk of hair I left out of my messy bun back, twisting the end just a bit in a move I've grown to love.

"Are you mine?" he asks in a low voice, the kind of voice that makes butterflies float in my belly, banging into the sides.

"I . . . I . . ." This is a conversation I've been avoiding for weeks.

Am I Zach's?

If you asked the version of me that drove to the island in May, I would have laughed and said hell the fuck no whether I knew who Zach was or not.

But now?

This man, the way he talks to me, the way he looks at me, the way he treats me?

God.

Am I ready to put aside the panic that giving myself to someone else induces? The risk of opening to someone, of letting them be part of my life knowing at any moment, in theory, they could hurt me?

His eyes are warm but firm as he looks at me, taking me in, waiting for a response.

I bite my lip, not breaking eye contact, but eventually, I give him an answer.

The only correct one really.

"If you want me to be," I whisper nervously. It takes five seconds for me to realize that was absolutely the right answer when the dimples come out, when his arm moves, wrapping my waist and pulling me into him, catching me when I fall against his chest because I can't move quick enough in my high heels before he finally speaks against my lips.

"Baby, a man like me wants to show off a woman like you. A man like me knows a woman like you will always wear whatever the fuck she wants, and a man like me knows if he wants to keep a woman like you, he'd better learn how to fight."

Then, he gives me a slow kiss which scrambles my brain just a bit before he breaks it, letting me whisper against his lips in confusion.

"Fight?"

"Just in case," he says with a smile, and I just . . . stare at him. "Anyone even looks at what's mine in a way I don't like, I'll fight them." That smile grows and so does my confusion.

"You can't keep doing this," I say with a slight shake of my head.

"Doing what?"

"Passing all of my tests," I whisper, and I almost take it back, almost laugh it off, but for some reason, I don't.

I don't because a part of me wants to know what he'll say.

Instead, I keep staring, watching thick brows come together in confusion as he works to decode my words.

"Passing your tests?"

"Yeah. You keep passing all of my tests." Thoughts flash across his eyes and I watch as he tries to tear my words apart, as they come back together in a way that makes sense to him.

"This is a test?" A hand moves over the shimmery sequins, from my back to my bottom of my ass, and I can't help it. A small smile comes to my lips.

"I mean, yes and no. I'd be wearing this no matter what. But men . . ."

"I am not most men."

"You're not, are you?"

"No." His words are firm and the hand on my ass moves to my chin to hold me in place so I can't move. "And you need to come to understand that, Cami. I'm not most men. I'm *your* man. And because I'm your man, I know what you need. I know you need to live independent and free, do whatever you want, wear whatever you want. I know you don't want a man who will smother you and make you fit some mold you were born to break. I know you didn't come here looking for this, but it's what you found, and angel, I'm not letting you go anytime soon, do you understand?"

I have no choice.

I nod, a tiny nod, and his lips tip up.

"So no, Cami. I am not like most men. I'm *your* man. You're gonna have to get used to it."

"So I'm learning," I whisper, and then he steps back, warm hands leaving my body. He moves back and sits on the edge of the bed, legs wide, hands on the bed next to him and he stares at me like he's still decoding me.

I feel naked, and not because of what I'm wearing.

"Do you feel good in your outfit?" he asks.

"What?"

"Do you feel good? You feel hot, gorgeous in it?" I lick my lips but I don't lie. I nod. "I know you do. You like wearing tight clothes. You like showing off." He reaches out, grabbing my wrist and tugging until I'm standing between his legs, looking down at him as he looks at me.

"You're mine, right?" I nod again. "Then we're good." A hand moves to the outside of my thigh, bare skin on warm bare skin.

"I don't understand," I say in a breathy whisper, both because of the way he's looking at me and the feel of his calloused hand on my thigh, the way his hand is moving up and down, warming my skin, thumb creeping to my inner thigh, each time getting closer to the short hem of my dress.

"You wear what you like, baby, and I'll back you up. You wanna go to a fine-dining restaurant looking like Billie Eilish in my shorts and tee, I'll bring them to you. You want to go out in a tiny dress, I'll watch your ass all night. You're a big girl, Camile. You can choose what you wear. You are not my property. I do not decide how you dress." His thumb moves up, up, up, grazing the fabric of my panties, and my breath catches.

"I might own your body, Cami, but that means I protect it. I don't police it. The only request I have is if you go out like this, I come with." My mouth opens to protest, but the thumb finds my clit through my panties. "Not because I don't trust you. Not because I want to hover, but because I don't trust other men. Because I want to make sure you're safe. You go out with your friends like this and you don't want me there, I'm in the corner. I'm silent. I'm your DD. I'm your unofficial bodyguard. I'm whatever you want me to be, but I'm yours and you're mine. And I hope you're starting to learn by now, I keep what's mine safe."

"But . . ." There's another hitch in my breath as his thumb presses on my clit. "But you don't mind if I dress up."

"You're an adult, Cami. I told you, I can fight if I need to."

His hand slips out from my skirt, over my dress, holding me at the hip.

"You can't be real," I say, and my words are so low, I wonder if he can hear them.

I kind of hope he can't, but then he responds.

"Why not?" I sigh.

"Because you're everything I thought didn't exist in the world."

"I'm right here, Cami. I'm real, just like we are, and I'm yours."

I have no words for him as he continues to stare at me, but I don't think he expects me to say anything at all. Instead, he leans forward, pressing his lips to mine briefly before stepping back, his hand moving to mine.

"Come on. Let's go celebrate."

It's hours later when Zach has to make good on his word because I'm dancing with Kat at the raging success that is the Anti-Bitch Pack Party when hands touch my hips.

Her eyes go wide but I don't need that clue to know the hands on my hips are not Zach's.

I know in an instant.

I can't tell if it's because calluses don't catch on the sequins of my dress or if the size of the hands isn't right or if I just *know* somehow with that simple touch, but I know all the same.

And when the air in the crowded club moves, wafting familiar cologne my way, I know I'm right.

Instead, when I turn, Jason fucking Demartino is standing there.

Why the fuck he's here, I do not know, but he's here all the same, staring at me like I'm food and he's starving.

But not in a hot way.

In the way that makes my skin crawl.

FIFTY-TWO

ZACH

I'm not totally sure what I expected when Cami got that gleam in her eyes and ran off with Livi, but a huge party with a cover charge that spilled out into the parking was absolutely not it.

But I've been behind the bar with Rhonda and the three part-time kids, who normally are out enjoying the weekend these last days of the summer season, serving drinks nonstop.

When Cami told me I needed to up the inventory, I laughed at her.

She stared at me like I was being an idiot.

Pretty sure that won't be the last time I'm grateful I listen to her.

They promoted the last-ditch effort to save the bar as an anti rich-bitch party, something I wasn't too sure about, but it worked.

With the cover charge alone, they've done it, made it so the doors will stay open through the season for locals and Rhonda and Frank can stay on until the summer picks up.

I don't know why I even questioned them, the two hardest working and hardest headed women on this planet.

It's an honor to have them on my side, truly.

The patrons have been a mix of tourists and locals all coming to celebrate the end of the summer, even a handful of Beach Club employees who, from what Cami whispered to me with wide eyes, were staff expected to work the twins' event.

But the biggest shock of the night was when the Beach Club members themselves started to make their way across the street, coming for drinks and dancing since Cami and Livi pushed the tables and chairs to the side of the room, creating a makeshift dance floor. That shock was mirrored on Cami's face when more than one came up to her, thanking her for planning this *wonderful new event*. Seems even the wealthy members can get burnt out on tea sandwiches and martinis.

But hands down, the best part of the night has been watching Cami *shine* in her element, talking to clients, both past and potential, schmoozing them, and giving them her card with a wide smile. Even the way she's combatting the anxiety I know she feels at events like this by dancing with Livi, Abbie, and Kat.

But she never loses sight of where I am.

Without sounding like I'm more important than I am, I think that's the key, just another factor in the give and take of our relationship. When the anxiety starts to slide in, she finds me, locks eyes with me, and I smile at her because she's so fucking pretty and I'm so fucking lost for her.

That's when the panic slides off her face, when she smiles back, when she shakes her head like she needs me to think she finds me annoying and overbearing.

Instead of a lifeline.

That's fine. I'll let her have that, so long as I get her.

It's late into the night, not long before closing time, when my need to keep my eyes on her pays off. I'm standing at the bar across from Damien, occasionally talking over the loud music but mostly watching our respective women dance, when it happens.

It's not the first time, of course.

Throughout the night, since the women have wandered onto the crowded dance floor, men have come over, tried to dance, and accepted the gentle letdown without one of us having to come over.

But this time is different.

I recognize the man from the Fourth of July party, when he was on one of the twin's arms but staring at Cami's tits like he was having some kind of flashback moment.

And I haven't forgotten when she told me all about how he tricked her when she was barely 18 and how he was the catalyst for how she viewed relationships.

I think I would have been more annoyed the night he called when she was at my place if her need to avoid relationships wasn't the exact reason she found herself in my bar that second night. But if he hadn't twisted her up all those years ago, there's a good chance Cami wouldn't have been coming in night after night to tell me her various issues while I took the time to slowly tear down her walls until she let me in.

I remember thinking if it weren't for him, there was no way gorgeous, kind, self-assured Camile would still be single now and how I should send him a thank you gift.

But as I watch Cami turn to face him, anger on her face as she pushes his chest, clearly telling him to back up, I can't find it in me to be grateful for him at all.

Especially when he steps closer, his hand moving to her wrist, fingers wrapping there. His face isn't in my line of sight, but Cami's is and the panic there stops time for me.

My hands go to the bartop as I jump over it. I'd probably have kicked Damien in the head if he wasn't already moving in that direction, eyes locked on the same situation as mine are.

"The *fuck* is going on?" I shout over the music, Livi turning to me with wide, shocked eyes.

"Man, this has nothing—"

"It sure as fuck has something to do with me when your hands are on Cami's wrist and she's looking scared as fuck."

"We're old friends. Go back to your job and let us chat."

"Jason, stop it."

"Cams, come on. We need to talk and you've been ignoring me all summer."

"I thought I told you on the phone she has a man and you have no need to even contact her." His face drops as his eyes move from me to Cami and back before finally dropping her wrist. Instantly, I move, pushing her behind me.

"Zach—"

"This is him? This is the asshole who turned you into a whore on the phone?" Jason shouts over the music, eyes locked behind me at Cami, his hand moving in my direction. "God, Cami. I thought you were better than that."

"Jason, please. You should leave. I—"

"You know, I guess I was right all those years ago. You're fucking nothing, Cami," he says, and even though I can't see her, I know she goes still.

I can picture the look of pain, of a well-aimed remark on her face. She might be over him, might be healed from the way he treated her, but there will always be a part deep inside of her, the young girl who believed this was her first love, who will always be hurt by him.

And that? That's unacceptable.

"Alright, you need to leave my bar before I call the police."

"Just a fucking whore, good for nothing but a quick fuck. I mean, you should know, right?" he asks, tipping his chin to me. "You were the one who told her to moan for you on the phone, weren't you?"

A fire builds in my gut both from knowing eyes are me and from the warmth of Cami's hand on my lower back. Rage burns for this piece of shit who deigns to even *look* at Cami, with too much money and not nearly enough sense.

"Zach, honey, it's not worth it," Cami says softly behind me, her hand on my lower back a grounding force.

She's right.

He's not.

Cami won by being free of him, by succeeding and thriving despite how he treated her.

He's not worth it.

"Aren't you with Staceigh, Jason?" Livi asks, her voice taunting. "What, is she not enough fun for you? You have to come and slum it over here?" His gaze moves to my left where my daughter is standing and something tells me no amount soft touches from Cami are going to stop the impending rage.

"Why, do you want a chance next?" he asks, and my blood boils. "I bet you're fuckin' wild in bed, yeah?"

And then it happens.

I snap.

It's not the words, but him stepping forward, reaching around me, and grabbing my daughter's wrist.

"Let her go," I say, my voice a growl that can still be heard over the music.

"Zach," Cami says, her voice raising a frantic octave.

"Let go of me!" Livi yells.

"Make me, asshole," he says, looking straight at me, and fuck.

He *did* ask.

"Oh fuck," Cami says in a groan.

And as I pull my hand back then launch forward to hit him square in the face, a satisfying crunch coming as I make contact, I can't help but let those dimples Cami loves so much show.

"Dad!" Livi shouts as Jason stumbles back, holding his face. Blood starts to leak from his nose between his fingers.

"Now get the *fuck* out of my bar," I say, voice calm despite the growing crowd watching us.

"I'm gonna fucking sue you for all you're worth!" Jason screams, spit flying as he does.

Cami's standing next to me and instead of keeping my eyes on him, I look to my woman, already knowing what I'll see there, what thoughts are running through her mind.

That it's all her fault, that she's more trouble than she's worth.

God, how long is it going to be before she realizes *I don't give a shit?* Before she understands I'd lose the bar and everything I built if it meant keeping her safe—not just physically, but emotionally.

The way she treats Livi with love and kindness, the way she bends over backward for anyone she deems to have been wronged in order to make it right—those are the things that make Cami *Cami* and what I love most about her.

I know her internal dialogue is screaming about how there's no way this guy doesn't have an entire law firm at his beck and call and there's no universe where I could match that. If he comes after me, he'll win, for sure.

And I'm okay with that.

"I don't think you are," a deep, low voice says, interrupting. It's smooth and cultured with a hint of a New York accent.

The room shifts a bit and Damien Martinez is standing there with his arms crossed, Cami's best friend standing behind him with a hand on his shoulder as if she's worried he'll be next, he'll take his own hit at Jason.

Didn't Cami tell me he once punched someone out at a holiday party for talking shit about Abbie?

My kind of guy.

"The fuck I'm not. He just hit me, completely unprompted. There's a hundred fucking witnesses." He turns to me, blood dripping onto his ill-fitting dress shirt. "Your bar, you said? It's going to be mine."

"Jason, come on, let's—" Cami starts, and I move my arm out to ensure she doesn't take a single step closer to him.

"Oh, what, you want to talk now? I'm good. I forgot what a useless whore you are. I don't need to talk to you."

Instantly, the urge to hit him again makes me stretch my fingers.

Fuck, if he's going to sue me, might as well make it worth it, get a few more good punches in.

"You know what?" Damien says, and when I look at him, he's got a smug smile on his lips as he reaches into his pocket, grabbing his wallet and tugging out a card. The smile grows as he hands it to Jason and it's a little twisted. "You're right. I'd absolutely love to see you again in court."

Jason stares at his hand but doesn't take it.

"Go on. Take it. Have your people be in touch. I cannot wait to tell a judge about how you assaulted not only Mr. Anderson's partner, but his daughter in his own establishment." Damien turns his face to me before speaking, his smile huge.

"All while trespassing on your property, correct?" I have to fight my own smile.

"Absolutely. This man is not welcome on my premises by any means."

"Perfect." Damien looks back to Jason. "And these witnesses—it's convenient they work closely with Camile and Olivia, since we'll likely be able to contact them easily for eyewitness reports." He waves the card for him to grab but Jason keeps staring, blood dripping from his nose. "Not just tonight, but from what my girlfriend has told me, Camile has claimed on multiple occasions you have repeatedly harassed her this summer, not leaving her alone when she asked."

Jason's face goes white and it's not from blood loss.

"That's bullshit!"

"We'll see. Either way, take my card and leave the property."

"Fuck this. You're not even worth it, Cami. Enjoy the trash." And then he walks out, the crowd parting easily to let him out, booing as they do.

"A round on me!" Abbie shouts gleefully, and the entire bar cheers. When I look to Damien, he's shaking his head at her.

"Why do I feel like that round is actually on me, *naranja?*"

The word makes zero sense to me, seeing as she's tiny, blonde, and I've never seen her wearing any color other than pink, but it seems to make her smile.

"Because it is."

He smiles back and we make our way to the door to watch Jason leave.

FIFTY-THREE

ZACH

Livi walks over after we make sure the douchebag has left my property with no further issue, her arms crossed on her chest, a smile on her lips.

"So, what happened to *never throw the first punch?*" I glare and she bursts out laughing.

"A man putting his hands on a woman is always fair game, Olivia. Good to learn that now, though if you're ever in a position to need to use that information, I swear to fuck I'm going to lose my mind." The thought of my daughter getting caught up with her own Jason makes me sick to my stomach.

"Yeah, yeah, yeah. You know what I learned from this whole debacle?"

"To pick your exes wisely?" I ask with hope in my tone. Cami reaches out and slaps my arm.

"No, to have Damien around anytime I think about hitting someone." Damien lets out a deep laugh and even I can't fight the smile.

"Okay, I'm over this. Who wants to dance?" Abbie asks. There's not a person on this planet who could convince me this woman ever has less than 100% energy.

"Me!" Livi shouts, grabbing Abbie's outstretched hand.

"Give me a bit. I have to talk to Rocky Balboa over here," Cami says, her hand moving to mine and lacing there.

"Sure, *talk*," Abbie says with a wink as Cami leads me back toward where the door to my tiny office is. It's a disaster, papers strewn everywhere, extra bar tees I need to take home and wash in a pile, the desk covered in so much shit you can't even see the calendar underneath.

But all of that is forgotten as Cami uses the toe of one of her ridiculously high heels to kick the door shut behind her before her hands are twisting in the front of my shirt, pulling me close. She stumbles as we move, as I navigate her through the mess of my office.

"I am so fucking turned on right now," she groans against my lips, and instantly, I'm hard. "You *hit him*."

"He touched you," I say then bend my knees as I move to grab her thighs, lifting her and pressing her to the door. Once she's pinned there, I move my hand to press the lock on the door, my mouth moving to her neck. She moans as I suck on the spot she loves beneath her ear.

"That was the hottest thing I've ever seen, Zach." I would smile but my free hand is moving up her thigh, my thumb moving to her clit over her panties, the same place it was just hours ago.

Cami moans, her head tipping back and hitting the steel door with a thunk, but with the way her hips are moving, the noises coming from her, I know she doesn't care.

Fuck, she's so keyed up, I bet I could make her come just like this: touching her, kissing her, never even dipping below her underwear.

"You liked that? Fuck, Cami, I'll fight for you every goddamn day if this is how you get, moaning for me, soaked through your underwear." She moans again, a deep sound reverberating through her chest. My cock throbs with the noise.

"I need you," she whispers, and that's it.

That's all I need to move from under her dress to her ass and walk her over to the desk. Her arms hold herself around my neck as I use a hand to swipe office supplies to the floor, sitting her on the edge and using a hand to tug her underwear down her legs and over her heels. She's pulling the stretchy dress over her head as I tug off my shirt, and then she's completely naked on my desk, one leg dangling off the edge, the other on the top, leaving her spread open for me.

Fucking marvelous.

"Stay there," I say, reaching in my back pocket and grabbing my phone. Opening the photo app, I take a few shots, then I get closer to take a photo of just her dripping wet pussy.

"Zach," she moans impatiently, her hand moving down her body to touch her clit.

My phone slides into my pocket before I use it to slap her thigh, listening to the yelp and moan she lets out.

"Mine. You don't touch until I say," I scold, using my thumbs to spread her pussy wide. "And right now, I'm doing the touching. We don't have much time."

"Then *do it* or I'm taking care of it myself," she says with a groan, and I wonder if I'll ever get tired of the way she loves to push me, to test me.

Definitely not.

Especially when we both want the same thing.

Without any kind of ceremony, I lean forward, my hands moving to her thighs to keep her spread, and I flatten my tongue along her from entrance to her clit before sucking it into my mouth, listening to the sound of pained relief leave her lips.

Any other time, I'd sit back on my heels and stare, watch her, make her beg me for more, drag this out.

But I'm keyed up and I know she is too.

I can take my time later, when we're alone and at my place, when she's writhing in my bed.

Instead, I gaze at her, my mouth never leaving her clit as I slide two fingers into her. Her hips buck as I move them in and out, fucking her gently as I continue to suck and lick her clit the way I know she loves, driving her closer to the edge faster than ever.

"God, you look good like this." She moans, her fingers barely able to thread in the hair which needs a cut. "On your knees for me, eating my pussy." I crook my fingers, hitting her G-spot the way I know she loves, and she groans again. I've never been into a woman talking dirty to me but *fuck*.

Cami doing it?

My cock continues to throb, begging for relief.

I groan against her pussy and she moans, her eyes drifting shut, her head tipping back, her hand pushing my head closer.

"Fuck, fuck, Zach," she cries. "I'm going to come. *Fuck*."

Her head tips down again and I meet her eyes and I know what this is.

She's waiting.

Waiting for the go-ahead from me, for permission to let go.

Fuck, she's perfect.

I nod barely, my teeth scraping her clit as I do, my fingers moving against her, and that's all it takes.

Not my teeth or my lips or my fingers.

My *permission*.

Then she's screaming my name, falling apart on my desk, and I know I'll never forget this night.

Even when I have an entire fucking library of filthy moments with Camile, I'll choose to jack off to this undocumented moment, the time she fell apart in an instant.

I suck for a few more beats, slowly fucking her with my fingers as I let her come down before removing myself and standing.

I can tell from here that only took the edge off, she still needs more of me.

Needs my cock.

Thank fuck.

"*Now*," she moans, reaching for me as I stand between her legs. "I need you inside me *right now*." I groan in approval, moving her leg off the desk and grabbing her behind the neck, tugging her in close until her lips meet mine, letting her taste herself.

But just as her hands move to my belt, a knock comes from the door, both of us freezing.

"Fuck," I murmur. "What is it?"

"Know you two are busy in there, well deserved, thanks for saving my job, Cami, but if you could speed it up, that'd be great. Orders are piling up and I think Rhonda's going to have a mental breakdown." I sigh and groan, looking at Cami, who's smiling.

"Rain check?" she asks, already stepping off the desk and pulling her dress back on.

"Easy for you to say. You already came once," I grumble, adjusting my painfully hard erection. I reach into my clean pile of bar tees and pull one over my head, unsure of where I threw the other one.

"Aww, poor baby," she says with a joking pout. My hand moves behind her neck, pulling her in hard against me, my lips brushing hers as I speak.

"You're going to get it for that later, you know?" A smile spreads on her face, a gorgeous carefree one I don't think I've ever seen before, like a final weight has left her shoulders.

I'd risk my business every single day if it meant I got to see that smile.

"I'm counting on it, dimples," she says, then she steps back and walks out of my office, letting in the raucous noise of the bar, while I shake my head, watching her disappear into the crowd.

It's long hours later, way after the normal closing time, before we get the bar cleaned and closed up, Damien, Abbie, and Livi heading back to the Beach Club and Cami sitting in the passenger seat of her car as we head to my place.

I'm going to fall off your bike if we ride it home, Zach, she argued when I suggested it.

"What now?" Cami asks with a yawn as we turn right out of the parking lot, the Beach Club becoming a shrinking spot in the rearview mirror.

"Oh, now I'm taking you home so I can fuck you sideways." Her laugh fills the salted sea air as I drive along the bay, the windows open.

"Works for me, dimples."

And you know what?

That name is really starting to grow on me.

FIFTY-FOUR

TUESDAY, SEPTEMBER 5

CAMI

Do you know what the Little Mermaid and I have in common?

> You're both delusional?

We both want to be part of your world.

> Ahh

Did it make you smile at the very least?

> Yes, which is a feat considering I'm most definitely about to get fired.

No matter what happens, we'll figure it out. Just survive today and then come to the Fishery. I'll feed you and you can get drunk and then I'll fuck you until you can't worry about anything but my cock.

> Sir, I'm at work.

Did it help you forget?

> Maybe a little.

> Mission accomplished. Love you. See you soon.

On Tuesday, after the Anti-Bitch Pack Party, Olivia's sitting in my office with me, both of us working on closing any open accounts and events and contacting vendors to make sure everyone is paid and happy. The Beach Club closes each winter and my contract ends in just a week and a half.

And to be honest, whether I'll be invited back next season is a total fucking crapshoot at this point.

We're both engrossed in our work when the knock on the door comes, both of our heads popping up to look.

In the doorway, wearing a well-fitting, expensive suit, his grey hair perfectly in place and his arms crossed over his chest, stands Jefferson Kincaid.

It's funny because I decided in just thirty seconds while sitting in Zach's kitchen while he told me those girls had fucked not only with his income and business, but with Frank and Rhonda's, I didn't care about the repercussions. Until that moment, I had decided I would try my best to explain the wedding situation to Jefferson and pray it didn't destroy my career.

I figured with Olivia on my side, there was a tiny glimmer of hope we could talk ourselves out of this mess.

And really, I should feel anxiety in my gut looking at him, knowing I ruined the end of summer event his new stepgranddaughters were throwing, knowing I dragged his granddaughter into my chaos, knowing I took his clients away from his location and to another when my job is quite literally to plan and execute events *within the Beach Club*.

There is an incredibly high likelihood I will not be asked to return to the Beach Club next year.

And you know what?

I'm okay with that.

I have no idea what the next two weeks will hold.

I have no clue what the next six months or year will look like.

But I know I have new friends who will cheer me on no matter what.

And I know I have a man who will do anything in this universe to put a smile on my face.

And because of that, I know I'll be okay.

"You two. My office," he says then turns and walks away.

Olivia and I look at each other, our cringe mirrored on one another's face.

Well, fuck.

But still, we stand and walk the plank over to his office. And we do it hand in hand.

"So, this past weekend was . . . interesting," he says, hands clasped tighter on the desk in front of him, looking fully at ease with this conversation. Ironic considering the sweat on my upper lip. I wouldn't be surprised if he could see my pulse throbbing in panic.

"It was," Olivia says, and when I look at her, there's none of the panic coursing through my veins evident on her face. Her shoulders are back, her chin high, and she's staring right at her grandfather, her own Bitch Pack upbringing kicking into high gear.

It inspires me to kick mine in, too.

I'm Camile fucking Thompson.

I can handle this.

"Camile, would you like to explain what happened to me?"

I take a deep breath, nod, and open my mouth, unsure of what I'm going to say, but like always, I know I'll figure it out along the way.

But I don't get the chance.

Instead, a warm hand is suddenly in mine again, gripping tight in a *in this together* kind of way before Olivia speaks.

"I'd like to go first, Grandfather," she says, and Jefferson's face is full of surprise but still, he nods and moves his hand in a *go on* gesture. "I've spent four years since mother met Huxley enduring the barbs of Staceigh and Laceigh. You know as well as I do no matter what they did, she was going to try her best to marry Huxley. I know you also know each summer, I always try my best to stay under the radar with my mother, to play the game so to speak and . . . survive." Jefferson raises an eyebrow and nods, and I'm not going to lie—I start to get irrationally angry.

What I'm learning here is Jefferson knows the mild torture his daughter puts Olivia through each year and lets it happen because, what? Everyone is afraid of a 5'2" blonde with Versace heels?

Jesus Christ.

These people need to get a fucking grip.

"I went into this summer with one mission alone: to make it through this wedding so my mother would release my trust early, allowing me to begin my career without having to bootstrap nearly as much. It was also going to give me freedom from her and her new life. Having my own income and business would give my mom less leverage over me."

There's a pause and I expect Jefferson to speak, to say something, anything, but he remains quiet, casually watching his granddaughter.

"I was going to do that no matter what this summer brought. Cami was a bit of a wrench because as much as I wanted to ignore it, I like her. I thought she was cool and I liked how she had ideas and was working here to play the game, just like me. I could . . . I could relate to her." I twitch my nose just a bit, trying not to allow any emotion to cross my face.

Right now, we're a united front.

"As you might have figured out, the twins decided Cami would be their game this summer." A shadow crosses over Jefferson's face.

"What was the catalyst?" he asks, finally breaking his silence.

"I'm sorry?"

"What turned them against Camile?"

"Oh." Olivia looks at me then at her grandfather and then at me again. "I don't—"

"It was an ex from college. Staceigh decided she was interested in him and he . . . was interested in rekindling an old flame."

"You weren't interested?" I make my lips straight, trying not to let the disgust cross my face.

"No, I was not. Not in the least. In fact, I tried to warn them about a cruel trick he played on me back when we were together but . . ." My voice trails off and finally, I get my first hint this might not be a *complete* train wreck.

"Like calls to like," Jefferson says in apparent understanding.

"Yes," I confirm with a nod.

"So what happened?" He leans forward like he's invested in whatever tea Olivia and I will be spilling rather than getting ready to reprimand us.

"Staceigh asked me to invite Cami to the Memorial Day party and we told her there was a . . . theme."

"I'm assuming the theme you shared wasn't all white?" he asks with a raised eyebrow, and there it is—a bit of disappointment is written on his face.

"No." There's a pause before she speaks again. "Anyway, things after that were . . . tense. The twins were trying to do anything to rile Cami, and I . . . well, I let it happen. I tried to keep my head in the sand about it all and just survive the wedding until . . ."

Another pause.

"Look, there's no point in telling you this step by step. I—"

"Oh, I'm quite enjoying the story," Jefferson says with a smile. I fight one of my own because even though he's absolutely about to fire me, it's kind of funny, this old man wanting all the dirty details of the mean girls and his granddaughter battling them.

"At the Fourth of July party, I became intoxicated. It was my own fault. I should have known better, but Cami's friend overheard the girls talking about how they were going to humiliate me, make it so my mother would be mad at me and I wouldn't get my trust." She looks at me and smiles. "Cami saved me and we decided they shouldn't be allowed to treat people like entertainment. We created a united front."

"Jefferson, these girls terrorize everyone around them. Employees, staff, friends, family—no one is safe. It's ridiculous. And while there were a few tricks here and there, nothing was harmful and they it brought it upon themselves. The staff, their friends—everyone gave us the information we needed, and they did it completely willingly. We weren't the only ones fed up with how they treat others. We may have pushed them in, but they dug the hole. You can't blame Olivia for—"

"And what about last night?"

I sigh, looking at Olivia. "That one was me. I asked Olivia to help me plan since it would be so last minute but that was me. And no one else should take the heat for it."

"I have"—he looks at a paper and I cringe—"twenty-five employees who didn't show up to work yesterday to run the End of Summer Bash." I chew my lip.

"I understand. I invited them all to our party at the Fishery. It turns out the twins weren't just playing with Olivia and me. They were playing with the livelihood of Olivia's father."

"And your . . . boyfriend?"

Well, fuck.

I was hoping that wouldn't come up.

But if I'm jumping in . . .

"Yes. Zachary and I are dating."

"So, it's safe to assume you'll be available to work here again next summer, correct?"

A pause.

A long one because—

"Seeing as you'll be living on the island with Zachary."

"I don't—"

"You know, I told Melanie the day she brought those brats to me that they were trouble. She insisted they were innocent, wouldn't hurt a fly, but I also raised Melanie herself. She's mellowed out these days, turning her angst mostly to those she works with and staff, but she was a brat for some time. The only reason she stopped was she had Olivia and I told her if she didn't get her antics under wraps, I was cutting *her* off. Being a single mom with no income didn't sound appealing at all to her so it worked well enough. Unfortunately, she took that tactic and used it against her own daughter."

"I don't understand—"

"Camile, I've heard nothing but rave reviews on your events both for the Beach Club and privately for members. The only negative commentary was from Staceigh, Laceigh, and . . . what does everyone call them?" There's no fucking way he— "Ah, the Bitch Pack, correct?"

I look at Olivia, whose face mirrors mine, eyes wide, jaw loose, full of shock.

"Even the event last night, which, am I understanding Zachary was able to raise the money he needed for the winter season?" I nod. "I've received no less than five calls this morning alone from members saying they can't wait for the next Anti Bitch Pack Party next year. They loved getting out of their comfort zone, changing the scenery."

Olivia and I look at each other in shock.

Of course, last night was a blast. All the Beach Club employees we had worked with over the summer came, Livi and I buying them all a round each, but it wasn't just them.

It was Beach Club members too, those who realized the End of Summer Bash was a wash, who saw our last-ditch attempts at marketing and traveled across the street where there was food and drinks and music and celebration.

And from what we saw, they all had fun.

"I cannot in good conscience allow you to leave this company without at least trying to retain you on staff for next year."

Retain you on staff for next year.

Is that . . .

Am I . . . ?

"But I helped ruin your daughter's wedding."

"Huxley was already on his private jet and long gone when the slideshow started, and most of Melanie's friends had left not long after their first dance." I *had* noticed that. "All that was left were mostly friends and acquaintances of Staceigh and Laceigh."

We did do the slideshow pretty late . . .

"But Staceigh and Laceigh . . . I mean, Staceigh was in prison."

"Do you think Staceigh St. George lasted this long with her attitude and need to tear others down without being smart and devious? Huxley will never be approached with that topic, at least not by Staceigh or her sister. That would mean certain death to their current lifestyle."

"But—"

"The reason I was content with Melanie marrying Huxley was because while he is a very closed off man and deeply invested in his business rather than his social life, he doesn't take shit. Not from Melanie, not from his daughters. So instead, they keep that quiet."

"He must know—"

"Oh, I'm sure he hears stories about his daughters and what pains they can be, but he doesn't have the full picture. Now, I raised Melanie, which means I have ears everywhere, just in case."

"Jefferson, I . . . I really appreciate this. I do. But . . . if I return next year, there will absolutely be talk—"

"If you don't, there will be more talk. And even more, the twins will assume they got away with something. I'm willing to double your salary in order to keep you on staff."

Double my salary.

Jesus fuck.

And it's then I realize where Melanie gets it, where Olivia gets it, even. The cunning, cutthroat ability to see what they want and get it.

Let's be honest—Olivia definitely didn't get it from her father, king of dad jokes and winning you over with sweet words and affection.

"And I would like to hire you on retainer for future Kincaid

Incorporated events. I, of course, will be recommending you to colleagues, so you'll need to build a staff quickly over the next few months since I guarantee your calendar will fill up, but I would expect you to work on-site in the Beach Club from May to September." There's a warmth in his face I can read. He knows about Zach and he's giving me the opportunity to build my business, but also keep Zach.

To stay on Long Beach Island, to be chained here all summer.

I hear his offer.

I think about it.

I panic, momentarily, but I know in his world, you need to act fast.

I look to Olivia who has a small, easy smile. It says, *Take it. At least you'll get something good from this summer.* I can read her the same way I can read her father, the same way I can read my best friends, and I wonder if she can read me just as well.

Probably.

Definitely.

But she's wrong. She's wrong because this job wouldn't be the only thing this cruel summer brought me.

It brought me Zach.

It brought me an understanding of who I am and it helped me understand how I cut people off without letting them in.

It brought me closer to Kat and Abbie, who have been worried about me for some time.

It gave me guidance for what I want my life to look like.

And it gave me Olivia.

"I would like to accept your offer," I say, and it feels like a sigh of relief runs through the room, though I can't tell if it's from Jefferson or Olivia. "But I have a few requirements." Olivia's hand in mine tightens and her face swings to me, eyes wide like she's begging me to shut the fuck up before I ruin my chances.

"Of course. You wouldn't be a cunning businesswoman if you didn't." His smile is kind as he nods his head in agreement.

"I don't think I'll need room and board," I say, hoping Zach wasn't in a lust-filled haze when he asked me to move in with him. Again, Jefferson smiles. "But I'd like Olivia to have my room for herself." She's been staying in the large condo her mother takes up, and on many occasions, she's mentioned how much she hates having to see Melanie each day.

"Okay," he says with a nod.

"Okay?" Olivia asks in shock.

Her shock is only going to get higher with this random idea I'm running with.

But I'm tired of living carefully and calculated and closing myself off to the help of others.

"And Olivia and I have agreed to form our own firm. She's going to be in charge of all marketing and press for events in the future, and I need you to hire her on as well each summer, same salary. We'd work to get your business out there, but also to improve the image of the Beach Club. Get fresh members, a broader, younger clientele."

Panic is fueling me as I word-vomit an idea I had midsummer when I realized most of the customers were aging, having been members for some time and continuing to return. That was definitely going to negatively impact the future of the Beach Club.

"Cami, that's—" Olivia starts, but her grandfather cuts her off.

"Done."

"Done?" Olivia parrots.

"Done. I think it's genius. This club has needed a revamp for some time, I've just never had the initiative. I thought one day long ago Melanie would take over this aspect of the business, but she has no interest in it." He looks at us and smiles. "I think you two will make an amazing team. I'll have Jeanne send over the contracts today. What will the retainer fee be?"

Olivia starts to shake her head to say no, but I speak over her.

"Twenty thousand a month," I say, my palms sweaty, but I know this business.

It's a good price.

"Done," he says then puts a hand out.

I stare at it.

Olivia stares at it.

We stare at each other.

And then I smile, moving to shake Jefferson's hand. "Excited to work with you," I say then watch Olivia do the same.

"Me as well. I think this is a great move, ladies. Alright, well, I have to be out. Lots of meetings before the club closes for the season." Then, he's standing, tipping his head, and grabbing a briefcase. "You two can stay in here however long you need."

Olivia and I both stay seated, staring at each other and him and back to each other.

It's a mix of panic and shock and awe and genuine confusion, and from what I know about Jefferson Kincaid, he loves leaving people in this kind of state.

He proves that when he stops at the door before leaving.

"Oh, and ladies?" he says, and we turn to look at him seemingly in sync before he smiles wide. "Pretending to cancel her card and then paying the tab was a good touch."

And I have no option other than to burst out laughing.

EPILOGUE

8 months later, Friday, May 24
Cami

> Good morning, angel. How's your morning?

>> What, no joke today? I already had my coffee at home.

> You were so pretty this morning, I forgot my pickup line.

>> There. That's my favorite one ever.

> Love you.

"Livi, did you see this?" I ask, rounding the corner of her office at the Beach Club and holding a clipboard in my hands.

It's strange being back here after last year and even stranger knowing Liv and I take up a good chunk of the third floor between her apartment, our offices, and the meeting room.

Just a few of the requirements we negotiated before the summer season.

Olivia and I hit the ground running with our business once we left the Beach Club. There were a few small events I had scheduled before we made the decision to merge our business, birthday and anniversaries, but in October, the Kincaid Corporation allowed us to have our big break by handing us full reins to the charity gala they host each October.

The very next day, we had three new clients on retainer and countless inquiries for everything from events to build good press to planning the *wedding of the year*. Or weddings, since we have six this summer alone, three at the Beach Club.

"See what?" she asks, sitting at her desk. It's actually the first time I've seen her all week, with her working in our office in the city while I work from here.

Another term we negotiated with Jefferson, a term that allowed me to move in with Zach and stay on the island full-time.

"What Patricia Bridgestone wants on the invitations?"

I think my favorite part about working closely with Olivia is being able to laugh together about some of the outlandish requests clients have. Last week, we had to gently let one know we weren't comfortable with supergluing a horn to a white horse's head in order to fit the unicorn theme for her daughter's first birthday.

"Which part?" she asks with a smile.

We've officially been business partners for just over eight months and not a single moment in that time have I regretted the decision to form a business with her. She is most definitely the peanut butter to my jelly, able to efficiently organize the people while I manage the details of the events.

Which is great when we have clients like this.

"What the fuck does *Vermont formal* mean?"

"Oh, that part." She smiles knowingly. "I thought you'd like it."

"I have never in my life heard of that term. Is it like Bernie Sanders at the inauguration? Or is it more lumberjack chic?"

"Truly, I have no idea." I plop into the chair in her office and sigh.

"Honestly? I think this is a next week issue," I say.

"Fair." She clicks a few times before looking back at me. "Okay, so this week we have the Memorial Day brunch and the all-white party." I widen my eyes and smile at her.

"Oh, so it's an all-white party? I thought we were going to change the theme this year?" This is a joke I've made every time she mentions the godforsaken Memorial Day party that, in a way, changed both of our lives.

This year, its 'host' is Jefferson himself as Melanie is just *too busy* doing rich bitch things across the country to grace the Beach Club with her presence, and, for some strange reason, the twins opted out of spending the summer here, despite the warm invitation from Olivia.

No idea why.

"God, you really need to spend less time with my dad. His shitty jokes are rubbing off on you," she says with an eyeroll. I put a hand to my chest and gasp.

"What? I can't believe you would even put my utterly hilarious barbs in the same category as your *father's dad jokes.*"

"Yeah, well, the truth hurts, Cam,"

"*Look,* it's not my fault you played a horrible, mean trick on me and I'll never let you live it down," I say with a smile.

"What aren't we letting Liv live down?" Cici asks, rounding the corner with a stack of papers in her hands.

"What a bitch she was to me," I say with a smile, standing to grab the copies I asked her to make me. Cici also works for Anderson-Thompson Events. After Liv and I stole her for the summer last year, I just . . . never let her go back.

"Ooh, my favorite topic. Can we talk about how she was a bitch to me next?" Her smile is almost evil and I laugh out loud, watching Livi roll her eyes in annoyance.

"If I buy you guys lunch, will you stop?"

"Probably not," I say, standing and leaving my clipboard on the chair. I can grab it later. "Especially since we're most likely going to the Fishery and you won't be paying either way."

"Yeah, in order for us to stop with that, you'll need to pay out big time," Cici says with a smile my way as Olivia stands and loops her bag on her shoulder.

"I seriously hate you guys." I hook my arm in hers and give her a kiss on the cheek.

"Back at ya, babe."

Monday, September 2
Zach

"I don't like him," I say to Cami as I put a basket of fries in front of her. She grabs a fry, dipping it in ketchup before turning back to look at the corner where Livi is standing fucking canoodling with her *boyfriend.*

He's a fucking douchebag.

I have no solid evidence for this other than I just *know* it in my bones.

"Zachary," Cami says in a teasing tone.

"What kind of name is *Brad?*"

"Okay, to be fair, that is a terrible name. It sounds like a high-class Chad."

"Jesus fuck, are you telling me my daughter is dating a Chad?" Cami sighs and rolls her eyes.

"No, I'm telling you your daughter is 24 and dating a man name *Bradley* and she looks happy. She's a big girl; she can make decisions about people without her father giving his two cents." I look back to where Liv is standing with the frat boy looking weasel and sneer. I guess she met him this summer while working at the Beach Club, which is red flag number one.

"She'll always be my girl and I'm telling you, there's something off with him. She's too good for him."

"Cool it, Daddy," she says, her smile widening. "Gotta put your own feelings in the back seat."

She's right and I do. Anytime she brings the kid—fine, man, seeing as he's almost Cami's age—around, I am personable, keeping my thoughts only for Cami to hear.

"Mel likes him, which should say everything you need to know about him," I say and watch her tip her head from left to right as she chews like she's weighing her options. She knows that's a pretty solid argument.

Olivia's mother has been blissfully married for nearly a year, and she's stayed out of my daughter's hair since her wedding, enjoying life as a wealthy man's wife. According to Livi, she's in the interview stages of being accepted to some kind of reality show about rich wives.

But that also means she will heavily favor our daughter hitching herself to any man who can somehow improve her own social standing.

"But Livi likes him and *that's* all I need to know about him," Cami counters and it's also a fair argument. Kind of.

"This wouldn't be the first time she's made a bad decision." She rolls her eyes, reaching over to smack my arm.

"Stop. No one's perfect. Look at me and all of my shitty decisions."

"But your shitty decisions led you into this bar a year ago," I say, lifting the bar top to walk around to her. She spins on her high-backed stool until she's facing me, and I stand between her legs.

I love this most of all.

When it's normal, when it's just us at the bar, me feeding her and her looking at me like I said something that meant something to her.

"Thank God for that, you know?" I say, wrapping an arm around her waist.

"Why's that?"

"Oh, you know. If you hadn't fallen in love with clam baskets and Aperol spritzes, I wouldn't have a couple hundred customers coming in tonight." She rolls her eyes and slaps my chest.

Tonight is the second annual *Anti Bitch Pack Party* at the Fishery, though it's been renamed the *So Long Summer* party since, according to Cami, there's no need to have Anti Bitch Pack since there is no more Bitch Pack at the Beach Club.

"And I'll die keeping it that way if I have to," she had told me late one night which made me laugh and, in turn, her glare.

But secretly, I'm grateful Cam didn't have a reason to plan her petty revenge again this summer, instead spending most nights at the bar and *all* nights in my bed.

It was a really fucking good summer.

Heavy emphasis on the fucking because it's been over a year and I still can't get enough of her.

I wonder if that will change, if the need will ever temper.

I look at her, her long dark hair and her orange nails and her gorgeous eyes she unshutters for me alone, and I know my answer.

No.

I'll never have enough of Camile.

Her phone vibrates on the bar and she looks at it and groans.

"Client?"

"Worse. A text from Cici."

"Something wrong with Cici?"

"No, but she finds it entertaining to keep me up to date on the questions the members ask her. Someone has requested Dom Perignon on ice with crystal flutes for when they arrive."

"When they arrive *here*?" I ask, a laugh in my voice. Cami groans again.

"Yes. They don't understand this isn't one of the the high-class, all-inclusive experiences. Most of the members have been loving when we do events around the island, and it's great that we've been able to help out some local businesses, but I swear to God, if another person asks if you'll serve caviar here, I'm going to lose it." I can't help but snort out a laugh.

"It's not funny."

"Come on, it's a little funny. Think of Frank smearing créme fraîche on crostini and topping it with *fucking caviar*." She bites her lips, trying to fight a smile. "Or Rhonda carrying out a bottle of Dom. Fuck, half of the shit she carries from behind the bar, she drops. That's why we don't see the fancy shit here."

Now she smiles a different smile.

A sweeter smile.

"You carry Prosecco."

"I have Prosecco on hand for *one* person alone, Camile. Anyone comes in asking for a fuckin' Aperol spritz, I've never heard of it in my life."

"Ooh, Aperol spritz sounds delish," a customer down the way says. I look to the sky and beg God to give me patience to make it through the day.

As if she's reading my mind, Cami puts a hand on my should and pats gently.

"Don't worry, big boy. Tomorrow, we're both off and we can hide away all day."

The first day all fucking summer we'll both be off and I'll have her all to myself.

Thank fuck for that.

Tuesday, September 3
Zach

I woke well before Cami, leaving her sleeping soundly in our bed to go to the other side of the island to get breakfast sandwiches and coffee before she wakes up. I drove her car, her only rule about the bike being she be awake and functioning anytime I get on it so she knows if and when I arrive at any destination in one piece.

It's a pain in my ass, but it's a small ask, so I give it to her. Plus, then the saddlebag of my bike doesn't smell like fucking everything bagels.

When I unlock the front door and push it open, though, I almost drop everything when the sound hits me as soon as I step in.

Moaning.

Fucking *moaning*.

What in the—

"That's it. Look at how pretty you are when you take my cock. Fuck."

A man's voice.

A woman's moan.

"Arch your back more, make it real pretty for the camera, Camile."

Fuck, that's my voice.

My voice and Cami moaning.

"Fuck, yes! More, Zach, please!"

My cock is already hard, and I'm pretty sure I know where the fuck this is going.

"*Oh, god.*" This moan is lower, quieter, less frantic, and I instantly know it's Cami.

Not video Cami, right now, real life Cami.

I put the coffees and sandwiches on the counter and walk with purpose toward our room, kicking Cami's heels she took off last night to the side as I do and leaning in the doorway as soon as she's in sight.

I was right.

I have never been so fucking happy to be right in my *life*.

Miles and miles of dark skin against white bedding.

Hair mussed and wild like she took her bonnet off and dove right in.

My laptop propped further on the bed, playing a video from a few months ago. Cami's on her hands and knees and one of my hands is in her hair, the other pushing on the small of her back as I fuck her mercilessly. She's moaning the whole time, her breasts swinging in time with my thrusts.

And Cami, legs sprawled, hand between them, works herself.

"Morning," I say, staring at her. Her head moves to look at me as her hand continues in lazy circles, a smile on her face.

"Morning, babe."

"What's going on here?"

Video Cami screams as she hits her first orgasm.

If I recall correctly, I gave her three that night.

"I woke up and you weren't" —a low moan leaves her lips, her eyes drifting shut just a bit as she slides a finger inside—"you weren't here."

"I was getting bagels and coffee," I say, reaching behind myself and tugging my shirt off. Cami's eyes lock on me, her teeth moving to bite her lip.

"So, you took it upon yourself?" I ask with a smile, my hands moving to the button on my jeans.

"A girl's gotta do what a girl's gotta do," she says then moans deep as her hand flexes and I know she bent her finger inside of herself, grazing her g-spot.

"Well don't let me stop you." Pushing my jeans and boxers down at the same time, I'm naked when I grab the chair from the corner and position it near the bed where I can watch Cami.

"W-what?" I can't tell if the stutter is from confusion or arousal, but both have my cock twitching. I take it in hand, stroking slowly as I stare at her. Her eyes move from my face to my hand, a small moan leaving her lips before moving back to my face.

"Put a show on for me, Cami. I'd like to watch."

"A show," she says whisper soft.

"Play with your pussy for me Cami." She moans as her eyes move to my cock in my hand, my hand leisurely moving up and down. "But watch the screen while you do."

"Fuck," she groans, but does as I ask, her finger continuing to make circles around her clit, her hips bucking to get more of what she isn't giving herself yet.

"Actually, I need something from you," I say, then stand, moving to where she lays on the bed. Her legs spread wider as I approach, her hand moving faster. I slap her inner thigh, rubbing it with the same hand to ease the ache. "Eyes on the screen, Cami. If I remember correctly, you're about to come again."

And then I'm sliding three finger inside her without pretense, her dripping wet pussy giving little resistance as I do.

"Fuck, Zach," she moans, her pussy clamping on my fingers as her eyes widen, locked to me. Again, I take my freehand and slap her sensitive inner thigh in the same place, forcing a deep moan from her lips.

"Here's how this is going to go. I'm going to get my fingers nice and wet in your drenched fucking cunt." She tightens. "Then I'm going to jack myself off while I watch you play with yourself, get yourself close. You're not going to come, Camile."

She groans in irritation, her head falling back and rolling back and forth.

I know if I let her, she could come right her, right now.

I smile, loving her misery.

"We're going to do just that while you watch." I tip my head to the video where I'm sitting with my back against this bed, Cami in my lap. Her head is tipped back with a moan, her hair brushing the top of her ass. "You're going to hold out until you come again on that screen." I crook my fingers and Cami's hips jolt.

"No, no, Zach, no." Her voice is already desperate, her hips moving in time with my fingers. "I can't—"

"You can and you will. Then you're going to keep holding on to it, climb on my cock and ride me." Another low, anguished moan. "And neither of us will come until the video ends."

"Fuck, Zach, that's—" I remove my hand from between her legs, stepping back and sitting on the chair again, using her wetness as lube while I stroke my cock, watching her squirm.

"Keep going," I say when her fingers stop over her swollen clit.

"I can't."

"You can, and you will. Be a good girl and keep touching yourself, Camile." I keep stroking, avoiding the sensitive tip of my cock where precum is pooling.

"Zach, baby, I can't, if I do I'm gonna—"

God I love how much she wants to do what I say, how much she wants to be good and hold out on her orgasm until I give her to go ahead.

"She's almost there, Cam, god do you hear her? Come on, fingers inside, fuck yourself good, baby." She moans in pain and pleasure obliges, the moans on the computer screen getting more and frantic. "Fuck do you hear her? She's right there, about to fall."

"Oh., god, fuck, fuck, I can't—"

Video Cami screams, coming in convulsions as she does and instantly I move, laying on the bed next to my girl, just as desperate to fill her as she is to be filled.

"On," I say, my voice gruff.

"Finally," she whispers to herself as she straddles me. My hand moves back, swatting the side of her ass with a satisfying smack.

"Drop the attitude, angel, or I'm coming in you and you'll have to wait until I'm ready to have you again." She pauses, her pussy hovering over the head of my cock and stares at me with horror.

"You wouldn't."

"Wanna bet?" I ask, raising an eyebrow. She rolls her eyes and I'd give her more shit except her hand is around my dick, sliding the head along her wetness before it notches and she slowly slides down, both of us groaning deep as I fill her.

"Fuck, you feel perfect," I groan, fighting the urge to buck my hips.

"Shit, Zach, I can't... I'm already right there. *God*." The way she leans back, the head of my swollen cock is directly on her g-spot, already sensitive from the deprived orgasm I know she desperately needs.

"What is it, what do you need?" My hands span her hips and I don't think I'll ever get over how fucking beautiful we look together.

"I need.... I need....." She's leaning back, her fingers circling her clit as she lifts and falls.

Any thought of waiting for the video to end before we come is gone with that image alone, of Cami using me for her pleasure.

"What do you need, baby?"

"I need to come, Zach. God, please."

"Then go, baby. Fall for me," I say, hand moving to hold her cheek, to brush my thumb over her full bottom lip.

"I want to go with you," she moans, canting her hips as she does. "Fill me with your cum, Zach."

Well, fuck.

She always surprises me.

I groan out loud, wrapping an arm around her waist and moving quickly, keeping myself planted inside of her as I move to flip her onto her back, take one leg by the knee and place it over my shoulder, before I start to viciously pound into her.

"Fuck, yes!" She's shrieking now, her pussy convulsing around me.

"You want me to fill you, angel?' She nods. "Use your fucking words, Camile. Tell me what you want." The sounds from the video ratchet, adding to the insanity of this moment as the headboard slams against the wall.

"Yes, god, yes. Please fill me up and make me come." Her voice is shaking as she moans and gasps for breath between the words.

I can't speak as my hand moves between us, my thumb pressing to her clit as I slam in deep and throb, coming deep inside of her as she shrieks and convulses around me, dragging out my orgasm for what feels like an eternity.

"Jesus Christ," Cami moans long minutes later as I pull out and roll off her, using an arm around her waist to bring her in close to me, nuzzling into her neck.

"Good?" I ask with a smile, pressing my lips to warm skin. Her hand move haphazardly behind her, slapping at me.

"Shut up."

"So no?" I laugh when she puts her face into a pillow and groans. "Alright, I guess I'll have to try harder next time, let's go." The hand on her waist halfheartedly move to turn her to face me.

"No, no. I need recovery time, Zachary! It was good! It was great! Put your ego and you dick away, please." I can't help but laugh. "I was promised coffee and bagels," she says in an exhausted whisper long minutes later.

"Are you telling me you're ready to eat?" I gently run a hand from her shoulder to her hip and back again.

"Yeah but I also don't want to get up."

"I'll get it. I don't think I'll let you out of this bed all day." She sighs as I press my lips to the smooth skin on her shoulder.

"Fine by me."

It's hours later, the sun starting to set when Cami's fingers are drawing shapes on my chest and my world stops spinning.

This has happened three other times in my life.

Once when Melanie told me she was pregnant.

Once when Livi was born and put into my arms.

And once when Cami walked into the Fishery with her friends to celebrate her new job a little over a year go.

And now this.

"You know I love you, right?" she asks, her voice shaking with nerves she wants to hide as she does.

I don't reply.

I can't.

The words swirl and swirl around me like stars in a night sky and I try to grab at them, try to put them in the right order to understand their meaning.

You know I love you, right?

The answer is yes, but also . . . no.

Of course I know what Cami feels for me is as close to love as she might ever get, old wounds deeper than she ever would recognize stopping her from crossing that line.

From the first time I told her how I felt, I became resigned to the fact there was a very good chance I would never hear the actual words come from Cami's lips.

I was okay with that.

If I had her, had her trust and smile and her sleeping in my bed at night, that was enough.

And now, in the dark of night with what I realize are shaking hands, I have her love.

God.

God.

I don't think I've ever heard anything more beautiful.

"Say it again," I say, moving so I can turn on the side table light. She blinks at the sudden brightness but I don't care. I need to see her face this time, need to see her eyes and watch the words come from her lips.

"What?"

"Say it again, Camile. Say it again." Her brow furrows before her lips part and she speaks, voice low and hesitant but understanding, I think.

"I love you, Zach." I roll so she's under me as I balance on my forearms.

"Again." A slow smile spreads on her lips.

"I love you, Zach."

"God," I groan, letting my eyes shut, the words wallpapered behind my eyelids.

I love you, Zach. I love you, Zach. I love you, Zach.

"Again," I whisper when I open my eyes, and this time, it's strained.

Her smile widens and her hand lifts, thumb brushing over my temple.

"I love you, Zachary Anderson. I love you and I love your dimples and I love how you take care of me. I love how loyal you are and how *kind* you are and how true to yourself you are. I love that you pass all of my tests and I love that you love me, scars and bruises and all. I love that you know I'm broken and are okay if I never heal. I love that you raised an incredible daughter and I love that you tell shitty dad jokes even though I rarely laugh. I love that you leave me messages underneath the paper on the coffees you bring me—"

"You've seen those?" I ask, confused. She's never once mentioned it, the tiny thoughts I leave in messy black Sharpie beneath the brown paper cup liner I bought in bulk the first time I brought a coffee to her at work.

And it's Cami, so I was sure if she saw them, she'd mention it. Since she never did, I assumed it was a no. I'm not totally sure why I kept writing them, but I did. Maybe it was a space to put my thoughts without scaring her off, maybe just a way to get the more mushy jokes out.

Or maybe wishful thinking she'd see them and become more comfortable with the idea I am completely, totally, irrevocably in love with her in every way.

"I saw the very first one. I was about to throw it out and the sleeve slipped down." Her thumb strokes over my cheekbone before she whispers, "You drive me to distraction." I groan, rolling again until she's on top of me, the feeling of love and adoration filling any empty space it can find.

"You do too," I say then kiss her neck before I distract her some more.

Two years later

Zach

Cami's hands are at my neck, tying the stupid fucking bow tie Olivia insisted I wear.

"*It's her wedding day, Zachary. You can handle wearing it for an hour.*"

"*An hour?*" *I had asked, glaring at the black strip of fabric.*

"*Once the ceremony and photos are over, you can take it off.*"

"*Livi will be okay with that?*" *I asked because as annoyed as I would be to wear it, Cami isn't wrong. It's Livi's big day and she's my baby girl.*

"*I negotiated for it on your behalf.*"

I think I fell for her again in that moment, and when she saw my face, I knew she knew it and it made her laugh.

But now we're here.

"Ever wish we did this?" I ask her, my eyes locked on her face.

Her own eyes never leave her own hands as she needlessly adjusts my bow tie.

"Do you?" she asks. There are nerves in her words, uncertainty.

"Angel," I say, one hand moving to grab her wrist and the other moving to her chin, tipping it so she looks at me. "You are mine. Period. I don't need anyone or anything to make that true—I just need you."

"Yeah, but—"

"If it was what you wanted, I'd call Livi right now and beg her to reschedule so we could get married today. But just know, that would be for you. I don't need it. Every day, you wake up and *choose* to be mine, no strings holding you there. That's more powerful than any vow or certificate on this planet."

There's a long moment where she stares at me before her eyes start to water.

"No, no. You can't cry. Not just because I fucking hate it, but if you mess up your makeup, Abbie will come in here guns blazing. She'll probably find something for Damien to sue me for. Damage. Emotional distress. Who knows, that man is sneaky as fuck." It does the job, making her lips tip and a soft smile leave her lips.

"God, you're really good at this," she whispers, her hand moving to my face, thumb brushing my temple.

"Avoiding getting sued? I mean, so far so good." She rolls her eyes, steps back, and slaps me on the chest.

"You're such a pain, you know that?"

"Takes one to know one, angel." She rolls her eyes, hands touching the bow tie once more before she steps out of reach.

"Let's go, dimples. You've got a little girl to walk down the aisle," she says, my heart breaking and healing in the span of a breath as she reaches the door where my daughter is waiting for me to give her away.

Her phone rings before her hands can touch the knob, her brow furrowing before she reaches into her bag and checks it.

"It's Livi," she says then presses to answer and puts the phone to her ear with a smile. "Hey, Liv, I—" Her brows come together in confusion. "Hey, hey, calm down. Calm down. What's going on?" A beat of silence and even from where I stand, the sound of Livi frantically speaking to my woman travels through the room.

Cami's face falls, her mouth dropping open.

"He *what?* Okay, it's okay. It's okay, Liv. I'll be there in"—she pauses, staring around the room we got ready in. then shakes her head like she decided something could wait—"five minutes. I'll be there in five minutes. Less. I'll take my shoes off, I'll run. I'll be there in two minutes, Olivia. Stay calm, okay?" She nods to herself, sitting on a chair and working the tiny buckle on her heel as she balances the phone on her ear.

Panic continues to fill me.

Something bad happened.

And Olivia is at the center of it.

"I love you, Liv. We've got this." She takes the phone from her ear, hits end, and instantly turns to me.

Both of her shoes are off now and she stands, grabbing her bag. Her eyes break my stare once more as she looks to the bar cart and grabs a bottle of vodka before looking back at me.

"What the fuck is happening, Cami?" She sighs and reaches for the door in a rush.

"He left her at the altar," she says.

ACKNOWLEDGMENTS

I've said it before, but writing acknowledgements is such strange thing. I was raised primarily by a single dad and emotions, affirmations, and words of encouragement were more in the form of a back pat and a thumbs up. (Love you, Dad.)

But I thrive off of giving people words of affirmation (not receiving because it makes me uncomfy and v awkward so you guys will just have to endure me bragging about my favorite people and the people who made this book happen.

So here we go.

Forever and always, thank you Alex. Thank you for taking chances with me. I never ever know what I'm doing but you always believe in me. When I whisper my scary goals in the middle of the night, you tell me they're too small. You've been self sacrificing from the very beginning, letting me follow every single dream of mine. When people tell me I write fictional men who are unrealistic, I smile and know I have one of my own. And I'm not just saying that. I usually complain about you more than anything, but everyone who works with me, who watches you bring me snacks and make sure I've drank enough water from the other side of a video call know you set the bar sky high. Love you. Thank you for marrying me when we were too young to know what we wanted and then growing up to be everything I needed.

Next: Ryan, Owen, and Ella. I say this every time, but thank you, thank you, thank you for being the coolest kids and letting me be your mom. Also, close this book, you are so totally grounded for reading it.

Thank you to Madi, my emotional support human. Thank you for being codependent with me and listening to me while I work through plot holes and have a crisis of faith. Thank you for *never* having a crisis in faith in me and sitting there patiently until it clicks. Thank you for gossiping with me about everything and nothing and for giving me Matilda. Thank you for the most gorgeous covers and bookmarks and inserts and stickers. I love you forever and always.

Thank you Lindsey. Forever the ultimate cheerleader, my first hire and I am eternally grateful I sent you a random ass DM once and told you I didn't want to do my own Facebook group. I'm *so fucking proud of you* and what you've built.

Thank you Norma Gambini for fixing my incessant typos and telling me to take a breath when I send you unhinged, panicked emails. I couldn't do this without you.

Thank you to Shaye, who is unbearably patient with my flighty ass and gives me a million reminders and makes the most *gorgeous* PR boxes that everyone clamors for. Thank you for keeping us on track during work calls and telling me to stop being mean to myself.

Thank you to Rae, for keeping the ship afloat, giving me gentle reminders of things I've forgotten ten times already, and spending three hours talking about literally nothing every time we get on a call.

Thank you to Lo for sensitivity reading, helping me plot this baby out, and being so incredibly open and supportive. You've taught me so much, doing so with kindness I don't necessarily deserve but appreciate all the same. Sorry I fall off the face of the earth sometimes.

Thank you to Good Girls PR for giving me a real marketing plan and making me stick to it instead of just flying by the seat of my pants.

Thank you to Chelsie for being so amazing and kind and never holding it against me when I fall fo the face of the earth and forget to text her back.

Thank you to my beta ARC's who receive this story and point out typos without holding them against me.

Thank you to my ARC team, the true stars of any hint of success this book will receive. Thank you for your honest insight and undying support.

Thank you to Booktok - yes, the whole damn thing - because without you, this would all be a pipe dream. It's easy to see the shitty parts of the platform but when you push that aside, there's a glorious, supportive, beautiful mix of people who are so kind and amazing. I'm honored to be a part of it.

But most of all: thank YOU, dear reader. I never thought this would be my life, writing stories and having you fall in love with the pretend people I create. I don't know how to tell you how much you've changed my life, changed my *family's* life, but I am eternally grateful. I owe everything to you.

I'm sure I'm missing people which will haunt me in the middle of the night for years, but thank you. From the absolute bottom of my heart. I love you all to the moon and to Saturn.

WANT THE CHANCE TO WIN KINDLE STICKERS AND SIGNED COPIES?

Leave an honest review on Amazon or Goodreads and send the link to reviewteam@authormorganelizabeth.com and you'll be entered to win a signed copy of one of Morgan Elizabeth's books and a pack of bookish stickers!

Each email is an entry (you can send one email with your Goodreads review and another with your Kindle review for two entries per book) and two winners will be chosen at the beginning of each month!

ALSO BY MORGAN ELIZABETH

The Springbrook Hills Series

The Distraction

The Protector

The Substitution

The Connection

The Playlist

Holiday Standalone, interconnected with SBH:

Tis the Season for Revenge

The Ocean View Series

The Ex Files

Walking Red Flag

Bittersweet

The Mastermind Duet

Ivory Tower

Diamond Fortress

ABOUT THE AUTHOR

Morgan is a born and raised Jersey girl, living there with her two boys, toddler daughter, and mechanic husband. She's addicted to iced espresso, barbecue chips, and Starburst jellybeans. She usually has headphones on, listening to some spicy audiobook or Taylor Swift. There is rarely an in between.

Writing has been her calling for as long as she can remember. There's a framed 'page one' of a book she wrote at seven hanging in her childhood home to prove the point. Her entire life she's crafted stories in her mind, begging to be released but it wasn't until recently she finally gave them the reigns.

I'm so grateful you've agreed to take this journey with me.

Stay up to date via TikTok and Instagram

Stay up to date with future stories, get sneak peeks and bonus chapters by joining the Reader Group on Facebook!